"I REGRET THAT I CANNOT CONCUR . . ."

Heads turned. Spock felt the disapproval at his impertinence; it could not be helped.

"Someday these children will seek to know their place in the Universe. They will need a home—"

"Do not presume to speak to us of our principles, Spock!" Sarek's voice cut like a knife through the shocked, uncomfortable gathering. "Your . . . dissent . . . has been noted—and you will keep your place. This does not concern you."

But it did. Spock regretted it had come to this. "I am constrained to point out," he said into the chilly silence, "that the Federation Council would agree with my concern. The children of Hellguard require a home."

"You would speak to *outworlders* of this?" S'tvan, philosopher and physicist, was on his feet. "You would threaten disclosure? Public humiliation?"

"If I must." Simple blackmail. They all stared at him in disbelief; Sarek closed his eyes in shame.

"Spock," his father said. "You are dismissed from these proceedings."

Look for STAR TREK Fiction from Pocket Books

Star Trek: The Original Series

Star Trek: The Next Generation

STAR TREK®

THE PANDORA PRINCIPLE

CAROLYN CLOWES

POCKET BOOKS

New York   London   Toronto   Sydney   Tokyo   Singapore

The author gratefully acknowledges permission to quote from the following sources:

"I to my perils . . ." by A. E. Housman, copyright 1936 by Barclays Bank, Ltd., copyright 1964 by Robert E. Symons. Reprinted from *The Collected Poems of A. E. Housman* by permission of Henry Holt and Company, Inc.

"Goin' Home" by William Arms Fisher, copyright 1922 by Oliver Ditson Company. Used by permission of the publisher.

An *Original* Publication of POCKET BOOKS

POCKET BOOKS, a division of Simon & Schuster Inc.
1230 Avenue of the Americas, New York, NY 10020

This book is published by Pocket Books, a division of Simon & Schuster Inc., under exclusive license from Paramount Pictures.

ISBN: 0-671-65815-8

First Pocket Books printing April 1990

10 9 8 7 6 5 4 3 2 1

POCKET and colophon are registered trademarks of Simon & Schuster Inc.

Printed in the U.S.A.

To my mother,
who read me books before I was born

Acknowledgments

Vondra N. McIntyre, for Hellguard and a perfect heroine.

Diane Duane, for her insight and inspiration.

Don Maass, who pulls rabbits out of hats—and twitchy writers too. Without him this book would not exist.

Karen Haas, who liked the beginning so long ago.

Dave Stern, for his editorial guidance and Vulcan patience.

Kevin Ryan, for his kindness and enthusiasm.

Mary Ellen Mathews, for unwavering sanity (despite our long acquaintance) and for teaching Max and me everything we know.

Richard Fortener and Julian Webster, chemical engineers, for their bemused advice on secret weapons of the 23rd century: "No, of course it can't *happen!* Natural law as we know it . . ."

Dr. James K. Woosley, physicist, for hypothetical explosions.

Rockford Halleron, for Navy savvy, words of comfort, and for footing all our phone bills.

Lynn and Becky Fox, for Saturday nights, fabulous dinners and their complete *Trek* library: "Sure, we can watch that . . . again."

Marianne Petersen, for musical notes.

Molly Clowes, journalist, editor, beloved aunt—for just being there: "Well, it's nice, dear, but . . . who *are* those people?"

And "those people," the inhabitants of a starship, who beamed us all aboard and let us "boldly go . . ."

I to my perils
  Of cheat and charmer
  Came clad in armor
By stars benign.
Hope lies to mortals
  And most believe her,
  But man's deceiver
Was never mine.

—A. E. Housman

THE PANDORA PRINCIPLE

Chapter One

SOMEONE WAS SCREAMING.

She hated that sound, hated this trap of strange weaving lights, this place of nowhere to hide. Beyond the light was darkness . . . no! She couldn't hide there. That was where It waited, where It searched and screamed for her. Because of her. Because of what she'd done—

If only she could remember what that *was* . . .

But the screaming was so loud she couldn't think. Hunger gnawed at her. Fear hammered in her brain. And a new pain—a tearing, racking pain she didn't understand. She huddled tight, curled inside herself, hugged her knees and held her breath to make the hurting go away. But that didn't help, and she tasted blood. Her own.

If only that screaming would *stop* . . .

Not move. Not now. Not ever make a sound. Make It never see me, make It never hear me, make It go away . . . but It was always there, waiting for her in the shadows, sharp, deadly as a blade.

Then suddenly, It wasn't waiting anymore.

Run! run, run, run . . .

Pain. Ripping, cutting, sharper than the stones that slashed her feet. Icy sweat poured down her face, seeped and burned into her eyes, and made her cold. So very, very cold.

Make It never hurt me! Make It never get me! . . .

She ran down dreadful corridors of light, past curving walls of solid rock, along twisting narrow tunnels until the light was swallowed up and she saw nothing more at all. The terror owned her now, and she was running against the pain, running for her life, on and on into the deep and screaming dark. Not fast enough. Shouts, footsteps rang behind her getting closer, closer. And she remembered something then, a thing that drained her will away and turned her heart to ice: It would get her in the end, because she couldn't run forever, because this place was a trap. With no way out.

She was going to die.

On planet *Thieurrull* the nights were cold. By day twin suns broiled its surface, scorching and squeezing dry unfortunate life-forms that found no shelter. Relentless heat whited out the jagged mountain range against an orange sky and melted barren plains into a shimmer. Between the mountains and the waste lay the remains of what had once been a colony. Dust swirled in empty doorways. Slag heaps blackened in the suns, and servo-miners stood abandoned in craters gouged from the land. Heavy boots no longer tramped the burning clay. Rough, angry voices no longer cursed the choking dust. Harsh laughter and oaths and drunken shouts no longer echoed on the wind. The soldiers were gone. The workers and women and ships were gone. The food was gone.

A world and its few remaining souls had been left to die.

When darkness fell on derelict mine shafts and fissures in the parched ground, living creatures crawled or slithered to the surface hunting for the day's dead. If more than one scavenger happened upon a rotting carcass the fight was to the death; the deadliest survived. Battles fought and feeding done, they began the search again for safety and shelter from the planet's cruel dawn. Painfully, impossibly, life still clung to Hellguard.

It had no moons. At night with only starshine burning through thin atmosphere, the rusts and umbers of searing daylight bled to shades of gray and black. The distant suns that blazed in the deep skies of Hellguard were fiery and cold, and they flung their terrible, taunting beauty across the endless curve of space.

Far beyond the colony, out on the open plain, a circle of tents stood under the star-drenched sky. The wind swept around them, howling over the waste, and their lamps made a dusty ring floating in the dark. And in the shadows of the colony, unseen by those who brought this strange new light, a tiny flicker of it caught and burned in hollow, hungry eyes that watched the night.

Spock sat by himself in the shadows that flickered against the walls of the main tent. Around the flame of a single lamp, twelve more Vulcans gathered, sat down together and waited. Somewhere outside a tent flap came loose and whipped and rattled in the wind. The recording device looked incongruous lying there on the mat-covered ground, a gleaming metallic piece of technology, out of time with lamplight, men in robes, and the keening wind that blew through this treacherous, alien night.

Spock watched his father switch on the recorder. The only change in Sarek's composed, expressionless face came when the lamplight caught his eyes; for an instant they burned like flames. Then Sarek began to speak. And Spock was grateful for the shadows, grateful for the dark, grateful that his part in this was done. Tonight his elders met to testify to tragedy; he had only been a messenger, bearing news from beyond the grave.

Vulcan's fleet had lost four ships in the past fifteen years: *Criterion, Perceptor, Constant* and *Diversity,* all science survey vessels, all Vulcan crews, all gone missing in space. One by one they simply vanished—the last, *Diversity,* six years ago. In every case transmissions were routine, from sectors bordering the Neutral Zone but within the Federation. Then silence. No signals, no log buoys, no debris. Nothing. Until three months ago.

Enterprise was crossing Gamma Hydra sector, patrolling

up the uneasy perimeter of the Romulan Neutral Zone, when the bridge heard a faint, frantic Mayday in obsolete Federation code. It originated from a Romulan cargo craft fleeing toward Federation space, with a warship of the Empire in pursuit and gaining. As *Enterprise* breached the Line and drew within transporter range, the warbird unleashed a bolt of fire enveloping its prey. The only occupant, a Vulcan woman, was beamed aboard unconscious and too badly burned to live. Spock reached her side in sickbay just before the end, touched gentle fingers to her charred face and joined her fading mind so she would not die alone. His log of the incident read "Explanation: None." But when *Enterprise* docked at starbase he requested leave and hired transport home to Vulcan.

That all took precious time. Vulcan's Council took even more with private inquiries to the Empire and lengthy discussions of Federation law, which Vulcan was about to break. In the end the Federation was not informed. *Symmetry* carried no complement of weapons; Vulcan's survey vessels never did. Crossing the Neutral Zone and penetrating the sovereign space of the Romulan Star Empire were tasks better left to long-range sensors, secrecy, and speed. Even a starship, a *Constitution* or an *Enterprise,* would stand no chance in the Empire's front yard. A single ship of Vulcan registry would be doomed, but a single ship it had to be.

For this mission flew only on the last thought of a dying Vulcan in the final mindtouch of her life, a thought that sent shock waves through Council and families alike: On an abandoned world called Hellguard—the fifth planet of 872 Trianguli—there were children, Vulcan children, dying on a burning rock in space.

". . . but no trace at all of our science ships or their small crews," Sarek said, speaking for the record. "Five hundred and fifty-six citizens of Vulcan, our sisters and brothers, daughters and sons, are lost to us. If they are alive," and the deafening thought of thirteen minds was a prayer that they

4

were not, "they are beyond our reach. In memory I speak their names . . ."

The Empire had denied everything. No, it knew nothing of Vulcan ships! What evidence did Vulcan have to make such charges? . . . Children? How could there be *children?* It was biologically impossible; their scientists had said so; regrettable these ships had gone astray, but did Vulcan have some *proof?* . . .

Now they had proof, living proof. And Vulcans would keep no more secrets tonight, at least not from each other. Sarek spoke the last of the names. Lamplight flickered in the dusk. Shadows danced up the walls of the tent; the air hung heavy, and time seemed to be standing still. The recorder went on blinking.

"The remaining inhabitants range in approximate ages from five to fourteen. Life-scans confirm what we were told. They are indeed half Vulcan." He switched off the recorder to allow a moment of grief. Heads bowed in silence and in pain. There was no need to state what every Vulcan knew, no witness to reconstruct events. Only the shattering, irrefutable truth: a band of starving children who should not exist at all.

Vulcan males and joined females are subject to a season as primitive and unrelenting as their planet's windswept sands. At other times mating (or not) is a matter of personal choice; but every seventh year it becomes a matter of life or death, a matter of being Vulcan. *Pon Farr:* eternal paradox of the Vulcan nature, its private pain, its illogical, secret soul. When their times approached, Vulcans would never choose to venture off-world in survey ships. Vulcans would never choose to mate far from home. And Vulcans would never choose to mate with Romulans. Somehow on this remote, decaying world, internal chemistries had been tampered with. Vulcan minds had been broken. The sacred personal cycles had been disturbed.

Vulcans had been raped.

Sarek lifted his head and reached for the recorder once

more. The flames in his eyes came not entirely from the lamplight, and his quiet voice filled the tent like a tolling bell—or a peal of distant, dangerous thunder. "I conclude the statement of fact. Now Salok will speak of the survivors and what is to be done."

Salok was old even by Vulcan reckoning, a healer with a very special skill: he was extraordinary with children. When Salok told them not to be afraid they weren't. When Salok told them that it wouldn't hurt it didn't. And whatever else he said, they neither questioned nor explained. Salok always healed them, and he always understood. But not tonight. Tonight he looked worn and frail. His hands trembled. His eyes clouded. Here were things he did not understand and had never encountered before. He mourned with Vulcan for the lost, but the pain he felt was for the found.

"As Sarek has spoken," he began, "we meet to consider the children. Spock's information was correct: they were left here to die. Many have. Survivors hide in the empty buildings and rubble of the abandoned colony. It is a vicious life, a wonder that they live at all. Malnutrition is their immediate problem, but not the most serious. That is their minds, their savagery and ignorance. I observed no system of values, not even a primitive code of behavior. They kill without thought or regret over a morsel of food. They even kill each other—the youngest, weakest ones. The bodies," his voice became carefully remote, "are used for food."

Thirteen pairs of eyes closed briefly. Vulcans killed no living creature for food, and cannibalism was beyond their imagining.

"This planet is dying. We cannot help them here. I suggest our research station at Gamma Eri, a protected environment where they can be healed and taught. I shall go with them, and we must send them our finest, our most adept physicians and teachers. When the children have attained some measure of civilization and rational thought, they can be relocated on worlds for which their progress and their gifts are best suited. This will take . . . a very long time." He paused, exhausted. Consenting silence, nodding heads, and a vast unspoken relief answered his words. "Then it shall be done. Tomorrow the ship returns. At dawn we must begin the—"

"I ask forgiveness." Spock was standing, hands clasped behind his back. "I regret that I cannot concur."

Heads turned. Spock felt the disapproval at his impertinence; it could not be helped. He took a deep breath and went on.

"Someday these children will seek to know their origins, their identities, their places in the Universe. Gamma Eri is an orbital science station, not a world, not a home—"

"We save their lives, Spock!" The thunder in Sarek's voice was not so distant. "We seek to repair their minds. What more would you have us do?"

"Treat them as we would our own," Spock said quietly, "for in fact they are. To uproot them from their birthworld as we must, to tend them on a station that does not even orbit Vulcan's sun, to instill in them a 'measure' of Vulcan thought and then to send them on their way—is that the sum of our debt to those we named tonight? These are their children. They deserve a home."

Sarek's face was stone. The others averted their gaze, allowing a father to deal with his wayward son, who was behaving so incorrectly. "These children, Spock," Sarek explained, "are the products of coercion. Rape. Living reminders of Vulcan nature torn apart and shamed. Our kindred were violated. They did not choose their fate."

"Nor did their children." Spock looked at his father across the tent, across a lifetime. "Our world is their birthright. It is for *them* to decide what measure of Vulcan shall be theirs."

"Now, now, Spock," old Salok intervened, "we mean to help them, and we will. We do not blame them for the poverty of their natures, but we must recognize it. Adapting to life on Vulcan would be painful and difficult—for *them*, as well as for us. We must seek to do the greatest good for the greatest number."

"Forgive me, Salok, but that equation fails to balance

when the greatest good is merely the avoidance of difficulty, and when it is purchased at the expense of a helpless few. We say we value diversity in its infinite combinations. Are we to abandon that principle simply because it becomes inconvenient?"

"Do not presume to speak to us of our principles, Spock!" Sarek's voice cut like a knife through the shocked, uncomfortable gathering. "This decision was never yours to make. It is not now. Your . . . dissent . . . has been noted."

Spock regretted it had come to this. "I am constrained to point out," he said into the chilly silence, "that the Federation Council would agree with my concern. A homeworld is considered mandatory for displaced populations, and displaced populations are a matter for the Federation."

Simple blackmail. They all stared at him in disbelief; Sarek closed his eyes in shame.

"You would speak to *outworlders* of this?" S'tvan, philosopher and physicist, was on his feet, his voice unsteady with the effort at control; his only daughter and his youngest son had been aboard the *Constant*. "You would threaten disclosure? Public humiliation? How dare you! This is *not* a Federation matter—this is a *Vulcan* problem! We will care for these half-breeds in our *own* way!"

Spock let that pass. "I am an officer of Starfleet, S'tvan, sworn to uphold a Federation law that Vulcan itself helped to draft. Violation of the Treaty on this mission would result only in our own deaths, since we come unarmed, and the loss of yet another ship. We do not provoke war, so my silence, like my life and my commission, was my own. But now we speak of others. I could not keep silent. They are children—and they are Vulcans."

"They are *not!*" Sickened, S'tvan sat down again, and one by one the others turned away. Spock thought he saw a glimmer of respect in the old healer's eyes, but then he stood alone.

"You are dismissed from our proceedings, Spock!" said Sarek.

Spock nodded. It was just as well; the thing was done. He picked up his tricorder and walked to the tent's only exit. As he unfastened the flap, his father spoke sadly at his shoulder.

"You would betray all of Vulcan, Spock?"

"If I must." The tent flap caught in the wind, tugged at his hand. "I did not believe it would be required. Or that all of Vulcan would be so fragile."

"Before you do, Spock, consider this: You did not speak from logic here. Perhaps your human nature betrays *you* . . . once again."

"Perhaps. It sometimes does. I am what I am, Father." Spock let go of the flap and stepped outside. When he turned to fasten it behind him, he found it was already closed.

He left the circle of the camp and walked out on the plain, so absorbed in thought that he was unaware of a shadow, not his own, moving after him in the dark.

What happened in the tent came as no surprise, even Sarek's reminder of his human failings. Spock hardly needed reminding.

Only months ago he had knelt upon the plain of Gol to leave behind the things of Earth, to belong at last to Vulcan in the peace and freedom of *Kolinahr*. But the Time of Truth was not within his reach. And his teacher watched him fail. *Your answer lies elsewhere, Spock* . . . not on Vulcan. Spock walked away from Gol that day, knowing that he would never be free, knowing that some things could not be left behind.

Now he stood on another plain, watched the skies, and knew his father was correct: his human nature did betray him, then and now. But he'd known all that before. It changed nothing. Tonight he spoke *because* of what he was, because of what he'd seen.

Spock had seen their faces. Darting, fearful, wasting faces. Starving bones and starving minds. Dull, empty eyes that held no promise, that watched and waited for the dark. Half-children and half-dead, half-animal . . . and half Vulcan. He walked upon their world well-fed, nourished by

9

millennia of civilization, by blessings and aspirations, by all it meant to be a Vulcan. And except for a fortunate circumstance of birth, any one of those savage, starving creatures might as easily have been himself.

No, he could not keep silent. *I do what I must,* he thought, *but the children's fate is not the only question here.*

There were far too many questions here. He must find answers, or other ships and other lives might never see their homes. If it happened to Vulcans, it could happen to anyone.

But why had it happened at all?

Spock turned his back against the wind, set his tricorder on the ground, and shielded it from blowing dust as he monitored its readings. They confirmed his earlier data and told him nothing new: seismic instability. Recurrent planetquakes would have made mining too hazardous, which could account for the Romulans' departure, but so could many things on this inhospitable world.

Why had they been here in the first place? And what had they been mining? He'd found no resources of scientific or military value. At the excavation sites his scans showed only common iron ores: hematite, pyrite, a few more useful minerals that could be mined anywhere else with far less trouble. Investigations of two mine shafts revealed both blocked by cave-ins; the expedition had no time to explore further. But Spock knew he must.

Because neither *Symmetry's* instruments nor their own surface scans could penetrate the damping field emanating from those rocky cliffs. A natural phenomenon? Or something of value buried there? That might explain the mining colony; it did not account for missing Vulcan ships. If there were answers here they lay beneath those mountains, and he had until dawn to find them.

As Spock reached for his tricorder he felt a pricking at the edges of his mind—and at the back of his neck. A new awareness intruded on his thoughts, sent a warning ripple down his spine.

He was not alone. Something was watching him.

With every appearance of unconcern he keyed the bioscan, rose to his feet and began a sweep of the horizon. Halfway around, it registered. Life-form: small, Vulcanoid; distance: 30.2 meters—between himself and the camp. He stared into the windy dark, saw no one, then continued scanning and considered what to do. He perceived no danger, no hostile intent, only the palpable sensation of being observed. So this watcher was allowing him to study and to think undisturbed. For the moment he decided to do likewise. Shouldering his tricorder he set out across the plain and did not glance back. He knew he was being followed.

A long-ago rockfall from the mountains created a natural barrier, partially separating the colony from the plains. Spock should have gone around it. It yielded no new information, provided no shortcuts, and came to an impassable dead end. He retraced his path through the maze of boulders, and in sight of open ground again resigned himself to taking the longer—

A split instant's warning wasn't enough. The attacker dropped from the rocks above, slamming him down against jagged stone. The sickening crack he heard was the impact of his skull, and to Spock's profound annoyance the world began to fade. He fought to remain conscious, aware of his right arm pinned beneath him, his left arm flung back over the rock, and the glint of starlight on a sharp piece of scrap metal pressing into his throat.

A ferocious face with teeth bared in a snarl belonged to a young boy, a surprisingly strong young boy. Too late Spock knew he'd underestimated the danger here, but he'd been so certain—

The boy growled a warning, jammed a knee into his chest.

Spock's vision swam. His left hand seemed far away, but free; if he could distract this youth for a moment . . . the point of the metal jabbed into his flesh just below the angle of his jaw, and Spock felt blood trickle down his neck. Any movement at all would drive it deeper. A groping hand found his ration pack, ripped it from his belt. After some hurried scrabbling Spock heard it hit the ground. That ration pack was empty, and the grim purpose in the face looming closer was unmistakable. Spock knew then that there would be no distracting him. There was no more time.

Suddenly the boy jerked upward, stiffened. His mouth opened in a scream that never came. The light went out of his eyes, and he toppled backward to the ground, then lay still.

Spock pushed himself off the rocks to kneel beside the body, searching the shadows, steeling himself for another attack. None came. But if the boy was alone, what had killed him? The body lay sprawled on the ground, the mouth a silent scream, the eyes still open, staring up at a sky they would never see again. He had been young. Gently Spock closed the eyes and turned the body over.

Then he saw the knife.

It pierced the rib cage neatly on the lower right side, where the heart would be, if this half-Vulcan's anatomy were similar to his own. Someone out there was efficient—and so far, invisible.

He found his tricorder, shut it off, and tried to ignore the throbbing in his head. His mysterious watcher seemed to want him alive—or intended to kill him next. Then his ears caught the faintest of sounds: a pebble pinging against rock, scattering to the ground. Mindful of the risk, he sat down in a patch of dim starlight and waited. So did his silent sentinel. Just when he was ready to concede defeat, a shadow moved soundlessly from behind one rock to another. It moved again. Finally, from between large boulders, the shadow separated itself from the blackness. It crept toward him and stepped into the light. At last his elusive watcher stood revealed—and an eyebrow lifted in the dark.

Fascinating. It was a little girl.

She was starving. Naked, except for some rags tied about

her waist, she was a walking skeleton. Every rib, every bone in her body stood out in stark relief, covered only by skin and layers of dirt. The child was filthy. Dark hair hung down her shoulders in shaggy, matted tangles. Sores blistered her feet and legs, and a lifetime of dust crusted between her fingers and toes. With wary eyes on Spock, she circled until the corpse was between them, jerked her knife free, then prodded and shoved to turn the body over. She seized his empty ration pack and searched it with a practiced hand. Never glancing at the boy's face, she pried the sliver of metal from his grasp, examined it and stuck it in the rags at her waist. Then holding her knife ready, she advanced.

Spock sat very still. A sudden feeling of disquiet grew as he watched her approach, and the reason for it was impossible.

She peered at him under her dusty snarls of hair with bright, hollow eyes. Intelligent, crafty, curious eyes. *How old?* he wondered. *Nine? Ten? And how often has she killed?* She stopped out of reach, leveled her knife at his face and sighted along its blade. They studied each other in silence. What was in Spock's mind simply could not be: it was absurd, but . . . he felt he *knew* her. Nonsense. He was obviously concussed and must alert himself to further symptoms. She sidled closer, inspecting him inch by inch. His face, hands, clothing and shoes were all gone over with acquisitive interest. Eyes lit on his tricorder. She pointed with her knife. Reluctantly, Spock pushed it toward her on the ground.

"What?" she hissed, displeased that it contained no food. Her language was Romulan, and Spock answered her in kind.

"It . . . tells me things," he said. Her eyes went wide. She snatched it up and held it to her ear, listening, then scowled.

"Tells!" she ordered, shaking it soundly. When it refused she bashed it with a bony fist. "Stupid sonabastard!" she swore, and flung it back to him. *"You* tells!"

"Certainly. What do you wish to know?"

"Stars!" She pointed up at them, and Spock stared. *She spoke that word in Vulcan. When—and how—did she learn it?*

"You know what they are?" . . . *and what else do you know?*

She swept a scrawny arm across the sky. *"My* stars!" she said fiercely, aiming her knife at his heart lest he disagree.

"Yes, I see that." This encounter was becoming stranger by the minute, and Spock thought it wise to reassure her. "I mean you no harm. I go that way." He nodded to the mountains beyond. "If you wish you may—" A look of sheer terror crossed her face. She turned where he pointed, then whirled around in fury.

"Not!"

"But why? What about those—"

"Notnot!" She stamped her foot; eyes flashed, nostrils flared, and she brandished the knife for emphasis. She backed up to a rock in sight of the open plain, shoved the boy's piece of metal under it, and sat down to watch. The knife never wavered. With her free hand, she shook his empty ration pack and began picking crumbs out of the dust. The wind whistled around them, and she shivered in the cold.

Spock's head throbbed. He sought to identify that disturbing impression, which he could neither understand nor dispel: she still seemed *familiar.* Or reminded him of . . . whom? The Vulcan woman beamed aboard the *Enterprise* had been T'Pren, but T'Pren was on board *Diversity,* gone missing only six years ago. This child could not be T'Pren's daughter; she was far too old. No, he could *not* know her . . . yet he did. Explanations eluded him, and time was slipping away. When he tried to shift his legs into a more comfortable position, she menaced him with her knife.

"As you wish, but I must go now," he said, starting to rise.

"Not!" The knife sang past his face, missing him by inches, to lodge in a crevice in the rock beyond. She darted over, yanked it out—and hadn't missed at all. Something small wriggled on her blade: a species of rock-dweller about

three inches long writhed on the sharp point that impaled it. She thrust it out by way of example. *"Not*go!" she hissed, and seemed very firm about it.

Spock concluded that he was overmatched and might do well to keep it in mind. The child retreated to her rock and unstuck her prey, whose muscles went on twitching even after she sliced off the head, popped it into her mouth and began to chew. Resolutely he concentrated on the open plain where lights still burned in the Vulcans' tents, but he couldn't shut out the sounds of crunching bone and sharp teeth gnawing through tough, leathery skin. He felt quite ill. No doubt that blow to his head . . .

"You eats," she ordered him, holding out the last piece of meat. A precious gift indeed . . . but it ended in three claws, and dark blood dripped between grimy fingers onto the ground.

"No," he said, hoping she wouldn't insist. "It is yours."

Frowning, she crammed it into her mouth. Blood ran down her chin. She licked it away, licked all her fingers and bent over the drops of blood on the ground. She scraped them up with the dirt and ate that too; all the while, she guarded him relentlessly.

Spock looked up at the sky, trying to judge the hour by the movement of the stars. They burned near and bright and beautiful against a faint glimmer of the dawn. *Dawn*—no time to reach those mountains now. Out across the plain the Vulcans were emerging from their tents, beginning to break camp. Today would see the success or failure of their mission. *Symmetry* would be making its rescue run across the Zone—a calculated risk, marginally safer than remaining in orbit without defenses or a cloaking screen. But if it failed to elude patrols and never arrived at all, they would be stranded here, along with the children of Hellguard.

With a start he realized the child had moved so stealthily he never noticed. Now she stood at the far edge of the rock where he was sitting, watching him watch the stars. After a moment she climbed onto it and sat with him looking up at the sky, so intense and quiet that Spock felt he was witnessing some private ceremony. Her knife dangled forgotten in her hand.

"Stars," she whispered, her face solemn and expectant. She searched the sky as if she were waiting for something to happen—or trying to remember something. *Where did she learn that word? Why did she save my life? And why,* Spock questioned his own rationality again, *why should this all seem so . . . important?*

"I am going there," he murmured, "to see your stars. And you shall come with me." She stared at him transfixed, eyes huge and wondering. "My people come to take us there. They bring you food. You will eat. And then we go—"

"Not!" She scrambled off the rock and backed away, clutching the knife and ration pack in her hands, shaking her head in fear, looking from him to the approaching Vulcans and to the mountains behind her. Then she pointed at the sky. *"Run!"* she cried, and to Spock's utter consternation, she vanished into the dark.

The incident left him profoundly disturbed. Her last word was also Vulcan, meaning *flee,* run for one's life. Whatever his words meant to her, the attempt to win her trust had failed. But she was hungry; she would come with the others to be fed. Of course she would. If she didn't, her face would haunt him all his days.

He lifted the body and carried it out onto the plain, the body that so nearly was his own. He lived because this boy died, because an intelligent, dangerous child had saved his life for reasons known only to herself. Spock vowed under Hellguard's blazing stars that today he would return the favor. And he began to build a cairn of stones.

"The decision has been made, Spock. Do you wish to know?"

A bloodred dawn was rising in the sky, already hot and fading all but the brightest stars. The wind had died with the morning light, and dust swirled around the silent Vulcans as they went about their tasks. An open-sided shelter stood on poles in the center of the compound. Spock pried open crates of food, cakes of high-moisture nutrient specifically formulated and laced with sedative to make the children docile, calm their fears and ease the shock of their transport to the *Symmetry*. If it ever came.

"I do, Salok," he paused, grateful to the tired old man.

"I thought you might, as you were absent from our discussion. No doubt your scientific studies were more pressing."

Spock detected a gleam of humor in the old healer's eyes. So his confrontation in the tent, his embarrassing words, his abrupt departure from the gathering would be acknowledged in typical Vulcan fashion: they never happened. Beyond the colony the ragged mountains towered over them, stark and broken in a crimson dawn. He thought of ships and lives and the sudden terror on a small, hungry face. "My studies were of interest to me, Salok."

"I am gratified to hear it, Spock. And profitable?"

"Perhaps not, Salok, but only time will tell."

"Ah, time," said Salok, "time will tell us many things, Spock. Our meeting was of interest also." The light in his old eyes brightened. "Your elders think it best to offer the children places with their kindred families on Vulcan." Carefully, Spock betrayed no sign of relief. "It seems that to do otherwise would necessitate cumbersome discussions with the Federation, which would entail the outworlders' questions regarding our mating cycles, which we would then be obliged to answer. To say nothing of the questions, Spock, about our disregard for Federation law and the Interstellar Treaty with the Romulan Empire." Spock was well-aware of these consequences; he had relied on them. "But the children must agree. If they wish to identify their kin and declare themselves citizens of Vulcan, the medical procedure will be administered. The right to demand it will always be theirs."

"But they are only children, Salok. Surely—"

"As will be our laws and customs. They are not exempt. Their natures are untrained. It will be difficult—for everyone. Those incapable of understanding will be cared for—

17

but not on Vulcan. We cannot make this choice for them, or for all the lives they will affect. Our decision is just, and it was not made lightly. This choice must be theirs, Spock, not yours or mine."

Vulcan justice: What was given would be earned, and what was earned would be given. These children must choose what every Vulcan child was born to—and would come to realize that their Vulcan kin wished they were never born at all.

"Their circumstances must be explained to them, Salok."

"I have no doubt that they will be," he murmured.

"Forgive me. I do not question your diligence."

"That is wise, Spock," Salok folded his paper-thin hands, "for it is not I who will do the explaining. Since you seem able to speak what passes for their language, the task is to be yours. That, you see, has also been decided."

Inwardly, Spock sighed; this was not precisely what he had in mind. It could not be said that he had an affinity with children. In their behalf he would risk his life gladly; in their presence he much preferred to be elsewhere. But he was in no position . . . "Then I shall make it clear to them, Salok. I understand."

"I am not certain that you do, Spock." The gleam in his eye showed signs of becoming a twinkle. "They must be cared for, you see, prevented from inflicting damage to the ship and to each other, or becoming a source of disruption on our voyage home."

"But," Spock frowned, "that would require . . . constant supervision, Salok. I regret that my duties on board—"

"Have been redefined."

"I see." What was earned would be given. There was a certain elegance to Vulcan justice, and it would be a long way home.

"After all, the children are why we came. You and I shall work together in this important undertaking."

"Then my duty becomes my honor, Salok."

"Perhaps. As with so many things, only time will tell."

Twin crescents of fire broke the horizon, and search parties began setting out. Exhausted as he was, Salok started after them.

"Ah, Salok, I think the ground here becomes rough underfoot. It might be best for the children if you remain to meet them."

"The ground is the ground. But for the children, I shall wait. And you need not be concerned about your duties, Spock. The old and the young are not so different, you see, when the ground becomes rough underfoot. In some ways, we all are much the same." Salok could take the sting out of anything. Even Vulcan justice.

The search teams moved in twos and threes with scanners and translators in hand, seeking out hiding places, stopping to speak softly. The suns climbed in the sky. The rocks, the ground, the air shimmered in the sweltering heat. Not a breath of wind was stirring, and every movement raised the dust. It tainted the air, burned their eyes and throats, and hung about them in a sulfurous cloud as they walked among the ruins of the colony.

Only Sarek was speaking now, his voice carrying on the still, thin air under the beating suns, echoing through the translators in the children's common tongue. He spoke of simple things: food for everyone, every day; a place where people didn't hurt or kill and there would be no need to fear; shelter from the heat of sun, and rooms at night where no harm came and they could sleep.

And one by one, from rubble and doorways and in between the rocks, children crept out to listen. For some this sunrise would have been their last; none looked savage now. Their shriveled bodies wasted, bellies distended from the lack of food. Their skins parched and blistered, cracked and bled from dehydrating, merciless suns. Behind vacant eyes their dying spirits waited, uncomprehending and resigned to whatever fate life's torture held in store. Their hair was the only thing that grew. Defenseless, young and terrified, they stood blinking in the burning light of day, an empire's forgotten legacy of brutality and neglect. Few even resisted when the Vulcans approached, or when kind hands lifted and carried them across the burning clay. Sarek's words meant nothing, except for the promise of food. But there was truth and goodness in the voice beckoning them, and another sound they didn't understand: they were being saved.

As the day wore on the search continued; suns passed their zenith and started down the sky. In the inferno of Hellguard's afternoon, even Vulcan skins drew taut and painful, then began to blister underneath their robes. Rocks grew searing to the touch. The ground itself scorched through their boots, and everywhere the dust surrounded them. It choked their lungs, coated their scanners and stung their eyes, while they counted the living and counted the dead. They found bones bleaching in the suns, picked clean long ago by scavengers; decaying bodies crushed by rockfalls from the mountains; a little boy trapped under a fallen building, whose life ebbed away in their hands. And they found eleven more, unresponsive and too weak to move, but alive. None of them, however, possessed a knife or curious, intelligent eyes.

Nor did any of the others. The shelter was busy and crowded when the last search party returned. Thirty-two survivors were eating, receiving medical attention, and growing sleepy in the shade. Spock walked among them, looking into every face, every pair of dull, bewildered eyes. She wasn't there. She wasn't anywhere.

Then a new sound floated on the air above the calm resonance of Sarek's voice, a sound that should have been sweet and welcome to Spock's ears: the clear, sharp trill of a ship's communicator.

The *Symmetry* had come at last.

"But they are all accounted for, Spock . . ." Sarek listened impassively to his son's news. The first groups of children were being carried from the shelter to a point beyond the rocks where the beam-up would take place. Sedated or not, the sight of people disappearing before their eyes would terrify them. Spock was grateful for this foresight; it granted him some time. ". . . their number agrees with our scans. Your readings indicate otherwise?"

"No, Father, they do not." Precious seconds ticked away. Desperate strategies collided with inevitable logic in his mind: remain in orbit? scan the planet? risk all their lives for one? None of that would happen. "But there *is* another. Last night I saw a child who is not here now."

"And who is uncounted by our scanners—and by yours? How do you account for this?"

How indeed? The same way she followed him unseen across open ground, saved his life, held him at knifepoint, spoke to him in Vulcan . . . the facts would neither enhance his credibility nor advance his cause. "I do not account for it, Father. The child exists. She will die if she is left behind. I shall not put others at risk, but while there is time, I ask to search alone."

"You *ask,* Spock? Or you *inform?*"

"I would prefer your permission." Spock reset his tricorder.

"It is illogical . . . to search without assistance. An officer of Starfleet should know better. Take those who can be spared."

"Thank you, Father—" Something caught Spock's eye, tugged at the periphery of his vision: only a flicker beyond the crowd, a vanishing impression of furtiveness and stealth. Only a glimpse, but that was enough. "—it is not necessary, after all."

She stood at the far side of the shelter, watching and unnoticed, listening to the voices around her the same way she'd searched the sky—as if she were trying to remember something. She moved again. In her hand was the empty ration pack, and she inched forward, intent upon her goal: an open crate of food, just a few yards away. Under their very noses—how did she *do* that? Spock held his breath and began threading his way through the groups of sleepy children, past the Vulcans moving them from the shelter and carrying the ones too weak to walk. He wasn't in time to stop what happened.

Backs were turned as she reached into the crate and began stuffing food into her newly acquired pack. Sensing a presence and movement behind him, S'tvan turned around to look. That startled her, and the pack slipped from her hands. She shrieked with rage and scrambled off into the sunlight, out of reach.

Then she pulled her knife.

It flashed in her hand, threatening them all, while she eyed her cache of food and schemed to get it back. Her raw, blistered feet bled onto the fiery clay, but her eyes were cunning, and the knife was sharp, steady in her hand. Behind her lay open ground, a clear route of escape to the huts and rubble of the colony. She had planned it well.

"You may have food." S'tvan kept his distance and spoke into the translator. "Give me that knife, and I will give you food."

His translator rendered back an oath.

"S'tvan," Spock moved beside him, "perhaps I can—"

"That one is vicious, Spock. She must give us the knife before she is fed. There is no time to waste."

Spock pushed back the hood of his robe. Her eyes flickered in recognition. Then she scowled, defiant, furious with everyone.

"*My* knife!" she screamed, gripping it tighter in both hands. The stakes had just gone up: it was now a matter of pride. Behind them the evacuation went on. The shelter was emptying quickly.

"S'tvan, I believe that I—"

"By all means, Spock." S'tvan managed to imply that Spock was better equipped to converse with someone as illogical as himself. "She must give up the knife," he insisted, "or be left behind."

"She understands, S'tvan. You do understand, do you not?" he asked quietly. She glared venomously at the groups of children being led beyond the rocks, then turned on

Spock seething with fury, her thin, sharp face a study in betrayal.

"Spock, you must—"

"Be silent, S'tvan," Salok's calm voice interrupted. "Spock will know what to do."

The trouble was that he didn't. He estimated his chances of catching her if she ran—and didn't like them. "If he fails," another voice muttered, "we will lose her. There is no time . . ."

Fail? There was no room for failure here. Spock sensed a crowd gathering behind him and fervently wished they would all go away. He did not require an audience—

". . . there is some difficulty here?" —or his father.

"Yes, Sarek. Spock attends to it. Do not interfere."

They all fell silent, waiting for him to utter some pearl of wisdom, some piece of logic to convince her. He picked up the ration pack, held it out, and took a step closer.

"The food," he said, "is yours. Eat." He tossed it to her on the ground. She grabbed it up and reached inside. Then eyes narrowed in her crafty face. She looked again at the dazed, sleepy children—and at the waiting Vulcans. Slyly, she hugged the pack and scowled at them under a tangle of hair. "The knife," Spock said, "is also yours."

This pleased her. She drew herself up proudly and tossed her head, sending a cloud of dust into the air.

"No, Spock! She may not bring the—"

"Be *silent,* Sarek . . ."

"There is a way," Spock lowered his voice, moved another step closer. So no one else could see, he opened the pocket of his robe. "We can hide it—here. They will not know," he said, as her glance shifted to the Vulcans, "because we will not tell them."

Eyes lit, then narrowed shrewdly. Secrecy appealed to her; so did her knife. She fingered its cracked hilt with affection.

"My knife!" she whispered desperately. Tears gathered in her eyes. Her mouth began to tremble, and she clamped it into a small, tight line. Spock nodded, knowing what he asked. All this child had in life was her weapon and her

pride; in front of everyone, she was losing both. She was also hungry, tired of hiding, and mortally afraid. But he would win now, he knew that too, and all at once it mattered *how*.

"I will keep it safe for you," he said. On impulse, he held out the tricorder in his hand, touched a key, and let it dangle by the strap. Her eyes widened. "Remember this?"

"Notknife."

"Better," said Spock. "It can tell you things." It swung back and forth, glinting in the light, looking more attractive now. Its dials and keys glittered like rows of jewels; lines of data streamed mysteriously across the small display on a field of royal blue, and setting suns in the reddening sky struck its gleaming metal, turning it the color of burnished gold. It filled her eyes, filled her mind. She had to see it, touch it, have it—

The knife wavered. She took a step. Another—to within reach.

"This," Spock said, "is *mine*. You may keep it safe for me."

Slowly, suspiciously, she held out her knife. For agonizing seconds it hovered inches from his palm. At last she let go and watched his fingers close around it. Shielding their transaction from prying eyes, Spock slipped it into the pocket of his robe. Then in full view of everyone he placed the tricorder in her grasping hands. She snatched it away and glared at the others in triumph.

"My!" she crowed importantly, bony arms full of prizes, and set about twisting and poking at the tricorder's keys. Spock gave a passing thought to his stored data. That unit was field-issue, said to be impact-proof and tamper-resistant. She would be the definitive test of its durability— and his own, he felt certain.

The Vulcans observed these proceedings in stony silence. As they departed with meaningful looks and gravely shaking heads, Salok's voice drifted back to him. ". . . and *compose* yourself, Sarek . . . so difficult for fathers when sons are like themselves."

"Come along now," said Spock firmly, starting after them.

Out of sheer perversity the child hung back, scowling, refusing to move. Spock sighed. It seemed to him that this had been a very long day and that Vulcan justice had a very long arm indeed. His arm, unfortunately, was too short to render her unconscious. A phaser on stun would solve the problem, but he had none. And there was nothing left to bargain with . . . or was there?

"You told me something else is yours," he reminded her. She understood at once and searched the daytime sky.

"My stars *go!"* she sneered, scornful of such tricks.

"Your stars are *there,"* he said with absolute authority. "But now the sky is too bright for you to see them." She looked up again, frowning. "Of course," he shrugged casually, "I know about stars, and you do not. But the others will know. The others are going to *see* your stars. Must I tell them that *you* were too *afraid—"*

"Notnot*not!"* she screeched and started shaking her fist, hopping up and down, and cursing him proficiently to prove it. "Sonabastard yougo *dies* in sonabastard *dust!* Sonabastard *things*go eats you sonabastard *eyes! . . ."* and so forth. After a lengthy malediction, she finally ran out of words.

"So," said Spock, "you are not afraid. Then come with me, and you shall have your stars." He turned and walked away. Nothing happened. He forced himself to keep on walking . . .

"My knife! *My* stars! You sona*bastard! . . ."* She began to follow.

The suns sank behind the mountains, and shadows stretched over the world. Dust and wind began to wear away the footprints left behind. By morning they would all be gone. As the planet turned toward the dark, stars came out to spatter the sky, shining down on emptiness.

And deep inside, Hellguard rumbled in its sleep.

Chapter Two

SOMEONE WAS SCREAMING.

That was always the same. And she was trapped in the place with the walls of eyes, lights that moved like dust in the suns, with colors that only came in dreams. They grew and changed and fell back inside themselves forever like the sky. They knew all about the screaming and how she hurt inside. They hated her. She hated them. She didn't want to die. *Run, run, run . . .*

Blood rose and bubbled in her throat. Fear ripped apart her mind. A trap, a trap with no way out, nowhere left to hide. No place dark enough, no running fast enough, no sky forever anymore. It would live, and she would die—but she wanted something first. Revenge. She hated It, hated harder, *harder . . .*

And then she wasn't running anymore.

A chance, one last chance to save herself: she would kill It—before It killed her. The screaming grew and fed her rage. Her grip tightened on the knife—its hard, sharp steel would let her live. Too dark now to aim and throw, but she knew another way: she would stab Its heart out! Her spirit soared. She tasted blood—and triumph. *Make It hurt! Make It die! Kill It now!*

She turned—and there It was, coming at her out of darkness, forming, taking shape. She *knew* that shape. She'd always known. It . . . It . . .

Exploding, impossible horror blotted out the image in her mind, and every nerve, every muscle, every cell in her body shrieked a last command: *Kill It! Kill It NOW!* Her arm swept up to strike the blow—but never fell.

Her hand was *empty.* There *was no knife.* No . . . NO! That was *wrong!* That couldn't *be!* Where was it? *Where?*

Existence plunged and swirled away in freezing black despair—and the screaming, endless screaming, followed her down. She could smell her own death. Cold, sick dread was choking her, cheating her, killing her. In a dying frenzy of terror and pain, she clutched at her waist, where her knife used to be. But it was too late now. And there was nothing there. Nothing, except—except . . .

. . . cloth. Red cloth. A uniform.

Saavik jolted awake, and reality burst into life around her: her uniform, her desk, her equation on her screen. Her room.

Starfleet Academy.

Damn that dream! Hot, angry tears stung her eyes. Her fingers were raw, aching from digging into the armrests of her chair. Beads of cold sweat still trickled down her forehead. Deep inside her chest, her heart was still hammering. And somewhere in another time and place, somewhere beneath an abandoned world of dust, where broken mountains cut like scars into a cruel, burning sky . . . somewhere, someone was still screaming. *Damn that dream! Damn that hateful, horrible, filthy world! Damn the Romulan Empire! And damn all Romulans—for making me one of them!*

She pushed the hair out of her eyes and looked around her room, gratefully drinking in its soft light, its clean, white surfaces, its compact, functional design. She ran her hand along her desk, lingering over the comm console and the keypad of her built-in computer terminal. The equation she'd been working on stared back at her from the screen, still incomplete—and still wrong. That was real. Nothing had changed.

I am here. I am really, truly here.

She smoothed the fabric of her uniform, wanting to erase the unsightly creases made by a dreaming, twisting hand. Magically the wrinkles fell away, disappeared as though they'd never been there at all. So easy. So . . . civilized. *I am no more a Vulcan when I'm asleep than when I'm awake,* she thought bitterly. *Humans only think so because they know no better, an honor I do not deserve. Real Vulcans never dream such dreams. Real Vulcans never hate or fear or feel such shame. Real Vulcans never want to kill.*

But Saavik was not a real Vulcan. In spite of all her progress and acquired veneer of civilization, underneath the proud red uniform of Starfleet Academy she would always be half Romulan. And no amount of progress could ever make up for that.

It is not logical to dream of the past, she told herself firmly, as she straightened up and tugged her jacket neatly into place. The past was over. She had much to contend with in the present, and it was shameful of her to want to kill anything.

But she did. She wanted to kill that dream.

I just won't think about it, she decided, and left her desk to open the window. *I won't ever dream that dream again!* Damp cool air rushed in, defeating her room's environment controls. The campus slept. A soft spring rain was falling, and lights along the tree-lined walks made the drops on her window shine like stars scattered on the night of space. The hour was late—or more precisely, very early. It would be daylight soon. The only sound she heard was the strange gentle patter and trickling of the rain. Water. So plentiful here that it fell from the sky.

What is it like to belong on this world, to swim in oceans of water? Never to die of thirst or rot burning in the dust? No! I won't think about that . . . she turned to contemplate her

28

living quarters. Its shelves were bare, storage compartments empty. The hard mat she'd asked for rested on the platform of her bed. A row of standard-issue cadet uniforms hung in the closet along with a few simple outfits of her own. Personal items occupied one drawer. Her study tapes were in her desk.

The polite young man who showed her to this room when she arrived had looked awkwardly at her two small cases, which she refused to let him carry, then remarked that when the rest of her stuff got here, he was sure this would seem just like home.

Saavik wondered what he meant by that. Since she'd never had a home and she had no other possessions, it was not possible to agree. She saw nothing wrong with her room the way it was. Perhaps he intended to be kind, a quality she sought to develop in herself. Not knowing how to respond, she simply stood there until mercifully he went away. Unpacking didn't take long.

When she sat down to work her thoughts were disturbed by a faint but (to her ears) distinct exchange taking place in the next room. It was proper to ignore it, but that was easier said than done. Those voices were human. And Saavik was curious. So she'd listened, at first alarmed, then utterly confused.

The occupant of the next room was announcing loudly that her life was *over* because she was unable to locate something called her CoffeeTech. Her male companion said to forget about it, come here and have-some-*fun!* She accused him of being insensitive; she had *lost* her *CoffeeTech* —how could she have *fun?* He offered to show her, but she was too distraught: without her CoffeeTech how could she stay up? He would show her that too; *he* could stay up—all night if necessary! She wished he would get serious; what she needed was a *CoffeeTech!* He, dammit, would buy her a new one if she would come here this instant—or she could go drink Starfleet coffee like everybody else. That *sludge?* From the slot on the *wall?* He was a *beast* to even *suggest* it!

And no, she would *not* come here—she'd rather be *caught dead!* Why, there was just no telling what a *beast* . . . like him . . . might . . . do . . .

Caught dead. Saavik shivered remembering that careless phrase. She felt an unreasoning surge of anger at these pampered foolish humans who required luxuries and possessions to survive, and who didn't know the meaning of the words they used.

But those words were their own. Could they not speak their language as they wished? Why should that make her angry?

Suddenly she felt confused. Out of place. Very much alone.

And perhaps her room *was* too empty.

On her comm station lay the tape of a message waiting for her when she first arrived. Having played it twice already, she found no logical reason to hear it once again—and suspected that there was none. But she dropped it in a slot, touched a key, and sat down to watch. The shifting squares and code patterns rearranged themselves into a familiar, craggy face on her screen, and a hand lifted in the traditional Vulcan greeting.

"Live long and prosper, Cadet Saavik," the image said. *"I trust this finds you in good health and on schedule. You are now a cadet, first class, of Starfleet Academy. I congratulate you, and I am confident that you will attain even more distinction in your studies than you did on your entrance examinations.*

"Regarding compliance with Starfleet's information directive: We have discussed the options available to you when you report to the Registrar. I feel it my duty to remind you once more that claiming your Vulcan family and citizenship—and thus avoiding the question of your birthworld—is a simple matter of requesting the antigen scan. That is always your choice and your right. You have overcome much and accomplished much already in life. Your reluctance to reveal this to Starfleet or to Vulcan is somewhat understandable. But your

refusal to acknowledge it to yourself is illogical. Your achieve-
ments do you credit, and one must face the facts, Cadet
Saavik, even when they are pleasant.

"For everything there is a first time, Saavikam, and many
are in store for you. Your greatest challenge at Starfleet will
not be classwork, for which you are well-prepared, but
learning to communicate and work with humans. Our physi-
cal forms are similar, but their concerns and thought pro-
cesses are vastly different. To you humans will seem
irrational, frivolous, full of contradictions and continually
exasperating—all of which is true. They are also inventive,
capable of greatness, and worthy of study. Try to employ
benevolence and tolerance in your dealings with them.
Should these attributes momentarily elude you, practice
removing your thoughts to reflect upon the principle of
Infinite Diversity. I find that sometimes helps.

"No doubt you already have many questions, and no doubt
you are about to ask them all. I suspect it is futile to
recommend that you rest in preparation for your day tomor-
row. Nevertheless, I shall do so all the same. You have
attained a desired goal, Cadet Saavik. Tomorrow you embark
upon a new journey. Good night, Saavikam. Live long and
prosper . . ."

Saavik froze the image and stared at it for a long time.
Outside the rain had stopped. The sky was growing light, all
pink and golden in a watery dawn. A scented breeze drifted
through her open window, where the branches of a tree hung
dripping, heavy with blooms. And in the morning stillness a
bird began to sing.

On this extravagant planet even the trees had flowers.

She touched a key, and the face faded from her screen.
Saavik knew no words to explain it, but now everything
seemed changed: she no longer felt angry or confused, only
like an explorer on a strange new world. And her room
wasn't empty anymore.

No, Cadet Saavik had no need of possessions; she had
quite enough to do just keeping track of herself.

She removed the tape, put it away carefully, and opened her comm channel with a series of destination codes. Another mode of address was proper now, she reminded herself, as she straightened her uniform again and remembered to push back her hair.

BEGIN MESSAGE, the screen read, and Cadet Saavik sat tall and proud. She raised her hand and gazed into the recorder's lens.

"Live long and prosper, Spock," she said. "I am beginning my first day at Starfleet Academy . . ."

". . . and I would appreciate further discussion of the term 'fun,' which seems to be the underlying basis of human behavior. On that subject, I have a number of questions . . ."

Spock left his quarters on the *Enterprise* and walked down Deck 5's empty corridor, turning his reply tape thoughtfully in his hand. The lift opened, and still deep in thought he stepped inside. As so often in recent years, he'd spent his meditation hour today answering Saavik's questions. Curiously, the effect was much the same. Perhaps it was also curious that this thought occurred to him only when there was no time to wonder why.

The turbolift opened, and Spock stepped onto the bridge. Pleading glances from senior crew told him the situation had not changed: their monotonous, uneventful patrol was adversely affecting the captain; the captain was adversely affecting everyone else, and the problem was compounded by his constant presence on the bridge.

"Commander Uhura," Spock murmured, "at your convenience, could you do me a favor?" He placed the tape on her console.

"Certainly, Mr. Spock. Where this time?"

"To Starfleet Academy, Complex Three. The terminal access is encoded. Thank you, Commander." No doubt Uhura had puzzled for years over his daily messages, but she'd never asked what they contained. Admirable restraint —for a human.

"You're welcome, Mr. Spock, and—" her eyes slid toward the captain "—welcome to the bridge."

"Indeed," Spock said with a sigh.

Admiral James T. Kirk fidgeted in the command chair, tapping his thumbnail against his teeth and staring at the uneventful starfield on the screen—as if staring hard enough might produce some action. Not *trouble,* of course not. But *some* reason to justify sending *Enterprise*—and himself, dammit—or a certain Admiral might start cutting orders for a certain Acting Starship Captain to get back behind a desk at HQ, where the only challenge in life was how to stay awake in those damn staff meetings . . .

"Captain?"

"Spock—" Kirk spun around. "Early, aren't you?"

"No, Captain. And you have been on the bridge for sixteen point two five hours. As there appears no immediate cause for concern, I thought perhaps you could . . . use the time."

"To do *what?*"

"Perhaps some . . . fun, Captain: a leisure activity, an intellectual pursuit, an athletic exercise—"

"Captain." Uhura turned from her board. "Message incoming from Starbase Ten. One-way Priority. Would you like to take that in your quarters, sir?" she suggested hopefully.

"I would not. Put it on, Uhura, we'll all take a look."

"Welcome to the sector, Jim." The kindly face of Commodore Stocker filled the screen. *"We've got an errand for you. Our probes are tracking an unidentified vessel approaching Federation space—sublight speed. No cloak, no signal, no response to our attempts at contact. It's not one of ours, and commercial lines report all craft accounted for. Given its nonaggressive posture, we doubt the Romulans are involved—but we'd appreciate it if you'd take a look. Proceed at your discretion, Captain, but ID that ship. Coordinates and probe data follow. Report back ASAP. And thanks, Jim."*

This is more like it, Kirk thought as the probe's data

flashed on the screen. "Mr. Sulu," he said, "lay in a course. Uhura, tell the Commodore we're on our way." He stabbed a button on the armrest. "Scotty, can we go to warp five with no problem?"

"Aye, sir, but—"

"We've got a ship heading in from the Neutral Zone on impulse. It won't acknowledge, and Starbase wants an ID."

"I don't wonder, sir! Standin' by."

"Sulu?"

"Course plotted and laid in, sir."

"ETA von hour, tventy minutes, Keptin," Chekov added.

"Long- and short-range sensor sweeps, Mr. Spock. If the Romulans are out there, I want to know *before* we run into them—and before they duck behind their cloaking screens. Monitor that ship, Uhura—and keep your ears open."

"Aye-aye, sir!" Uhura turned to her board, smiling.

"Here we go then. Warp five." . . . *yes,* much *more like it.* He watched the view on the main screen freeze for an instant, then burst apart and streak away in trailing rainbows of light as *Enterprise* plunged into the stars.

"Having fun, Captain?" his first officer murmured in passing.

"Fun, Spock?" Kirk turned, outraged innocence itself. "This could be very dangerous, you know. We're ordered off course, that ship has no business in the Zone, any Treaty violations get hung around *my* neck—and you ask me if I'm having *fun?"*

"I . . . see what you mean, Captain."

"I'm so glad you do, Mr. Spock." Kirk leaned back, and a slow, satisfied grin spread across his face. "Hell yes, I'm having fun," he said softly.

The blaring klaxon finally stopped. Battle stations stood ready. The image on the screen grew steadily as *Enterprise,* her shields raised, nudged closer and closer. Everyone waited. In the tension on the bridge the only sound was a single, patient voice.

". . . this is U.S.S. *Enterprise* . . . please respond. Federation vessel *Enterprise*, requesting communications . . . please respond . . ."

It plowed through space, running lights on, ports glowing, ship's beacon winking eerily as it turned atop the bridge and sliced the surrounding gloom.

Enterprise's sensors reached into the Neutral Zone and detailed the menacing lines, the space-worn hull, and the yellows, reds and greens of its feather-painted wings. A giant bird of prey had ventured far from its hunting ground— somewhere in the Romulan Empire.

And far from the light of suns or inhabited worlds, the two ships approached an invisible line, first drawn a century ago by grateful astrogators on their starcharts in the carnage and ruin at the end of the Romulan War. A mutual border had been impossible then; it still was. From those final, bloody battles that drove the Romulans homeward in defeat, a treaty was born—and a neutral zone, into which incursion by either side technically constituted an Act of War. Satellites and substations ringed its narrow corridor. Signal buoys warned straying ships away. Although the Zone had been violated often in recent years by Romulan raids on Federation space, "occasionally breached" by Starfleet on missions of rescue and espionage, routinely ignored by merchants, smugglers, and pirates—both the Federation and the Empire patched and clung to their fraying net with determined vigilance. Because in a hundred years no one had thought of a better way. And because the alternative was war.

". . . please respond . . . this is the U.S.S. *Enterprise* . . ."

"Full stop, Mr. Sulu. This is close enough." Kirk's eyes were riveted on the screen. "Report!"

"Romulan Bird of Prey, sir," Sulu said. "Plasma and photon torpedoes."

"Spock, what's on sensors?"

". . . I am reading . . . no life aboard, Captain."

"I can't believe that."

"Nor could I. I scanned it twice, and—"

"Once more, Spock. For luck."

Spock began to repeat the futile procedure.

". . . please respond . . . Captain," Uhura turned, still listening intently, "they aren't jamming us. I'm getting chatter from their instruments, only . . . no response, sir."

"Third scan, Captain," murmured Spock. "No life aboard."

Kirk took a deep breath, let it out slowly. "All decks, this is the captain. Go to Yellow Alert and stand by . . . Spock? It doesn't look damaged. Life-support failure? *What?*"

"The hull has not been breached, Captain. Seals and airlocks are intact, radiation levels normal. Life-support systems are functioning." Spock frowned at his viewer; mysteries annoyed him.

"Chekov, Sulu, keep scanning. Any shadow of anything. If they're out there behind a cloaking screen—"

"We'll get it, sir. We know what to look for."

Of course they did; Spock had trained them. And sensors were upgraded during *Enterprise*'s refit: a cloaked ship on short-range scan produced a negative visual echo, a slight distortion in the field. Since a cloaking device was limited over distances to sublight speeds, they should have fair warning of any approach.

Kirk looked up to find Spock standing beside him. "Something wiped out that ship, Spock," he said quietly. "And we've got to find out what."

Kirk waited until the Romulan ship had drifted across the Neutral Zone: then he had Spock, McCoy, and Mr. Scott beam over to the Romulan ship in full environmental suits, phasers set on stun.

The three officers materialized to a glimpse of lifeless bodies through a haze of vaporous red smoke, which immediately fogged their faceplates. Spock began reading his tricorder's data, a catalogue of chemical toxins.

Scott said it faster. "Phaser coolant, Captain, enough to

choke a regiment. A leak's got into the system. I'm tracin' it, sir." He groped his way to a well in the deck and descended its ladder.

McCoy ran a gloved hand over his visor and knelt beside a corpse in battle dress. "Dammit, Jim, this one's just a kid."

"Four dead on the bridge, Captain," Spock reported, "none above the rank of sub-commander. Senior officers must have been below. I see no sign of emergency life-support packs . . ." He began examining various stations and panels, "and controls regulating airflow are inoperative. They were unable to vent the substance, but the board does not register a coolant leak. I cannot give you visual; those circuits have been disabled. Weapons are on line, all systems on automatic, and their course is locked into the helm. Sir, this ship is on a direct heading for Starbase Ten."

"Is it now? An attack gone wrong, Spock?"

"It would seem so. Apparently, they went sublight when the malfunction was detected. One torpedo bay has opened and closed."

"Jettisoned log buoy?"

"Possibly. For that and other reasons, I should like to interrogate the computer. Romulans are aggressive, not foolhardy. Launching a single ship at Starbase Ten simply is not logical."

"All of them kids, Jim." McCoy ran his scanner over the fourth body and sat back on his heels. "Dead at least two days. There's no doubt about what killed them. Coolant gas is so toxic they never had a chance. God, this ship's a mess! How the hell—"

"Worse'n a mess!" Scott's angry voice came through the link. *"Ruptured coolant line down here in engineerin's what did it, sir. Exploded, where it runs along the air duct, and it's still leakin' into the system. No backups, no cutoffs, conduits rigged together any old how. A sorry sight, sir, but I'm sealin' off the line. The ship'll take hours to vent."*

"When you're finished, check out the engines, Scotty.

Spock, leave the computer for now. Conduct a search. I want to know how many were aboard. You go with him, Bones. Make sure they all died for the same reason."

"What about these bodies, Jim? They should go into stasis—"

"Yes, Bones. We'll beam them over. Now get going."

"Very well, Captain. We shall attempt to use the lift."

They made their way across the bridge, waving away the fog that still swirled around them. McCoy reached the lift first.

"Look here, Spock! What's this?" He pointed to a niche in the wall. Displayed inside it was a brightly glowing object. Spock came to observe and scanned it with his tricorder.

"What's that, Bones?"

"It is," Spock stated succinctly, "a three-dimensional, six-sided object with two sides of unequal length, approximately sixty by forty-five by thirty point five centimeters. A rectangular polyhedron, which apparently contains a luminescent, electromagnetic field, and which—"

"Forget the geometry, Spock! Jim—it's a *box*. A clear box. Only pretty thing on this flea trap. It's got colored lights inside it, making spiral patterns . . . wonder how they *did* that?"

Spock stared, feeling himself drawn by the vibrant color spectrum and the chains of turning designs within. "Captain," he studied the readouts from his tricorder, "I have never seen anything resembling this. The outer layer is primarily silicon and contains some form of shielding, which my tricorder scan does not penetrate. There are no controls of any kind. It . . ." *is beautiful,* he thought, but said aloud, ". . . its purpose is not apparent."

"So maybe it's *art,* Spock. Maybe it doesn't *have* a purpose."

"Doctor, all things have a purpose. Particularly art. Your haphazard view of the nature of things is most—"

"Gen-tle-men." The captain's tone was soft and dangerous. *"My patience is wearing very thin. I want a search of that ship—now! I'm not interested in Romulan art."*

"Understood, Captain." But Spock doubted that it was. This bridge had no emergency life-support; why should it have art? "Come along, Doctor," he said with some reluctance. They entered the lift, but Spock couldn't dismiss the object from his mind. It was aesthetically appealing, and oddly hypnotic . . .

Their footsteps echoed as they walked the dingy, narrow corridors and looked into utility cubicles, what passed for a sickbay, and into crew's quarters. There was no sign of anyone. But a clear box with sparkling patterns of light occupied a niche in the wall at the junction of the second level's main corridors. On the next deck, resting on a pedestal, another sat in the corner of the largest cabin.

"Here is another one, Captain," Spock reported. "This makes three so far, and they all look the same. I should like to—"

"Later, Spock. Nothing yet?"

"No, Captain. This appears to be the commander's cabin, judging by its comparative luxury. But we have found no person of such rank. No one at all, in fact. It seems I made an error."

"Spock, this doesn't make sense. A kamikaze run with a skeleton crew? They'd never get through Starbase's defense. Why would they waste a ship on—"

"Captain!" Scott's voice broke in. *"I think I know. I found somethin' very interestin'. Mr. Spock, can ye come straight away? Port side, fourth level down."*

"What, Scotty? You found the crew?" Kirk tensed in his chair.

"Nary a soul, Captain. But there's another of those pretty baubles—and a wee gadget for Mr. Spock to feast his eyes on. I'll be needin' his opinion."

"On my way, Mr. Scott. Come along, Doctor . . ."

Kirk hated waiting. And suddenly he hated that Romulan ship, with its empty decks and questions with no answers; the only thing he hated more was not being there.

"Dammit, what 'gadget,' Scotty? What do you *think*

you've got?" . . . this was ridiculous, no one telling him anything . . .

"Spock here, Captain. What is it, Mr. Scott?" Spock sounded calm as ever, but then the silence seemed to go on interminably. *". . . ah, yes,"* he finally said. *"Yes, I see."*

"Well, I *don't* see, gentlemen!" snapped Kirk. "So will one of you kindly tell me what the *hell* is going *on?"*

"No, sir!" Scott replied firmly. *"Not just now, sir! Ye would not want us speakin' of this over the comm link."*

"Speaking of *what?"*

"I quite agree, Captain. We must not discuss this on an open channel."

Kirk rubbed a spot in the middle of his forehead, trying to erase his frustration. "Then beam back aboard immediately —unless, of course, you have some *objection!"* He didn't wait to find out. "Uhura, take the conn!" he said, entering the lift.

As the door hissed shut behind him, his anger began to fade, replaced by a growing sense of unease. Just what had they found on that ship?

". . . an' that's that," Scott finished gloomily. "Not exactly good news for the Federation." They sat in the briefing room's silence, while Kirk's mind reeled around what he'd just heard.

"A cloaking screen with unlimited range—in *warp drive?"*

"It appears to exist," Spock agreed, "as an integral function of the drive itself. Instead of depleting antimatter reserves, it collects and recycles energy from their coil emissions. With the power-consumption factor solved, their weapons could be fired without decloaking first. A ship with this advantage approaching at warp speed would give our defenses insufficient time to react. Starbase Ten would sustain critical damage, at the very least."

"So . . . a test run with a skeleton crew, a load of fire-power, and warp speed all the way? But they had this little problem?"

"That is the obvious explanation, Captain." Spock looked uncomfortable. Kirk waited. "I can offer no other."

"If they risked the one," Scott reasoned, "it means they have others. They'll be back."

Spock nodded. "This device renders the Federation vulnerable and bodes ill for this area of the galaxy. Without further study we cannot know if it was developed by the Klingons, Romulans, or a collaborative effort. We must assume that both empires possess it."

"And now we do. We won't be giving *this* one back!" Kirk said grimly. He touched the intercom. "Uhura, message to Starbase Ten, Priority One. Use that new code and scramble it."

"The new code scrambles itself, sir."

"Fine. Send to Commodore Stocker, Starfleet Command, this sector. Item: Romulan warship, on course for Starbase Ten. Leak in coolant line killed crew of four. Item: cloaking screen designed for use in warp drive. Ship's engineer and science officer project weapons' capability with cloak in place. Will proceed to Base with ship in tow, pending further orders."

"Yes, sir. That's going out now."

"Thank you, Uhura." Kirk leaned back, welcoming a moment's distraction. "A new code, gentlemen, the Rosecrypt. 'By any other name'—get it? Someone has a sense of humor. It encodes and decodes by individual ship's and destination's Ops manuals, and then it's cross-ciphered by Starfleet Calendar dates. But that's as far as I get. Uhura must know what she's doing."

"No doubt she does," said Spock, "since it was she who invented it. Captain, request permission to reboard that ship and interrogate its computer. Although I believe record tapes were completely wiped, the terminal I examined appeared to be functional. We must check for potential traps. It should be possible to program and navigate the ship on automatic from our helm, without the drain of a tractor beam on Mr. Scott's engines."

"Aye, an' they'll be grateful, Mr. Spock. Captain, Starfleet'll be adaptin' that design. I'm thinkin' we were very lucky."

"Damn lucky—this time. Gentlemen, you've earned your pay for the week. Spock, go to it. I'll be on the bridge. Scotty, maybe you'll get a crack at that ship when we get to starbase . . ."

They left the briefing room and went their separate ways.

After nearly three hours, Spock found no information anywhere in the computer banks, no record of what was sent out the torpedo bay. Ship's log? The obvious explanation, but those were piling up. So he reprogrammed the nav computer warily, but meticulous checks and rechecks revealed no hidden traps.

Then he crossed the bridge and stood staring into the glowing box. Its vivid ebb and flow of colors unfolded, expanded, turned back in upon themselves. He ran his hand across it, feeling the cool, seamless surface. He lifted it from the niche and set it back again. Surprisingly heavy, surprisingly beautiful. Four of them. A form of surveillance imaging? Transmitted by some carrier wave not registering on his tricorder? Or simply a pleasing object with no explanation, obvious or otherwise?

He should not be delaying; the captain was anxious to get under way. He could request permission to bring it back, run a complete spectroanalysis, and satisfy his curiosity on his own time. But he continued to watch. Really, quite fascinating . . .

"Spock, how's it going?" Kirk's delighted voice broke into his ear. *"There's something I want you to hear."*

"Navigational programming is completed, Captain. I find no suspicious relays to indicate overloads or triggers to detonate the engines. But these artifacts . . . may I bring one—"

"Not now, Spock. We've got new orders. Stand by. Uhura, patch him through on commlink . . . All hands, this is the

captain. Message from Starbase Ten to U.S.S. Enterprise*: 'New potato too hot for starbase to handle. Orders per Starfleet Command: Secure ship and all systems intact. Proceed best speed to Earth.' And very well done, all of you. We'll be getting under way shortly. Spock, come on back aboard. That's it, my friends—we're heading home. Kirk out."*

Spock heard the cheers that went up all over the ship, but he was frowning as the transporter beam took him . . .

. . . and he frowned all during the perfectly executed test maneuvers, even when the ships accelerated and winked away together at warp speed. Before Kirk left the bridge, he strolled over to the science station, wishing Spock wouldn't frown like that when things were going so well.

"Spock. Is something the matter? If you'd like time off or—well, anything . . ."

"I see no reason to disrupt routine," Spock began stiffly. "However . . . a personal request, Captain. When *Enterprise* docks, may I invite a guest aboard? A student of mine at the Academy." He didn't elaborate further.

"Of course." Curious as he was, Kirk didn't pry; that frown was finally gone. "And about that ship—we'll take it apart, get all the answers."

Spock nodded, then frowned again and turned back to work.

And Kirk left the bridge feeling uneasy. But when he stepped out into the festivities in full swing on every deck, his uneasiness was forgotten, and he was swept along with the happy tide. Today had turned out right after all.

And *Enterprise* was homeward bound.

In a remote, forgotten province of the Romulan Star Empire, Praetor Tahn cursed the dampness and the cold. He adjusted the voice-changer he wore about his throat, wrapped his cloak tighter, and pulled its hood down over his head. His hands shook. His stomach cramped in fear, and he cursed the twenty long years he'd been coming in the dead of night to rooms like this one. Then he opened the door.

He was last to arrive, last of The Ten, an alliance born in secret, fed by an Empire's arrogance and disregard. And if Tahn could put a name to any shrouded figure in this room, he didn't want to; he preferred to stay alive. There was great power here: commands of ships and troops, private funds for weapons, private contracts with the Klingons. And occasional mistakes—the government's investigation of one incident had led almost to their doorstep. But mostly their efforts brought results, escalating distrust at least, with the Empire outraged at Federation charges, furious when its Word was not believed. This was all to the good.

For their business here was the overthrow of government. No names, no faces, no unfiltered voices betrayed identity. Secrets went deep, and plans were whispered here. Very soon now, that was going to change. Everything was going to change—or so The First had promised on that dark night twenty years ago, when his words had reached into their hearts and changed their lives forever. Tahn was young then; he was older now, old enough to know the fate of a traitor discovered in their midst. Which was why his belly ached and his hands trembled so. He was running out of time.

The First, who knew all their names, made a sign, a ripple in the folds of his black cloak. The Second activated a soundshield and turned out the lights. Then someone spoke into the dark.

"First, there is great news! It is just as you said—they have taken the ship!"

"Excellent. And the probe?"

"Deployed and undetected—or the fools believed it was one of their own. Transmissions to and from their base were in an unknown code, but they spoke freely between ships. As you said, they take it to their Starfleet. Your ship goes to Earth."

"Excellent," First said again. "Now you will hear why. Our Cause does not depend on haste or plans that lack the vision to prevail. Tonight I tell you of another plan, two decades in the making, and the world where it was born. You know its name; you do not know its secret. Your attempts were tests of character, skirmishes, mere rehearsals for a Grand Design—a Design that cannot fail, not even by treachery from within . . . Tenth?"

Tahn's heart stopped inside his chest. *He knows! O gods . . .*

"Tenth, I have need of ships and soldiers. Yours."

"But—" *Without them I have no protection! He knows that too! O gods . . .* "First, I have but one, and two modest outriders."

"Modest sacrifice then, Tenth. Prepare them."

"I—am honored." *What else can I say? O gods . . .*

"Yes, Tenth, *honored.* Remember that. For soon," the voice hummed through its resonator, "soon there will be many ships and many new worlds. This time the Enemy will fall. And the cowards in our government who sell honor to buy peace—they will join us. Or *they* will fall! There can be no honor in appeasement! No glory in this cage of stars! And no peace in surrender to this Federation foe! Our Enemy is hasty and predictable, and therein lies its doom. So today they have taken a ship, and for the rest—have no fear . . ."

The voice sank to a whisper; the room waited on his words.

". . . the rest they will do to themselves."

45

Chapter Three

SUNWARD FROM THE glow of Mars, a distant point of light winks blue and green in the night of space: an elegant island jewel tossed on black velvet amid mightier, drabber neighbors. It grows into a turning cat's-eye marble. Trailing wreaths of cottony clouds drift across its land masses and oceans. Serenely, as it has done billions of times before, a lush, tranquil planet winds along its way in placid revolutions around a fifth-magnitude star. In three short and colorful spacefaring centuries, this sapphire face has become famous. Hub of the Federation, home of Starfleet, playground of the galaxy. An unlikely, out-of-the-way little place to become a legend, but there it is: Earth.

"Captain," said Sulu, who was due for shore leave, "Dock's got our feathered friend now. There it goes." The Romulan ship tracked toward the great double mushroom of Starfleet Spacedock. The mammoth doors opened, and it disappeared inside. "And sir, looks like we'll be home in time to celebrate."

"What a world!" McCoy gazed at the main screen with affection. "I can celebrate just looking at it."

"Let's get there first, gentlemen—then we'll see." Kirk breathed a sigh of relief, glad to see the last of that damn ship. As he turned his attention to the shore leave roster in his hand, he heard Uhura muttering into the comm.

"Yes, he's still got it . . . No, I *can't* see the *names* . . ."

Spock observed the glances, the nudges, the air of heightened excitement, then rose from his station and came toward Kirk wearing a perplexed frown.

"Captain," he said, "something has always puzzled me. Why should this port of call evoke such euphoric anticipation? Although performance remains adequate, the duty personnel seem more . . . exuberant . . . than the situation warrants."

Exuberant? Kirk looked around the bridge and saw nothing but smiling faces and unflagging efficiency. Of course they were *happy* . . . "We're just glad to be home, Spock. Earth in the spring—there's nowhere else quite like it."

"Precisely my point." The eyebrow spoke volumes.

"Well . . ." Kirk covered his mouth with his hand, apparently in deep thought, but McCoy took up the challenge.

"Never mind, Jim, I'll handle this. *Home,* Spock, is where we can really un*wind,* kick up our *heels,* let ourselves *go.*"

Spock's puzzlement deepened. "As opposed to *what,* Doctor?" he inquired. Kirk could stand no more.

"Bones, leave it alone. Spock, I . . . I don't know *why,*" he pronounced with what dignity he could muster. "I guess it's just one of those . . . *things.*" Perversely, Spock seemed enlightened.

"Indeed. Thank you, Captain. No doubt that accounts for it." He returned to his haven of data banks and rational explanations.

Now, Spock started that on purpose, Kirk thought. *I'd swear he's in a good mood.* He was wondering why when the voice of Approach Control interrupted.

"Standing by for your helm, Captain. And sir, regarding your shore leave parties: HQ's transporters are scheduled for maintenance tonight, and City Station's went down this afternoon. Spacedock pads are fine, though, and we have plenty of shuttles for crew going planetside. Sorry, sir."

"Acknowledged, Approach Control. Kirk out." *Oh, well,* he thought, *nothing's ever perfect.* And *he* wasn't going anywhere, except to his quarters—to assign shore leaves in peace.

Uhura was feeling a lot less philosophical. Now she had to deal with *shuttles* tonight—and an officious, junior voice ranting in her ear.

"Starfleet Command to Enterprise! Acknowledge, Enterprise!"

"Enterprise here," she answered sweetly.

"Lieutenant-Adjutant Michaels here! Relaying orders from the Admiralty! Priority! Encoded! Transmitting now! Acknowledge that relay, Enterprise, and state your name and rank!"

"Why, certainly, Lieutenant-*Adjutant* Michaels," she said in honeyed tones. "This is Lieutenant-*Commander* Uhura acknowledging." Pleased with the nervous gulp on the other end of the line, she extracted the tape and intercepted Kirk on his way to the lift. "Orders from the Admiralty, sir."

"Oh?" Kirk eyed it warily. "What do they want?"

"Encoded, Captain. But about our *shore leave* assignments, sir? With all those shuttles docking—"

"Yes, Uhura, I'll go straight to my quarters and do my homework." He snatched the tape and escaped into the lift.

Uhura stood with her hands on her hips; the beginnings of a nasty headache lurked somewhere between her temples. This whole night was going to be a mess. *Shuttles stacked up, people at the wrong airlocks, everybody complaining . . .* she sat down, thoroughly irritated, and flipped a switch. "Bridge to all decks! The shore leave roster will be *posted*—when it becomes *available.* Consult your *displays.* Do *not* call the *bridge!* Repeat! Do *not* call . . ."

Spock cast a watchful eye around the bridge, grateful that instrument dockings were unaffected by emotional homecomings. Not so the crew. Personnel at engineering were recounting a very old, very improper anecdote, so convulsed with mirth that they couldn't utter the punch line. Misters Sulu and Chekov were conducting an elaborate wager on their respective tolerances to toxic amounts of ethanol, which they planned to consume before the night was out. The chief medical officer was leaning over the command chair and, despite the fact that no one was listening, proceeded to air his views on transporter repairs —and transporters in general.

Uhura glared at the blinking lights on her panel and vowed revenge on all who assumed that "do not call the bridge" couldn't possibly apply to *them*. She drew a finger across her board, wiping all the calls away, and looked up to find Spock standing over her. "If it's important they'll call back!" she fairly snapped at him. Promptly her board lit up again. "See? They'll even call back when it *isn't!*" Her headache no longer lurked; it throbbed in time with the winking lights. "It's *been* like this!" she moaned. "'Fascinating'—right?"

"Not in the least." Spock studied her blinking panel with overt distaste. Then it squealed, the way it always did when the captain leaned on the button.

"I WANT SPOCK! NOW!" The channel cut off.

"Now that is somewhat more interesting. In your opinion, Commander, does the captain seemed perturbed?"

"Nooo, Mr. Spock," she sighed. "In my opinion, sir, the captain is having a fit. Sir, can you get that shore leave roster away from him? Until people know what's going on—"

"Understood, Commander. You have the conn. No one is dismissed."

"Yes, sir." Uhura glared at his retreating back; getting the conn in Spacedock just made her whole day . . .

"Uhura, what's wrong?" McCoy watched her, concerned.

"I—I don't *know,"* she confessed. "I mean, I have a headache, but—" Immediately McCoy produced a hypo-spray and began adjusting it. "Now, watch it, Doctor, I also have the conn."

"So? Who needs *two* headaches?" The spray hissed against her arm, and like magic the pain began to recede. Within moments she felt refreshed, brighter . . . wonderful . . .

"What *is* that stuff? Do you carry that around all the time?"

"Of course, Uhura. I'm a doctor. Now listen." McCoy leaned forward confidentially, patted her hand, and turned on the charm. "Can you do me just one little favor?"

"He's conning you," Sulu warned. "We're only going dockside."

"What *kind* of favor, Doctor?" she asked, fearing the worst.

"Can you find me just one little *shuttle?*"

In Spacedock shuttle bay #27, Lieutenant Robert Harper stepped through an open airlock into the waiting travel pod as the Romulan ship tracked past its curving viewport. Fred DiMuro was already there, his ebony face pressed close to the window.

"Hi, Fred. Look at that monster we'll be working on! Some job, huh?"

"I'm looking, Bobby. Security's really squeezing on this one. Wouldn't tell me a thing."

"All they told me is we report to Commander Dorish. But *some*thing's going on. I had to ID to even get in here."

"Yeah. Bet it's some new kind of weapon. Why else would they bring it . . . hey, where's the kid?"

"Fixing a drink dispenser in the bar. Shouldn't take long. Some jerk tried to reprogram it for doubles." Harper began a routine check of the flight panel. At the Academy it was always Harper—with his sandy hair, freckles, mild manner, and razor-sharp mind—who'd been at the top of everyone's list.

"I hear you turned down another assignment," DiMuro said critically. "That's crazy. *Nobody* turns down the *Enterprise.*"

"Aw, mind your own business, Fred. You don't know—"

"I know your little buddy isn't going anywhere, so you're still on the ground. A career won't wait forever. There's such a thing as losing it, you know."

"Well, a Dock assignment's not exactly on the ground. I *like* it. If I want other worlds, I can always go home."

It had been fun growing up in a museum. Life City sprawled in the blistering California desert under its glittering biodomes. The huge xenoculture project was the largest in the Federation, a galactic tour in artwork and holo displays. Bobby Harper spent his childhood stalking the caves of Epsilon Indi V, playing with the raincats of Menkar VII, building castles in the purple sands of Beta Algenib III, and helping his mother catalogue the artifacts of over a thousand cultures within and beyond the Federation. She was the museum's director. Her office walls were plastered with degrees and awards, so many she'd lost count—and *she'd* never told him he was "losing it."

"They'd never let the little guy join Starfleet, Harper. Face it."

"You don't know that. That 'little guy' is tougher than—"

"I *do* know, Bobby. There's just no room for someone who can't take it—even a whiz with machines."

Harper's jaw set stubbornly. "So, Mr. Academy Goof-off, now *you're* the authority on who can take it and who can't?"

"You can't even keep a *girlfriend* with the kid tagging along!"

Tired of the argument, Harper turned to watch the view.

The Romulan ship was out of sight. Along the curving expanse of docking bays, *Enterprise* settled on her moorings. Harper imagined streaking through the stars, imagined being aboard her. And he'd be aboard right now, except for one little—

"Bbbobby?" A gurgling cry sounded from the corridor.

"In here!" he called.

DiMuro started shaking his head. "Sounds like a talking water cooler! Hey, I'm sorry, Bobby, but that *is* what it sounds like."

"Yeah, I know." Harper grinned. A scuffling in the hall was followed by a soft thud against the door and a plaintive sigh.

"Wwwoops, Bobby!"

"Ya gotta ID. Put your hand up."

"Oookay, Bbbobby!" With a soft chime the door whooshed open.

A Belandrid padded in, blinking its neon-yellow eyes. Barely one meter tall, weighing only 12 kilos, it moved on delicate webbed feet, waving its fragile webbed fingers at Harper in greeting. The species was classified as "humanoid": two arms, two legs, and bilaterally symmetrical. But its skeleton was composed of cartilage; it possessed both gills and lungs; its toes and fingers (seven on each limb) ended in filament-like tips, which performed tasks with equal efficiency. Its head was egg-shaped and hairless, its eyelids vertical, and its mouth made a tiny round O. Even on land, its voice gurgled when it spoke. As it climbed through the airlock, its translucent, pale-blue skin began to blush pink with delight, and it reached out to pat Harper affectionately.

"Hhhiya, Bbbobby!"

"Hiya, Obo." Harper patted it back, thinking how little he knew about his friend, including how to spell its real name.

All Belandrids looked alike, but only this one had left its ocean planet Belandros and returned to Earth with the Federation contact team. No one knew why. Or why its uncanny knack for machinery went unnoticed until it encountered a new officer on Spacedock: engineering Lieutenant Robert Harper.

Clad in a tiny suit of coveralls, Obo had followed Harper around his first day, offering to hold things, making itself useful. Harper assumed it belonged there. And when Commander Dorish stood over him, chewing him out because a set of relays wasn't on line yet, Obo said "Eeeasy fix," reached bare fingers into the circuitry, and synched the entire panel in a matter of seconds.

Word got around. Obo's scheduled departure day came and went. No one questioned talent. Obo was so sought-after that even the higher-ups—certainly Commander Dorish—just naturally assumed this small presence was somehow authorized by Starfleet. Truth to tell, no one wanted to learn otherwise. So Obo stayed. And Harper stayed—and hoped no one would dig too deep.

Because DiMuro was right: Obo could never serve in Starfleet.

Although its vocabulary was limited and childlike, Obo could speak English; it could understand and follow orders. But it had no concept of rank or discipline. It was incapable of defending itself or anyone else. It did not comprehend deceit or anger or malice. It fainted or burst into tears when criticized harshly; when praised it hugged its supervisor. (Harper had explained about that, over and over, but sometimes Obo forgot.) So people were grateful, but they made little jokes and dismissed Obo with a pat on the head, which was all it seemed to want out of life: to be loved and to fix things and to be with Bobby Harper. Obo didn't mind if no one took it seriously. Only Harper minded that. Only Harper believed there was more to Obo than met the eye and that someday everyone would realize it. Meanwhile, he wasn't going off without his friend. And if a girl didn't like Obo "tagging along"—then she was the wrong girl for Bobby Harper.

"People getting their drinks okay now?"

Obo nodded vigorously. *"Eeeasy* fix! *Verrry* quick! Gggood, gggood Ooobo!"

"And what've *you* been drinking tonight?"

"Wwwater! Mmmy *fffavorite!"*

DiMuro grinned. "You're a cheap date, Obo, ya know that?"

"Yyyes, Fffred."

The display on the panel came to life with a visual of their position, destination, and designated traffic lane. The flight computer relayed instructions. "DOCK CENTRAL TO POD 27: PROCEED TO REPAIR DOCK 4. YOU ARE CLEARED FOR DEPARTURE. DUTY OFFICER, CONFIRM FOR VOICEPRINT AND ENTER SECURITY CODE."

"Acknowledged, Central. Lieutenant Robert Harper. Code 8121."

"See what I mean?" DiMuro whispered. "We can't tell anyone what we're doing up here!"

"*Sssecret,* Bobby?" Obo's eyes elongated and blinked in amazement. "Secret for *mmme?*"

"Big secret—*especially* for you," warned Harper. He worried about secrets. Sometimes Obo forgot those too.

DiMuro guided the pod out into the streams of traffic, and Harper watched the *Enterprise* as they approached. Lights played across her shining hull, and her call letters NCC-1701 fell away beneath them as they climbed into their programmed flight path.

"*Nnnever* tell! Oookay, Bbbobby?"

"Okay, Obo. Now you be good tonight. You do what I say. Don't wander off, and don't fix anything without permission . . ."

The pod accelerated as it flew along the curving labyrinth of docking bays into the constant twilight of Spacedock's harbor.

"Perhaps it is merely routine, Captain," said Spock, frowning at the decoded message on Kirk's screen. Kirk shook his head.

"Routine? You don't be*lieve* that, do you?"

"Difficult to say, Captain. The lack of clarity with which—"

Kirk wasn't listening. *"Damn* that Nogura!" He looked at the message again himself, in case somehow the words had changed. They hadn't: ADMIRAL JAMES T. KIRK, CMDR., U.S.S. *ENTERPRISE:* RE: DISCOVERY/ RECOVERY OF ROMULAN SHIP: FILE INCIDENT REPORT IN PERSON BY 0800 HRS, THE 15TH. ADMIRALTY SENDS REGARDS AND HAS SOME GOOD NEWS. HOW ABOUT LUNCH? . . . HEIHACHIRO NOGURA.

"The 15th—that's the day after tomorrow." Kirk slapped the flat of his hand down on the desk. "I beat him, you know, when I ducked out on the Admiralty, and he can't *stand* it!"

Spock stood patiently, hands behind his back, waiting for his captain's temper to cool. "I *more* than justified my command out there! We brought home a *Romulan warship!*"

"Which further enhances your reputation," Spock pointed out, attempting to interject some perspective. "But to conclude—"

"That's just *it,* don't you *see?* Now he can pin a *medal* on me, stick me behind a *desk* again—and *congratulate* me while he does it! So all along I was damned if I did and damned if I didn't. I should've seen this coming."

"I am not certain that I follow—"

"It's the fundamental principle of bureaucracy—to rise to the level of one's own incompetence."

"Surely not, Captain. That would be absurd."

"It happens all the time. Here's how it works. There's this guy, see, and he makes—oh, say, widgets . . ."

Not wishing to interrupt, Spock tilted his head and tried to look well-informed.

". . . and he makes widgets—real *good* widgets—which he *loves* doing. So he's always on time, and he works real hard, even finds ways to make *better* widgets. So, what do they do?"

Spock shook his head, mystified.

"They make him a vice-president! Which he knows nothing about! Which he's no good at *doing!* And they train someone else to make the widgets, which was all this guy wanted to do in the first place . . ." Kirk looked around at his cabin, as though he were seeing it for the last time. "All I've ever wanted was to command a starship, Spock. *This ship.* It's what I do best. Nogura doesn't need me. Why can't he just leave me alone?"

Spock thought a moment. If the captain had wanted sympathy, he would have summoned Dr. McCoy. While he didn't begin to fathom the irrationale of bureaucracies or Admiral Nogura's intentions, he had an uneasy sense his friend was probably correct about both.

"Can you not simply decline a ground assignment?"

"Theoretically." Kirk was glum. "On paper, maybe, but

to his face . . ." Not a second time. The worst moments of Kirk's career, worse than Klingon disrupters and alien entities, were spent in Nogura's office in a battle of wills to regain command of the *Enterprise.* He won that one, because some unidentified power was bearing down on Earth and Nogura had to admit that Kirk's experience in dealing with the unknown just might improve the odds, which were then too slim to even calculate. Kirk beat them anyway. In the rosy afterglow of public gratitude, he found he could write his own ticket, and he did. But that was a long time ago.

There was no emergency now, no lever Kirk could think of to use. *Enterprise* nestled snugly in her dock; Earth turned safely beneath them, and Kirk felt himself being manipulated by a hand he could no longer control.

"Well, then . . . so be it." His anger began to give way to depression and a cold inner voice, telling him that he might not be able to get out of this one. Spock didn't know Nogura the way he did. Spock couldn't be expected to read between the lines. *What did I expect Spock to do, anyway? Pull a rabbit out of his hat?* Ashamed of himself, Kirk realized that was exactly what he'd expected—and aside from being impossible, it wasn't fair to Spock. He recovered himself abruptly. "Sorry, Spock, not your problem. You go on. We'll talk about this later."

"As you wish, Captain, but . . . would you satisfy my curiosity on one small point? Why do you feel that you must meet with Admiral Nogura on the 15th?"

Kirk stared at him; it wasn't like Spock to miss the whole point. "Because those are my *orders!*"

"No, Captain. I do not wish to seem presumptuous, but those are *not* your orders." Kirk's mouth hung open, and he stared at his screen in disbelief. "As I previously indicated, the wording is imprecise and therefore open to interpretation . . ."

Finally, Kirk saw it. He began to grin.

"You're right, Spock—you are *right! 'By'* 0800 hours!"

"Which could mean that you must be prompt, or—"

"A deadline!"

"You must file the *report* in person, that much is clear. Lunch, however, seems optional. This sort of error does not occur among Vulcans. Perhaps the inherent ambiguity of your language—"

"Or perhaps," laughed Kirk, "I'd better go file that report right now."

"Tonight?"

"Well . . . why not? Nogura won't be around. Hardly anyone will. The brass'll be in the officers' lounge." Kirk began to pace again; the pieces were falling into place: a quick trip down and back, irrefutable proof he'd been there—they wouldn't find his entry until the 15th, and by then . . .

"Spock. We're shipping out at 2300 tomorrow night. Inform the department heads. This ship has a mission to complete!"

"Ah. Indeed. And will you be granting *shore leaves,* Captain?" Spock asked pointedly.

"I'll have a mutiny on my hands if I don't. But let's keep it simple. Two twelve-hour rotations, half the crew each . . . oh, damn." Kirk noticed the padd and stylus lying untouched on his desk.

"Allow me, Captain," offered Spock, deftly taking possession of the elusive document. "Shall I call for a shuttle?"

"Right away. Want to come along? Dabble a bit in conspiracy?"

"Really, Captain," Spock did his best to look affronted, "I am unaware that any conspiracy exists. I plan a visit to HQ tomorrow, but tonight I am expecting a guest on board."

"Oh, yes, that student of yours. I'll be back in a few hours. If there's time, I'd like to meet him."

"Why, that would be . . . most interesting. Thank you."

"Thank *you,* Spock."

"Not necessary, Captain. I simply assisted you in carrying out your orders. That, of course, is my function."

"Of course." *And some things,* thought Kirk gratefully, *like the sun and the moon and Spock just never change—and whatever would I do if they did?* "So how about seeing me off? Or do you need to get back to the bridge?"

"I think not," said Spock, relieved to avoid conditions that had likely deteriorated in his absence. "I shall join you on the hangar deck. And if I may express an opinion, I am gratified that your prompt compliance with the admiral's directive will prevent unwarranted disruption in our routine. The loss of efficiency would be regrettable. Now, if you will excuse me, Captain . . ."

"Why certainly, Mr. Spock . . ." Kirk watched the door close, then laughed aloud. *Don't worry, I won't tell a soul—no one would believe me anyway* . . . but for just a second there, he was positive that he'd seen his efficient, logical, imperturbable Mr. Spock . . . calmly pulling a rabbit out of an empty hat.

When Spock called the bridge moments later, Uhura answered breezily: *"Bridge, and I* still *don't know!"*

"Spock here. Commander, are you quite well?"

"Just fine, Mr. Spock! No problems here!" There was a chorus of guffaws in the background. Prudently, he chose to ignore them.

"Very well. The shore leave schedule is appearing now on all displays. You may wish to inform the crew."

"Why, Mr. Spock! Has anyone ever told you you're a wizard?"

"Certainly not, Commander. That would be preposterous." There was no magic involved in making a request of the ship's computer or in the one point five minutes it required to comply, without misunderstandings, temper tantrums, or exhausting exuberance. "Dismiss bridge personnel and yourself when your relief arrives."

"Oh, I'll stay on, sir. I wouldn't wish this on anyone—and I feel fine now, really I do. Just fi—"

"Indeed. How very commendable. I am expecting an arrival in twenty-six minutes. Please inform me when it signals and direct it to the hangar deck. Immediately, however, the captain requires transport planetside. When is the first shuttle available?"

"About ten minutes, sir, but . . . it's on order for Dr. McCoy."

"In that case it will do nicely. Direct it to the hangar deck as well and divert all other craft to airlocks."

"Aye, sir. But, uh, what should I tell the doctor?"

"You may tell him, Commander, that he is . . ." the pause was filled with possibilities, ". . . outranked. Spock out."

Fortunately, he never heard the doctor's response.

Harper and DiMuro stood on the Romulan bridge, re-reading the dispatch order and inspecting two bright objects placed side by side on the navigation station. The boxes looked identical: the same weaving lights in spiral patterns, the same changing rainbow hues, the same transparent surface.

"Beats me, Fred. I've never seen anything like it."

"Me neither. Does Mr. Spock say which one he wants?"

"Nope. Just one, delivered by hand to Exo-Sci down at HQ—all the off-world artifacts get analyzed there. Most of this order deals with the transport specs: antigravs, no pressure changes, no transporter beams. He doesn't know what these are any more than we do."

"Sure is *picky,* isn't he," DiMuro grumbled.

"So I hear, but picky is Standard Operating Procedure when you don't know what you're dealing with." Harper activated the air cushion in a shipping container, lowered in a box on antigravs, sealed the lid and tagged it. Then he stared into the remaining one, wondering what was in there. "Wish Mom could see this. Due respect to Mr. Spock, but *she's* the specialist. It ticks her off how Starfleet gets first crack at things. Say, maybe—" He reached for his communicator.

"C'mon, Harper, all the action's down in engineering!"

"Take it easy, Fred—Commander Dorish? Harper here, sir. Mr. Spock's cargo's ready for the courier. We found four. They look like some sort of art form, but it's kinda hard to say without—"

"Not our department, Harper. I need you boys down here—and that fellow with all the fingers."

"Yes, sir. But could Life City take a look at one of these?"

"Drumming up business for your mother, eh, Harper?"

"Well, sir, she'd be happy to, and she has clearance. Should I check with Mr. Spock? It'll only take a minute."

"No, I cleared his request, guess I can clear yours. If she doesn't mind, what could it hurt? I'll call it in. Your courier's docking now, so finish up and get down here."

"Aye, sir—thank you, sir! Harper out . . . good old Dorish!" He began working on another container as he snapped his communicator shut. "Didn't go all regulation on me. Could've, too, because—"

"Come *on*. You heard what the man said."

"Slack off, Fred, we're waiting on that courier." He sealed the second box. *Hi, Mom!* he keyed on its tag, *Fresh from the Romulan Empire!* He didn't notice the ensign who strolled onto the bridge. But DiMuro perked up immediately.

"Hel*lo* there! Can I help you?"

Harper turned—and found himself staring at a young woman, his age (or maybe a year or two older), medium height, with a trim figure, soft brown curls, and a winsome face. Right now, the ensign was all business as she consulted the orders in her hand.

"Yes, if you're Mr. Harper. I'm Korbet, and I'm supposed to . . . wow!" She peered around the dingy bridge. "A real live Romulan warship—what a hunk of *junk!*"

"Sure is. Those Romulans are very predatory, you know. Now what's a nice girl like you doing on a bridge like—"

"Fred . . . hi, I'm Harper. Don't mind him. Someone must've let him off his leash." *She's pretty,* he thought as she smiled. *I'll bet she gets this all the time. At least she thinks it's funny.*

"That's okay." Korbet grinned. "Lots of people get affected by their surroundings." She and Harper laughed together, enjoying the joke. Then their eyes met, and they kept smiling at each other for no reason at all. Finally, blushing, Korbet collected herself. ". . . um . . . these go down to HQ? What are they?"

"Huh? Oh, nobody knows. This one to HQ . . ." *How could anyone's eyes be that blue?* ". . . and this one goes out to Life City. Dorish is calling in your orders now. Gee, I'm sorry about the extra trip . . ." his voice trailed away. He couldn't stop smiling, and she kept smiling back.

"No problem. They're predicting storms over 'Frisco tonight, but the desert'll be real nice flying." Very slowly, she checked the tags and transport specs; they took some time examining each other's duty logs. "Well, um . . . will that be all . . . Mr. Harper?"

"Bobby. Yeah, I'm afraid . . . I mean, thanks, uh . . ."

"Jessie." The blue eyes twinkled. "You're welcome."

Harper bent down to switch on the containers' antigravs, and DiMuro salvaged what was left of his ego for a parting shot.

"You be careful with 'em, Korbet—or Mr. Spock'll get you."

"I'm always careful," she said, guiding her cargo into the lift. "So tell him not to worry, whoever he is." She waved at Harper through the closing doors. He turned to DiMuro, smitten.

"Oh . . . she's the *one,* Fred! She's *perfect!* She's smart, she's beautiful—she *likes* me! She'll even like Obo, I can *tell*—don't ask me *how,* but . . . oh, no!" Harper snapped back to reality. "Where *is* Obo? I haven't seen it since—oh, this is awful . . ."

"We'll be on report, *that's* what's awful!"

". . . could be anywhere by now! Aw, I told it not to wander off . . . Obo?" He searched frantically, hoping it was somewhere on the bridge. At last he heard a faint, miserable hiccup.

Obo sat in a disconsolate heap, wedged under the comm station, arms wrapped around itself and eyes blinking distrustfully. "We go *hhhome,* Bobby!" it whimpered fretfully.

"No, we just got here. Hey, what's wrong? You sick or something?" He knelt to take a closer look.

"Bbbad place, Bobby! Go home *nnnow!"*

DiMuro groaned. "Jeez, this is all we need—Obo with a case of the vapors. Can you imagine on a *ship* under *fire*—"

"Stuff it, Fred. Listen, Obo, we can't go home. We've got work to do. Now, do you want to stay here? All by yourself?"

"No!" it wailed, terrified. "Stay with you!"

Obo extended an arm out to Harper, who pulled it to its feet. The Belandrid was scared, Harper realized. "Wonder what's bothering it," he wondered out loud as the three of them piled into the lift. "There's always a reason—"

"Who *cares?* This whole thing's been a big waste of time."

"No it wasn't, Fred. We were just doing a favor—and like Dorish said, what could it hurt?"

It is illogical, mused Spock, *to look forward to events. They seldom unfold as planned.* But as he watched his captain's shuttle depart and contemplated the empty landing bay before him, Spock admitted that he was looking forward to this night.

It was a long way from the dust of Hellguard to the hangar deck of the *Enterprise.* Only he and Saavik knew how far. Tonight people would meet a cadet on her first tour of a Federation starship, find nothing unusual except that she was a Vulcan, and never know why their easy assumptions were the highest form of praise. And even as he looked forward, Spock couldn't help looking back—to a very different night, only six years ago.

She had dismantled his computer that morning and broken his last padd and stylus that afternoon. Believing himself prepared for this occasion, Spock produced a large stack of paper, a box of graphite pencils, and a hand-drawn chart of intricate runes. The evening lesson was a single sentence:

My name is Saavik, written in Vulcan.

The pencils snapped. The papers tore. Spock's parentage was maligned, and the gods were invoked with increasing venom. Unaware that these were merely storm warnings, he met each outburst serenely with a fresh pencil, a fresh piece of paper, and implacable encouragement.

"You can make your name on the computer, Saavikam. Now you are learning to write it yourself. Do not be impatient. For everything, there is a—"

"*HATES* YOU FIRSTTIMES!" she shrieked, unleashing a barrage of pencils, papers, fists and screams. "*HATES* YOU STUPID SONABASTARD WORDS! HATES *YOU!*" She hurled the chart across the room and knocked its stand to the floor. "GO, SPOCK! GO *A-WAY!*"

"Saavik. You are overtired, and I believe that—" the pencil box whizzed past his head, shattered against the wall, "—has made you cross. Come along now. It is time to go to sleep."

"*NOT! NOT*SLEEPS!" Her eyes went wild with fear, and she scrambled over the table out of reach, poised to run the opposite way if he came after her. "*YOU*GO STUPID SLEEPS! *YOU*GO WRITES YOU STUPID SELF! YOUGO A-WAY, SPOCK! GO *A-WAY!*"

"Very well, Saavik, there is no need for further damage." He eyed the armchair she was swinging above her head. "Our lesson is *over.*" He turned, dignity unruffled, and left; the chair sailed across the room and splintered as it smashed against the closing door. It was a long night. Silences were punctuated by spates of cursing and bashing, followed by more silence. Spock lay on his bed, staring into the dark and wondering where he had gone wrong.

In the morning he opened her door to a scene of devastation, amazed there could have been so many breakable objects in one room. He waded through the ankle-deep debris and shreds of crumpled paper to the table on which Saavik was curled asleep, clutching a mangled page in her hand. He eased it from her fingers. The words were malformed, torturously carved, but they were legible and correctly spelled: SPOCK NOTGO MY NAME IS SAAVIK.

He looked at the words and at the permanent frown on Saavik's sleeping face. He looked at the room. He wondered where they would be living after Saavik was required to write a paragraph. And he folded the paper carefully and put it away.

Spock knew nothing of children, except that he had once been one, had managed to get over it, and saw no need to dwell upon things that could not be helped. It was one thing to save a life, quite another to undertake its education—for a reason he could never explain to anyone, least of all to himself: the deep and disturbing conviction that this small destiny must not be left to chance. More to the point, Saavik would tolerate no one else, and no one else would tolerate her. At Gamma Eri she refused to claim her Vulcan kin and attacked other children at every opportunity. So Spock took a year's leave (time to make her presentable, make her change her mind—a very *long* time) and took Saavik elsewhere.

Dantria IV, a remote, bucolic world, was ideally suited to his purpose. Its gentle, gray-skinned inhabitants seldom wondered at the tall man and darting child who lived in a house beyond the forest. Spock wondered a great deal. Unaccustomed to proceeding without theory or expertise, he had the sensation of teetering constantly on the brink of disaster. Knowing about children would not have helped in this case, so he applied himself to knowing about Saavik— and took life one crisis at a time.

She often demanded to see her knife, particularly when being chided for some offense, and she knew exactly where it was kept: in a box, high up on a shelf. Spock always showed it to her, reminded her she must never use it, and tried not to think what would happen if she did. But he could never bring himself to lock the box. In fact, he treated Saavik the same way he treated everyone else—with kindness, dignity, and respect. And in time a curious thing began to happen: Saavik began trying to imitate his courteous approach. She even began to obey him, in her own fashion and after exhausting all the whys, which seemed to him a fair exchange. If that did not exactly serve the cause of

Vulcan propriety, it served Spock and Saavik well enough. And she kept her word: she didn't kill again, but she didn't give up hunting either. Not for food—now there was more than she could be coaxed to eat—but this planet teemed with creatures she'd never seen before, and Saavik took to bringing them home alive. She led a steady procession of Dantrian wildlife in and out of the house: rodents, reptiles, birds—and, one harrowing morning, a child.

Hearing her voice, Spock stepped outside and stared at what he saw: a gray-skinned, wispy-haired Dantrian infant (of indeterminate gender and no verbal skills) tethered firmly to a tree by a rope around its waist. It sat bewildered and sucking on its fingers, while Saavik (hands clasped behind her back) paced to-and-fro, instructing it in the rudiments of behavior.

". . . and now I tells how you be a Vul-can! Notkills anyones anymores! Noteats lit-tul an-ni-mals! Stops you cur-sings! Wears you shoes! Trynot in-ta-rupt! Be la-gee-kal, like Spock! *Notnot!* You *stupid!* Noteats *own* fin-gers!" she cried, exasperated, and plucked them none too gently from its mouth. "Not la-gee-kal! You eats someones *else's!*" Deprived of its only sustenance, the child began to wail, and Spock hastily intervened.

"Where did you get this, Saavik?"

"Finds it! Bro-ken!" she complained, as would any aggrieved consumer who had acquired a faulty product. "And *stupid!* It eat on *own* fin-gers!" she shouted over the screams.

"Allow it to do so," he advised, wincing at the intolerable sound, "so it will stop making that noise." She pried open a tiny fist, located the appropriate digits, and stuck them back in its mouth where they lay ignored, while the cries grew shriller and more insistent. Spock and Saavik stared at each other in mutual dismay. "Perhaps it is hungry. We must ascertain where it belongs and return it—immediately. And *carefully,* Saavik! Do not damage it!" *Abduction, kidnapping . . . how would he explain*— "No, no! Not upside down, Saavik! I am sure that is not correct!" But given this new perspective on life, the child ceased crying and began to squeal and chortle with delight.

At that propitious moment the search party arrived: two small guilty boys and a frazzled mother, all delirious with relief. Grasping the infant firmly by its ankles, Saavik started forward.

"Saavik, let me—" but a joyful reunion was in progress.

"Oh, look, they found *Baby!* And Baby is all *right!* Baby is so *happy!* Isn't that *wonderful!*"

"I do it! *I* finds it!" Saavik presented Baby, drew herself up proudly, and ignored Spock's quelling glare.

"My, wasn't that *clever!* Aren't you a *clever* little girl!"

"Yes I are! It notgo a-way! I *tells* it things and—"

"She meant no harm, Madam. She brought your child home to—"

"I *ties* it on a *rope* and *tells* it things and—"

"What a good *idea!* Better than trusting the *Boys!* The *Boys* took Baby out in the *woods!* The *Boys* went off and *forgot* it! The *Boys* just would be *boys,* wouldn't they!" The Boys were prodded forward and dolefully agreed. Saavik was bursting with her news.

"And you knows what it *do?* It *eat* on *own*—"

"Ex*cuse* me, Saavik. Madam, your child appeared hungry, but—"

"IT EAT ON OWN FIN-GERS!"

"Yes, dear, a Very Bad Habit, and Baby *must* be made to stop. *So* sorry for the trouble! So grateful! What can ever repay—"

"Nothing, nothing at all, Madam—*truly.*"

"Why, the nice little girl must come for a *visit!* Would the nice little girl *like* that? A nice little *visit?*"

"NO!" Saavik scowled and ducked behind Spock, narrowly escaping a pat on the head. The Boys looked on enviously.

"Shy little thing, isn't she!"

"Not . . . precisely . . ."

"But so *good* with *babies!* Just a *little* visit? Not today? Well, then *soon . . .*" At last they departed, taking turns holding, hugging, and kissing Baby, whose gender was never alluded to.

Spock took a moment to recover from the encounter, then turned to Saavik with a number of things on his mind. He began with the easiest. "You were interrupting, Saavik."

"I spea-kings first. You in-ta-rup-tings me! They wants it, Spock, and it so stupid." Puzzled, she watched until they were out of sight.

"They are its own people. The child belongs with them . . . and you have people of your own. On Vulcan. Do you want to find them too?"

"Why?" she asked suspiciously. "Theygo lost?"

"No. But you belong together."

"They notfinds *me. I* notgo lost." She gazed at him, eyes dark and solemn. "You notwants me too, Spock? Be-cause I in-ta-rupt? Be-cause I makes you tells me things? You wants mego a-way?"

"No, Saavikam. We need not speak of it again."

"If Igo lost, yougo finds me?"

"Yes, Saavikam. I will."

"Well, if yougo lost, Igo finds you too. But you trynot go lost, Spock. And I trynot in-ta-rupt anymores. Tells me somethings new now! Firsttime!"

"Indeed. You have expressed a wish to join Starfleet, so—"

"Not a *wish!* It what I *do!* Ex-cuse me."

"So you must learn to follow our most important rule. Now listen carefully, Saavikam. It is called the *Prime Directive . . ."*

Spock's sense of impending doom gradually gave way to the daily marathon of life with Saavik. She was energy in constant motion. She possessed formidable intelligence, acute perception, and a ruthlessly logical mind. Her moods were turbulent, her attention span exhausting, and she was even more compulsively curious than himself. He found he enjoyed her company. He hadn't expected that. Or to begin telling tales of his captain and his ship and all the worlds and peoples he had seen, night after night as they watched the stars. To teach her, he told himself. And had he admitted it, to see—just once—if she would smile. But Saavik never smiled. And if she cried, he never saw it.

And Spock found something else, which he didn't examine too closely: the respect and trust of someone who needed him, who needed precisely what he had to offer, who never asked for what he could not give. Sympathy and sentiment were of no use to her at all. Saavik required information—constant, endless, complete information—and Spock possessed an inexhaustible supply of that. Saavik gave him something in return, a thing so simple, so rare that he had never found it in his life: acceptance. Unemotional, matter-of-fact acceptance of himself exactly as he was. She never judged him as the Vulcans did (and as Spock judged himself) by a rigid code of correct behavior. She never watched and waited as the humans did for him to slip, to betray a trace of feeling, to "be human" . . . to fail. What did she know of humans or of Vulcans? She was only Saavik, and Spock was only Spock, who answered questions. Spock always answered. He found he couldn't help it.

But once he did come very close. Near the end of that year one quiet afternoon in the country, Saavik glanced up from her tricorder, pointed out across the field, and said:

"Look, Spock! Rabbits!"

"Yes," he murmured, eyes on his journal, "introduced for the predators after the drought. Terran, *Oryctolagus cuniculus;* family Leporidae, order Lagomorpha, class Mammalia, subphylum—"

"What are they doing?"

". . . mating, Saavik. Subphylum Vertebrata, phylum—"

"To make *more* rabbits? But they have too many already!" She frowned, propped her chin on her hands, and observed the process critically. Spock contemplated the cloud formations and wished for rain. "Vulcans do mating. Are there too many Vulcans, Spock?"

"No, Saavik." . . . and no rain in sight.

"Why are there too many rabbits, but not too many Vulcans?"

Yes, a logical mind. Spock addressed himself at length to various species' population problems: gestation periods, number of young at each birth, and frequency of mating. "Rabbits," he concluded, returning to his journal, "mate as often as every six weeks, whereas Vulcans must mate only once every seven years."

"Must?" she fastened on the word like a bad taste in her mouth. A poor choice; she had never cared for it. *"Must?"*

". . . Vulcan males . . . must. Yes."

"But that might be *inconvenient!*" This word, however, was her current favorite. "What if they don't want to? What if they're busy doing something else? What if . . ." Spock put it as gently as he could, but Saavik's face went pale. ". . . *Die?* We will *die* if—"

"Not unless, that is . . . females . . . seldom die. Do not distress yourself, Saavikam. It is . . . different for you." *I am doing this badly,* he thought. *Perhaps a study tape, at a more appropriate—*

"Then you go do that mating right away, Spock! So you won't die! When did you do it last? What kind of Vulcans did you make? And where are they?" She looked about as if they might appear in the field along with the rabbits. Spock got to his feet abruptly.

"Saavik, we must go now. It is growing late."

"No it isn't. And this is important. I want to know—"

"Do not argue, Saavik," said Commander Spock of the starship *Enterprise.* "Now put on your shoes and come along."

"No. I prefer *not* to put on my shoes and come along," she informed him, scowling. "That would be inconvenient. I want to know about making Vulcans—and what you did with *yours!*" She sat on the ground glaring up at him. Spock glared back.

"You are being de*lib*erately difficult, Saavik!" The instant he said it, he knew it wasn't true. She was deeply frightened.

"You say I am a Vulcan, but—" her voice shook, "—but you won't say what will *happen* to me! Why is that a bad question?"

And then it all came back to him, another afternoon seen through seven-year-old eyes: hot Vulcan sun streaming in the window, sand outside shimmering in the heat, the strangeness in his father's voice. Tomorrow Spock must go to see T'Pring; it was all arranged. They would touch each other's minds; they would meet again someday . . . and then, Sarek told him *why*. Motes of dust had floated, trapped in their sunbeams. The sand outside still shimmered in the heat, but it would never be the same again. The sand, the sun, his father . . . after that day, nothing was the same.

Spock knelt down beside her. "There are no bad questions, Saavikam, only complicated ones. And personal ones, which we shall discuss tomorrow. I do not know how it will be for you. I only know how it was for me. If I tell you," he bargained patiently, "will you promise not to argue and come home now?"

Wide-eyed, she scrambled to her feet. *"Must* I wear my shoes?"

"No, just . . . try not to interrupt . . ." They left the field and walked along the lane in the deepening shadows of late afternoon. And very quietly, as though it all happened to someone else a long time ago, Spock told her the truth. Saavik didn't interrupt once. She walked beside him in troubled silence for a while.

"I am glad you did not die, Spock. You or your captain."

"I, too, Saavikam."

"She was a bitch!"

"That is, among other things, inaccurate. The term refers—"

"Oh, I *know* what it refers—and that's what she *was!* What she did was *bad!*" Saavik stopped in the lane and stamped her foot, temper brewing. "You say it is bad to hurt people, but she made people hurt each other! That is much badder! She was a *bitch!*" Spock didn't trust himself to comment; he came perilously close to agreeing with her. "And why didn't she do her own fighting?"

"Because . . . it is not allowed. Men do not fight women."

"Why not? That's stupid! *I* would have fought you *myself!* I can fight anyone—kill them, too! Except," she added virtuously, "I don't do killing anymore. And I won't do that mating either!"

"I quite understand. You have a long time to decide." Shadows were gathering in the lane as they started off once more. Saavik walked closer beside him, kicking her toes in the dust.

"I just decided, Spock. My Vulcans would not be good ones."

"Now why is that, Saavikam?" he asked in spite of himself.

She began counting reasons on her fingers. "They would argue. And be de*lib*erately difficult. And interrupt, and curse, and hate to wear their shoes. And ask com-pli-ca-ted questions." She looked up at him wisely. "They would be *very* inconvenient, you know."

Spock's eyebrow actually ached, and it was a long moment before he spoke. "Not . . . necessarily," he said.

But through that year of Saavik's questions, some complicated questions of his own went unanswered—even more puzzling than how he could "recognize" this child he never saw before. And the most baffling question of all was Saavik herself. On that world where children killed to save themselves, why had she killed to save a stranger? Who taught her those words in Vulcan? Why her constant obsession with the stars? And now, despite his sincere approval of her progress, why did she attack her studies with such driven fierceness, as if the unknown were the enemy itself? And why, when she prowled the woods at night unafraid, why did terror leap into her eyes at any mention of the word *sleep?* Saavik would recount her discoveries to him in relentless detail, admit to him (with embarrassment) her uncertainties and failures, then trustingly follow his advice. She confided to him her troubles of the present and her aspirations for the future. But Saavik would never talk about her past. Never. And Spock would never insist.

A year was not so long after all. He prepared her for the day when he would leave. But when the moment came, he found himself less prepared than she. For the first time in his life, Spock thought about returning from a mission, wondered whether or not he would survive. She had no one else, and that was a disturbing thought.

Back on board the *Enterprise,* he opened his case to unpack his few belongings and found things not quite as he'd left them. Tucked in at the bottom under all the folded clothes, Saavik had hidden away her knife. Spock stood in the privacy of his cabin turning it in his hand, remembering every word of their good-bye.

". . . but *why* can't I come with you on your ship?"

"Because you are still too little, Saavikam. You must attend the Academy first. We have discussed this many times."

"I don't like being little!"

"Then eat your food and learn your lessons. Time will do the rest. Send me your questions every day, so I can send you answers and study tapes. Soon you will travel on a ship—in the stars. When the time comes, I will tell you exactly what to do, and I shall be waiting for you. A new world, Saavikam, with a real school. You will like that."

"Yes. But I don't need that family to take care of me."

"We know that, but they do not. And it is only for a short while. So be polite. Those children respect you, Saavikam. You must remember to be gentle with them."

"I will, Spock. I'll remember."

"And time passes more quickly than you think. Until we meet again, Saavik—live long. And prosper."

"Live long and prosper, Spock. I'll learn everything, I promise! And I'll stop being little! And someday I *will* come on your ship! I am going to *do* it, Spock! You will see . . ."

". . . to Mr. Spock, bridge to Mr. Spock," the comm was saying.

"Spock here."

"Sir, a shuttle's asking to dock on your authority," Uhura

said with a trace of amusement. *"The pilot says a Cadet Saavik requests boarding permission."*

"Thank you, Commander," Spock replied, with grave formality and no amusement at all. "Please acknowledge. Say that permission is granted. And that *Enterprise* welcomes Cadet Saavik aboard."

Chapter Four

I AM HERE . . . really, truly, here! Saavik's pulse was racing.

The moment she stepped onto the bridge, all Spock's stories came alive, in the very place they all began. It was here Spock watched the Tholians weave a web while his captain was trapped in nonexistence; here the doctor fell on his own hypo and nearly changed the Universe; here officers lay dying when Khan cut off their life-support; and here the captain played some high-stakes poker when his ship had only ten minutes to live. And hundreds of other things happened here, which Spock had told and (when she begged him) retold over the years. She knew them all by heart—and wanted to hear them all again. Once he even sent her a Starfleet training tape of this bridge on an uneventful day, and she played it over and over, memorizing every face, every inch of every panel she could see, longing to touch those consoles herself, to be one of those people, to *belong* on this ship in the stars.

So it didn't matter now that the people were all gone and the viewscreens were all dark and they were hanging anchored in a berth in Spacedock. Just standing here at last, on the bridge of the starship *Enterprise,* Saavik might as well have been flying.

An emotional reaction, she scolded herself, *to the best first*

*time I ever had! I won't show it. I belong to Starfleet now. I
have my own number, my own uniform. I'll remember to say
"Mister" Spock, and I'll do nothing to disgrace him, I
swear . . . no, I won't do that either . . .* and the people
weren't all gone. Someone was sitting at the comm station,
her chin resting on her hands. She appeared to be meditat-
ing, but Spock went over and spoke to her.

"Commander Uhura. This is my student, Saavik. She is in
her first term at the Academy. Saavik, this is Lieutenant-
Commander Uhura, our chief communications officer."

"Live long and prosper, Lieutenant-Commander Uhura."

Uhura looked up into the most earnest, intense face she'd
ever seen, and one of the most beautiful. Long, dark hair
framed high cheekbones, upswept eyebrows, and curled
behind delicate Vulcan ears. Black lashes fringed enormous
eyes that were burning with curiosity and a very un-Vulcan
excitement. The girl stood tall, thin, impeccably correct in
the trousers and jacket of her red cadet's uniform; and the
sturdy old tricorder she carried was in a brand-new case.
Except for her solemn, aloof dignity she seemed very young.
Her eyes widened in surprise and studied Uhura merciless-
ly. Uhura couldn't keep from smiling.

"Welcome aboard, Saavik. First time on the *Enterprise?*"

"Yes. You invented the *Rosecrypt*. It is remarkable. How
did you think of it?"

"Oh, well . . ." Uhura found herself answering, "I got
tired of the Romulans and Klingons breaking all our codes.
It began as a game—but they don't teach that to cadets, do
they?"

"No. It was the subject of a study tape from Commander
Spock, dealing with innovations in the encryption of secure
transmissions over subspace frequencies and creative appli-
cations of computer logic. It was most informative." Saavik
glanced at Spock; he was gazing calmly into the middle
distance, so she pursued the subject. "What fascinates me is
that I know precisely how it works, yet I cannot break the
cipher . . ."

Uhura was dying to see that study tape.

". . . and it began as a game? Interesting. Games are considered 'fun,' are they not? I am studying that." Saavik frowned and continued her intense scrutiny. Uhura tried not to appear amused.

"Well, games can be a lot of things. But yes, generally they're fun . . . Saavik? Is something wrong?" she asked gently, wondering if her hair had come undone.

"No," said Saavik. "But I have never seen anyone so aesthetically pleasing. I was unaware of that quality in humans. Oh." She bit her lower lip, frowned, and looked to Spock again. "I believe that was a personal remark."

"Several," he acknowledged.

"I apologize," she said. "I did not mean to be impolite."

"Don't worry, Saavik," Uhura beamed, delighted. "That's not impolite where I come from."

"I dare say Commander Uhura will survive the experience," Spock murmured. "Shall we explore the rest of the bridge?"

"Yes." Saavik nodded eagerly, then remembered something. "I appreciated our conversation, Lieutenant-Commander Uhura. I would like to speak with you further, if time permits. I have a number of questions. I shall be on board until tomorrow."

"Good, Saavik, I'd like that too. Do you have a cabin assignment yet?"

"No. A cabin is unnecessary, since I do not plan to sleep. That would be a waste of time."

"I see." Uhura gave Spock a sympathetic grin, but he seemed to find nothing out of the ordinary. "Then I'll see you later—and Saavik, have you ever looked in a mirror?"

"Yes," she answered, obviously puzzled.

"Well," smiled Uhura, "maybe you should look again."

"I . . . shall." Saavik turned away in confusion to follow Spock around the bridge.

At the science station she peered over Spock's shoulder as he demonstrated the sensors, then sat down to operate them herself, scanning ships in the dock and traffic patterns outside. Uhura overheard snatches of their conversation, which was conducted in low voices and in Vulcan.

". . . but what did she mean, Mr. Spock? Why should I look in a mirror? Is my appearance incorrect?"

"No, Saavikam, the commander was returning your compliment."

"I don't understand."

"Humans consider remarks about their personal appearances to be either compliments or insults. How they distinguish one from the other is very complicated, since it depends upon the degree of flattery involved and the current fashion of the moment. Tricky ground, Saavikam. Best avoided altogether."

"Oh. I am relieved I gave no offense, but I intended no compliment, Mr. Spock. I believe I was being entirely objective. Games are very important to the humans, aren't they?"

"Yes, Saavikam, they are indeed, frequently to the exclusion of all else. It is illogical, of course . . ."

I wouldn't have missed this for anything, Uhura decided. *That kid's not giving Spock a minute's peace—and he's as happy as a clam. Just goes to show: with Spock, you never know . . .*

". . . yes, Saavikam, we can come back," he said as they started to leave. "Commander, I am expecting a call from Headquarters within the hour. By then I should be in my quarters. I trust you will withstand the excitement of coming home."

"And the same to *you,* Mr. Spock." Uhura grinned.

Saavik nodded politely, choosing not to hazard another conversation, but she murmured in Vulcan as they waited for the lift. "Mr. Spock, what is the significance of coming home? Why does it cause excitement?"

"Now that is also very complicated, Saavik . . ."

Uhura couldn't stop chuckling after they were gone.

. . . no, you just never know . . .

* * *

It was going to storm.

Kirk's footsteps sounded loud on the paved, tree-lined walk that led toward Starfleet Headquarters. A flicker of lightning lit up the low blanket of clouds moving over the bay, and he began counting off the seconds. At one-thousand-and-nine, thunder shuddered in the distance. All around him the sweet seductive smells of a spring night beckoned: flowers in bloom, new-mown grass, and that peculiar, charged scent in the air just before a storm.

Earth in the spring, nowhere else quite like it. And suddenly he was seized by a homesick, irrational desire—to get the hell back to his ship. The brightly lit Plaza lay before him, and he ducked behind a tree feeling a little foolish.

From the landing site someone was crossing the square, guiding a shipping container on antigrav handles. Kirk could see her brown bouncy hair shine under the lights and wondered what she looked like up close. At night you went in by the front door if you didn't have priority access from the shuttledock—or if you didn't want your ID in its entry computer. He waited until she'd gone inside, waited a moment more, then crossed the Plaza and climbed the wide granite steps of Starfleet Headquarters.

The outer doors opened and with a familiar hiss slid closed behind him. Through the inner doors Kirk nodded to the ensign on duty at the front desk and strode briskly to the bank of lifts.

"Admiral . . . Admiral Kirk—sir!"

Damn.

"It's really you—sir!" The ensign was standing at attention, blushing to the roots of his carroty hair. He was also goggling at Kirk with undisguised awe. Kirk sighed.

"Evening, Ensign," he said, wondering how in blazes he could cover his tracks. "Yes, last time I checked, it really was me. Why? Am I wanted—dead or alive?" The ensign's face got redder.

"No, sir! Not that I know of—I mean—" The boy was in agony. Kirk took pity on him and cracked a smile. "I mean I read about you in history class, sir. Never thought I'd get to *meet* you!"

"History?" Much worse than being wanted dead or alive! "Ancient or modern?" Kirk asked a bit sharply.

"Uh . . ." The ensign wasn't sure. "Organian Peace Treaty, sir."

"Oh. Well, don't believe everything you read—and I see you do a lot of reading. That's against regulations, you know." The ensign stared aghast at the book in his left hand, a traitorous forefinger still marking the place. Kirk opened his palm for it like a schoolmaster confiscating a slingshot. "Let's see what's more exciting than pulling desk duty at night."

"Kid's book, sir," mumbled the ensign, embarrassed. "Present for my little brother. I saw it in an antique shop and spent my whole . . . well, sir, then I just couldn't put it down."

Kirk held the book in his hands, and for a moment the years fell away. It looked nothing like his own copy—real paper, that one was, with some of the pages cracking away and missing part of its leather binding. This one was a late 21st century, acrylo-laminated, guaranteed-never-to-wear-out edition, but the title hadn't changed in four hundred years: *Treasure Island,* by Robert Louis Stevenson. And the words on the flyleaf were still the same:

> *If sailor tales to sailor tunes,*
> *Storm and adventure, heat and cold,*
> *If schooners, islands, and maroons,*
> *And Buccaneers and buried Gold,*
> *And all the old romance, retold*
> *Exactly in the ancient way,*
> *Can please, as me they pleased of old,*
> *The wiser youngsters of today . . .*

"Lucky little brother," said Kirk wistfully as he handed it back. "I've a good mind to confiscate this, Ensign—and read it myself—but I was a little brother once. Besides, if you're a fast reader, you might finish it before you go off duty."

"Aye-aye, sir! Thank you, sir!" The boy glowed with pleasure and set about redeeming himself. "Uh, if you'll just sign right here, sir, I'll announce you . . ."

"Well . . . be against regulations not to, now wouldn't it?" Kirk grinned shamelessly. "Thing is, see, this is sort of a surprise. I'd hate to spill the beans too soon. What's your name, Ensign?"

"Richards! Sir!"

"You putting in for starship assignment, Richards?"

"Yes, *sir!*"

"Fine, fine. I like a man who knows a good book when he sees one." Kirk winked broadly and escaped. *And I should be shot for that,* he thought, *but he won't breathe a word. Richards. Nice kid, good book, lucky little brother—I'll remember . . .*

A few minutes later he stepped through a door four hundred feet underground into a level of Starfleet few officers even knew existed. Only two other starship captains had ever had clearance all the way down to "the Vault."

The huge, subterranean complex was deserted, as Kirk knew it would be. This was the giant brain, the nerve center of Starfleet Command; its self-contained, independent life-support could sustain two thousand people forever if necessary. But the Vault's day-to-day inhabitants were machines, and except for occasional maintenance crews, no one ever came here. In the silent, half-lit gloom, bank after bank of screens monitored the deployment of the fleet, the security status in all sectors of the Federation, data dumps from every starbase in the explored galaxy, and incoming telemetry from probes and sensors of what lay beyond. The main missions room upstairs was replicated here in miniature with a vast array of tactical displays. Over a century ago, at the height of the Romulan conflict, the Vault was hollowed out of bedrock under the old Starfleet building for impenetrability, secrecy, and survival if Earth should come under attack. That, of course, had never happened. But not all planets were the home of Starfleet, and even after a hundred years of peace, not all star systems were friendly neighbors.

While diplomats served in the front lines at embassies and councils, while starships patrolled the outposts and perimeters of the neutral zones, while the scales of galactic peace balanced, tipped and balanced again, far beneath the streets of San Francisco the air was always fresh. The food synthesizers were always maintained, and the data flowed in a never-ending torrent. Because peace could never be taken for granted, because Starfleet had to protect that peace, and because someone had to think the unthinkable—the Vault was designed for war.

Kirk hated the place.

But he could work here undisturbed. He could tap into any data bank in Starfleet undetected, and no one except a worshipful ensign would ever know he'd been here—until he was long gone.

Piece of cake! he congratulated himself, as he sat down at a terminal near the door. "Computer, access current Admiralty records. Any pending orders for Captain James T. Kirk."

"IDENTIFY FOR RETINA SCAN," a metallic, vaguely masculine voice instructed. Kirk sat through his third in the last three minutes. The computer confirmed his ID and displayed a few printed lines. Kirk swore freely and long.

There it was: his ground assignment to HQ, his commendation, even a date for the decoration ceremony. Every single important thing in his whole life, all shot to hell by some crisp green words on a little black screen.

"Not this time, Nogura!" he whispered through clenched teeth. "Computer, stick that back up the Admiral's . . . database."

"INSTRUCTIONS NOT CLEAR. PLEASE REPEAT."

"Reappend that file! Delete my request to view it! Delete *that* request, and delete my access to all data from this terminal. Route my entry through Debriefing, Records Office, fourth floor, terminal two." *That should do it,* he thought.

Kirk leaned back in the chair, linked his hands behind his head, and propped his feet up nonchalantly on the counter. "Open new file," he said. "Incident report . . ."

In the Exo-Science lab on the 18th floor of Starfleet Headquarters, Drs. Goldman and Rakir were kissing. This wasn't unusual. The most difficult challenge of Janet Goldman's already distinguished career was keeping her hands off her colleague when other people were around— but no one was around just now. It was silly anyway, since the whole department knew they were actually going to get married, and everyone thought that was delightfully traditional and very sweet. Janet Goldman thought so, too.

But El-Idorn Rakir was shy, easily embarrassed, and culturally . . . well, *quaint.* His people always were, even to the extreme of celibacy until after a formal exchange of vows. She caressed Rakir's smooth, noble face and sighed. Oh, yes, if he believed they must now be *married* . . . then far be it from Janet Goldman to infringe upon another being's cultural integrity!

They were so absorbed in interspecies communication that they didn't hear the courtesy chime, or the door when it opened.

"Excuse me? . . . Ex*cuse* me!" Jessie Korbet stood in the doorway, her hand on a floating shipping container.

"This better be important, Ensign." Goldman made no effort to stop, but Rakir extricated himself and tried to look busy.

"It is," Korbet said. "It's your delivery from Spacedock." They stared at her blankly. "You're the duty scientists tonight? You're supposed to confirm delivery with a Mr. Spock on the *Enterprise.* Dock didn't post this on your update?"

"Oh, I'm sure they did," Goldman said quickly. "Must've slipped my mind. So what did Spock send us?"

"We do not know, because we did not see our update," Rakir informed Korbet with a guilty glance at the dark message screen.

No kidding, thought Korbet. She held the container while they lifted its contents out with antigravs and set it on the counter.

"What is it?" breathed Rakir. "It is beautiful!"

They all stared into the clear, rectangular object, where a point of light coalesced and broke apart, expanding in a turning geometric design, shimmering in a vibrant rainbow of the color spectrum. When the pattern filled the box, the light seemed to bend. Color and line folded back in on themselves and diminished to a glowing point of light that began the cycle again.

"Don't know," said Korbet, "but it sure is pretty, isn't it? Came off that Romulan ship *Enterprise* brought in tonight. I guess they can't figure it out."

"Not even Spock? Wow! Bet *I* can!" Goldman grinned. "Let's put it under the Infrascan. Then we'd better call him. How come he didn't do this himself?"

"I don't know that either, Doctors, but I've got to get going. Another of those things goes out to Life City, and there's a storm coming in fast. Traffic'll be a mess."

"Have a safe trip, Ensign. Hope you beat the storm."

"Thanks, Doctors. Don't work too hard, now," Korbet winked. Goldman laughed, and Rakir blushed as the door closed.

Then Goldman went on staring into the box. Its flickering lights played across her face. "Look at this, Dorn. C'mon over here," she invited, "and I'll show you something."

"You show me many things, my Janet," he hesitated, then moved cautiously to her side, "and all of them distract me. Perhaps we should call the Mr. Spock."

"In a minute. Now, look at that—gotcha!" she giggled.

"Oh, you are devious, my Janet . . ." Rakir began to laugh too. And when they stopped laughing, they started kissing again.

Jessie Korbet's shuttle climbed above the storm. A bright full moon shone down on the boiling blanket of cloud, but up here the air was calm and still. She checked the monitor on her cargo hold: all safe and sound.

Tonight's my lucky night, she thought. *He's cute, that Bobby Harper—and nice, really nice. I have a good feeling about him . . .*

She always listened to those feelings—and to that little voice that came from somewhere beyond the Ops manuals and instrument checks. Instinct or intuition, "flying by the seat of your pants" or just plain good timing—whatever anyone called it, in the end it was luck. Jessie Korbet believed in luck. And so far, luck believed in Jessie Korbet.

Life City's domes were in sight, and the storm was far behind as she crossed the moonlit peaks of the Panamint mountains.

A stopover tonight at Life City—and tomorrow, another visit with Bobby Harper . . .

". . . and you are all settled in now at the Academy, Saavikam? Is there anything you require?" In the dim warmth of Spock's cabin, Saavik wrenched her eyes away from the chess set on his desk to answer his question. Her formality tonight pleased him. He knew she would rather be out of her chair inspecting his possessions and asking questions of her own. Paradoxically this also pleased him.

"Yes, Mr. Spock, I am all settled in now. And everything is provided by Starfleet. There is nothing I require."

Spock studied her over his steepled fingertips. She was looking well, a far cry from that emaciated, dangerous, furious urchin of Hellguard. And although it was irrelevant, Uhura was entirely correct.

"Nevertheless, there may be some things which you do not precisely require, but which would be of benefit to you, or simply pleasure. If so, you are to obtain them. Your credit balance is adequate for any contingency, Saavikam. You need not have booked your passage here on a cargo freighter."

"The credits were not the reason, Mr. Spock—the flight

time was the longest. I like being on a ship, you know. It seems to matter more where people are going than where they came from."

"Quite so, Saavikam. May I ask how you chose to account to Starfleet for the latter? If you prefer, I need not know."

"I . . . I decided to claim the Act of Privacy." She knotted her fingers together in her lap, avoiding his gaze. "It was just as you said. The tape is made unwitnessed, sealed, and classified—not even in the Academy files. They asked what planets I have visited for medical reasons, but only in the last three years. I am grateful for this law, but . . . the humans assume I am Vulcan. If I do not correct them, is that telling a lie?"

"No. Humans make many erroneous assumptions, and although they allow for the privacy required by other species, to them it is a somewhat relative term. You must define it for yourself."

"But to them *every* term is relative," she sighed. "Human speech is very difficult—riddled with idioms, even when issuing orders. And that could present grave problems, 'if you catch my drift!' I learned that one yesterday."

"You are not obliged, however, to overwork it, or to participate in their eccentricities. Idioms are only . . . the tip of the iceberg, as it were. You must study their emotions as well."

"Yes. And I chose a subject for that very purpose, Mr. Spock. It—" she frowned, took a deep breath, "—is a game."

"Ah. You observe the humans' reactions to it?"

"Yes. I also . . . participate."

?

She sighed again. "I knew you would say that."

"I have said nothing, Saavikam . . . yet. What is this game, and how did you come to choose it?"

That was the difficult part to explain. The sun was so hot that day, the sky so blue and perfect when she walked across the playing fields on her way from the Registrar's office. She found herself remembering an orange sky, jagged mountains, and acrid, choking dust. She hated remembering that. She hated all those questions she could never answer: *Date of birth? Parent(s) name(s)? Present homeworld?* And as she walked, she wondered how it would feel to know those answers and not be ashamed, how it would feel to . . . belong . . .

A crowd of people gathered around white lines drawn on the ground, many humans and an odd assortment of aliens. Some took turns swinging a stick, while one of them threw a small white ball—and threw it very badly. Saavik watched a long time before approaching the two humans who seemed to be in authority.

". . . so Koji can catch. We'll play that cadet at third."

"But Coach, he can't *run!*"

"So? He can *reach,* can't he? Whaddaya *want* from me?"

"But Coach, we got no *pitching*—'less you count that Walker kid. Leastways he can throw straight."

"Yeah, but if he ever finds the plate, they'll cream him."

"Excuse me," said Saavik, pointing toward the inept thrower. "Am I allowed to do that?"

"You tryin' out for the team?" The human with pink, spotty skin looked depressed. The brown one buried his face in his hands. Saavik didn't know what The Team was, but she wanted to throw that ball. And she didn't know a breeze had blown her hair away from her ears.

"Yes," she said.

"What? Are you crazy?"

"Uh, Joe . . ." The pink human administered a swift kick to the brown one. "Sure, you all get a chance. That's the rule. Name?"

"Saavik. With two A-letters. May I know your names?"

"Huh? Oh, I'm Tommy. That's Joe, the coach. Hey, Joe," he muttered, "you want I should catch this?"

"Naw," Joe groaned dismally, "I'll do it." He went to replace a player who wasn't quite getting the hang of things. Saavik was at a loss to account for his disapproval; her uniform was neat and correct, which was more than could be said for anyone else present.

"Don't mind Coach," said Tommy, as they walked to a circle of dirt in the center of the white lines. "He's got problems. Now here's the ball, Saavik. You just throw it all the way to Joe there, hard as you can."

"Are you sure?" she asked doubtfully.

"Sure, I'm sure! Only . . . try to *aim* it, okay?"

"I understand," said Saavik.

"Oh yeah? Then you're way ahead of everybody else today. Hey, you!" he shouted to the person waiting to swing the stick. "Back off. This'll only take a minute."

Saavik's fingers closed over the ball, feeling its skin-like texture, the way it fit right into her hand. The sun beat down on her head, and she smelled the dust beneath her feet. But it was the heat of other suns, the smell of other dust that filled her mind. And something comfortingly familiar, something she knew how to do . . . shape and weight were different . . . easier, really . . .

"Aim for this, kid!" Joe held up his hand covered with thick brown padding. "Ya ready? We don't got all day!"

"I am ready," Saavik said—and threw the ball.

Before it left her hand (swore everyone who saw it happen) Joe was flat on his back, the ball embedded in his mitt. Shouts and whistles of approval went through the crowd. After a moment he rolled over and got to his knees, clutching his hand and grinning from ear to ear. "Are you injured?" Saavik called, alarmed; the shouts changed to hoots of laughter.

"Naw, naw! Hey, kid, what's-yer-name," he ignored an offered icepack and started toward her, "can ya do that again?"

"Saavik. And it does not seem advisable. Are you certain—"

"Naw, dammit," he growled, "quit askin', will ya? Hey, Koji! Get in there an' catch!" A large, husky cadet lumbered out and, with theatrical flourish, began donning the protective gear over his uniform. The crowd applauded wildly. "Okay," said Joe, "ya don't gotta kill him. Just toss a few."

She threw the ball again and again with smooth economy of motion, picking it neatly out of the air with her bare hand when it was thrown back. The crowd cheered each pitch. When players began taking turns at swinging the stick, she asked, "Shall I do it more slowly, so they can hit it?"

"*What*, are you *crazy? I* call the pitches, kid, you just throw the ball! Say, can you put a curve on that? Know what I mean?"

"Vary its trajectory? Interesting. I believe so."

"Yeah, well, it's not as easy as it . . . hot *damn*, that's a *slider!*" An hour later he muttered, "Okay, don't wanna wear out your arm," and looked her up and down in grudging acceptance. "You be here, 0800 hours, tomorrow. I guess you made the team, uh . . . what's that name again?"

"Saavik. But what does it mean, to Make The Team?"

"Means ya gotta *work*, kid. Ya gotta play the *game*. Ya gotta get *tough*—and beat the pants off the midshipmen in three weeks. Think ya can do that?"

"Yes," said Saavik, though the reference to clothing puzzled her. "May I throw the ball again tomorrow?"

"What, are you *crazy?* Oh, yeah, kid—you'll throw the ball!"

"Very well," she said, handing it back to him, "I shall attend. I would like to ask a question."

"Uh, what's that, kid?"

"What is this game called? . . ."

Saavik decided not to explain. "Base Ball, Mr. Spock. This game is called Base Ball, and I am the person who throws it. I also observe their emotional responses," she insisted, "and their verbal exchange consists entirely of idioms. There is no reason to disapprove of this, Mr. Spock, because the game is one of strategy, quite logical and complex. It depends upon mathematical progressions of—"

"I grasp the basics, Saavikam." Spock held up his hand to forestall the coming lecture. "And although I do not share the humans' enthusiasm for the pursuit of the ball, in its various forms it has pervaded most of the galaxy. Given your fondness for projectiles, I am not surprised that you succumbed to its allure. I trust you will maintain a sense of perspective."

"Oh, yes!" she promised instantly. "Later. But tomorrow is The Big Game. Cadets play the midshipmen, and have always lost. But this time," her eyes narrowed grimly, "we are going to *win*."

Spock had no doubt of it. "Consider their ancient proverb, Saavik: It is not winning or losing, but how one plays the game."

"Oh. Well, that must be very ancient, Mr. Spock, because they do not believe it anymore. Humans want to win all kinds of games. They even argue about which has the most merit. But I belong to The Team now, so of course I must want to win too."

"Of course. And when does this momentous event take place?"

"At 1400 hours, tomorrow."

"Then I shall attend, unless you prefer that I do not."

"Oh, by all means, Mr. Spock." Best not to mention how around campus they were calling her "The Photon Torpedo." In fact it was best not to mention anything more at all. Desperately, her eyes strayed again. "I would like to ask a question, Mr. Spock, if it is not too personal. What are those figures on the stand?"

Spock seemed to brighten. "That is a chess set, Saavik. When the pieces are in play, they are moved from one level to another on the boards. An interest of mine. Someday I shall teach you."

"In *play?* Then this is . . . a *game?*"

"Yes. A very *different* sort of game, however," Spock said loftily. "Chess is considered *mental* exercise."

"Oh. Pieces move on small squares? And that is all?"

All? Spock closed his eyes, as if banishing some momentary twinge of pain. "Hardly 'all,' Saavik. This may disappoint you, but they are not hurled through the air. Chess is a contest of *strategy*. Pieces are moved in logical progressions, based upon mathematical . . ." He paused. Saavik tilted her head, folded her hands in her lap, and waited for him to go on. Her eyebrows rose in a look of tolerant, quizzical appraisal, which reminded Spock of something he could not quite place. ". . . so do refrain from using them to practice your baseball."

"That would damage them," she pointed out. "I don't damage things anymore. And I practice Base Ball at dawn each morning."

"A fascinating order of priorities," Spock said. "Tell me, does your curriculum encompass skills beyond baseball and idiom? Have we abandoned physics and astronomy? Does the Academy now send its graduates into Starfleet armed only with baseballs and a working knowledge of colloquial speech? One might think the causal sciences had been declared obsolete."

Saavik frowned at him severely. Sometimes Spock went on this way, then watched to observe her response. Long ago she'd decided it was some sort of test. "Nothing like that has occurred. And I have told you all about my classes. At times, Mr. Spock, you say some very strange things."

"An occasional weakness," he admitted. "You may attribute it to the human half of my nature."

"Oh. Well, I wasn't going to mention *that,* Mr. Spock. I am trying to be correct tonight."

"And your efforts have not gone—" The intercom whistled softly. "—excuse me . . . Spock here."

"Mr. Spock, I have your call from Starfleet now."

"Thank you, Commander Uhura. I can take it here."

"Do you wish me to wait elsewhere?"

"Not necessary, Saavik. This will only take a moment. Feel free to examine anything you wish . . . ah, Dr. Goldman. I am pleased you are on duty tonight . . ."

Glad of any excuse to move about, Saavik rose from her chair to admire the glittering mosaic on the wall with its intertwining circle and triangle. She decided that Base Ball at Starfleet Academy was a case in point of Infinite Diversity—particularly if Spock were to attend.

". . . an interesting object, is it not?" he was saying. "I assume the delay was due to transport difficulties?"

"Well, no. Things have been a little . . . jammed up tonight, Mr. Spock," Goldman said smoothly. Out of sight her fingers teased the silky hair on Rakir's arm. He imprisoned them, then moved beyond their reach while she stared guilelessly into the screen.

Of course. I shall be there in the morning. If time permits I would appreciate preliminary data, composition of the casing and so forth. But I have no wish to burden you, Doctor. You seem overtaxed as it is. This is simply a matter of curiosity.

"No problem, Mr. Spock. It's set up under the scanner." She switched the viewer's angle to show him. It appeared unchanged: a transparent box on the transparent platform of the high-beam Infrascan, its sparkling lights weaving their designs, expanding and contracting. "Do you want more than the initial readout?"

No, that will be sufficient. But you may report tonight on what you find. The lateness of the hour will be of no importance. Thank you for your assistance, Dr. Goldman. Spock out.

"Certainly, Mr. Spock." His face faded from the screen. "Overtaxed!" she snickered and began calibrating the scan. "Sorry, Dorn, this won't take long. I'm kind of curious myself."

"That is normal for your species, my Janet, is it not? And for Vulcans also, though they seldom admit to it. You might learn from Mr. Spock's regard for the truth. You implied that we were working hard tonight, when you know that such was not the case."

"Oh no? Speak for yourself, my love!"

"I shall speak for us both and complete our duty log while you are occupied," said Rakir with great dignity. "If you allow me to concentrate, it will not take long either."

"Kiss me quick!"

"No, my Janet. I shall do that later—and thoroughly." He removed himself to a nearby console and began to work.

"It's a date," she laughed as she switched on the scan.

Twin beams from above and below pierced the box with a radiant blue-white light, so bright it seemed to wash out the patterns and colors inside . . . no, that wasn't it—

They were *gone*. And down the center, in the wake of the narrow scanning beams, ran a tiny, hairline crack. It grew.

Then with a sound like bursting glass, the box broke.

Uh-oh, Spock won't like this! Goldman tried to turn off the scan, but her hand wouldn't move . . . *not right, not feeling well.* Terrible white-hot pain stabbed into her. *Heart attack? But I'm too young! This isn't fair! Dorn!* She couldn't make a sound. Pain radiated down her arms and legs, burning in her throat, shrieking in her ears. This was no heart attack—every cell in her body was afire. Her vision blurred. Across the room, in another universe, Rakir was turning from his screen. She tried to take a step, felt herself falling . . . *Something in that box! GET OUT OF HERE, DORN!* her mind screamed at him. *Tell Spock! Tell them all . . .*

The pain became a wave carrying her away. She was lying on the floor, hearing the soft rush of air through an open vent. That was wrong, but she couldn't remember why. The edges of her vision were turning dark, closing down to a faraway point of light. And in that light were her mother and her father, her brothers and her friends, every day she'd ever lived, every thought she'd ever had—and Dorn. *So this is what it's like,* she thought quite clearly, *but I* can't *die now . . . just isn't . . . fair . . .* Then in the light she could see herself. Herself seeing herself. Leaving herself. *Dorn . . . should've kissed me . . . but I'm already . . .*

Rakir blinked his eyes. Pain exploded in his chest, seared down his arms and legs, hammered in his head. So hard to breathe, as if the air were solid, made of wax. So hard to turn around. He saw the scanner's light, the broken fragments shining under it. And Janet was falling to the floor, brown eyes open, staring, her face all twisted in pain, a mottled flush darkening over her skin. And El-Idorn Rakir knew that he was dying. He did not fear death, but no one ever told him it would be so sad. *Wait for me, my Janet! I am coming with you . . . first, must do . . .*

Red letters on the wall swam before his eyes. He forced himself to think only of the word: CONTAM-ALERT. A button sealed behind a pane of glass, a striker too many inches away. He closed his fist, smashed the glass himself. The edges of his vision were turning black. The shards of glass slid over his fingers, but the effort was in vain. Before he could push the button, he was sliding down the wall, knowing he had failed.

Only pain now, pain and bitter, welling regret. His icy homeworld, its blowing snows, even this failure faded from his mind. But his heart cried out for Janet, for all the kisses she should have, the one he refused a moment ago—and the distance that lay between them now: ten feet, ten light-years he could never cross. He prayed for time, began to pull himself across the floor, inch by inch. *So sorry, my Janet . . . never kissed you enough . . . but I would have learned . . . for you.* All his life dwindled down to one tiny light, one cruel truth: he would never touch her, never again. He lifted his hand anyway—and reached—as the light went out.

Ten seconds later, because no one had canceled the sequence that triggered automatically when a seal on a Contamination-Alert was broken, an alarm began to sound in the empty halls of Starfleet Headquarters. Ten seconds after that, because no one told it otherwise, the maintenance computer took over, dropping safety doors at every entry to the science level, bypassing all access by turbo lifts, shutting down air vents that fed the 18th floor to isolate the contamination at its source. And because no one came to turn it off, the alarm went on ringing.

". . . and equipped with a redesigned cloaking screen, which my chief engineer and science officer believe will function over long distances in . . . Computer, what the hell is that?"

ALERT ALERT ALERT ALERT ALERT . . . With its voice mode still disengaged, the words flashed in red across Kirk's screen.

"Identify!"

ALERT: CONTAMINATION EXO-SCIENCE

"Status! Nature of contamination?"

UNKNOWN

"Safety status!"

CONTAINMENT IN PROGRESS

All right then. He hit the intercom's audio.

"Richards! Kirk here. My screen shows a problem up in Exo. What's your status? . . . Richards?" The only answer was the hiss of empty air. In the background an alarm was ringing. *Left his post, dammit! Probably went to check . . .* He touched another key.

"Exo, report! What's your status?" A deafening alarm blared through his speaker. Kirk leaned on the button. "Report, Exo! A Contam-Alert is in progress. What is your status?" *Must be bad. Why weren't they—* "Science level! Anyone!" Nothing.

"Officers' lounge, this is Admiral James T. Kirk. We've got a problem in the Exo lab. Is everything under control up there?" *When someone gets around to it,* he thought, *they'll want to know where the hell I am!* But no one did.

"Richards!" Kirk tried again. *Maybe he was back. Maybe something went wrong with the comm . . . maybe—* "Operations calling HQ. Security check! Report immediately—any department!" Kirk felt an icy chill run down his spine. This was *impossible.* Even late at night, most departments had someone on duty up there. "Anyone, report! *Is anyone able to answer? Anyone at all?"*

Nothing. Except—

Kirk whirled around at a sound not from the intercom: a faint, pneumatic hiss and distant clang, followed by a loud metallic click from the giant, shielded door of the Vault. New words flashed across his screen.

*FAILSAFE*FAILSAFE* THIS LEVEL IS SECURE. CONTAMINATION-FREE.

"Who gave that order, computer?" he heard himself shouting. "Who sounded that alert?"

CONTAM SEQUENCE INITIATED EXO-SCI 20:52:32.07

NO INTERRUPT. NO ALL CLEAR.

PROCEDURE IMPLEMENTED ALL LEVELS

"Visual." Kirk was holding his breath. His heart was knocking against his ribs. He had to look, no matter how much he didn't want to. The words on the screen dissolved into a view of the main entrance from a point behind the curving information desk.

Richards hadn't left his post. A head of curly hair rested on an outstretched arm. The fingers that still gripped an open book were turning dark and mottled. The alarm was still ringing . . . in the Exo lab, a woman lay dead on the floor; a co-worker had died trying to help her, his hand only a few inches away.

The officers' lounge was littered with cards, backgammon pieces, spilled drinks . . . and dead bodies. They sprawled across tables, slumped in chairs, faces contorted in agony, skins dark and mottled. Most of them had been his friends. *What could happen that fast?* Bradley had almost reached the intercom before he died, and Conklin—it looked like Conklin tried to claw his way out the window. Poor Conklin. That window wouldn't open anyway.

And neither would the Vault—not now! Adrenaline and reflex took over. Kirk snatched the communicator from his belt and flipped it open.

"Kirk to *Enterprise!* Kirk to—*damn* it!" He snapped the communicator back in place. What was he *thinking?* This was the *Vault*—his communicator wouldn't work down here! He lowered himself into the chair, aware of the tremor in his knees. All those people up there—dead. From the 18th floor, to the first, to the 69th—in seconds!

Nothing happened that fast!

But there was another reason for the sudden wave of nausea and fear that gripped him: communicators weren't the only things that wouldn't work in the Vault.

Transporters wouldn't work down here either.

Empty stillness wrapped around him, and Kirk could hear the beating of his heart. He drew a ragged breath, unclenched his fists, and tried to think.

"Sure," he muttered, "piece of *cake* . . ."

". . . lateness of the hour will be of no importance. Thank you for your assistance, Dr. Goldman. Spock out."

The object's image faded as the transmission ended. Spock stared at his empty screen for a moment, then touched a pad and recalled the tape. At the point it switched to the scanner and the box, he cut out the audio, marked the place, and replayed the recording. *Indeed, a curious object— and strangely compelling.*

"Saavik," he said, "this item is of considerable interest. The details of its discovery are classified, but not the object itself. You may come here and see it if you wish."

She came to look over his shoulder: the box sat on the clear platform of the scanner, its lights weaving in rainbow designs, shimmering, expanding, folding up again . . .

Spock wasn't sure what made him look up, but the sight of Saavik's face brought him to his feet: it was stark and bloodless, her eyes wide with fright.

"Saavik!" He reached for her. She shrank away.

"No!" she whispered, backing off and shaking her head. She was trembling violently, but her eyes never left the screen. "No . . . *no* . . . it was a *dream* . . ."

"What, Saavik? What is it?"

"I've . . . *seen* that . . . *before!* In a . . . cave . . . on Hellguard—"

Spock's hand was on the intercom, signaling the bridge.

"—there were *thousands* of them!"

Chapter Five

"NOTHING, SIR, but I'd swear that signal's going through."
Uhura switched frequencies, tried again. Something was
very, very wrong. "And I'm sending on the captain's channel, Mr. Spock, but he's not answering. Didn't he take his
communicator with him?"

"He did. Are you trying all departments? All levels?"

"Yes, sir—but we just *had* HQ! Not five minutes ago!
Either that whole comm system just went down or . . .
where was the captain going tonight, Mr. Spock?" For a
moment, she thought he wouldn't answer; that cool Vulcan
calm, usually so comforting, was frigid and terrifying now.
His face looked carved out of stone.

"Headquarters," he said much too quietly. "We must
locate Admiral Nogura immediately—and discreetly if possible."

"Yes, sir." *Nogura?* She turned back to her board, and
Spock used the auxiliary panel to make a call of his own.

"Dock Central, this is Spock, on *Enterprise*. Please put me
through to Commander Dorish. He is aboard the ship in
Repair Dock Four . . . Commander, Spock here. It is my
belief that you and your crew are in grave danger. I must
insist that you suspend work and evacuate all personnel into
Dock . . . Yes, Commander, I realize that . . . No, Com-

mander, *no one* may remain aboard . . . No, Commander, I can *not* give you the facts, because as yet I do not *have* them . . . Then on *my* responsibility, Commander!"

"—but how do I *log* it, Spock? What about my *report?*" Dorish tugged at his graying mustache unhappily. "A dock *shutdown?* All right, I'll take it under—" He stared at the dead communicator in his hand. "Damnedest thing, Montgomery—now what're *you* doing? You passed up shore leave to get over here!" Dorish folded his arms across his portly midriff and glared. Scott had left the tangled machinery to gather up his probes and wrenches, and was polishing each one lovingly before replacing it in his tool kit.

"Ye heard him, lad. Spock says to be shuttin' it down."

"But—" Dorish looked around the dismantled engine room in frustration. "He won't say *why!* I don't think he even *knows* why!"

"Aye," Scott nodded, "an' he'll be the devil himself till he finds out. You've just heard a rare thing, Malcomb—the sound of a Vulcan playin' a hunch."

"What the hell do I tell HQ?" complained Dorish. "They're waiting for that report."

"Well . . ." Scott buffed a fingerprint off his laserseal and tucked it into a padded slot. "Start off by tellin' 'em how Mr. Spock outranks both you an' me—and then tell them about this." He handed a melted fragment of metal and wire to Dorish, who started at it, frowning.

"This looks like part of a *detonator.*"

"Aye. It was way back in what's left of that ruptured coolant line. This scow was *sabotaged,* Malcomb, and if Spock says to shut it down, I say we'll bloody well be shuttin' it down! Now, give me my sonic calibrator, Malcomb—oh!" He rescued it from irreverent hands. "Show a bit of *respect,* lad—'twas made in Aber*deen!*"

"I don't get it!" DiMuro peered out the viewport as their pod floated away under a green and yellow painted wing. "All that secrecy, and then they pull us *off?*"

"Uh-huh . . ." Harper said absently, patting one of the arms wound around him. Obo was still frightened, its eyes shut so tightly that the skin on its head puckered into wrinkles. "Talk to me, Obo. Tell me what's wrong."

"We go home *nnoww?*"

"No, Obo. I'm sorry. We have to stay until they tell us we're done for the night."

The Belandrid lifted its head from Harper's shoulder. One long, vertical eyelid parted from side to side, and a neon-yellow eye glowed balefully.

"No, Bobby. We go home nnoww!"

DiMuro chuckled. "Maybe we should go home now, Harper. Seems like the little guy knows something we don't."

"Maybe," Harper said, as Obo clutched on to him tightly once again. Something sure had his friend spooked.

He wondered what that something could be.

". . . because I want to *know, that's* why, Lieutenant! *Adjutant!* Michaels!" hissed Uhura furiously. "And I want to know *yesterday!* . . . Then you just *get* him, mister! *Ensign* Michaels can push a *broom* on some nasty little . . . Well, *thank* you, Michaels . . . yes, yes, very helpful . . ." Uhura signed off and turned to Spock. "Still on Dock, sir. He'll call back."

Spock nodded, fitted a comm plug in his ear and listened to the signal repeat at ten-second intervals. *"Enterprise* to Captain Kirk," he said, "come in please. *Enterprise* to Captain Kirk . . ."

That won't do a bit of good, and he knows it! Uhura watched him out of the corner of her eye. Apprehension and dread settled around her like a fog. Her board whistled; it was only inship.

"Bridge. Oh, Mr. Scott . . ." she listened closely. "Yes, sir. I'll tell him . . . Mr. Spock, Scotty found bits of a detonator in that coolant system, says it was sabotage, an inside job. They're all off the ship, and Commander Dorish is in his office. He's waiting for an ex—uh, an update, sir." The comm whistled again; she pounced on the incoming signal. *"Enterprise*—Captain!"

"Captain! Are you all right? Where are you?"

"HQ, Spock. You've got to reach Nogura—"

"We are trying, Captain. Can you give us visual?"

"I . . . yes, all right . . ." The main screen came to life with Kirk's face, and Uhura's gasp was audible: he looked drawn and haggard with shock. *"Spock, we've got a problem."*

"Yes, Captain. Where in Headquarters? We tried—"

"I'm . . . downstairs, Spock. They're all dead up there. Some kind of contamination in the Exo lab. Must've got into the—"

"No one is alive . . . at all?"

"No, Spock. No one."

"Sir," Uhura broke in, "I'll notify the transporter room. We can triangulate and beam you—"

"No, Uhura, you can't," said Kirk tightly.

"But Captain—" A look from Spock stopped her. He swallowed hard, seemed to understand more than he was telling. Her board signaled again. *"Enterpr—*yes, Admiral! Please stand by . . . Mr. Spock, the captain's on a secured channel, but I don't know—"

"Admiral, Spock here. Is your transmission secure?"

"Affirmative. What's the problem, Enterprise?"

"Stand by, sir," said Spock. "We're patching you through. Uhura, put them both on screen—and scramble our output."

The main screen split, and Heihachiro Nogura frowned out at them. His ageless, Asian face was completely unlined; silver hair made a striking contrast to bright and bottomless black eyes. His enigmatic presence evoked varied reactions: Spock responded with a deference accorded few humans; McCoy found him nerve-racking and unfathomable. The irritating mix of admiration and rebellion that Nogura produced in Kirk manifested itself in subtle contests of wits against the only tactical mind Kirk believed capable of defeating him. Even more irritating to Kirk was an uncomfortable suspicion that this knee-jerk reaction was childish, that any contest was one-sided and of his own making. Nogura seemed above such things, but was he? That was the trouble with Nogura: you never knew quite where you stood. Kirk didn't like that at all.

"Jim, what is it? Where are you?"

"HQ, sir. There's been a . . . disaster down here. Some kind of contamination from the Exo lab. I have visual, Admiral. The maintenance shutdown wasn't fast enough."

"What level are you on, Kirk? How bad is it?"

"No one's alive upstairs. I'm . . . down in the Vault."

"The Vault? *What for?"*

Kirk took a deep breath; it all seemed so stupid now. *"That incident report, Admiral. Your orders were . . . by 0800 . . ."* He didn't bother to finish the sentence.

"Got it," Nogura said; Kirk had no doubt that he did. *"Show me what we're dealing with. Has anyone else seen this?"*

"No, sir. It only happened a few minutes ago."

Nightmarish images unfolded on the bridge's screen. Uhura clamped a hand over her mouth, but her eyes filled with horrified tears. Spock watched, frozen, expressionless, and stricken. The lab, the lounge, the front desk, level after level, body after body . . .

"Note the time factor, Admiral. Seal broke on the Contam-Alert at 20:52:32." The view of the alarm casing in the Exo lab zoomed forward. *"The glass broke, but the button never lit. Maintenance tripped the alarm at ten seconds, the failsafe shutdown at twenty. Now, here's the front desk . . ."*

The tape showed Richards reading his book, toppling forward as he struggled in the throes of some unseen pain. When his curly head fell onto his outstretched arm and fingers on the security alert button froze without pushing it, Kirk stopped the tape and enlarged the running chrono display at the bottom of the frame.

"Look at that, Admiral, 20:52:46—a total of fourteen

seconds—and he was eighteen floors away! *Sir, they never had a chance. They were dying before that alarm ever sounded."*

"But air doesn't circulate through the system that fast. Nothing could do that. Do we know what caused it?"

"Yes, Admiral." On the bridge, Spock cued up his tape of Dr. Goldman's call. "This did. My conversation with Dr. Goldman ended at 20:51:33. The fragments now under the Infrascan were this . . ."

Once again, innocent and beautiful, the transparent box sparkled on the platform of Dr. Goldman's scan. Chains of rainbow lights wove and rippled, replayed themselves again and again.

"We found four of these on board the Romulan ship," Spock continued tonelessly, "on the bridge, in a corridor, in command quarters, and in engineering. There was nothing to indicate . . ." He paused. "I wished to . . . study one of them. I notified Dock authority, ordered regulation clearance at Exo, and requested preliminary data from Dr. Goldman. It seems the scanner beam has destroyed it. I speak for the record, Admiral. I am responsible."

"Never mind that now, Spock," said Nogura brusquely. *"What about the work crew on that ship?"*

"Evacuated into Dock, also on my responsibility. They found evidence of deliberate sabotage. The implications are grave, sir. Commander Dorish was in charge. He is awaiting further—"

"Let him wait!" Nogura snapped. *"Look, Spock, it wasn't your fault—that thing's intriguing. If you hadn't checked it out, someone else would, that's all. Jim, are all the doors secured?"*

"Computer says they are. Transporters were already off-line."

"I'm posting guards." Nogura tapped on his keypad, spoke quietly over his office intercom, and got back to them. *"Crisis standby personnel are being notified. Security's rounding up a task force to report to Life Sciences. We'll have to beam in probes. Recommendations, gentlemen?"*

"They will need access to classified files," said Spock. "Intelligence data on the Romulan Empire, for example. System security will have to be overridden. Captain, you have direct access but—all due respect, sir—not the expertise. Admiral, this will be delicate work. We'll need an expert in computer systems."

"Then get down there, Spock."

"Admiral . . . there is another line of inquiry I must pursue. It is . . . imperative."

On the screen, Nogura folded his arms, waiting for an explanation. None was forthcoming.

"This won't keep, gentlemen. Jim, access Command database and evaluate qualified personnel. Get me a team, a high-level scientist and a computer specialist. Send them to Administration's terminal room. Spock, you join them when you can. You'll brief them from the vault, Jim, and keep everything under wraps. This is a need-to-know situation— we don't want a panic on our hands."

Kirk gazed into the warm, empty gloom of the Vault and told himself there was no reason to feel such mounting panic or the illusion of walls closing in. Whatever this was, they'd clear it up, find an antidote or decontaminant or whatever. Until then . . . well, he had everything he needed to hold up here for a very long time. Somehow, that thought didn't comfort him at all. To keep himself from pacing, he reviewed the selections he'd made for the Task Force.

Dr. Ayla Renn, Lt. Cmdr.: Acting head of the Exo-Science lab while Dr. Syng was on leave. MD, XMD, Ph.D., ZBA . . . her credentials scrolled by. Six years in Starfleet, three on Earth, and an impressive list of field work. A notation read *Does not suffer fools gladly!*, and Kirk nodded, satisfied. Dr. Renn was a straight arrow.

Ensign Maxim Kinski: Computer rating A-7.1. Expert. Four months out of the Academy, not an experienced officer. But this wasn't a command-level assignment—and that *rating!* Only eight tenths of a point below Spock, who held the highest in Starfleet. Seven-plus ratings were hard to come by, and Kirk figured Kinski would do until Spock—

His comm whistled.

"Admiral Kirk here."

"Good evening, Admiral. I'm Dr. Ayla Renn, and I'm in the Administration Building, Room 2103. I was told to report here and call in on this number."

One thing her file hadn't mentioned: Dr. Renn was a knockout. She had the face of a china doll, all peaches and cream, emerald-green eyes and tumbling red hair, still wet from being out in the rain. The sight of her lifted Kirk's spirits.

"Yes, Dr. Renn. You're in the right place."

"But sir, I'm a scientist. There're just computers in here."

"'Scuse me." A pale, intense young man leaned into view. His black, electric-looking hair was due for a trim, and his Starfleet uniform hung on his bony frame. *"I guess I'm here for the computers. Ensign Kinski, sir."*

"Yes, Ensign. You're both in the right place."

"Is there some kind of emergency, sir?" Kinski asked, definitely on edge. *"We had to ID with Security—"*

"Yes, Admiral," Renn confirmed. *"There're guards all over the Plaza. And two of my people are in the lab at HQ. Can I just call and make sure they're okay, sir?"*

"No, Doctor, you can't. That's why we're here. I'm going to run some tape and tell you what we know so far, which isn't much. And I think you both had better sit down."

Kirk waited for them to get settled. Renn was calm and focused, Kinski quiet and scared—probably the first real crisis he'd ever faced. No, not an experienced officer . . .

What was taking *Spock* so long?

Saavik abandoned her meditation; it wasn't working anyway. In the warm air of Spock's cabin, her cheeks still burned with shame at the disgraceful way she'd behaved. Her hands still clenched into fists when she wasn't looking, and chains of weaving lights still danced on her eyelids whenever she closed them and tried to think. Spock had been gone too long, too long for this to be some dreadful mistake. But how could a dream be *not* a dream? How could a nightmare come to life? Questions whirled in her mind.

When the door chimed she felt a rush of panic, which she hated, and an absurd impulse to run away and hide. But there was nowhere to go; the past had found her, even here. She touched the button on Spock's desk, the door slid back, and one look at his face swept her questions away. The past had found them all.

He stood looking down at her, and for an instant she sensed a wave of regret so deep it was worse than pain. Then he drew up a chair, sat facing her in silence. "It is very bad, Saavikam," he said with utter calm. "That object shattered under the scan at Headquarters. Everyone in the main building . . . is dead."

Saavik closed her eyes and tried to stop the roaring in her ears. People had died. A piece of *her* world killed them. And she remembered it was Spock who told that doctor to . . .

"Many lives are already lost," he was saying. "If we do not act quickly, others could die as well. You recognized that object, Saavik. And you thought it was a dream?"

"Yes," she nodded miserably. "I've always dreamed it. I tried not to—but it kept coming back. I know Vulcans should not—"

"Saavik. You must tell me of this dream."

"I would tell you anything—" To her everlasting disgrace she began to tremble; with his everlasting kindness Spock ignored it. "—but I *know* nothing else!"

"You may know more than you realize, Saavikam, but you have no means of discerning what is important and what is not. I must have your help. I must know what you know, even what is beyond your ability to recall. I have only one way to do that."

"I understand." She clenched her fingers together in her lap.

"I must be certain that you do. We have practiced mental disciplines. At times I imparted knowledge, abstract concepts—but I have never looked beyond what you wished to show me. I must ask to do that now. It is necessary, Saavikam. I am sorry."

She nodded. Her fingers were freezing.

Spock leaned closer, speaking softly. "I am with you. You are safe on board the *Enterprise*. Nothing can harm you here."

Saavik wanted to believe him. His face was so close to hers that she could feel him breathing. She tried to take courage from that warmth and life, but everything inside her had gone cold. "What must I do?" she asked in a whisper.

Spock's voice whispered back, gentle and warm in her ear. "For once in your life, Saavikam, try to do nothing. Think of the dream. Think only of the dream . . ."

The room was dim. The air was dry and still. It was deathly quiet. Saavik watched long fingers moving toward her face. She shut her eyes, felt the heat from Spock's hand before a touch so light it almost wasn't there.

Then she was falling back into the past, back into fear and hunger and pain. Terrified, she fought to stop it, but a relentless power drew her down that dark, dangerous path. Old instincts stirred: the taste for blood, the thirst for swift revenge. An overwhelming urge possessed her to follow where they led, to see, to know, to *kill* . . .

Time spun backward. Guarded secrets, hidden doors flew open in her mind. Buried thoughts and feelings, sights and sounds and smells rose like living ghosts to batter down the barriers of the past. *Do not resist me, Saavikam. I need you . . . need you . . . need . . .*

Thin coverings of civilization ripped and tore, sheared away. The walls of her own will, the foundations of her very soul broke apart and crumbled in scalding sunlight, blinding rage. Fragments of existence—hunting, killing, hatred— shattered into shame . . . and fell . . . and some enormous gentleness caught all the falling pieces, sifted, reconstructed them, and inexorably moved on.

There was night and sky and stars. And underneath the

stars were dust and death, wind and mountains. And underneath the mountains, underneath the mountains . . . that place . . . of dreams and evil, nowhere to hide, death in those walls of strange, twisting light, where It was always waiting for her in the dark. Running and pain, running and blood . . . and someone was always screaming . . .

It was over. Dizzy, shuddering, Saavik felt herself sitting in a chair, icy fingers resting on her face. And when they pulled away they left behind a distance in her mind, distance from the fear and pain—and something new: a clarity, a knowing.

She opened her eyes to a glimpse of Spock's face she'd never seen before: pale, shocked, in agonizing pain. His breathing was shallow and rasping; his hand trembled as it drew away, and there was a look behind his eyes she didn't understand—but it wasn't blame. Some moments passed before he spoke.

"I did not know."

Saavik looked away; the gentleness in his voice brought tears to her eyes, but she refused to let them run down her cheeks. Never, *not once,* had she let Spock see her cry—and she would rather die than do that insult to him now. "I didn't *want* you to know! I didn't want *anyone* to know! I am so . . . *ashamed . . ."*

"There is no logic in that," he said quietly. "Admiral Nogura may wish to speak with you. You must answer his questions as best you can. I have only one. Could you find that place again?"

Go back there? Saavik experienced a horrible reversal taking place, a sense of time disintegrating. Her surroundings seemed insubstantial; reality was dissolving, her present becoming the dream. Only Hellguard was real. *Go back there?* Spock was silent, waiting for an answer. She forced the words from her throat.

". . . yes. I could find it."

Spock nodded and rose to his feet. He stood looking down at her, as if he wanted to say something more but couldn't find the words. "You were only a child, Saavikam," he said at last. "You are not the cause of this. Stay here. Prepare yourself for questions." The door closed behind him.

And the tears came. Furious, helpless tears of grief and rage—for the deaths of people who deserved to live, for this generous, beautiful world that offered her such opportunity. And for Spock. For reasons of his own, which she would never understand, he had given her everything and asked nothing from her in return.

Until now. Saavik began to shiver in the warmth of the cabin. Tears dried on her face. Even rage deserted her and left behind a crushing, thudding dread. *Only a child . . . not the cause . . .*

But she learned something new when that mindlink dissolved and her own horror and shame looked out at her from Spock's face. His soft words faded like an echo, and she could not believe in them. People had died. And Saavik *had* caused something; she knew that now. Because back there, all those years ago, back in that cave on Hellguard— she had done something terrible.

If only she could remember what it *was* . . .

"A blank, Admiral. No memory of the circumstances or events preceding them. She was terrified and badly injured at the time."

"Can she be made to remember?"

"I . . . tried, Admiral. It is beyond my skill. I do not think a further attempt is advisable or likely to succeed. Sir, there is no doubt about what she saw."

"Weapons." Nogura's face hardened dangerously.

"Yes. Transparent boxes, filled with patterns of light— rows of them, stockpiled underground on the fifth planet of system 872 Trianguli, well within the perimeter of the Romulan Empire."

"And you believe this was planned."

"I am convinced of it. Consider this, Admiral: an apparently aborted attack, an apparently disabled ship locked on course for Starbase Ten, with an advance we do not possess —and, given its nature, one we could not resist. We would take precautions, be alert for possible dangers, but we would also take the ship—to our most secure command base for study. And on board, arranged as ordinary, perhaps useful items, are the boxes. Interesting, but incidental in light of the military discovery. Even the evidence of sabotage—and that was unintentional—would not reveal the purpose of that mission. The real danger lay where we would least suspect. It was well-planned, Admiral, and for a very long time."

"And we swallowed the bait? They took a big chance."

"Did they, sir? Consider also the Romulan mind: wheels within wheels, an attack within an attack. You said yourself that if I had not investigated the object, someone else would have done so. I agree. We behaved predictably at every turn, Admiral—we were curious. And the Romulans were counting on it."

"If you're right, Spock, you know what this means."

"Yes, Admiral. Among other things, it means that Earth has come under attack."

"And all we know about these things—besides the fact that they kill people—is that a child remembers them? In a dream?"

"An eyewitness account. The only one we have."

"But what was a Vulcan child doing on a planet in—"

"Ask her, sir. I think you will believe us."

"All right, Spock. But I hope to God you're wrong."

The main screen went blank. Spock opened a private file he hadn't reviewed in years. The Hellguard scans recorded that damping field; perhaps they held some other clue he'd missed at the time. Kirk was briefing the data team now. His life—and a great deal else—would depend upon their expertise and judgment.

". . . they're all dead!" Kinski was on his feet, several shades paler than before. *"And their faces! What's the matter with their—"*

"Hush, Kinski," Renn whispered, unable to tear her eyes away from the screen.

"And sit *down*, Mr. Kinski. Dr. Renn, I'm sorry," Kirk said gently, switching off the tape. "Friends of your's?"

"The best," she nodded, fighting to keep back her shock and tears, *"the very best. Thank you, sir . . . Kinski!"* she snapped. *"Sit down before you fall down!"*

"I'm—I'm okay," he muttered, but clearly was not. He sank back into his seat. *". . . I—I trained for this, but . . ."*

"I know, Kinski. It's different when it's the real thing." Kirk was having serious doubts about this ensign, but there was nothing he could do now, except give the kid time to pull himself together. "Doctor Renn, you call the transporter room over at Life Sciences. They're waiting to beam in probes. Get linked up with them, you'll be evaluating the data. And Doctor, information on a need-to-know basis *only*. Admiral's orders."

Renn shook her head. *"I want to go on record as objecting to that, sir. It's extremely dangerous. It's going to slow us up and create a potential hazard. Everyone right down the line needs to know what we're dealing with."*

"Duly noted, Doctor. You can take it up with Admiral Nogura, once we know ourselves." Kirk let her glare. When she began a furious attack on the keys of the comm, he turned his attention to the other half of the team. "Mr. Kinski, I understand you're an expert with computers."

"Oh, sure—I mean, yes, sir." Kinski was still badly shaken, but breathing easier and looking painfully embarrassed. He ran a hand through his unruly hair. *"I'm sorry, Admiral. It's just . . . I've never seen anything like that . . ."*

"I understand. But you'll be looking at computers from now on. Your file says you're the man for the job—are you?"

"Yes, sir."

"Fine. Now, here's what we need . . ." Kirk began to tell him.

* * *

". . . no, Spock, no doubt at all," Nogura said unhappily. His brief talk with Saavik had killed any hope that this might be some schoolgirl fantasy. That self-possessed young lady probably never fantasized about anything—and would accurately report it if she did. "I believe her, but she's just a child. Command won't accept this on telepathic testimony. You know that."

"Which is why I urge you to act on my recommendation, sir, while it still falls within the scope of your personal powers."

"It's already out of my hands, Spock. The station's on alert. Nothing leaves Dock without verified orders. I'm accountable now to Council and to chain of command. The best I can do is make sure this gets before the Council."

"That will take time, Admiral. This weapon is very effective, even if we find the means to neutralize it. And Earth will not be the only target. The Empire has an arsenal, and we know where—"

"If they're still there, Spock. And that's a big *if.* I can't commit *Enterprise* to some fact-finding mission."

"Forgive me, Admiral. I should be more explicit. Facts would be welcome, but that was not what I—"

"Sirs," Uhura's voice cut in, *"Captain Kirk says his team is ready with the probes. You asked to be notified."*

"One moment. What are you suggesting, Spock?"

"Some sabotage of our own, Admiral. Without delay."

"Inside the Romulan Empire? That's suicide. I won't commit *Enterprise* to that either. We need to know what we're dealing with. Commander Uhura, put us through."

Ayla Renn stared at the row of monitors and keyboards that faced the clear, windowed wall and ran the entire length of the room. Outside it was still raining; fog was so thick she could barely see HQ's shadowy tower just across the Plaza —and a faint blur of light from the corner of the 18th floor. Inside Room 2103 the lights were bright; the status screen read 21:58, and Kirk, Spock, and Nogura stared out at her from separate screens. Three more displays glowed with the test patterns and serial numbers of the probes, and the next four terminals were set up for analysis and data retrieval.

"Let's get on with it, Doctor." Nogura frowned impatiently.

Renn could almost hear him tapping his foot. She gritted her teeth, held her tongue, and spoke to the transport officer waiting at Life Sciences. "All right, one at a time. And get it right. One to the eighteenth floor—center of the Exo lab. Then one to the first, then one to the sixty-ninth. Admiral, these med probes do basic analysis and scan for known contaminants and organisms. We're using them first, because they're on hand and—"

"Let's make it snappy, Doctor. I've got a briefing in ten minutes. I need to know what killed our people."

Renn bit back a sharp retort. "We're getting telemetry now, sir."

One after another, the displays in front of her came to life. Lines of data began to fill the screens.

Renn stared at probe one's monitor in disbelief. Kinski, peering over her shoulder, saw it too.

"That's wrong," he said, pointing at the screen. "We've got a glitch."

"No, we don't," Renn muttered. She froze incoming data on all three probes and checked the readout from the first floor. Same thing. And the 69th . . .

"Malfunction, Dr. Renn?" asked Spock quietly.

She shook her head, unable to believe what she was seeing. "No, sir, they're all reading—"

"What, *Doctor?*" demanded Nogura. *"What killed those people?"*

Renn's mouth had gone dry. She stared at the numbers and tried to find her voice. "Sir, it doesn't make any *sense,* but . . . there's no *oxygen* in the air!"

Chapter Six

THE SILENCE STRETCHED ON.

"Gentlemen, Doctor," Nogura finally said, *"I'm due in a briefing. I'll get back to you. Spock . . ."* With a slight motion of his head, he indicated a wish for privacy. Spock cut out audio on the other channels. *". . . ever heard of anything like this?"*

"No, Admiral. I have not."

"Make sure nobody else does."

"Is that desirable, Admiral? The time factor—"

"That building's completely secured?"

"As far as we know, sir, but—"

"And I take it this isn't some nerve gas we could neutralize and vent in the next half-hour?"

"No, Admiral."

"Then except to Kirk or to Enterprise, *no information leaves that room. Understood?"*

"There will be speculation, sir, from the scientists waiting to begin work. And Commander Dorish has requested—"

"The necessary people are being informed, Spock, and Dorish is one of them. For the moment just learn what you can and sit tight. I'll need a report."

The transmission ended before Spock could object further. He picked up on comm and studied the incoming telemetry. Kirk gave him a what-was-*that*-all-about look, but said nothing; Kinski was less restrained.

"Spock, I've got this idea. I was just thinking—"

"Mr. Kinski, one moment, please."

". . . not a microorganism, Mr. Spock," Renn was shaking her head, *"and it's not radiation. I'm cross-referencing Klingon and Romulan weapons' data for known chemical compounds. This is oxygen depletion on a scale I've never seen. Even decompression in space leaves some residual . . ."*

As Kirk monitored the data descrambling on his screen, he blessed the architects and engineers who, despite the expense, had designed HQ's independent, closed-system air supply and given the Vault its own. At the time it was an experiment; now it was mandatory for structures housing off-world or hazardous materials and standard for anyone requiring a controlled environment.

The normal breathing mixture in Starfleet Headquarters was manufactured, recycled, humidified, charged with negative ions and contained 22.76% oxygen, slightly higher than atmospheric levels. Double-door, "airlock" entry systems compensated for any exchange (with what was, after all, a compatible atmosphere) and accommodated security procedures as well. The design reflected and made use of what Starfleet knew best: starships. No sweet scent of flowers wafted through open windows, no weather changes or seasonal charms—and no dust, pollens, molds, or other outdoor irritants to cause downtime for computers, discomfort to many humans, and more severe reactions in off-worlders. Starfleet air was good for equipment and kept duty personnel alert. At least it used to.

Now the air inside those solid, transparent aluminum walls was 22.76% something else. *Exactly* 22.76%. And the probes hovering over the devastation in the officers' lounge, above the information desk in the lobby, and beside the scan in the lab all read the same level of available oxygen: zero. Not 2% or 1% or .001%. Zero.

"Excuse me, sirs," Kinski persisted. *"I have a suggestion. Maybe we could just—"*

". . . everything else is showing, Mr. Spock," Renn continued. *"Nitrogen, CO_2—even the traces. Just an X-factor of 22.76—and no oxygen. Med probes can't tell us what's happening in there. This won't be easy, sir, neutralizing some alien element we can't even identify."*

"The Romulans are not in the habit of making things easy, Dr. Renn. And these probes are inadequate. I suggest the deep-space 424's for extended atmospheric analysis."

"Admiral Kirk," Kinski appealed to him in a whisper, *"if they would just* listen *a second—"*

"Spock, Doctor. Mr. Kinski would like to make a suggestion. I think we can hear him out."

Spock acquiesced with infinite patience, Renn with somewhat less: *"Oh, for pity's sake—what?"*

"Well . . ." Now that Kinski had their attention, he didn't quite know what to do with it. *"There's no oxygen in there, right?"*

Spock closed his eyes. Renn wound her fingers in her hair.

"And we want to find out why. But they make *it, don't they? For hospitals and life-support packs? Well, maybe we could just beam in some. And put it* back *in the air!"*

After a moment of silence, Spock's eyebrow ascended. Kirk cleared his throat. Renn began relaying a request for oxygen cylinders.

". . . and put remotes on those valves. They'll have to work on computer signal." She looked up and sighed. *"Worth a try."*

Spock nodded. *"Indeed. Designate a test area and monitor the reaction. With the new probes, we may be able to determine what we are dealing with. A meritorious suggestion, Mr. Kinski."*

"Thank you, sir."

"Yes, good thinking, Kinski," Kirk added. "Now set up

some graphics on this experiment of yours. I want to see what all these numbers mean."

"Yes, sir . . ."

Spock ignored the conversation. While the data flowed through his computer and his mind, another analytical process occupied his higher realms of thought.

To perpetrate an act of terrorism on a planet they could never conquer, to stab at the heart of Starfleet Command from the safety of an empire half a galaxy away—these things were obvious but short-term gains. No, this was a plan long in the making, beyond random destruction or a single, successful strike. Saavik's buried memories were proof of that. Years ago the Romulans had built an arsenal out there, on that dead, forgotten planet; and their ancient quest for battle was alive today—even after a hundred years of comparative peace. But unlike Klingons in the affairs of war, Romulans tended to take the longer view. Spock believed that in the affairs of peace, humans should learn to do the same. If the weapon could be neutralized here, the Council might resist what Starfleet would propose. If not, it was an open question, and Spock didn't like the odds. And then there was Hellguard . . .

"—if you'll pardon me, sirs!" Renn was glaring from one screen to the other. "When are we going to let everyone in on this? We're about to run more data and projections than I can handle, and everyone else over at Sciences is sitting on their duffs. We've got guards out there with no idea they're standing on a contaminated building. With all due respect, sirs, this procedure really stinks!"

Doctors, Spock decided, must all take lessons from McCoy. She did have a point, but this was no time for a debate.

"Dr. Renn, we're under direct orders from Admiral Nogura," Kirk said sternly. "And must I remind you that this is a matter of Federation security? The admiral is concerned about preventing undue panic—"

"And I'm concerned about doing my job with my hands tied. This is dangerous, sirs. We wouldn't have armed guards out there if it wasn't. We wouldn't have ordered up probes from supply if we could get in there in suits and find out for ourselves. And now we're asking for oxygen?"

"I am on board *Enterprise,* Dr. Renn," Spock said, frowning. "And I assure you the contamination is contained. Headquarters is under maintenance lock and cannot be entered. The guards are stationed to insure that no attempt is made. I, too, regret the delay in informing personnel, but the admiral's instructions to me were quite specific. After chain of command is fully briefed, I trust our investigation will proceed in a more orderly fashion. Until then, we must do the best we can. Sir, a word with you, if I may." Spock cut out Renn's channel and waited until Kirk did the same. For the first time since the night's terrible events began, they were alone.

"Jim. Are you . . . all right?"

"Fine, Spock. Kinski and Renn are doing good work but—how long till you can get down here?"

Spock hesitated. This wasn't the moment to discuss Saavik's evidence—or the possibility of a mission Jim could not command. That would be difficult enough when the time came, if it came.

"There have been . . . developments, Jim, but I prefer to wait until we know more. I am concerned that local authorities may not have been informed, at least that a problem exists. Obviously the admiral did not order you to do so."

"No, Spock. No, he didn't."

"Then perhaps he already has."

"Maybe, but—you'd better check it out."

"Indeed. And Jim, every attempt is being made—"

"I know it, Spock. Go."

Spock nodded briefly, and went.

"Still in conference, Mr. Spock. He'll return the call."

Spock sighed, then signaled his own quarters. Saavik

answered at once, pale and composed. "I must be brief, Saavik. You are at liberty and free to explore the ship. Observe restricted areas. Obey orders from the crew."

"I spoke with Admiral Nogura, Mr. Spock. Do you wish to know what was said?"

"Indeed. You may report."

"Well, first he told me that I could refuse to answer his questions. I did not wish to refuse, so I told him everything—about where I come from and what I saw and how we know it was more than a dream. Then he asked if I would submit to a verifier scan, and I said yes, but that I do not lie and the mindlink is far more accurate. Then he said—"

"Briefly, Saavikam. There is little time."

Saavik frowned, and began speaking faster. *"He asked me the same thing you did—about finding that cave again. He asked a lot more questions about Hellguard and the Vulcan mission. He seemed unfamiliar with details. I told him what I know and said he could view my Privacy tape if he wished. I also suggested he contact T'Pau on Vulcan, but he seemed disinclined to do that."*

"No doubt," Spock murmured; T'Pau was perhaps the one being in the galaxy that Nogura went out of his way to avoid.

"Then he said my testimony would remain private, if at all possible. That is the substance of our discussion, except for the question of my exact age. Since I . . . am not certain, he asked who spoke for me in matters of consent. Why?"

"A human technicality," Spock said. "It is of no consequence, except to them. What did you answer?"

"That I speak for myself! And if that was insufficient, you would speak for me. Did I say wrong?"

"No, Saavikam. You have acted correctly in everything." And eliminated a personal dilemma as well. The problem of the Hellguard information was resolved: he was not forced to break a confidence; Saavik was not bound by one. Nor did she stand upon her right to privacy. "I shall not return to my quarters tonight, Saavikam. You may rest or work there as you choose."

"Mr. Spock, I would like to ask a question. Will I be going back to the Academy tomorrow?"

"Nothing is certain, but . . . I think not. When I—"

"Sir . . ." Uhura turned from her station. "It's Commander Dorish. He wants to speak with you, if you have time."

"Saavik, you must excuse me."

"Yes." Without another word, she cleared the channel. And that, Spock reflected, was the only straightforward conversation this night was likely to bring. It was most informative.

"About dismissing his crew, sir."

"Begin recalling our own personnel. Leaves are canceled on my order. Inform department heads to prepare for departure on short notice. Commander, Spock here."

"Dorish here, Spock. Can you tell me any more about this tragedy?"

"Not at this time, Commander."

Dorish shook his head. *"I don't understand why you pulled us off that ship in the first place. I mean, we weren't the ones in danger, now were we? It was those people down at—"*

"Commander! Are you scrambling this transmission?"

"Well, no. I just wanted to ask—"

"Please do so at once, sir!"

". . . done, Spock, but—"

"Commander, I was assured that you had been informed."

"About the deaths down at HQ? Yes, Spock, I got the information on that."

"And is that ship off Dock's air feed? Has the access been placed under guard?"

"Under guard? Why, no. The people there are authorized—"

"Shut it *down*, Commander! And post a guard *at once!*"

"Now hold on a minute, Mr. Spock. There's no need for that. Dock Four's a restricted area!"

"Commander, I . . ." Spock hesitated. This situation was intolerable, and the danger was clear and present. So was the need to know. "I am committing a breach of orders by telling you this, but—the contamination came *from that ship.*"

"But that's not . . . no, Spock. We're all just fine!"

"Forgive me, Commander." Spock reached for a tape still lying on his board. "My wording was imprecise. The contamination came from . . . this object. Three others like it were aboard—"

"That?" Dorish gasped. All the color drained from his kind, ruddy face. "That thing killed people?"

"A great many . . . Commander?"

"Oh, no, Spock," Dorish whispered. "Oh, my God . . ."

"Lieutenant Robert Harper, report to Commander Dorish in his office . . . Lieutenant Robert Harper, report to Commander Dorish . . ."

"Oh, not *now!*" Harper heard his own name blaring over the intercom. He hesitated in the corridor, then turned into Sector 20's lounge. Dorish could just wait. "Hey, guys, you seen Obo anywhere?"

A huddled group of officers glanced around, shook their heads and went on talking in excited whispers. Harper moved on, searching under the knots of people jammed into the bar, dimly aware that Starfleet's rumor mill was turning more than usual tonight. "Obo? Obo! Where are you?"

". . . but you can't call down now. You just get 'Circuits are busy, please try again later.' I'm telling you, something's going *on* . . ."

At a table by the window, with a prime view of the *Enterprise* floating in Dock 21, three officers ordered another round of drinks. Their progress was represented by rows of sake cups, vodka flutes, and metallic tumblers.

Harper's gaze wandered to the docking bay outside, and he felt an unaccustomed pang. Festooned with rigging of umbilicals and gantry lines, tended by service modules tracking across her hull, *Enterprise* floated in opposing gravity fields like a white, iridium queen.

Too bad we didn't pull duty in Dock 21 tonight, he thought. *Obo would've liked that. It's a privilege, a real privilege just looking at her* ... and a small, empty feeling tugged at him, a quick, disloyal thought: tonight just looking at the *Enterprise* didn't seem ... enough. *Forget it. Just forget it. I'd never go off and leave Obo behind. Wouldn't be fair. I've got so much—Mom and home and maybe if I'm lucky, a date with Jessie Korbet. But Obo only has me.* Where *was* Obo, anyway? It should have been—

"Harper!" A friendly brown hand clapped him on the shoulder. "Gotta talk to you! Guess what?"

"Hi, Fred. You seen Obo anywhere?"

"Naw. Don't worry, it'll turn up. Listen, something's going on down at HQ. They got guards all around the building—no one's going in or out. Didn't you hear?"

"Yeah, I guess so. I told it to wait right here for me, and now Dorish is paging me to his office. I already filed my duty log and everything! He'll just have to wait!"

"Yeah, let him wait. Obo too. Let me buy you a drink."

"Another time, Fred. I really have to find—"

"That's just *it,* Harper, there won't *be* another time! Listen, I just got the word . . ." DiMuro dragged him over to an empty table in the corner, where the only light came from the glow of floodlamps bouncing off the *Enterprise,* and the only audible conversation came from the next table.

A communicator's insistent chirping accompanied the senior officer's exchange. He finally snapped it open and growled into it. "This better be good, Uhura! This is my *shore leave . . ."*

"Listen to me, Harper, this is important! I got—"

"Shipping *out?* We just *got* here!"

"—new *orders*—just came through! I'm shipping out tomorrow!"

Harper stared at the excitement on DiMuro's face, and a lump began forming in his throat. It seemed like everyone was shipping out—and leaving him behind. "Way to go, Fred. You really worked for this. It's just . . . aw, it's just I'm gonna miss you. C'mon, tell me where you're off to," he grinned, "I'd better warn 'em."

"No need. No more pranks, Bobby, you're looking at a changed man. Tomorrow I take a transport out to Starbase Ten, then I transfer off to—" A sudden commotion from the crowd at the bar broke into DiMuro's tale. He glanced past Harper to the vid screen. "Wait, look at that!"

The blinking words NEWS BULLETIN were superimposed on a wide-angle view of Life City's shining domes glowing against a desert night. Searchlights from emergency hovercraft circling overhead swept the scene, picking out the shape and logo of a grounded shuttleliner and the jostling crowd of passengers who were being ordered back aboard by teams of uniformed, civilian police.

"That's *home*, Fred! What—"

"*. . . interrupt our scheduled event for a late-breaking story from California. You see the scene as it's unfolding now, outside the biospheres of Earth's most famous museum—the beautiful, desert community of Life City. This tragic story might have gone undiscovered for hours, except for a simple warning light on a shuttle's control panel . . .*" Harper watched, telling himself he'd wake up any minute. But the nightmare went on. "*. . . but no answer from Life City's flight station. We have a tape of that emergency landing, recorded by a photographer on board . . .*"

The giant domes of Life City, completely transparent after dark, shone like a cluster of beacons on the desert floor. As the shuttle began its near-vertical descent, the camera's view of the city inside zoomed into focus: scenes of walkways and trees, shops and planted parks—and bodies. Lying everywhere. In mid-stride, in mid-moment, everything had stopped.

In the bar, shocked murmurs ran through the crowd. People began surging forward for a better look.

"Harper! Where you going?"

". . . gotta . . . call Mom . . . make sure she's . . ."

"Wait. See what they—oh, God . . ." As the camera

panned down past the massive, closed iris of the hangar dome, the tape froze on a last image, startlingly close, painfully clear.

A Starfleet courier's shuttle sat on the landing pad, its hatch open, its flight compartment empty. Two white-suited ground technicians lay motionless beside it. The agony of death showed plainly on those upturned faces. So did the dark, angry blotches spreading over their skins.

"*. . . no official comment, but we have learned that initial scans register no life at all inside those biospheres . . .*"

"Harper . . . hey, Bobby, sit down . . ."

"*. . . or what went wrong out here in the California desert. So far all we know is that, apparently, Life City is dead.*"

Gentle hands pulled Harper down to his seat. The table-top rose to meet him as his legs gave way. Voices reverberated down a strange black tunnel, reaching him from a long way off. A firm hand closed over his arm. There was a whirring sound in front of his face, the faint odor of bourbon, and a pair of kind blue eyes.

"Take it easy, son. I'm a doctor . . . you knew people down there?" he was asking, and DiMuro was saying something, and Harper tried to catch his breath to tell them how it must be wrong. But breathing came so hard, and the blue eyes wouldn't listen. ". . . had some bad news, son . . . in shock right now . . . This'll help." Something hissed against his arm.

"*Lieutenant Robert Harper, report to Commander Dorish. On the double! Lieutenant Robert Harper . . .*"

"Oh, no! Forgot about him! I . . ." The hypo began to take effect. Harper sucked air into his lungs, pleading with the worry in those blue eyes, the fear in DiMuro's face. ". . . but, see, it's not true . . . my *Mom*? . . . oh, *no* . . ."

"I'm afraid so, son," the doctor said, still holding on to him. "Now all you need to do is sit right there a minute. I'm Dr. McCoy."

"From *Enterprise*?"

"That's right, son. Feel a bit steadier now? That's better.

Sounds like somebody's wanting you." The doctor patted Harper's shoulder. "Can you go along with him?" he asked DiMuro.

"Yes, sir. C'mon, Bobby. We'll go see Dorish."

Harper's mind began making connections: the things they sent off that ship, rumors about HQ, the news from Life City, and *that empty shuttle*—this was all adding up to something, something awful.

"Oh, God, Fred . . . what have I *done?*"

Ashen faces filled the comm screens. From Spacedock Nogura presided at a conference table with Admiral Komack and three other flag officers of Starfleet Command; the Council President and two more admirals attended on monitors. Aboard *Enterprise* Spock bent over his viewer. In the Vault, Kirk tapped his teeth and waited. Ongoing news coverage flickered in the backgrounds, including an interview with a hastily assembled panel of "experts" on potential causes of the disaster.

Ayla Renn scanned a sealed-off section of corridor on HQ's 18th floor and verified the signals from two new probes floating at each end. Twelve cylinders of oxygen sat waiting in that improvised laboratory, a hallway between the lab and offices already isolated by the maintenance shutdown and free of control switches, circuit panels, or anything electrical that could possibly malfunction. In the presence of so much oxygen, even the tiniest spark would cause a conflagration.

"Clear signals, Mr. Spock," she said, activating visual. The corridor appeared on monitors. She tried to shut the fury and grief out of her mind; at least the teams at Sciences were on the job. Even if they didn't know the whole story, there was no brainpower going to waste. "Stand by, Sciences. Cross-checks on everything."

"Just what will we be seeing, Dr. Renn?" asked Nogura.

"As I understand it, sir," Kirk spoke up, *"the new probes should tell us what this contamination is, and then we can*

determine what it will take to exhaust or neutralize it. Mr. Kinski has graphics for us on the readouts."

"Yes, sir . . ." Kinski kept an eye on the news while he keyed an overlay onto the corridor's image. "We'll be seeing blue dots, and yellow dots, and black dots. Blue's for oxygen, which we *don't* see now, because there's none in there yet. Yellow is everything else, black is the contaminant. And each dot represents the parts per billion . . ."

As the first cylinder of oxygen began to empty, the display showed a denser sprinkle of black dots around its valve, growing, spreading into a cluster, then a cloud. Like a swarm of virulent insects, the cloud hovered, thickening at its center, dispersing at its edges to fill the enclosed space in a matter of seconds. Renn watched the data, horrified.

"Are you getting this, Sciences? Verify that—"

"The probes are functional, Dr. Renn," Spock confirmed.

"Kinski," Kirk whispered, *"where are the blue dots?"*

"I don't know! I set it up right!"

"Your display is also correct, Mr. Kinski. Please be still."

Another tank, another cloud, another swarm—and darker and darker grew the screen. As the cylinders emptied, one by one, the graphic's overlay obliterated the image of the corridor itself.

"Remove the display, Mr. Kinski," Spock finally said. Screens cleared. The corridor looked the same as before, deceptively normal. Probes still winked and functioned, impervious to an environment filled with death. The only sound was the muffled murmur of a newscast.

On board the *Enterprise,* Spock stared into his science station's viewer, assimilating the flash-fed data as rapidly as it came in. At last he turned to the main screen.

"Mr. President, sirs," he said, "we were wrong." He keyed a computer simulation to their monitors, a helix of globular constructs of molecules in twisting rope-like skeins. "Here is our X-factor, gentlemen."

"Well, what is *it, Spock?"* asked Nogura.

"The identifiable component is silicon, but an isotope—a variant of elemental silicon, which has been engineered into a weapon. It has absorbed all the oxygen in the air supplies at HQ and Life City. And it is an isotope I have never seen before."

The significance of the news sank in: if Spock hadn't seen it before, no one else had either.

"When exposed to oxygen and to sub-microns of normal silicon, it reacts so rapidly that by the time our instruments record it, the process has already taken place."

"What process, Spock?" Nogura was growing impatient. *"What, exactly, are we dealing with? Some kind of chemical warfare?"*

"Reproduction, Admiral. As I said, we were wrong. In a sense it lives, as a gaseous, silicon-based organism—thus unidentified by our med probes. It is not metabolizing glass or other construction materials. But in the presence of oxygen and minute, airborne particles of silicon, it forms this complex chain of molecules similar to genes. It is a virus, gentlemen, a molecular virus. And it proliferates at an incredible rate."

"So we stop it. What will it take to do that?"

"Admiral," said Spock, "I have no idea."

"Commander Spock?" the president of the Federation Council spoke for the first time. *"How do you know this was deliberate?"*

"My . . . empirical evidence," Spock answered carefully, "is the weapon itself. Please observe." He touched a key.

And shining, beautiful, innocent as a rainbow, a clear box sparkled before their eyes. In its transparent depths, a point of light broke apart and grew, turned and twisted and teased the mind. Colors rippled in vibrant chains, from vermilion to violet and the scintillating spectrum between. "What you are seeing," Spock continued, "is, of course, unreal. The virus is visible only to instruments. The color and movement are aesthetic . . . enticement, probably generated from the inner layer of its shielded casing by holograph or energy field. But look . . ."

Superimposed upon the patterns, the simulation appeared in stark, functional monochrome. The technicolored lights inside the box unwound into an identical molecular chain.

"An ironic touch, is it not? Yes, Mr. President, it was deliberate. Molecular warfare, an entirely new class of weapon."

"And this . . . virus . . . was meant to escape into the atmosphere?"

"And would have," Spock said, "if Starfleet and Life City's environments were not self-contained—or if someone had walked through a door at the wrong moment. I suspect the weapon is also photosensitized to detonate under a high-intensity beam of light. An ingenious design, since worlds of advanced technology would be defended and difficult to conquer. But they would also possess instruments for spectrochemical analysis and inhabitants curious enough to use them. Make no mistake, sir, this weapon was meant to find its way to Earth. A bold strategy, but logical: what worked here would work elsewhere, with Federation defenses severely compromised. But the Empire seeks expansion, worlds to colonize. Perhaps the designers planned for this as well. Perhaps that virus has a limited life span, or some remedy exists to neutralize it—after which a planet's atmosphere could be reengineered. That is what we must discover, and quickly. If it escapes, there will be no time to stop it."

"How . . . long, Commander Spock?" the president asked.

"I fear the question is academic, sir, but . . . total oxygen depletion of Earth's atmosphere would occur within . . . ten hours."

In the Vault Kirk watched the faces on his monitors. Renn was nodding grimly as she pored over the stream of data still flowing across her screen. Kinski was biting his nails. Spock was back at his viewer. Everyone else wore angry, puzzled expressions of denial and disbelief, the looks of patients hearing their doctor diagnose an incurable disease.

"Spock," he began, "I know the virus can get the oxygen it needs to reproduce. But maybe if there's no silicon—"

"But there is, sir. In every cubic centimeter of the atmosphere, everywhere on Earth—even in the cleanliest computer rooms: dust. *Common dust and oxygen are all it needs."*

There was silence for a moment.

"Gentlemen." In Spacedock Nogura addressed the admirals around his conference table. *"Our scientists have their work cut out for them. We have other issues to consider. First, the question of security. I think we can all agree that . . ."*

"Admiral Kirk?" In Room 2103, Kinski moved close to Kirk's screen. The young man was clearly frightened to death. *"I'm—I'm sorry, sir, but I don't agree with* anything *these people are talking about! Sir, this isn't just some* industrial accident! *We're talking about the end of the* WORLD!" Kinski's gaze met Kirk's, locked with it. *"Do you understand what I'm saying?"* he implored.

From the empty reaches of the Vault, Kirk nodded.

"Yes," he said. "I do."

Chapter Seven

"I RECOMMEND standard procedure, Admiral. Quarantine regulations specifically state—"

"Thank you, Doctor," Nogura said quietly, but a vein in his temple throbbed. "I know what they state. You and Mr. Kinski will remain at your posts for the duration of this crisis. Around that partition, you'll find all the comforts of home. That will be all." Nogura cut off their channel. "Is *Enterprise* operational, Mr. Spock?"

"For what?" Kirk leaned into his screen.

"Marginally, sir. Nearly half the crew was on twelve-hour leave. The transporter situation has slowed their recall."

"Understood. I'll assign you additional—"

"Operational for WHAT?"

"Jim . . ." Nogura silenced him with a look, "you and your first officer have matters to discuss. You may do so now." And at a touch of his hand, two more screens went dark. "Gentlemen," he said to his admirals, "alert all starbases and outposts. Without more data on this new cloaking device, we must assume capability—and anticipate the use of unmanned craft aimed at Federation targets." With a courteous nod he switched off all the screens but one and waited until the conference room had cleared.

Then he turned to face the Council President. The burden of command never weighed more heavily, and his old colleague seemed to sense it.

"You face a dilemma, Heihachiro, do you not?"

Many, in fact, but only one he would discuss now.

"Yes. Earth is not the sum total of Starfleet's obligations. The Romulans monitor our media broadcasts. If they learn of the situation at Headquarters, they may be tempted to press their advantage. However, the quarantine must be invoked."

"You will find a way. And Council will convene off-world in emergency session—at an undisclosed site, I am told."

"Delegates are on their way up to Dock. Ships are standing by. Admiral Komack will be briefing the Council."

"Send me all your best minds, Heihachiro. I need them now."

"And I need time, sir. Other options are being explored, and other voices will be heard. Sarek is coming."

"I see. And you, Heihachiro?"

"No, Mr. President. I believe my place is here. I'll keep you informed . . ." The screen winked out. Nogura left his conference room by a private door and stood motionless when it closed, focusing his thoughts upon a sight designed to calm them.

In his Spacedock office grew an ancient piece of Earth, a family treasure handed down through generations. The elfin bonsai lived on a table of black onyx against a window full of stars. Gnarled and tinged with emerald moss, his willow trailed bare branches on its habitat's rocky ground. *It should have been an oak,* Nogura always thought, always knowing his ancestor had something else in mind. This lowly willow taught a lesson the mighty oak could not: how to bend. For Heihachiro Nogura that lesson was slow in coming. And it would not happen tonight.

TO DOCK CENTRAL/STARFLEET SPACEDOCK/0155 HRS.
RE: TRANSPORT OF COUNCIL DELEGATES. *ENTERPRISE, CONSTITUTION, POTEMKIN* TO DEPART ON SCHEDULE: *ENTER-*

PRISE 0300, *CONSTITUTION* 0330, *POTEMKIN* 0400 HRS. DESTINA-
TION COORDINATES FOLLOW. TIMETABLE CRITICAL. CONFIRM ALL
DEPARTURES.
HEIHACHIRO NOGURA, COMMANDING ADMIRAL, STARFLEET.

"Stand by for boarding: crews of Enterprise, Constitution,
and Potemkin. Enterprise *personnel have priority on the
pads. All leaves are canceled. Repeat: now boarding crews of*
Enterprise, Constitution, *and* Potemkin . . ."

The queue for Sector 20's transporter room backed up
into the corridor. Harper squeezed his way through the
milling crowd. Maybe if he'd just looked harder, maybe just
a few more minutes, maybe there was still time . . .

"Over here, Harper! I packed your gear." DiMuro pulled
him into line and lowered his voice. "Look, you don't have
to do this, Bobby. Forget what I said about—hey, where's
Obo?"

"Couldn't find it." Harper shook his head, very close to
tears. "It won't understand me leaving like this. They
should've *arrested* me, Fred. God, I wish they had. I *killed*
my own—"

"Stop it!" DiMuro snapped. "You'll go crazy if you keep
that up. Look, you don't have to *go.*"

"No! I have to do this! Find Obo for me, Fred. Make it
understand. You promise?"

"Sure. And don't worry—that kid's tougher than we
think, like you always—"

"You have business here?" A security guard's firm hand
landed on DiMuro's shoulder.

"I do," Harper said. *"Enterprise*—but wait, Fred! You're
leaving too! And I don't even know which—"

"Then get in there, mister! *Enterprise* people go first."
The guard began hustling him down the corridor to the
transporter room, with DiMuro tagging along. "Move it—
they're waiting on a sixth."

"Here, take your gear." DiMuro looped the duffel bag's
strap over Harper's neck and hugged him hard. "Do good,
buddy."

"Board that platform, Lieutenant. Hey, you—you can't go in there!" The guard barred DiMuro's way. Harper clutched his bag, stumbled up onto the pad, and turned back to see his friend ducking under a muscular, outstretched arm.

"Stand by to energize, hold positions please . . ."

"What *ship*, Fred?" Harper shouted over the crowd. "What—"

The guard grabbed DiMuro, who held a triumphant thumb aloft.

"Reliant, Bobby! Five years! See you out there . . ."

The transporter's whine filled the air. The room dissolved around him, and Bobby Harper left the world he knew behind.

". . . transmit a reply if hailed; otherwise, maintain silence. Beyond Vulcan disable your tracking signal and depart charted spacelanes. From there, Spock, you're on your own."

"Admiral," Kirk listened to the orders, trying to control himself, "if you could just give *Enterprise* some tactical—"

"I can't, Jim, and you know it. If you get caught, Spock, you'll be on your own, in Romulan space. Unauthorized. Command would never sanction this."

"Understood, Admiral. Telepathic evidence alone—"

"Spock's evidence!" Kirk shouted in frustration. "I don't understand about this eyewitness, but you can do better than—"

"Jim. All I can do is buy time. And hope the Council does nothing irrevocable. Spock, I'm making a statement to the press at 0255. I want Enterprise *out those spacedoors at 0300, sharp. And Commander . . . Godspeed."* Abruptly, he switched off.

Kirk felt the Vault closing in around him . . . *irrevocable . . .*

"*War,* Spock?" he whispered.

"Uncertain, Captain. The odds that those weapons remain on Hellguard are slim indeed. We must try to reach that planet before any chance to destroy them is lost. Jim . . . I

would prefer to serve here..." An old, familiar struggle crossed Spock's face: how to express in logical terms the emotion he wouldn't allow himself to feel. In all their years together that sight had never failed to touch Kirk—and to delight him. Now he couldn't stand it.

"Spock, most of engineering is still planetside. Nogura's sending you personnel?"

"They are boarding now, Captain. Shall I check in before departure?"

"Yes. Do that. Go on, Spock. You've got things to do."

Things to command. All Kirk had left to command now was a testy doctor and a nervous ensign. Well, by damn, command them he would. He reached for the intercom.

"Yes, Admiral," Kinski answered. Renn looked up from her work, hoping for some news.

"Doctor, Ensign. It looks like we're going to be here for a while."

Renn nodded. *"Do we report in to you, sir?"*

"Yes. I want to know what you know, when you know it. I'll be sitting in from time to time. Don't let it cramp your style." He smiled at them. "You have my comm-code. Call me if you need to."

"Anytime, sir?"

"Yes, Kinski, anytime," Kirk said, thinking how young they both seemed. "I'll be right here."

"Clear the pads, please. Clear the pads... they're all aboard, Mr. Spock," McInnis said into the comm. *Enterprise*'s transporter room was shoulder to shoulder with uniforms and no one going anywhere. "... yes, sir. I'll tell them. Mr. Spock's on his way, ladies and gentlemen. Just a few minutes more."

Harper wished he could sit down. He felt shaky, weak in the knees. The room buzzed with comment and speculation. Someone asked if he'd heard about Life City; he nodded, tried to stop the images torturing his mind. The strap of his duffel bag cut into his neck, so he slipped it off, shoved it to an empty corner on the floor, and tried not to think about home or Mom or Obo—or that empty shuttle on the landing pad.

Then the babble of voices quieted to shuffles. People came to attention for a tall, somber Vulcan who stood in the doorway.

"I am Spock," he said, "in temporary command of *Enterprise*. This ship departs in nineteen minutes. Despite our diplomatic status, this mission qualifies as hazardous duty. Any who wish to stand down may do so now, without prejudice." His gaze swept the room. No one moved. "Very well. Welcome aboard. Proceed down the corridor for cabin and duty assignments. You are off-shift until tomorrow. Lieutenant Robert Harper, please remain. The rest of you are dismissed. That is all, McInnis . . . now then. Mr. Harper."

"Sir." Harper stood stiffly, eyes front and center, his heart sinking to the toes of his boots. He felt Vulcan eyes boring into him and wished again that he'd been arrested.

"Dr. Katia Harper was your mother," the voice was deep, calm, almost kind, "Life City was your home. You declined a previous posting to this ship, Mr. Harper. Are you now fit for duty?"

"Yes, sir," he said staunchly, looked straight into those eyes, and found he couldn't look away. ". . . but . . . there's something you should know, sir," he heard himself saying. "I—I worked Dock Four tonight. I *sent* that thing down to Life City. It was my *idea,* sir—and it killed my whole—"

"I have reviewed the duty log and Commander Dorish's report. You made a request, which your CO granted. For the benefit of your mother's expertise, I would have done the same. My request simply went through other channels. As you must know, Mr. Harper, we have burdens in common." At that moment Harper knew he would follow this Vulcan to the ends of the Universe. "Your guilt and remorse are predictable human responses, Lieutenant. But they are useless to this ship. And dangerous where we are going."

"Across the *Zone?*" Harper blurted out that sudden leap of intuition, then looked away. "Sorry, just guessing, sir.

We'll do *something,* won't we? I mean, the Romulans can't just—"

"Our destination is not a subject for discussion," Spock said sharply, not contradicting him. "And I am not at all certain you are able to evaluate your own . . . please *explain* that, Lieutenant!"

"Sir? I don't—" but Spock was looking beyond him, frowning at the duffel bag he'd dumped in the corner.

It was moving.

"Oh, *no . . .*" he gasped, rooted to the spot. The bag wobbled and jerked, rolled about the floor. Tiny blue fingers poked out between its flaps, frantically unsnapping fasteners. And from the depths of its heaving canvas, a muffled voice began to wail.

"Nnnooo! Not Bobby's *fffault!* Don't be mad at—" In a scattering of socks, shirts and locker mementos, waving arms and glowing eyes erupted, teetered, then toppled into a heap on the floor. "*Bobby!*" Obo scrambled to its feet, clasping and unclasping its hands at Spock in supplication. "Be *nnnice,* okay?"

Spock regarded them both with disfavor.

"You are acquainted with this individual, Lieutenant?"

"Uh . . . yes, but I . . ." Harper wanted to die, from embarrassment or joy, he wasn't sure which. "How did you get in there?"

"Sssecret, Bobby! Nnnever tell! Fred said *nnnever—*" Eyes popped open, blinked fearfully. "—wwwoops!"

"Indeed." Spock studied the small person attired in Spacedock coveralls that bore no departmental insignia. "What is your name?"

"Ooobo," it replied.

"Nickname, sir," Harper explained. "The real one's too long for anyone to—"

"Your *correct* name," Spock insisted.

"Ooobbbooollloooddddrrrooobbbooonnnooo—"

"Very well, Mr. Obo. Your actions are highly improper. Your presence here is unauthorized. Was it your intention to stow away on a Federation starship?"

The creature brightened. "Yes!"

"No, sir. It doesn't understand. Obo's not official Dock personnel, not even in Starfleet—just sort of . . . adopted. Sir, this is all my fault. I'll go back and answer charges at—"

"Please, Mr. Harper. Refrain from assuming responsibility for events beyond your control. This all sounds most irregular. Mr. Obo, what, exactly, do you *do* on Spacedock?"

"Eeeasy fix!" Obo brightened at once and clapped its hands. "Vvvery quick!"

"Maintenance?" ventured Spock. Harper nodded weakly.

"You see, sir, Obo can fix anything—faster and better than anybody. It even knows *before* something breaks."

"Yes!" Obo scrambled over to Spock and clung to his trousers. "I am *gggood!* You will *lllike* me!" It reached for the Vulcan's hand.

"No, Obo! Don't—" Harper was too late. He watched, horrified, as Obo began using Spock's hand to pat itself on the head. Unresisting Vulcan fingers came to rest, and neon eyes shuttered closed. Obo blushed from blue to pink to brilliant lavender. Spock's hand finally slipped away. He folded his arms, lifted an eyebrow—and Harper abandoned any hope of ever serving aboard the *Enterprise*.

"Obo! Say you're sorry! You shouldn't—"

"Lieutenant Harper," said Spock severely, "at 0800 hours, you will report to sickbay. The chief medical officer will determine your fitness for duty. You, Mr. Obo, are a stowaway. Therefore, you will work your passage on this ship. What you have heard in this room is in *strict confidence!* Do you understand?"

It bobbed solemnly. *"Nnnever* tell!"

Spock frowned. "Now, that *is* your responsibility, Mr. Harper. You will see to it," he said, and strode from the room.

Harper stared after him, astounded.

The face on Kirk's screen inspired immediate confidence. Only those who knew Nogura well might notice lines etched where none used to be, eyes once bright gone dull with fatigue. But this was the face of command itself, the reassurance of wisdom, the voice of authority. His timing was perfect, and his delivery was flawless.

"... *Admiral Heihachiro Nogura, speaking to you from Starfleet Command. In compliance with Federation statutes, the Planetary Contingency Code is in effect as of 0300 hours Pacific time. This precautionary measure is mandated by the tragic and unexplained deaths at Life City, California. Until the cause of that disaster is determined, planet Earth has been placed under Federation Quarantine. We regret the inconvenience to citizens.*"

"... and you've got clearance, Spock? No hassles?" Kirk looked at Spock's face on one screen while Nogura's broadcast continued on another. The bridge appeared as normal as if he were making a routine call from his cabin. As if this were any other mission.

"*None, Captain. We are undocking now. Radio silence, sir. I regret no further communication will be possible.*" Spock nodded at the murmurs of moorings cleared, reverse thrust, one quarter impulse power. *Enterprise* was under way.

"... *transport to and from the planet will cease until further notice. All ground-to-orbit shuttle service is suspended.*"

"Spock, Scotty's been saying the warp acceleration 'feels funny.' He wants to check it out in flight. And that little light on my chair's panel doesn't always work—doesn't mean anything. I meant to—well, just sort of tap it. Or ask Uhura. Maybe she—"

"*Captain, I intend to return your ship to you in optimum working condition. All systems will be duly—*"

In the background there was a sudden commotion from the lift: an outraged voice began shouting on the bridge.

"*—finding out what's going on around here!*"

"Bones." Kirk tried to smile as McCoy shoved his worried face into sight.

"*Jim! I hear you're missing the boat! Earth's been quarantined, and we're off on some diplomatic errand—but I don't see any diplomats!*"

"Spock'll explain."

"Huh. That'll be the day."

"Take good care of my crew, Doctor."

"Well, God knows I try. Scotty's down there fussing over the engines, and he won't talk, and I've got a batch of new kids needing medicals . . . you picked one helluva time for a vacation, Jim."

"Sorry, Bones."

"Captain," said Spock, *"we are approaching spacedoors."*

This was it. Someone had to sign off, and Spock wasn't going to do it. McCoy glared at them both and fumed.

It was Kirk who finally broke the connection. "Good luck, all of you. Kirk out." The Vault seemed to echo with his words. Nogura murmured on.

". . . restrictions are temporary, legally required procedures. We hope to restore . . ."

He shut that off too. And was completely, absolutely alone. Panic rose in his chest. He fought it down, closed his eyes against it—and was back on the bridge, knowing every sound, every order, every move. Feeling the quickened pace and elevated heartbeats of his ship and crew heading into danger. Without him.

And without a prayer of ever coming back.

Kirk opened his eyes. The Vault loomed overhead, gray and uncompromising, all muted lighting, computer terminals and steel: an underground city with a population of one. No heartbeats here but his own. Up above, it was still spring, flowers were still blooming, and in spite of everything the world was still going on—

Wasn't it? The thought that it might not be sent Kirk's hand grasping for the comm like a lifeline, and he hit the wrong key.

Ensign Richards slumped over his open page, frozen in time. Kirk enhanced the image closer and closer. The print came into focus, and between those lifeless fingers, he could read the words:

"Is that all?" I asked.

"Well it's all that you're to hear, my son," returned Silver.
... *"Well," said I ... "I know pretty well what I have to look for. I've seen too many die since I fell in with you. But there's a thing or two I have to tell you ... here you are in a bad way: ship lost, treasure lost, men lost; your whole business gone to wreck; and if you want to know who did it—it was I! I was in the apple barrel the night we sighted ...* the page ran out of words.

And fear ran cold to the bottom of Kirk's soul. For his ship, his world, his Federation on the brink of war—and for all the little brothers. Everywhere.

Saavik stood on the observation deck and pressed her forehead to its transparent wall for one last glimpse of docking bays and ships in port drifting by. As *Enterprise* rose higher and higher in the towering twilight, Dock's massive spacedoors yawned across her view. Then with signals changing red to green and come-aheads flashing, the doors began to move. They parted slowly, opening wider and wider onto a deep and constant night.

"Now departing Spacedock. Prepare for warp speed."

She heard a step beside her, felt a quiet presence.

"Commander Uhura," she murmured.

"Not the visit you planned, Saavik. I'm sorry."

Saavik found nothing to say, and Uhura seemed to expect no reply. The commander had been on the bridge all this time—and must have heard ... everything. As they stood together watching the stars turn past, the ship's rotation carried Earth into sight. Saavik thought of oceans and rain, trees of flowers, baseball under saffron sun and cobalt skies. And people. All the people.

They were not likely to see those things again.

"Your world is very beautiful, Commander."

"Yes." Tears welled in Uhura's eyes. "You know, a lot of us have never even been here. And some of us don't get back much anymore. But this is where we came from, once. It's ... home."

That word again. "I used to believe," Saavik whispered, "that on a ship it mattered more where I was going than where I came from. I have much to learn."

"Well, you go right on believing it . . ." A tear escaped, streaked down Uhura's face; she never took her eyes from the view. The planet hung below them: a fragile, watery crescent of blue, its yellow sun peeking out and shedding light from the east, bringing a dawn still hours away from the domes of Life City and the windowed walls of Starfleet where no one was alive to see it come. ". . . because it's true. And we're always on a ship, Saavik. Whether we know it or not."

But now we're going where I came from, Saavik thought, *to a place of no beauty or goodness at all. Only a dream. But I am going to find that dream and that terrible thing I did—on my hateful, ugly world. And I swear, I swear by this beautiful planet and this ship that holds our lives, I am going to kill that dream—even if it kills me. I'll do whatever I must, so that evil place will never, ever hurt anyone else again . . .*

Earth sank below her field of vision, and when Saavik looked around she found herself alone.

"Warp speed in ten seconds. Stand by, please . . ."

There was no sound, only a kind of pause, a faint vibration in the deck beneath her feet. Then space went wild. Form and color fractured into spectra. Light streamed. Senses twisted and referents dissolved, and Saavik touched her hands to the window, longing to feel the quantum shift itself. Light bled away then; the galaxy contracted to a funnel of dark. From far ahead at its vanishing point, asteroids and planets detached themselves, hurtled toward her, rolled by beneath her hands.

And with the light-years slipping through her fingers, Saavik almost forgot where they were going. There was no Hellguard here, no anger, no shame. No past or future, birth or death. Life was a ship, bound for Infinity, and there were only stars.

* * *

Praetor Tahn was not an idealistic man, not even an intelligent one, and he would never be reckoned among the swift or the brave. But he did have the wit to keep to his house since that night's fateful meeting. Having long known there would come an end of his usefulness to The Cause, he'd planned well for the inevitable day—so that when it arrived, he would be elsewhere.

Safely, wealthily, elsewhere.

Small amounts at first, funds diverted from secret projects or purchases of Klingon ships, discreetly converted into gold and silver coin of the realm, sometimes a precious ruby—negotiable anywhere, anywhere at all. Over the years his talent for accounts and his fortune grew. But spending it on this pathetic holding, surrounded by estates far more powerful than his, would buy him only scrutiny and disaster. He hated this place anyway, hated this backwater world. He wanted wine, not weapons—silk, not ships. Life had dealt him a miserable inheritance and dangerous neighbors, but Praetor Tahn dreamed of better things.

So that night he rushed home, panic clutching at his heart, the First's words ringing in his ears: *treachery from within . . . ships and soldiers . . . yours . . .* and shivering inside his cloak, he sent the servants to bed, took his lamp and keys, and went down to a locked room deep in the moldering cellars.

It was gone. All his twenty chests, all his careful plans, all his dreams of warm sun and the good life someday—*gone!* Without so much as a scratch on the lock. *O gods . . .*

Somehow, the First had found him out. That empty room was his death sentence, to be carried out at the whim of a dark and deadly mind—whose identity was still unknown to him, whose Grand Design would bring the Empire down.

For the First had overreached himself this time: his weapon snuffed out worlds. And invader ships would not come in twos and threes provoking convenient conflict, no. They would come by hundreds, crushing the Empire's worlds, blasting the Romulan people out of the stars for what they dared to do. Protests would reach government officials, who would know nothing, deny everything, as they had so many times before. They would not be believed. And certain as the rising sun, those ships would come.

Tahn knew this, and he was afraid. The cup trembled in his hand; its wine was bitter and brought him no release. He'd spent these days marking portents, casting stones, seeking omens in the simplest of things. That in itself was a bad sign. Things were no longer simple. His life hung upon a slender hope, and he waited.

At last, from a high window, he saw that hope coming carefree to his gates: black cloak swinging, hood cast back, smiling at the guards who knew to let him pass. One hope, one chance . . . but it meant confiding . . . *O gods* . . . Tahn began to sweat when footsteps rang along the corridor, shivered when the door swung back.

"Old friend!" Tahn cried, and spilled a bit of wine. "By the gods, you've come!"

"Ever at your service, Tahn," the man said smiling, and helped himself to food and drink, as if in all the Empire there was nothing he could fear. "How goes the world?"

"O do not speak of worlds, old friend. One way or another, I am leaving this one soon. Plans . . . change, you see," Tahn clung desperately to generalities. "Events move more quickly than—"

"Why, you are not looking well, Tahn. The weight of office, perhaps? Some pressing concern of government?"

"Yes, yes . . . er, no. A small matter, a trifle, yet calling for discretion . . . er, secrecy, that is to say. Old friend," he cast pretense aside, "I need your help. I am in danger. But undertake this thing for me—and succeed—and you may name your price."

"When you have named the matter, friend. One depends upon the other."

Tahn checked the soundshield, then crossed the room and took his visitor by the arm. As his fingers sank into the folds of blackspun silk, he wondered how this man came by such luxuries, wondered many things about him—and felt a sudden fear. But there was no time to wonder. Their interests had coincided for many years, and Tahn had to trust in someone. What had been his, must have been his again.

"Then listen well, old friend," he whispered hoarsely, "and do this if you can. My life depends upon it . . ."

His guest departed as smiling and carefree as he came, and Tahn thanked the gods, just in case there were any. Whoever the First might be, wherever he might strike, now Tahn had a chance. Now he had a plan. Now he had the service and the word of his resourceful friend. And now, when there was time, Tahn could not afford to wonder anymore. Now he had to believe.

Three days later, a one-man ship drifted deep in Federation space, where it had come without alerting the network of probes and inspection stations monitoring the Neutral Zone. Its sensors scanned that vast and empty sector, overlapped and retraced, scanning again; when a single, moving dot appeared at the outer limits of their range, the automatic beacon responded exactly as programmed, sending the one message that would not be ignored:

. . . MAYDAY . . . MAYDAY . . . SHIP IN DISTRESS . . . MAYDAY . . .

Chapter Eight

IT WAS THEIR third day out from Earth. With Spock at his science station and senior crew on duty, the command chair sat strangely empty. *Enterprise* was crossing parsecs of star desert, heading "up the Line" behind inspection stations monitoring the Neutral Zone. Blind spots existed in that surveillance net (Sulu called them "smugglers' gaps"), where ion interference or passing comets obscured sensor drones—although some malfunctioned for less natural causes—and where outposts' eyes and ears could be outwitted, and sometimes were. Beyond Substation 36, ion storm NZ14 had been raging for months, scattering its noisy particles into surrounding space. There *Enterprise* would enter the Neutral Zone and skirt the outreaches of the Empire to make starfall at 872 Trianguli.

Spock had briefed his officers on the extent of Earth's crisis and the objective of their mission. Everyone on the bridge today knew the fate of worlds was riding on the *Enterprise,* but only Spock and Saavik knew that *Enterprise* was riding on a dream.

She spent her time working on lessons at the board next to Spock's, watching shipboard routine with endless fascination, and trying to learn the reason for his long, private consultations with Mr. Scott. Yesterday she asked if she could attend. But Spock only raised a frosty eyebrow, pointed out a syntax error in her essay on symbolic syllogisms in the poetry of T'Larn, and informed the crew that routine maintenance would be conducted in his absence. Then he left. And in light of what happened next, Saavik forgot all about those mysterious meetings.

The lift Spock summoned contained a passenger, the oddest being she had ever seen. Its eyes glowed bright yellow; its webbed fingers waved in greeting, and its voice gurgled, as if it were speaking under water.

"Hi, Sssspock! Watch me eeeasy fix?"

"No, Mr. Obo. I am due in a meeting. You may carry on."

"Okay. Bbbye. Hii, gggguys!"

And with that it worked its way around the bridge, chatting, using the hair-like extrusions on its gracile fingers and toes to remove panel covers, probe consoles' workings —often several at once—and reassemble them with impossible speed. Instrument response time increased. Uhura's board no longer screeched; it chimed. A passing hand banished the sticky action of Saavik's chair, which she hadn't mentioned to anyone. At the science station Obo found nothing to adjust. It stopped, turned a remarkable shade of pink, and stroked the viewer with great respect. "Sssspock!" it inferred correctly. After repairing the conn's armrest panel, it climbed up into the captain's chair and fell asleep. Which was where Spock found it when he returned to the bridge.

"Our stowaway appears fatigued," he observed mildly. "Commander Uhura, perhaps you could assist it to its quarters." Then he sat down to work, ignoring the open-mouthed stares of the crew.

Saavik hadn't seen the amazing person since. Today was just beginning, and she was wondering what would happen next.

"I'm getting comm, Mr. Spock. Starfleet channels," Uhura said into the quiet of the morning watch.

"New information, Commander?"

"Yes, sir. All nonessential travel's been *suspended,* and

ships are being recalled to starbases . . ." She listened, frowning. "It sounds like they're building up the fleet."

The news cast a pall. And the story behind it was apparent to everyone: no breakthroughs on Earth. Their captain was still trapped, their world still in danger of extinction.

"Is there going to be a war?" Saavik asked.

"We hope not," said Uhura.

"But you are preparing for one. It will not save your world."

"It might save someone else's," said Sulu grimly. "No one wants war, Saavik, but there's a principle involved: no one gets to wipe out planets either. It's Pandora's box, all over again."

"An apt allusion," Spock agreed and glanced across the bridge. Today Lieutenant Harper sat at engineering, the only new member of the watch. McCoy had declared him fit and in need of active duty, and Scott's in-flight checks were diverting all but the most nominal tasks below. Harper looked up, pale under his freckles, then bent to his board again. He seldom spoke at all.

"What is pandorasbox?" Saavik seized the opportunity to slip under the railing for another look at helm's controls.

"An old story," Sulu explained. "One of our creation legends says Pandora was the first woman on Earth, and she was given all the gifts of the gods. She was very clever and very beautiful. But the gods also gave her a little box, and the only thing they forbade her to do was to open that box and look inside."

"Why?" Saavik frowned. "If it was hers?"

"I'm coming to that. Now, besides being clever and beautiful, Pandora was willful—and very, very curious. And maybe she asked herself the same question you just did. So she opened the box. And in it was evil—plagues, and troubles, and wrongs. She shut it as fast as she could, but by then only hope was left inside. Evil escaped into the world, and it's been with us ever since."

"And this is what humans *believe?*" Saavik was appalled.

"Uh . . . no, not really. That's only a story, Saavik, a myth. But myths are part of our heritage, and they've stayed with us so long because there's some truth in them."

"And what truth is that, sir? I fail to see it."

"Oh, well . . ." Sulu was feeling a bit out of his depth. "I guess the point was that too much curiosity isn't a good thing, and, uh, that the gods should be obeyed, and—"

"The point of that story, Saavik," Uhura turned with mischief in her eyes, "which of course some *man* invented, is that all the troubles in the world were caused by a *woman.*"

"In Kiev," Chekov muttered, "who vill not return my calls!"

Judging by the laughter his remark provoked, Saavik deemed it intentionally irrelevant. She turned back to Uhura.

"But surely that is erroneous. In fact, an overview of your planet's political history would seem to suggest—"

"Saavik," said Spock, without interrupting his work, "humans consider it impolite to discuss their politics."

"Oh." She frowned, dissatisfied. "I beg your pardon. Then I would like to ask a question about your deities."

Uhura smothered a grin. "What would you like to know?"

"I would like to know why they would do such an immoral thing in the first place! And why should curiosity, which is a proper function of the intellect, not be considered a good thing?"

"Because those old gods didn't want questions, they wanted obedience. And people used to think that some things mere mortals just weren't meant to know. But Pandora didn't leave well enough alone, so the gods punished the whole human race for being curious, and hope is all they left us—or so the story goes."

"Hope?" Saavik's eyebrow arched. Uhura suppressed a smile. "But as I understand it, hope is an emotional attitude, a belief that all will be well, whatever evidence to the contrary."

"Yes, that's what it is." Uhura nodded, suddenly serious.

"I have no reference for gods or hope," Saavik admitted; her eyes smoldered, and her opinion of human rationality was being revised, sharply downward. "But when evil comes in boxes, *people* put it there. Perhaps this Pandora only wished to learn. Why does legend blame her, when it was your gods who were so treacherous?"

"Now, that's a *very* good question, Saavik." Uhura smiled, and Harper gave them both a look of undying gratitude.

"I also do not comprehend this worshiping of deities in the absence of any proof that they exist. And if superior beings did actually engineer—*create* your planet, would not intellectual accomplishment and advancement of your species please them more than worship, or mindless obedience to—"

"Saavik," said Spock from the depths of his viewer, "humans also consider it impolite to criticize one another's religious beliefs. We shall review acceptable topics of conversation at your tutorial this evening."

"No doubt," Saavik murmured, clearly frustrated. "Forgive me. I am unfamiliar with your cultural taboos. I must learn and abide by them. Even among Vulcans," she frowned at the back of Spock's head, "certain subjects are considered too embarrassing to discuss. I have difficulty with the concept, because it seems to me that if a thing *exists* one should be able to—"

"Saavik." Spock turned, noting general disappointment at his interruption. "The data you requested is now on your screen."

Saavik went silent. Yes, some subjects were embarrassing. She caught Spock's eye and flushed, feeling dishonest and ashamed. Without a word she went back to her seat. Spock watched her a moment then turned, arms folded and eyebrow raking the bridge, which sent everyone back to work covering their smiles.

Just then Uhura's board gave an unusual chime, but the

irate voice ranting in her ear was familiar enough. She flipped a switch to let it rant at them all.

"Why didn't somebody tell me we had a Belandrid aboard this ship?"

At his console, Harper turned in alarm.

"What seems to be the problem, Doctor McCoy?" Spock asked.

"The problem is it's unconscious on my table, and I don't know how to treat it!"

"Mr. Harper, you may report to sickbay," Spock said. Harper stammered a hasty 'thankyousir!' and dashed for the lift. "What is Mr. Obo's trouble, Doctor?"

"Obo . . . well, I don't know that either! Close as I can figure out, Scotty yelled at it!'

". . . didn't mean the beastie any *harm!*" Scott paced in sickbay and fretted. "'Twas havin' its wee fingers in m'*engines!* We're recalibrating the drive y'know . . ."

"No sign of injuries," McCoy said, running his scanner over the limp form. "What happened, Scotty? Did it get a shock or something?"

"Now don't start insulting my engines, Dr. McCoy! You've no call to be talkin' of *shocks!*"

"Obo?" A patter of footsteps sounded in the corridor, and Harper rushed through the door. "Obo, I *told* you . . . uh, Doctor, Commander Scott. I'm awful sorry about this." He peered down at Obo, and began rubbing the top of its head. "Come on," he said, "time to wake up now."

"You don't sound too worried. This happens a lot? This little fellow gets fainting spells?"

"Not exactly, sir. See, well . . . Obo is kind of different."

"You don't say!" McCoy was examining its fingers. "What's wrong with it?"

"Well, if Commander Scott . . . uh, *yelled,* that would—"

"The beastie was sittin' atop my dilithium regulator, an'—"

"Fixing it, sir. But Obo forgets to ask permission."

"We don't know the *problem* yet, laddie, so it couldn't know what to be *fixin'!* An' no tellin' the damage it's done! Recalibratin' the drive is a very, very delicate—"

"Hush, Scotty. It's coming around. Don't scare it again." McCoy shooed the engineer toward his office, and Scott went, muttering indignantly under his breath. Yellow spots began brightening beneath Obo's eyelids. Tiny fingers rippled and reached. Like shutters opening on a window, one neon eye parted and shone up at Harper and McCoy.

". . . Bbbobby?" Both eyes flew open. "A bbbig man yelled at me."

"You didn't *ask* first," Harper said firmly. "And that man didn't know you. You *scared* him, too. Ever think of that?"

"Nnnoo, Bbbobby." Obo hung its head.

"Well, you *ask* next time. Obo tries to be good, Doctor, honest. But when people yell—"

"Hurt fffeelings! Sssadness! Bbbad, bbbad—"

"Now, that's all *over,* Obo. I have to go back to work. You do what Dr. McCoy says, and I'll come back as soon as I can."

"Oookay, Bobby."

McCoy stopped Harper on his way out the door. "How're *you* feeling, by the way?"

"I'm okay, sir, thanks, only . . ."

"I know, son. Some things take time. Stop by this afternoon, if you want."

"I will, Doc." Harper waved at Obo. "Bye."

"Bbbye, Bbbobby!" Obo called out.

"Now, Obo, you be real good and let me have a look at your little—aw, no! Now put that down! It's expensive, and it's on the fritz."

"Eeeasy fix!" pronounced Obo, holding up a partially disassembled scope: rings, lens elements and circuitry fanned out like playing cards in spidery, webbed fingers.

"No! That's my DNA analyzer, see. I have to send it back—" Tears welled in Obo's eyes; its whole being seemed to droop. ". . . Aw, shoot, go on and play with it. Damn thing never worked right anyway." Hands maneuvered above McCoy's head as he plunked his patient back on the table.

"All dddone!" Obo thrust the scope under McCoy's nose. "Did I sssscare you?" it asked anxiously.

"Lemme see that!" McCoy snatched the scope away. It was all reassembled. Its light shone bright; at a touch, the lenses moved and focused. Readouts began to flow across its small display. "Well, I'll be! Scotty, come on out! You won't believe this!"

"Oh, aye?" Cautiously, Scott sidled from McCoy's office. "What'll I not be believin'?"

"Engineering to sickbay," the intercom interrupted with a squawk. *"Doctor, if you see Mr. Scott, would you ask him to—"*

"Aye, McInnis," Scott answered. "Do ye have that damage report, or will ye take all day?"

"Uh, got it, sir, but there's no damage! The drive's up to ninety-nine two. We can't figure how. That whateveritis was only in there a few minutes. We'll check it, sir, and run another—"

"Ninety-nine . . . *two?*" Scott goggled in awe at Obo, whose eyes began to fill with tears.

"Didn't fffinish," it confessed. "Bbbad, bbbad—"

"Leave it, McInnis! And from now on mind your manners. The wee beastie's worth *ten* of ye!" Scott switched off and tiptoed across the room. "Mr. Obo," he said gently, "can we start over? I don't know how ye do it, but if ye're feelin'—"

"Oh, no you don't!" McCoy scooped his patient up possessively. "This one's mine. And you already scared the living daylights—"

"Go *fffinish?*" Obo gurgled ecstatically.

"Aye, laddie," Scott beamed. "Will ye come with me?"

"Ooo, *yyyes!*" Obo turned to McCoy, eyes bulging. "Please? All *wwwell* now!"

"Yeah, I guess so . . ." McCoy said reluctantly. He watched the two of them walk off down the corridor together, clearly the best of friends. "Now I'm not finished!"

he called after them. "You come back later, Obo—hear?" An answer of sorts echoed down the corridor.

"Easy fix . . ."

Saavik leaned close to the screen, staring hard at the ugly, pitted surface of Hellguard as it appeared to *Symmetry*'s cameras six years ago. Even from orbit it was hideous. She'd never seen these tapes before, never wanted to, never wanted to remember this vile place or the savage, ignorant creature she used to be. Desiccated land unrolled before her: a world already dead, where suns burned cruel and dust swirled thick, blotting out her new life, mocking everything she wanted to become. Panic gripped her, and incoherent rage. She snapped off the screen, but its image hovered in her mind, a malignant ghost that left behind a mockery of its own: *You see, I am winning.* Just when she'd forced her breathing to slow, an intrusive voice began speaking on the bridge—but what it was saying made no sense at all.

"*. . . understanding—and a little human emotion,* Spock! That's all that little fellow needed! Just some good old—"

"Doctor, please." At the science station, Spock closed his eyes. "I am told Mr. Scott's *emotion* made the Belandrid ill in the first place."

"But you should see them now. And you know what it *did?* You know my new microscope? That fancy one I—"

"Doctor. To *what* do we owe the pleasure of your company? Is there some actual *purpose* to this visit?"

McCoy folded his arms and smiled crookedly. "Why, it just so happens, there *is!* Some Academy cadet named Sahvek hasn't seen fit to report for his physical yet!"

"*Saa*vik!" said Saavik, whirling in her chair, a green flush spreading over her cheeks. She stared at the human whose demeanor conveyed a profound disrespect for Mr. Spock's authority—which none of the senior officers seemed to think strange. To Saavik, that made it stranger still—and they were all looking at *her* . . .

"Omigod," breathed McCoy, "another one!"

"My *name,*" Saavik informed him coldly, "contains two A-letters pronounced as one. And I do not require medical attention because I am never ill." She turned back to work.

"Now just one damn minute! That was a *medical order,* Cadet! And *I'll* be the judge of who's sick and who's not around here!"

Saavik stole a glance at Spock—hands poised over his keypad, apparently oblivious to their exchange. She knew better. She studied McCoy dubiously, as she would some unlabeled specimen in a laboratory jar. "You are a doctor?" she inquired.

"Yes, I'm a doctor. Dr. McCoy. And you're the *patient.* So come along with me, young lady!" He entered the lift and held the door. Saavik's eyes widened in consternation.

"One moment, sir," she said, and rounded on Spock to begin a vehement conversation. Even in the ponderous syllables of Vulcan, her displeasure was evident. ". . . and all those doctors at the Academy, so *why* must I go to *this* one? I am not *ill!*"

"One of the reasons would be obvious, Saavik, if your state of mind were clearer: we had no time to append Academy records. Dr. McCoy is our chief medical officer, and even I must submit to his orders. Do you question the wisdom of Starfleet regulations?"

"Yes! And its choice of doctors!" she declared hotly. "Is there some other reason, Mr. Spock? You said *one* of the—"

"The other reason is that I requested it. Now, go with the doctor, Saavikam. Our lessons begin at 1600, at which time you may prove the existence of the dimensional tangent in abstract and concrete terms. I shall look forward to it."

"I also," she said grimly, approached the lift as if it were the gallows, then turned back to address the crew. "I appreciate our discussion of human beliefs," she told them. "It was," eyes narrowed at Spock, "for the most part, very informative."

"Now don't you worry," McCoy smiled, "this won't hurt a bit."

"Pain does not concern me, sir. And I do not *worry.*"

"I might've known . . ." The lift doors closed.

"You know," Uhura said, leaning back in her chair, "maybe that old myth got it wrong. Maybe something else was left inside the box, and we have to discover it for ourselves. What do you think, Mr. Spock? Do you suppose the gods left us *logic* instead?"

Spock looked up from his viewer in deadly earnest.

"Commander," he said, "you might be wise to hope so."

". . . uh-huh, and how about this? Does it ever bother you?"

"No." The human's touch felt cold to Saavik as he probed the scar on her shoulder. She tried not to shiver or flinch, but the contact was disgusting. So was his outrageous disregard for the Act of Privacy: *Childhood diseases? Childhood accidents? Things okay at home?* After a battery of scans, unpleasant proddings, and fatuous, interminable chatter, she had been here for an hour. She wanted to put her fist through the wall.

"Nothing *bothers* me, sir. Your instruments' findings are within acceptable norms, are they not?"

"Well, let's talk about you. Have you known Spock long?"

"Yes." She disliked talking about herself with this person. His tone was vaguely patronizing. He asked stupid, irrelevant questions while evading her own, sensible ones. And she was going to do something dreadful if he didn't stop saying—

"Uh-*huh.* Is he a relative of yours? Or a friend of the family?"

"No! I do not see how this concerns my health, but Mr. Spock is my teacher. *Now* will you tell me the results of my scans?"

"Well, I think your health's a little more complicated than a bunch of readouts." The doctor's mouth stretched into a silly smile. "I've known Spock a long time too. I'll bet he's a real good teacher, isn't he? Knows all the answers?"

"Of course. Or he will find them out."

"And he always expects the very best from you, doesn't he?"

"Certainly!"

"And I'm sure it's important for you to . . . live up to what he expects, isn't it?" the doctor asked.

Suddenly Saavik was sure she'd fallen into some trap, that any answer she might give would condemn her—or Spock. She wanted to get out of this cold, nasty room, away from this human with his clammy hands and smiling face and fuzzy mind. He made her furious.

"Doctor, why *shouldn't* I always do my best? Don't *you?*"

"Sure, but nobody's perfect. It can be quite a strain, always trying to do the right thing. Teachers don't always understand that. But I'm sure Spock does, even if he doesn't show it."

"I see no reason to apologize for the pursuit of excellence! Many things are beyond my understanding, but nothing is beyond Mr. Spock's. I have no difficulties with my teacher. Unlike *some* individuals I have met, he *always* does the right thing!"

"Oh, he *does,* does he?" McCoy glared, and Saavik was pleased to be the cause of it; she preferred her battles in the open. "Well, Saavik, why don't you just ask him about that time he . . . uh, no . . ." he waved his hand in the air, as if that could erase his words. ". . . on second thought, better not." He programmed a dispenser, and it spilled tablets into a bottle. "Now I want you to take three or four of these every day, hear?"

"Acutely. What are they?"

"Something the *doctor* ordered!" McCoy snapped, then managed to recover himself. "Sort of Vulcan vitamins. Spock takes them, so they'll be good for you. And in your pursuit of excellence, young lady, you might try eating and sleeping once in a while."

"Very well, Doctor," Saavik agreed so as not to prolong the visit. He grunted a final "Uh-*huh!*" and left her to dress in private. She did so hastily, ignored the noxious tablets sitting on the counter, and made such a furious exit that she collided with someone waiting in the corridor.

"Excuse me, I—oh, good afternoon—Mr. Harper, isn't it?"

"The name's Bobby," he said and broke into an admiring grin. "Wow, I'm sure glad to finally talk to you!"

Saavik couldn't think why. She didn't want to talk to anyone just now. And down the corridor beyond Harper, Spock was emerging from the briefing room and heading their way. Saavik wanted to talk to him least of all. "Forgive me, I'm afraid I don't—"

"Are you *kidding?* Why, you're the *Photon Torpedo!* Listen, I watched all your practice games back home. Talk about *smoke!*"

No escape; Spock was still coming, hearing every word.

"Talk about *what*, Lieutenant Harper?"

"Oh, uh, Commander!" Harper snapped to attention. "Well, I was just saying how Cadet Saavik here—"

"Perhaps *some other time,*" she suggested desperately.

"No, indeed." Spock came to a halt and folded his arms. "Do go on, Lieutenant. I shall find it fascinating. This cadet has somehow distinguished herself?"

"Uh . . . yes, sir." Caught between a rock and a hard place, Harper looked an apology at Saavik, but her eyes were closed. And he couldn't contain his enthusiasm. "In baseball, sir. Cadet Saavik pitched three no-hitters—all *perfect games!* She just blew it by 'em, right on the money every time. Too bad about the big game, sir. The midshipmen would've lost for sure."

"Ah. I see." Spock was now staring at Saavik intently.

Harper blushed under his freckles, feeling suddenly superfluous. "Uh, well . . . guess I'd better . . . be going now . . ." he edged away, then turned and fled. Saavik glared after him and simmered under Spock's stony gaze.

"It was either that or 'the Vulcan Vector,' Mr. Spock!" she finally burst out. "And under the circumstances I thought—"

"Very wise, I am sure."

Saavik was not at all sure. "May I go now?"

"Mmmm," said Spock. Saavik chose to take that for permission and marched off to the lift, head held high, and wondering if she would ever hear the end of this. A reproving murmur followed her.

"The Photon Torpedo . . . *really,* Saavik . . ."

She kept right on going.

"Come on in, Harper, be right—oh. It's you." McCoy frowned at Spock over his monitor. His voice turned cold, eyes unfriendly. "If you're here about Saavik, I'd say you're a bit late. Do you mind telling me what I was supposed to be looking for?"

"Doctor, I believe I did: any condition that might explain her inability to recall certain events during the first ten—"

"She was *starved,* Spock! That child never got enough to *eat.* Still has a borderline protein deficiency—and you worry about *total recall?* All right: no cranial damage, no evidence of brain trauma. *Satisfied?"* he asked acidly. "Then tell me—just what the hell do they *do* to little kids on Vulcan?"

Spock almost winced. "Doctor, what did you find?"

"Take your pick." McCoy gestured bitterly to a series of images on his display. "She's had shattered ribs, a punctured lung, multiple fractures, internal scar tissue—and they didn't get *treated* at the time. *Dammit,* Spock! What *happened* to that child?"

"I do not know." Spock had gone very still. "And neither does Saavik, which is why I asked your opinion."

How does he do it, change expressions like that without moving a muscle in his face? "Hell, unless she got thrown off a fifty-story building and by some miracle—"

"No."

My God, he's damn near devastated, McCoy realized. "Didn't think so," he said more gently. "The injuries are wrong for that. Look, I can only give you my best guess. I haven't seen much of this in my time, thank God, but I'd say somebody *beat* that child to within an inch of her *life*. Now, how could that happen on—"

"It did not happen on Vulcan, Doctor," Spock said quietly; he kept looking at the screen. "Saavik has never been there. And Vulcans do not beat their children."

"Well, Spock, I never thought they did. But damage like this . . . if she can't remember how it happened, it's probably because the experience was so traumatic her mind couldn't assimilate it. If she ever does, it'll happen in its own time—*her* time. Don't you make it into some kind of *failure* if she doesn't."

"Doctor, I assure you that I—"

"Listen to me, Spock. Those are *old* wounds, they healed a long time ago. I'm concerned with what's hurting her *now.*"

Spock stared at him. "Saavik is . . . in pain?"

"Yes! The kind she can't identify, the kind *you* won't admit *exists.* Her psychomonitor scans indicate pervasive guilt and fear—*fear!* Acute anxiety, displaced anger, deep-seated feelings of inadequacy that account for this *perfectionism* in everything she does. Self-hatred is a terrible thing, Spock—and your student's suffering from it. I think I know why."

Spock nodded. "This mission is a stressful—"

"I'm talking about *you,* Spock! That child worships you! She's knocking herself out to live up to your impossible standards, which even *you* can't always do. You want to put yourself through hell—go ahead! I've known you too long to hope you'll ever change. But don't do it to *her.* She's been through enough—not that she volunteered the information. Damned uncooperative, as a matter of fact. Quoted me the Privacy Act every chance she got. These," he held out the tablets, "would fix the protein problem, but she left them here. I even told her *you* take them too."

"But that is untrue, Doctor. I do not. Did you also lie to Saavik about these scans? Or withhold the information?"

"Dammit, it was the other way *around!* She didn't want to give me the time of day. Truth is, Spock, we didn't exactly hit it off. And talk about withholding information—you're not telling me *why* her memory's so important."

"I shall encourage Saavik to tell you herself."

McCoy sighed and threw up his hands. "Well, unless somebody tells me something, I'm working in the dark. Look, all I meant before was . . . go easy on her, Spock. She's a young *girl.*"

"An astute observation."

"You know what I mean! Try to encourage her, lend a hand when she stumbles, that sort of thing. That's what she needs now."

"How little you understand her, Doctor. What Saavik needs is the truth. I insist that you provide her with it, unvarnished and complete. She recognizes anything less and invariably finds it offensive. You incurred her distrust by withholding facts she has a right to know. It is your place to tell her, and I order you to do so. Your theories are quite beside the point in this matter."

"You're heartless, Spock—and she's paying for it. You just can't admit you might be wrong."

"And you, Doctor, consistently fail to look beyond the value judgments of your own species. To the best of my knowledge, Saavik has never 'stumbled' in her life. She would not appreciate the suggestion. I fear your sympathy is wasted on her, and I believe you know already that it is on me. Good day, Doctor."

"Wait one damn minute, Spock!" McCoy pointed to a readout. "Her blood chemistry says she's half Romulan. Does *that* have something to do with her anxiety? Does she even know?"

In the doorway Spock turned and sighed. "Of course she knows, Doctor. And that has everything to do with it." He left McCoy shaking his head and swearing to himself.

"That son of a . . . *now* he tells me . . ."

Saavik slumped at Spock's desk jabbing at the keypad and looking rebellious. Across the room he scanned a journal and ignored her scowl and muttered oath. All attempts to persuade her that swearing evinced a limited vocabulary had never produced the desired result. Saavik simply increased her vocabulary to avoid appearing limited. She did this by researching languages with which Spock was unfamiliar, logically reasoning that he could not object to what he did not understand. Her repertoire had become extensive, eclectic, and was always a storm warning. Finally Spock turned his viewer aside and beckoned the storm.

"Disharmony of the spirit requires no translation, Saavikam. Other than the dimensional tangent, what is troubling you?"

Her scowl darkened. "It . . . it is those *humans!*"

"Ah."

"They are a self-limiting species, Mr. Spock! And they *know* it! They are always saying so: 'I am only human' and 'What do you expect?' and 'Nobody is perfect'—but how can they ever *improve* if they think that way? They expect so *little* of themselves—just listen to their words. When Vulcans wish one another 'Live long and prosper'—the *humans* say 'Have a nice *day!*'"

"And why does this make you angry, Saavikam?"

"Because . . . because things are so *easy* for them. They laugh and cry, and they get angry—and then they excuse themselves for doing exactly as they please. And they think all their troubles came in a box from some gods, who were every bit as hateful as the Romulans. And they think that *hope* will fix their world. Well, I think they are very silly . . . some of them . . . sometimes . . ."

"And I think," said Spock gently, "that perhaps you have found exceptions to your indictment of the species as a whole. Perhaps you wish them to think well of you. And perhaps you wish that for yourself things could sometimes be so . . . easy."

Saavik glared at him long and hard, trying to think of a way to refute that. She paced the room and glared some more. Finally she came to stand looking down at him. "But I don't want to be like them, Mr. Spock. I want to be a

Vulcan, and . . . it isn't those humans who trouble me. It is myself. I try and try to remember, but I *can't!* I don't know what I *did,* and we'll be there soon, and I . . ." She threw herself into the chair beside him. "I want to be a *real* Vulcan, but I get so *angry.* And sometimes—most times, I don't even know why."

"I believe that you have a great deal to be angry about. I do not dispute your right to the emotion, only its usefulness to you. For example, you were angry with the doctor today, were you not?"

"That doctor appeared quite irrational to me!"

"Mmmm . . ."

"And he wouldn't *tell* me anything!"

"And I suspect that you told him even less than he told you. That is, of course, your right as well. But you wish to recover your memory, and he does possess medical knowledge. I am somewhat surprised that you left the possibility unexplored. But then when one is angry, one does not see all the possibilities."

Saavik digested that in scowling silence; Spock let it ride. She curled up in her chair, and it was a long time before she spoke.

"I dream another dream," she said softly, "but only when I am awake. Does that make it an imagining?"

"I cannot say, Saavikam, until I know the dream."

"It happens . . . on a ship, when we're going very fast and the stars come rushing at us. I watch them very hard. And it seems to me that there's . . . a *place* where all those stars are coming from, and that I am going toward it and *being* there, all at the same time. I can't see what it looks like, but I know how it will be. There's no anger there, Mr. Spock. Only stars. And I *know* them. I *belong.* If only I could get there, I would know everything in that place, and what it all means, and even my own reason for being born. And I would be everything I want to be. My place is very beautiful, but . . . if I look away, even for a second, it's gone. And then I know it isn't really there. I think I make it up, Mr. Spock," she said sadly, "because I want it to be true. And I would like to ask a question. Could I learn to be a Vulcan and still keep my imagining—just this one? Even when I know it isn't real?"

"It is real." Spock's voice was almost inaudible. "You are many things, Saavikam, but never doubt that you are also Vulcan. That . . . place . . . you speak of is not in the stars; it is in you. In me. In all of us. And you must keep it, always. You experienced a glimpse, a brief awareness, which is not uncommon. There is much, much more. The fusion of intellect and spirit, the peace of pure logic, is a state of mind we call the Time of Truth. *Kolinahr.*"

"You mean—I can *learn* this? I can find this *Kolinahr* in me?"

"It is a path, Saavikam, a way of life. And those who seek it must leave everything behind, all emotion, all attachment. Only then will the mind be truly free to reason clearly, to see things as they are, not as we wish them to be. Only then do we learn the true meaning of our existence, our own . . . reason for being born. *Kolinahr* is . . . Enlightenment. A deeply private experience."

"I never knew—you mean, more private even than *Pon—*"

"Yes, even more than that. We do not write or speak of this. The meaning comes to each person differently, the Masters say. But its truth cannot be taught. Its peace cannot be shared. It cannot be given to another. It can only be lived. You have known the desire. But even that must be given up in order to attain it. You must give up everything, everyone . . ."

Your answer lies elsewhere, Spock . . . and Vulcan's sun burned bitter that day on the ancient stones of Gol. It still did.

"But it is *possible?*" Saavik's eyes were shining. "If I study and learn everything and stop being angry? Even a half-Vulcan—"

"I do not know, Saavikam. I thought so, once. And if that is the path you choose, on Vulcan, with the Masters, it may be possible for you. But not for me. I tried. I . . . failed."

"But—" Saavik couldn't believe it. "—you are *never* angry! I have never *seen* you angry! Not even that time I broke your new computer, or that time I watered your memory crystals, or—"

"You were only a child, Saavikam, you never gave me cause. And my failing . . ." the words came slowly, ". . . was not anger."

"Then what—" She frowned at him, troubled. Spock waited for the inevitable question, knowing he must answer, wondering how. But the question never came. "—what I think," she whispered, suddenly unsure of herself, "is that this is a very Vulcan thing, and I do not understand it at all. But perhaps you didn't really *fail*, Mr. Spock. Perhaps, for half-Vulcans, it just takes a little longer. Don't you think that must be it?" She watched him anxiously.

Spock could not have said why failure should grow easier in the telling, but he was grateful all the same. He had never known her to deny herself a question. Saavik was becoming kind.

The intercom whistled. He went to his desk, then paused to look back at her curled up in her chair. "Saavikam, I believe you may be right," he said. ". . . Spock here."

"Mr. Spock . . ." Sulu had the conn, and his face was worried. *"We're picking up a ship's distress signal. It's a Mayday, sir. On heading 038, mark 7. Do we respond?"*

"Are any other ships on scan?"

"No, sir, nothing out here at all. We'll have to go sublight in twelve minutes or we'll overshoot on intercept. And it's still off the grid. We don't even know what it is."

"Estimate of time loss if we divert?"

"Our arrival on planet will be delayed at least one and one-half solar days, and that's only if . . . Mr. Spock," Sulu hesitated, *"Uhura says it's an automatic beacon. It doesn't vary, sir."*

Which meant all aboard could be dead. Breaking radio silence so close to the Neutral Zone might divulge *Enterprise*'s presence to Romulan surveillance probes. That they could not risk. And time was of the essence on this mission;

investigating a dead ship would squander it. But there was more to the equation: What if *Enterprise* reached Hellguard to find the weapons already gone, while people died because their Mayday went ignored? Less than two days away in Federation space. In flagrant violation of Federation law. By a Federation starship. That signal was strong enough to intercept at this range, indicating a large vessel. There could be hundreds of people on that ship.

"Mr. Sulu," he sighed heavily, "we will be going sublight. Plot your referent, and maintain radio silence. I am on my way." He switched off, frowning. "A complication, Saavikam—and no," he anticipated, "you may not. You may conquer the dimensional tangent instead."

"Yes, Mr. Spock," she followed him to the door, "but I would like to ask a question. This *Kolinahr*. It is very difficult?"

"Yes."

"And this is what it means to be a *real* Vulcan?" She waited, but he didn't answer. "This . . . is everything a Vulcan can be?"

"No," he said with sorrow in his voice, sorrow and old longing. "No, Saavikam, it is only the beginning. Study well."

She sat down again, trying to concentrate, then remembered something. She accessed Linguistics, spoke a word, and frowned at the definition on the screen: HIJACK (COLLOQ.): TO UNLAWFULLY APPROPRIATE PERSONS, GOODS, OR SERVICES (ESP. TRANSPORT) TO AN UNSCHEDULED DESTINATION BY MEANS OF THREAT, WEAPONRY, OR FORCE.

Well, that doctor *was* irrational! Or more likely he misused his own word. Humans often did that. *Yes, that must be it,* she decided, and turned her mind to a far more puzzling question:

What, in all the Universe, had caused Spock to . . . *fail?*

Kirk couldn't sleep, except in exhausted, fitful dozes from which some internal alarm would clang him awake, heart pounding, adrenaline coursing through his veins until the sight of Renn or Kinski on his screen told him Earth was still alive and he was not alone. He grew tired. So tired that shadows turned to people at the edges of his vision, so tired they sometimes spoke in clear, familiar voices, so tired the Vault became *Enterprise*'s bridge from one blinking of an eye to the next, and he ached to surrender to illusion—but that way lay madness. So he plotted his ship's course every hour, exercised until he sweat, explored passages and living spaces, switching on monitors as he went to banish empty silence with the sounds of life. Time passed slowly in the Vault.

And one by one, experiments failed. The virus resisted all attempts to poison it, neutralize it, or disrupt its molecular structure. Research centers from Earth to Vulcan were on link with Starfleet over coded channels; theories were discussed, experiments set up, and now robots wheeled along HQ's corridors, carrying out instructions by remote control. Hopes rose with the release of each cylinder of oxygen—and fell again. Analyses and lengthy consultations followed, leaving Renn and Kinski with little to do but eat or sleep.

At the moment, Nogura was on the line, and Renn was reporting the day's disappointments.

". . . and the second try didn't work either, Admiral. We haven't begun to crack its genetic code. The Vulcans are working on a method of molecular gene-splicing to make it vulnerable, but what they're doing is over my head, I'm afraid."

"Thank you, Doctor. Anything further?"

Renn hesitated. *"Just speculation, sir. Mine."*

"Then I'd like to hear it," Nogura said kindly, and Kirk felt a rush of affection for the old man. Renn was obviously upset, and trying not to show it. The strain was getting to her, too.

"This virus, Admiral. We've been assuming there's some designed weakness—or some antidote. But I think the Romulans built something worse than they knew. When it can't breed it just goes dormant, and so far nothing affects it, not even total vacuum. Sir, that means it could survive

beyond the atmosphere, be carried by ships or solar winds. If it got loose, I think it could contaminate a whole star system. And I don't think they planned on that. I think this may be the first use on a planetary target. Sir, I think maybe they just wanted to see if it worked."

Nogura listened intently. *"That is very interesting, Doctor. I want your speculations on the record. Send me a report, append the data. And try not to be discouraged, Dr. Renn. You're doing good work."* He turned to Kirk. *"A moment of your time."* Kirk found that an ironic choice of words. *"Jim,"* Nogura asked when they were alone, *"how are you getting on?"*

"Oh, just great," Kirk said dryly. "What's the word?"

"We should hear from Enterprise *tomorrow. But nothing so far from the Empire, and Council's at a standstill. Komack briefed the delegates. Sarek's held the floor for six hours now, and he's not about to yield. A vote's a long way off, but he won't compromise: they will assist in life-saving measures, but Vulcan will not accept our preparations for war; it's simply not an option. He and some of the others are going at each other, and the time it's buying us could tear the Federation apart. Member worlds are in an uproar, say Starfleet's supposed to protect them—and no one's putting any faith in scientific solutions."*

"But why the hell is Komack doing the talking? Heihachiro, why aren't you there? Don't they understand that—"

"You're the one who doesn't understand, Jim! The delegates are scared. I need that report from Dr. Renn because there's some talk going around in Council that the Federation should develop this virus. Everyone needs to know that kind of research could kill us all in the process."

"But . . . you can't let it happen!"

"Who the hell are you to tell me that?" The anger Nogura had held in check for days came boiling to the surface. *"Jim, you play your career like a game! You think* Enterprise *is your personal property, and you want to make the clock stand still! 'Send me your best minds,' our President said—and*

mine's stuck four hundred feet down because of some school-boy prank! But you signed on to serve where you were needed, Jim—and I need you here. I want you to think about that!"

"Dammit, I *have!"* Kirk said angrily. "I'm just not your man! Sooner or later, I'd punch someone out."

"Grow up, Jim," Nogura sighed. *"You don't punch people out. You keep them on a short string—where you can watch them."*

"And that's why I don't belong in your office! I don't *work* on a short string! I took back my ship because it's what I'm *good at doing*—and I'll do it again if I ever get out of here. But we know the odds on *that,* don't we! You might win yet, Admiral. Too bad you're not a betting man." Kirk heard himself sounding petty and exhausted, and hated himself for it.

"You are so wrong . . . Admiral!" Nogura said, and hung up.

"Damn you, Nogura!" Kirk swore at the empty screen, furious, sick at heart. His words rang in the velvet silence of the Vault, where there was no one to hear them. No one at all.

Chapter Nine

"ONE ABOARD, Mr. Spock, life signs low." Chekov frowned from his scan to the screen, where a ship hung motionless in space.

Black on black, a silhouette against the Universe, wealth and power were evident in every sweep of its light-absorbent lines. Wing tips spun out in filigrees of sensor webs; two needle-like nacelles streamed behind. Its sleek, expensive hull was bare of name, planetary registry, or Federation ID—and that sent Spock to his library computer, searching for a clue to its design.

"And one utility phaser, high-power," Sulu reported, "but it's not targeted or locked, not even on line. Sir, all systems have been cut to minimum. It must be cold in there."

"Ship-to-ship, Commander Uhura, tight beam."

"Yes, sir . . . this is starship *Enterprise*. Are you able to respond? . . . *Enterprise* to craft in distress, do you copy? . . ." She finally shook her head. "Nothing, sir. Mr. Scott says we can't dock with it. Transporter room's standing by."

"No, Commander. Inform Mr. Scott we are bringing that craft *aboard!* Medical and security personnel to the hangar deck. Mr. Sulu, you have the conn." Spock left the bridge looking ominous.

Chekov restrained himself until the coast was clear. "But it is too *small,* Sulu, for us to have heard its distress call."

"And too much power and too many sensors for its size. We've spent all this time rescuing a *smuggler!* Did you see Spock's *eyes?*"

"I did, Sulu. Not a happy Wulcan."

At the hangar deck's observation window, the medics waited. Security personnel quietly drew and set their phasers. McCoy twiddled with his tricorder, and Scott gaped in admiration at the ship. It tracked in, settling in the landing bay, and its matte-black surface reflected no glare from the floodlamps. And even before the hangar deck repressurized Spock was on intercom to the bridge, giving orders that put *Enterprise* back on course for Hellguard.

"I advise caution, gentlemen," he said as they crossed the deck, their breath frosting in the thin, space-cold air. They stopped at the ship's single airlock, and Scott moved to try its wheel. As he reached for it, the wheel began to turn from inside. With a hiss of vapor the hatch swung down, came to rest forming an exit ramp. A tall figure stood in the doorway, wrapped in a voluminous black cloak and hood against the cold.

"I am grateful," said a deep, male voice in perfect English, "I thought I was in for a long, long . . ." He swayed, then pitched forward in a billow of black cloth. Hands caught him, lowered him to the deck. The cloak's hood fell back from a chiseled, weathered face that looked sinister even in repose, a head of silvery hair, and a pair of prominent, elegantly pointed ears.

"He'll be all right." McCoy eyed his scans as medics lifted their patient onto a stretcher. "Probably thought he'd be stuck here awhile and took some Metabonil. I want him on monitors before I bring him out of it. He won't be talking tonight."

"Very well, Doctor. Mr. Scott, search that craft. Thoroughly. I want to know where it came from, what went wrong, and what it carries. Report to me whatever the hour."

"Aye, sir. I've never seen the like of this ship! I didn't know Vulcans were buildin' 'em like this. Come along, lads." He ran a gloved hand over the hull, then climbed into the airlock. The security team followed him inside. The medics were on their way across the hangar deck with the stretcher, and McCoy stood shaking his head, still frowning at his readouts.

"But he's not a Vulcan, Spock. He's Romulan. Now that's one helluva coincidence, isn't it?"

The following morning the patient was awake, alert, and pronounced fit for questioning. He appeared at ease, but his dark eyes were watchful, and behind them Spock sensed a keen, powerful intelligence. He answered questions freely: the ship, he said, was his own; he was a businessman, and his name was Achernar.

These preliminaries were interrupted by a weary, disgruntled Scott, who trundled in a sample of the ship's cargo on a floating cart: a ceremonial Vulcan chalice, bloodstone from the Klingon Empire, kegs of Romulan wine, cases of Romulan ale, and two ancient Orion sculptures considered long-lost religious relics. All of those items were illegal for trade. McCoy goggled at the ale, and as Scott tendered his report, his gaze kept swerving to several old, dusty bottles of something labeled "Glenlivet."

". . . no *proper* cargo bay! It was more like a hidey-hole under the deck, which took a day of lookin'—the deck plates were scan-proofed, and this is only a small piece of what we found." He eyed the Glenlivet morosely. "That ship's a regular palace inside and it's got warp drive, a single-unit transporter, and sensors that would do a starship proud. Flight data says he came out of Romulan space, but why he sent a distress—"

"My stabilizer was malfunctioning, gentlemen," Achernar said with a smile. "Invalidated my guidance system. Navigation input couldn't compensate. I was traveling in very large circles, you see. It might have been weeks or years before help came, out here on the edge of nowhere. Or never. So I cut power, set my beacon, took some— Metabonil, I think you call it—and settled down to—"

"Wait for some *other* rascal dodgin' the spacelanes?" snapped Scott. "One ye could buy off with a wee dram of—"

"Mr. Scott. Doctor . . ." Spock motioned them outside and waited until the door slid closed. "His medical condition?"

"Metabonil," McCoy confirmed, "saves a lot of lives when ships get stranded. He must've just been going under. Says when he heard our hail, we were already bringing him aboard. Typical. That stuff slows reaction time as well as metabolism. He'll be weak and wobbly for a few days. Needs to move around."

"In the *brig!*" Scott opined. "He's a smuggler, sir, no mistake. And we'll see about that stabilizer of his."

"An investigation should confirm or refute his claim?"

"Aye. But the ship, Mr. Spock. Will ye want us to fix it?" Scott flushed as Spock raised an eyebrow. "I don't mean for *him,* sir! He's a bad one, but his ship's a beauty. Custom-made. Those engines cost a pretty penny, an' to leave 'em . . . well . . ." Scott's voice trailed off. Spock frowned thoughtfully.

"Very well, Mr. Scott. Effect repairs, but inventory and impound his cargo. It will be required for evidence."

"Aye," Scott sighed. "That'd be . . . all of it then?"

"Yes, Mr. Scott, *all* of it." Spock reentered the inner room and considered the man who called himself Achernar. He carried contraband from two hostile empires, a neutral planet and two Federation worlds, one of them Spock's own. What he carried in his head might be more useful. The subject of these musings was sitting up in bed, regarding Spock with sardonic good humor. Intelligent, potentially dangerous, not to be underestimated.

"So," Spock said, "you are a smuggler."

"Please . . . a businessman." Achernar smiled.

"If you like. It does not mitigate your circumstances. You

transport restricted goods in Federation space without permits; you navigate without proper ID or assigned subspace codes. You violate the Neutral Zone, and you divert a Federation starship, for a reason we have yet to verify."

"I regret the inconvenience," said Achernar solemnly. "Believe me, I do. Perhaps we could . . . work something out?"

"I hardly think so," said Spock. "You are Romulan. Are you also an agent of the Empire?"

At that Achernar threw back his head and laughed. "No, friend Spock. No, I am not. I was only *born* a Romulan."

"To what world do you owe allegiance?"

"My world is my ship. My . . . *allegiance,*" the word amused him, "is to a principle far more enduring than permits or empires."

"How noble, that is if Federation authorities share your views. I should be interested to hear them."

"Certainly. Governments obsess themselves with loyalties and regulations. I deal in reality. You see, people will always trade something for something, no matter who they are or where they live. And in all my travels, I find that everyone has a price. Now, may we speak plainly? Grateful as I am, your assistance could prove . . . awkward. And as it happens, I possess information of value to your Starfleet. It is, of course, for sale."

"Of course. So much for principles. Yours, I fear, are sadly wanting. What is this information? What is its price? And what assurance will I have that it is accurate?"

"My information," said Achernar, "is the latest Romulan plot to bring your Federation to its knees. Interested?"

"Ah. A plot." Spock sighed in apparent boredom. "Rumored, no doubt. I must say, I am disappointed. You lack originality."

"A thousand pardons. Yes, plots are common in the Empire, common as cloaks, but I rather think you should hear this one. If I lack originality, the plan does not—and you lack knowledge of those you call your enemy. My price is modest: repair my ship, let me be about my business. My cargo is yours, call it a token of my gratitude. As for assurance, well, you must take my word—as I must take yours that my ship would not explode around me when I leave. Come now, friend Spock," he murmured, "I believe the risks are in your favor. Set aside these philosophical objections. I am a businessman, so let us do some business."

Spock appeared to weigh the matter carefully, then shook his head. "In conscience, Achernar, if that is in fact your name, I can make no agreement until I hear this 'plot' of which you speak. It could be last year's crisis, known to us already, or of no consequence at all. If it is none of those things, I may consider a bargain. The choice is yours."

Achernar laughed again. "I see you also are a businessman, friend Spock. Very well then, I accept. I shall even answer questions if I can. This much is what I know . . ."

Three sobering hours later Spock rose from his chair. "Your ship," he said, "will be repaired. When our mission is completed you will be free to go. Until then, you may leave your quarters only when accompanied by security personnel and wearing a surveillance transmitter. Any attempt to remove it or to enter restricted areas will trigger a security alert and forfeit our arrangement. I trust you understand my caution."

"Of course," Achernar said graciously. "Most generous."

Spock started from the room, then paused at the door.

"And regarding your 'greater principle,' Achernar: not only is it morally bankrupt, it is simply incorrect. People do not always trade something for something. Sometimes they manipulate the trader. And sometimes they prefer what they already have. One day, in all your travels, you may find that out."

"And one day, friend Spock," Achernar smiled, "you may find something worth trading for. Then, I think, even you would pay the price. A pleasure doing business with you, friend Spock . . ."

No, but it was enlightening, Spock decided on his way back to the bridge. That information was accurate, confirmed by events on Earth, and more: A secret military faction in the Romulan Empire had long been funding troops, ships, private missions—all without knowledge or consent of the government. That would explain the decades of diplomatic failures, broken contacts, each side certain the other was lying through its teeth. Now, with Earth hanging in the balance, the Empire's official intransigence and well-worn denials would not sit well with members of the Federation Council. And hours away from the Neutral Zone, on a covert mission under radio silence, Spock had no means of telling them that the Empire just might be speaking the truth. Or might not.

Was Achernar what he claimed to be, this man so disturbingly well-informed who would name no names? Why was that, if his only loyalty were to himself? And if his loyalty lay elsewhere, then friend Achernar would have little to lose by explaining the mousetrap to the mouse, once it was already sprung.

That evening Saavik sat in Dr. McCoy's consultation room doing her best to be polite, while he lectured her on the dangers of buried emotions, their relation to traumatic memory loss, and his peculiar belief that feelings were somehow beneficial. Saavik found this so absurd that she couldn't bring herself to discuss her own. At last he relinquished the tapes she'd asked for, muttering that *someone* must want to talk to him, and left her alone. The scans confirmed her memories of pain, but an hour of staring at them shed no light on how she came by those injuries.

She found Lieutenant Harper waiting outside.

"Hello, Saavik. I'm sorry about the other day. If you have time, I'd still like to talk to you."

She nodded. Perhaps it wouldn't take long.

"It's kind of a long story . . ." He told it as they walked along. ". . . and the whole city died that night. My mother, people I've known all my life, and someone . . . someone very special I'd just met. All because of me."

Saavik listened, horrified. The lieutenant's tale struck a chord inside her, deep and frightening—and his honesty made her ashamed. It took courage, she realized, to speak of such a thing.

"I talk to Dr. McCoy about it every day. He says the mind protects itself in funny ways. Sometimes people feel guilty all their lives instead of admitting they couldn't've changed what happened, because that would be even scarier. At first I didn't believe that. I mean, I *could* have . . ." he paused. "But that day we talked about Pandora, remember? I got to thinking—and you know what? I think Pandora was set up! The gods *knew* she was curious enough to open their box, and they knew exactly what was inside. So if *she* was set up . . . well, maybe Dr. McCoy's right. Maybe I was too. I have to live with what I did, and I don't know how to do that yet. But what you said helped me a lot. I just wanted to tell you."

"I believe," said Saavik, wanting to scream at the injustice of it all, "that the deaths of people you knew saved the lives of many you did not. But that is little comfort. Oh, you *were* set up, Mr. Harper. Your world was *attacked*. Your species' curiosity was part of a *plan*. You are not to blame, and *you* did not kill your city—the Romulans did. You must hate them for it. I do." The instant she said it she knew how wrong it sounded. Harper looked pensive. They reached the lift, and he held the door open for her. To cover her confusion she followed him inside.

"Well, I hate whoever did it, sure. But to hate a whole race of people I've never even met . . ." He shook his head. "See, Mom wouldn't have wanted that. She always used to say, 'There is no *them*—only people.' And I guess I grew up believing it."

Oh, but there is a "them," Mr. Harper, thought Saavik. *There is.*

The lift opened onto the light and noise of the rec deck, and she hung back. "May I ask why we are here, Mr. Harper? My tutorial is in one hour."

"It's a party," he confessed, "and I didn't tell you earlier because I was afraid you'd say no. Tonight's our last chance to have some fun. C'mon, Saavik, I'd really like you to be there."

"I—I should prepare my lessons, but . . ." Fun? An opportunity to observe it in progress? She had no experience with invitations or emotional appeals—and no experience in refusing them.

So on the ship's last night in Federation space, Saavik found herself at a party with the off-duty crew instead of studying.

She saw no evidence of "fun." All they did was eat. Large trays of exotic foods (far in excess of nutritional requirements) were piled on tables, and between mouthfuls all their talk was of the smuggler, his amazing ship and his illicit cargo. Chekov and Sulu called him a scoundrel in admiring tones and said he shouldn't be trusted. Uhura, who had run an errand to sickbay and actually *seen* him, said she'd never trust anyone that good-looking. Obo worked its way from lap to lap, drinking something fizzy, making slurping noises through its straw, and patting as many people as possible. No one seemed to mind. When Saavik's turn came, she was surprised to find that she didn't mind either.

"Mr. Obo," she looked into glowing eyes as the Belandrid sat down beside her, "I would like to ask a question. How do you effect repairs without first testing the equipment and without using tools? I saw you—"

"Eeeasy fix! *Vvvery* quick!"

"You do indeed. But *how?"*

"I'm afraid that's all you'll ever get," Harper said. "Those fingers get hot enough to solder metal, and they're so fine you can't see the real tips—but we don't know how Obo does it. Belandros has no technology at all. Obo just sort of picked this up."

"You are gifted, Mr. Obo."

Uhura had been strumming a guitar; now she began to sing—a new song, she told them, one she'd just written.

" 'Good ship Earth,' your children say,
'We'll be leaving you someday,
Bound for other worlds beyond your sky . . .' "

"And you are bbbeautiful, Saavik," Obo whispered. Soft, blue fingers tickled her own with warm, spidery tips.

" 'Where we'll love the stars we roam,
And sing of coming home,
And know that we were always meant to fly . . .' "

The music went on, and Saavik realized that Obo was holding her hand. Notes seemed to flow in the air around her. Her mind flowed too, undisciplined, somehow at ease. Now Bobby Harper was smiling, Obo was stroking her cheek, and feelings she didn't understand were overloading her senses.

Colors and shapes swam before her eyes, intense, brilliant as the faces around her. *Self-limiting, yes, and sometimes foolish, but . . . beautiful,* she thought, as if she were seeing them for the first time, *how they belong to each other.* And for a moment, Saavik almost understood about humans and love and coming home. She wanted to tell them that. She wanted to tell them everything, to be part of them, to *belong*—

Saavik froze.

In the doorway stood a security guard with a tall man in a black cloak. He had silver hair, a fine-boned face, and pointed ears. His eyes scanned the room, came to rest on her and didn't look away. He smiled—and Saavik knew she was looking at the face of the enemy. Obo moved away. Saavik's heart was beating in her throat.

"Come in," said Uhura, and to Saavik's horror, she smiled too. "This is Achernar. He's the one we rescued. He been giving you any trouble, Nelson?"

"Nope," the burly guard grinned and shook his head. "He's a real gentleman. The doctor says he's too weak to be anything else."

"And much too grateful," said Achernar. "You saved my ship and may well have saved my life."

"We know," said Sulu casually. Uhura began performing introductions. Even as Saavik's senses righted themselves, it still seemed that the world was mad. They all studied the stranger with interest, except for Obo who had gone to sleep in Harper's lap. ". . . and this is Cadet Saavik."

"Ah, 'Little Cat,'" Achernar murmured, eyes boring into her.

A wave of killing instinct swept over Saavik, dizziness and raw fear. Her fingers dug into the table beside her chair, inches away from an unused knife on a tray. Someone asked him something, and he glanced away from her a moment. When he looked back, the knife rested hard and cold in her sleeve. No one saw. No one heard the pounding of her heart.

"I must go," she said, rising.

"Oh, don't go now, Saavik," Uhura protested. "Is that what your name means? It's lovely."

"As its owner," smiled Achernar, mocking the hatred in her eyes. "And this ship," he smoothly changed the subject, "is full of wonders. I am not permitted access to your computers, but perhaps someone can enlighten me. What is our destination?"

"Sorry," said Sulu easily. "Orders."

"Sssecret!" Obo roused itself, blinked a bleary eye. "Ssspock said—"

"So what happened to *your* ship?" Sulu interrupted quickly, as Harper gave Obo a warning glare.

Achernar shrugged. "As I told Mr. Spock—"

"Ssstabilizer," Obo gurgled happily. "Easyfix—"

This time, Harper groaned out loud. "Obo . . ."

"Whoops! Secret, Bobby?"

"Excuse me!" muttered Saavik, stepping over cushions and outstretched feet. "I really must go now . . ." She was desperate to leave before they noticed she was shaking. The Romulan knew, she was certain, but he only watched, smiling his horrible smile. She made a hasty exit to a chorus of "thanks for coming" and "see you later," torn between fear for the humans and fear of what she might do if she stayed.

Back in her cabin, she locked her door, leaned against the wall, still shaking, and drew the knife from her sleeve. It gleamed dully in her hand, a blunt, useless thing. Revulsion and shame swept over her. In one blind moment of instinct she had betrayed years of Spock's teaching and trust; she had betrayed herself. She would throw it down the disposal chute right now, consign it to the ship's recyclers, wipe the object and the act out of her mind, and no one would ever—

The comm whistled, and her heart turned to ice. She jerked open the drawer of her small desk, flung the knife inside, and slammed it shut. Then she answered the call.

"You are sixteen minutes late for your tutorial, Saavik. Is there some difficulty of which I am unaware?"

"I . . . I apologize, Mr. Spock. I am on my way." She switched off, staring at the closed drawer, remembering that mocking face, remembering why she'd stolen a knife in the first place.

When she left she set the door to lock behind her.

". . . but he is *Romulan!*"

"Yes, Saavik. We know that."

"You *knew?* And you let him—how did you find out?"

"By medscan, of course. It registers the identifying blood component, a slight difference in the cellular—"

"Lock him up somewhere!"

"Saavik. He is under guard, and you are overwrought. For the moment I shall ignore your impertinence. Do you imagine that we take no precautions? Do you advocate incarceration for anyone aboard whose blood components—"

"Then lock me up as well! He is *dangerous,* Spock! Do not trust him! He will harm us if he can!"

Spock watched her closely. Her eyes glittered; feverish spots of color burned on her cheeks, and the look on her face was deadly. "Why do you say that? *How* will he harm us, Saavikam? You must tell me why you believe this."

"I—I don't *know!* But I am *right! Listen* to me, Spock! He is *planning* something! I saw it—in his *eyes!* I felt—oh, this will not sound logical to you, but that feeling has kept me *alive!* He is *Romulan,* and he knows . . . what I am. He said what my name *means!* Out loud! In front of everyone, just to—"

Spock raised his hand for silence and turned to the intercom. "Bridge, Spock here. Where is our subject now?"

"Rec deck, sir. Lounge area three. Sitting with—"

"Acknowledged. Spock out . . . you see, Saavikam, we do have the situation in hand. Now sit. Compose yourself. And explain why you were on the rec deck and not on time for our lessons." Spock's astringent presence was having its usual effect, and the Romulan was being watched by many people, here on this mighty ship . . .

Saavik's breathing slowed. Her fear began to seem irrational even to herself. "Cheering up Mr. Harper," she mumbled, shifting uncomfortably in her chair. "He asked me to their party. He said it would be fun, and I wished to observe that, but they never got around to it. They consumed no intoxicants, but they ate a lot of food and Lieutenant Commander Uhura sang a song." She fell silent.

"Are you concerned about tomorrow, Saavikam? Shall we speak of that?"

Tomorrow. Hellguard. "Will I remember when we get there?"

"There is no way of knowing, Saavikam."

"And what if I do? Can that place make—" she looked away, "—make me what I used to be? I mean, is it possible—"

"No. Do not fear your memories. What we *learn* makes us what we are. Life moves forward, Saavikam, and so must we. We cannot choose our pasts, only our futures. The past has no power over your progress. It has been lived. It is already behind you."

But it isn't, she thought, *it's ahead of me, waiting there on Hellguard. And I am so afraid . . .* "Then tomorrow—what must I do?"

"What you must always do: determine your duty and accomplish the task. But tomorrow," he said purposefully, "your duty is well-defined. You will follow my orders—*at all times*. Many lives depend upon what we find there. You must obey me, Saavikam, and there may be no time for questions. Do you understand?"

Saavik nodded. She saw a stolen knife lying in a drawer, the tiredness in Spock's eyes. She thought of all their nights of questions, answers, schools he'd found for her on worlds across the galaxy, study tapes that always came no matter from how far away . . . and how it felt, that learning. Always Spock, unfolding the secrets of the Universe from subatomic particles to the life cycles of the stars . . . and she wanted this night to last forever.

"But there is time now," he was saying. "I am not due on the bridge for five hours. We may spend them as you choose."

"Then I would like to study, as we always do. Tomorrow I might not . . . have time." He nodded his approval, settled back in his chair, switched on his viewer, and began on a stack of tapes. Saavik worked awhile in silence. "Mr. Spock? I would like to ask a question."

"Mmmm . . ."

"If I had taken the antigen scan all those years ago, you would have had much less . . . inconvenience, wouldn't you?"

He considered a moment, then shook his head. "Unlikely, since I would have asked to teach you in any case. But I could only give you knowledge, Saavikam, not a proper home. My urging was on your behalf. For myself . . . I would not have had it otherwise."

"Nor I," she said quietly, and went back to work. Nearly an hour later she glanced up to ask something else, but Spock's chin was resting on his chest. His eyes were closed. He was sound asleep. He hadn't done that in years. Saavik watched him a long time before she slipped away.

Dreading the return to her cabin, she rode the lift from deck to deck and walked the corridors of the *Enterprise,* staring out viewports at the stars, drinking in the ship's precision and beauty, feeling the light-years melting away outside. On the rec deck she stepped out of the lift before she saw him.

He was leaning against the wall, watching, as if he had been waiting for her all along. Fear slammed into her, a force that knocked her breath away, and a rush of blood drummed in her ears.

"Well, hello, Little Cat," Achernar said, and smiled.

"Do not call me that!" she hissed, hating how her voice shook. "Where—*where is your guard?*"

"Indisposed, but only for a moment. Do not worry, Little Cat. I promised to wait right here."

"You lie! He would never leave his post! Nor would he trust your promises!" *Alert the bridge,* she thought, but the intercom was on the wall, inches from his head. He leaned on his right shoulder, right hand concealed in the folds of his cloak. Saavik wondered if it held a weapon.

"And you trust nothing, do you? But answer me a question. What is a little Romulan cat doing on a Federation starship?"

"I have a *right* to be here! You do not—criminal!"

"So, you would have left me to drift in space?"

"I?" Saavik felt the heat rising in her face. "I would have blown you to dust. I know about you."

"Then you have me at a disadvantage. About you I want to know more. I like you, Little Cat. Tell me, is it the meaning of your name you so despise? Or your Romulan blood? Or is it only me?"

"You. And your lies. You know *nothing* about me!"

"I know you try to be what you are not. A pity. No Vulcan could ever be so beautiful. Well, I shall keep your secret, Little Cat, but there are lies and lies."

Saavik clenched her fists at her sides. "Let me tell you something, Mr. Achernar. I know you for our enemy. If harm comes to this ship or to anyone aboard her, I'll come after you. All the Universe won't keep you safe. I will hunt you down and rip your heart out—I *swear* it!"

Achernar laughed, and the sound curdled Saavik's blood. "You may not get the chance, if we are going where I think."

"Think what you choose. Where we are going is none of your—"

A door opened down the corridor, and an embarrassed security guard emerged and hurried toward them.

"Thanks for . . . oh, hello, Cadet. Pardon me," he said, reaching across Achernar to the intercom. "Bridge, Nelson. I'm back, no problem . . . no, just a call of nature. We're on our way." He took a small metal cylinder from his belt. With a maddening smile at Saavik, Achernar moved his cloak aside and held up his right hand, as far as its security bracelet would allow. The cylinder freed it from his wrist, then from the heavy grillwork of an air vent where it was attached. "Sorry about that," Nelson said to him as he signaled the lift. "Regulations."

"I understand," said Achernar, ever gracious, "but our cadet does not. She would rather see me drawn and quartered."

"No need, Cadet." Nelson grinned at Saavik. "We know where he is every second. We've had worse. Why, I could tell you stories that . . . Cadet, you okay? You look like you've seen a ghost."

"There . . . are no such things, Lieutenant. I am well."

"Then join us," Achernar invited. "We were having such a pleasant conversation. It could be even more so, I promise."

"No. I have seen your promises," Saavik said, trembling with rage as the two men entered the lift. "Do not forget mine."

"I shall treasure them . . . Saavik." Achernar was smiling, and Nelson looked confused as the lift took them away.

Oh, the foolish humans! They didn't see the danger, and Spock saw only logic. That skill was new to Saavik; she did not trust it now. Her life had depended for too long on seeing things, doing things not even Spock would understand, things of no logic at all. *Seen a ghost* . . . yes, that smile was like familiar poison.

There are lies and lies . . . the words stung; the truth stung.

She rode the lift back to her cabin, stopping only once. In Deck 6's corridor a fig tree's branches grew almost to the ceiling. She had admired it every time she passed. Now she looked at the oval sandstones covering the soil at its base. And took one.

Alone in her room, she drew the knife's dull blade across the stone again and again. It made a small, bitter sound. *You try to be what you are not . . . Yes! Yes, I do! I want to be better than I am—but I cannot be a fool.* So in the quiet dark of her cabin, she went on sharpening her knife.

She didn't mean to fall asleep. She didn't mean to dream the dream. But after eluding her for nights it came again, through a swirling mist of Hellguard's dust. Past the walls of twisting light, she ran from a death that wouldn't die, turned to fight with an empty hand, cursed the darkness dragging her down. And like an echo of her life, the screaming went on forever.

Only this time there was another sound: a voice from a time before, a place beyond the dream. It called clearly in her sleep, wrenching her awake; and its words left her sweating in fear, sobbing in the dark, and cringing with remembered pain. *Look up, Little Cat,* the voice said. *Look up, and see the stars* . . .

"On approach, Mr. Spock. Scans read clear."

System 872 Trianguli contained one fierce sun (its even fiercer neighboring star rose and set like a malevolent twin in Hellguard's sky) and five planets—four singed to lifeless hunks of rock eons ago, with poisonous atmospheres or none at all. The fifth was dead by Federation standards, red and brown, arid and uninviting. Most species would need environment suits to survive its thin, scorching air and sulfurous, corroding dust.

"Mr. Spock," Chekov was already at the science station, "a small dead spot on my scan—under those mountains. I get no—"

"No readout, no scan data. Yes, Mr. Chekov, a damping field." The same one that puzzled the Vulcans six years before. "That is our destination. Sensors and transporter will not penetrate it. I shall establish a check-in and beam-up point from the surface. Any questions, Mr. Sulu? . . . Very well, you have your orders."

"Aye, sir," Sulu nodded, but he didn't like them. Neither did Scott. They'd met that morning in the privacy of Spock's quarters to listen to his plan, and Sulu couldn't even tell Chekov what it was. Now, as the planet's wasted surface curved on the screen, a single, shiny speck rose on its horizon.

"Wait—*not* clear, sir! Scoutship! Weapons on line!"

"Jam them," Spock said to Uhura; she'd already done it. "Hold your fire, Sulu. Engage tractor beam, Mr. Harper— now!"

The tiny ship turned to run behind the planet, but the beam lanced through space and dragged it toward them. Its weapons, even at full power, wouldn't penetrate their shields. Scouts were built to look, listen, run—not to battle starships, and they need drop only one shield for transport. This tiny craft was no threat to them, and Spock had no taste for executions.

"Clear a hailing frequency, Commander Uhura, and engage translator. Scoutship," he said into the comm, "we have no wish to harm you. Cease your attempts to escape. The stress will destroy your vessel. When our mission is completed here, you will be released. Do you understand? Please acknowledge." No answer came, but the ship stopped its struggle to break away. "An unwelcome encumbrance," Spock sighed. "How many are aboard?"

"Just one, sir. He's all alone."

"And he cannot run or alert anyone to our presence. It should pose no danger, Mr. Sulu. Do not fire unless he gives you cause."

"Aye, sir," said Sulu unhappily, preferring a little cause and no enemy presence at all. Just then the lift doors opened, and McCoy strolled onto the bridge.

"So we're here, huh? Just thought I'd come up and see what's—"

"Doctor, your presence is unnecessary and will constitute a distraction." Spock touched the intercom. "Saavik," he said, "report to the transporter room. It is time."

"Time for *what?* You're not taking *her* down there?" McCoy pursued Spock to the lift. "That's *crazy,* Spock! This isn't—"

"After you, Doctor. Mr. Sulu, the ship is yours."

An unnatural quiet settled around the bridge as Sulu took the captain's chair. Chekov turned, unable to keep silent.

"Sulu, I have a wery bad feeling—"

"Stow it, Pavel. We've got our orders. We don't have to like them." And Sulu didn't, not one little bit.

"Yes, Mr. Spock." Saavik switched off the comm and opened the drawer of her desk. The knife lay inside, honed to a razor's edge. She took it in one hand, the sandstone in her other, despising them both. Her fist closed tight around the rock; it crushed, ground to powder, spilled through her fingers into the drawer. She dropped the knife in after it, slammed the drawer, and left.

She didn't set her cabin's lock; that no longer mattered.

"Deck Seven," she said to the lift. When it opened she stepped into the corridor, staring at the door of the main transporter room, wanting to run away. But she'd been running all her life.

Spock was there now. And Hellguard was waiting.

Enterprise was overdue.

Kirk ran the calculations again and again, telling himself they didn't mean anything, that word would come any minute now. And when it didn't he would swear in helpless fury at the safety of his prison, starving for some challenge, some risk, some way to make a difference. But there was none in this cocoon, this useless existence without another soul, where minutes passed more slowly than eternity and the only dangers were played out on the battlefield of his mind. In his darkest moments the panic won, when he could no longer imagine that door ever opening, or the faces of his friends, or the touch of a living hand—for the rest of his life . . . not long. Not on those terms.

And then he would fight his way back from the brink, hoping, believing, because there was nothing else to do. His voice grew hoarse, his hands shook. He forgot to eat, and he'd long since passed the point of exhaustion; if he slept at all anymore, he didn't remember it. Reality had narrowed to Room 2103 and his companions in exile. Another day was drawing to a close, a day that had seen two more theories fail.

"Sir, are you feeling all right?" Kinski asked.

"Yes, Admiral." Renn looked up from her report. *"Pardon me, sir, but don't you ever take a break?"*

"Why? Am I getting on your nerves, Doctor?" Kirk smiled.

"No, sir. It's just that you look exhausted. You should go see a doctor. When's the last time you slept or ate a good—"

"You tend to your knitting, Doctor, I'll tend to mine."

Renn shook her head in disapproval and went back to work, but Kinski hovered at the comm.

"Admiral," he said, *"have you got a minute, sir?"*

"It just so happens," Kirk said gravely, "that I do."

"Well, I've been thinking a lot—about what I'll do if I ever get out of here."

"That's normal, Kinski. But you're doing good work."

"Thank you, sir, but it's not the work—it's me. Do you think people should do what they're good at? Even if they have to change careers to do it? Even if it means . . . leaving Starfleet?"

"Doubts are normal too, Kinski. You're under a lot of stress. This is no time to make career decisions," Kirk cautioned him. "What else would you like to do?"

"What I did before," Kinski said, looking embarrassed. *"You see, sir, when I was younger, I . . . made computer toys.*

I started this company when I was fourteen, but then I got into the Academy, and there wasn't time—"

"Kinski *Toys!* I *knew* that name was familiar!" Kirk studied the nervous young man with new interest. "You made the Infinity Loop, didn't you?"

"Yes, sir," a smile transformed Kinski's face, *"that was my best one. You've heard of it?"*

"I've played it," Kirk admitted. "And so has my Vulcan first officer. He got all sixteen solutions, too."

"Seventeen, sir. Some kid out in Iowa or somewhere found a new one this year. The thing is, sir, I think I'm better at making toys than I am at serving in Starfleet. You're right about the real thing being different. Compared to this, the Academy was just a game. I can't stop feeling scared, sir. I don't think I ever will. And if I ever get out of here, I just want to go home and make my toys—you know what I'm saying?"

"Actually," Kirk sighed, "I know exactly what you're saying. And I'll tell you something, Kinski. There's no shame in being scared. And there's no shame in resigning from Starfleet. Now, I meant what I said. Don't rush into anything. You've put in a lot of work to get where you are. So wait till all this is over, and give it some thought. Then, if you still feel the same, you go home and make those toys. Because the only shame in this life, Mr. Kinski, is not doing the work you're cut out for. And once you find it, don't let anyone take it away from you."

"Yes, sir," Kinski said, self-confidence dawning in his voice. *"I'll do that—and thank you, Admiral."*

"Anytime, Mr. Kinski—"

A light began blinking on Kirk's panel: Nogura, calling for the first time in two days. *Enterprise? . . .*

"—but I think I'll take that break now. Hang in there, Kinski. Things'll get better."

"Yes sir."

But the instant Kirk saw Nogura's face, he knew things had gotten worse, much worse.

"Admiral."

"Jim," Nogura said grimly, *"at 0920 hours today, we received the Empire's formal denial of all charges. Debate was suspended, and Council took a vote. The nature of this threat, the lack of progress from science . . . it all factored in. Not even Sarek could persuade them that peace is the way, not this time. The whole Vulcan delegation walked out."*

"Then we're . . . at war?" Around Kirk, the room seemed to dim.

"We will be. Council has authorized a tactical strike. Battle groups are stationed to blanket the Neutral Zone from Starbase Ten to points—"

"My ship's still out there! It won't have a *chance!*"

"Jim . . . it never did. Spock knew that. Enterprise *went in because we had to try. We would have heard by now if—"*

"They're *alive,* Admiral!" Kirk heard himself shouting, knowing that only betrayed his exhaustion and ragged nerves. "It hasn't been that *long—*" The pity in Nogura's eyes infuriated him. "I'd know if . . . *dammit,* I'd *know!"*

"Tell that to the Rigel worlds, Jim. Tell it to the billions who'll die if this weapon works just once. And tell it to the Federation Council. We do its will—or have you forgotten that? And for God's sake," he waited through a silence, *"get hold of yourself. You know what we're up against."*

"Time, Heihachiro." Kirk strove to sound reasonable. "Just give Spock a little more *time.* That's all I'm asking."

"I don't think you grasp the situation, Jim. One city's dead, one starship won't be there when the orders come through—and now you want me to obstruct a Council mandate?"

"Yes! I mean—*no!* I—" Kirk fought the exhaustion he knew was muddling his brain. "I just mean . . . push where it *gives,* Admiral! Orders for the fleet come directly from you. As long as my ship's alive, there might be a chance to *stop* this. Now, isn't that worth every second you can beg, borrow, or steal?"

"Not one single flag officer would support me on it."

"I will!" Kirk heard himself saying. In that instant he was certain the cobwebs in his mind were gone. It was grasping

at straws, but maybe—even in the Vault—maybe he *could* make a difference after all. "Hear me out, Heihachiro!" he said desperately. "With ships in position, the Zone's defended. You find a way to stall that order, and I'll . . ." there was no going back from this, but suddenly the words came easy. ". . . I'll *take* that ground assignment! You'll *have* my support, and I'll be around to make it *stick!* That'll *mean* something, Admiral—with Command and with the Council—and you *know* it!"

Nogura sat watching him, saying nothing. *That old fox,* Kirk thought, *what's goes on in his head? Dammit, I just never know . . .*

"I won't back out this time. No tricks. No games. Word of honor."

"You understand, Jim," Nogura said carefully, *"that we're only talking about twenty-four hours—at the most. The Council's voted, and even my discretion won't cover it longer than that. You'd be staking a lot on one day. Are you sure you want to—"*

"My *ship's* out there . . ." *and I'll do anything, anything!* But Kirk couldn't get the words past the lump in his throat.

Finally Nogura nodded. *"I know, Jim,"* he said gently, *"you always were a betting man."*

The screen went blank, and Kirk's vision blurred. Monitors were dark now, and exhaustion came over him in waves. His body ached, arms and legs turned to lead, and he sank into the empty silence like a stone, while winning and losing chased circles in his thoughts . . . *but I did win, didn't I?* . . . and the circles widened into pools, reflecting memories of air and light. Worlds where he had walked—young green worlds, where people lived and laughed beneath their stars, knowing nothing of Federations or Empires. And the friends who had walked with him, touched and loved and fought, and sometimes died. And the deep wide Dark of never-ending oceans and never-setting suns, where a captain steered the course, and a ship sailed on . . . forever . . .

Kirk slept.

* * *

Nogura shut off the intercom, knowing that Jim had overplayed his hand only because he was so tired. But victories were few and far between these days, and this one was an unexpected gift—or a promise from a drowning man.

He crossed his office to the viewport spanning its outside wall. Earth slept, a dark disk edged in light. And on the onyx table, his bonsai's branches stirred. He was thinking of oaks and of Jim Kirk when the courtesy chime sounded.

"Sir?" His adjutant stood in the doorway. "That was Admiral Komack. Ships are in position, except for *Enterprise*. He says *Enterprise* didn't transport any delegates to the Council. He's . . . upset, sir."

"And what did you tell him, Michaels?" Nogura contemplated his tree: a willow still bending, an ancestor long dead, a lesson from the past that failed him in the present.

"Uh . . . what you said this morning, sir. You said that whenever he called I should tell him *Enterprise* was en route, her ETA was one solar day, and the fleet wouldn't move without her—"

"That's right." And Jim should have thought of it himself, should have known an old admiral would find a way—but Jim was so exhausted he wasn't thinking straight. *Word of honor,* a promise from a drowning man . . . had an old admiral come to that?

"—so that's what I said, and Admiral Komack said . . . well, he said a lot of things, sir. Do you want me to—"

"I know what he said, Michaels. When he calls back I'll be busy, understand?"

"Aye, sir. Admiral? Can I get you anything, sir?"

The bark was green, showing tiny buds. Spring came slowly in space, but it came. Behind him feet shuffled on the carpet, young, anxious. "Not now, thank you. How are you, Michaels?"

"Fine, Admiral. It's just all this *waiting!* But that's what they say, isn't it, sir—that the waiting's always the worst."

"Do they?" . . . *every second you can beg, borrow, or steal* . . .

The willow bent at his touch, as it must have bent that day three centuries ago beneath the weight of his ancestor's body, that day the sky turned to hell at Hiroshima. A miracle, this tree. No miracles that day for ancestors.

"Then they're *wrong*, Michaels," Nogura said sharply. "The waiting is *not* the worst."

· Chapter Ten

872 Trianguli V; *Thieurrull;* Hellguard. Fire and brimstone
by any name. Twin shimmers of the transporter set Spock
and Saavik down inside the old compound to a furnace blast
of heat, a fading ember sky, clay that scorched their boots
and cracked in jigsaw fissures as far as the eye could see.
Suns sank low behind the mountains, and daylight died over
the ruins of a colony reclaimed by an avenging world. Dust
no longer blew through empty doorways; there were no
doorways anymore, only piles of rubble crumbling with
time. Spock swept the scene with his tricorder.

Quakes had racked the mountains circling the colony's
western rim, hewn away great chunks of stone and flung
them down where buildings used to stand. New-fallen
boulders showed magnetic traces, but the disruptive field
that repelled ships' sensors was coming from beneath the
mountains, not from the stone itself. No life registered at all;
in this rock-strewn wasteland they were completely alone.
He opened his communicator.

"Spock here. We are proceeding toward the mountains. I
will check in at intervals. Status, Mr. Sulu?"

*"Scans read clear, sir. And that scout's in tow, nice and
quiet. It's not talking or going anywhere."*

"See that it doesn't, Mr. Sulu. Spock out . . . Saavik?"

She stared about her, face pale in the failing light, holding her tricorder like a talisman, as if it could ward off the evil of this place. Spock felt a sudden foreboding, an urge to call the ship, beam her back aboard. "Saavikam. Regulations did not permit me to issue you a phaser. Indeed, weapons may be of little use to us here, but I believe this one belongs to you."

A knife lay in the palm of his hand. Its hilt was cracked, its blade gone dull after all the years. Saavik caught her breath and took it slowly, reaching for some memory as her hand closed around it. She looked up trying to thank him, to tell him of that other knife she'd left behind, but she found no words at all.

"We must go now," he said. "Can you find the way?"

She nodded, and they set off due west in the gathering dark. The night wind began to blow, lifting dust to swirl around their feet. She crept from rock to rock, keeping to the shadows, watching, listening before she crossed a patch of open ground.

"Saavikam," Spock said, "there is no one here." He didn't know if she had heard, if they would ever reach the cave, or what might be waiting for them if they found it; he only knew they had to try. The dust blew, the night came down, and the stars came out in all their glory as he followed Saavik into the wind.

Stars. Always stars at night on Hellguard, always dust, always wind . . . and it whispered to her—old, cruel things. Strange to walk this ground in shoes with food she didn't need to eat, clothing warm against her skin, a presence at her back she didn't need to fear. She tried to think of lessons learned in clean fine rooms on other worlds, where people and their skies were kind. But those lessons were for other times; those rooms were far away. The empty pain clawing at her belly wasn't real, couldn't be; she wasn't hungry anymore. But it was there as if it never had been gone: old, triumphant pain telling her she was *alive*. Not dead of thirst or caught by Guards or killed by Bastard Others, like the stupid Little Ones who cried out loud and fell asleep at night. No, lessons learned were different here: to watch and wait; to throw her stones in secret, hard enough to smash a skull when someone needed killing; to hate, and hide, and never ever die, because then They would win, and then Everything would stop, and then she couldn't hate Them anymore . . .

Saavik ducked into the shelter of a rock and wiped the grit out of her eyes while Spock called the ship to confirm their new coordinates. He switched on the carry lamp when they set off again; its wide beam sliced the dark, played over boulders in their path and sharp stones littering the ground. Saavik didn't need the light. She found her way by starshine, as she had always done, and heard familiar echoes on the rising wind . . . *sounds of tramping feet . . . scrabbling, cursing fights . . . a dying shriek of someone caught. Someone else. Not me. Not tonight . . .*

"Saavikam, there is no one here."

. . . but ghosts . . . gaunt, tall shapes of tattered robes and sunken eyes: the Quiet Ones who watched the skies and gave away their food, who never killed or did her harm, and never fought to stay alive. Strange, and stupid, *not to fight! Stupid not to hide, when Guards always came and Quiet Ones always disappeared. And some just walked away. Watched the sky all night, fingers on another's face, and in the dawn went out onto the plain, cast off their robes under killing suns, and knelt waiting in the dust to die. Sometimes it took all day. And sometimes she ran after them screaming,* "Notnot! Yougo back!" *in such a rage she hardly felt the skin burning off her feet. But they never did, those stupid stupid Quiet Ones . . .* she heard her own breath choking in a sob.

"What is it, Saavikam? Are you in pain?" Spock's voice reached her out of the wind. His face bent close, inquiring eyes in swirling dust. Her heart seized in fear and shame. She couldn't tell him how it was, how the wrong ones always died, how they didn't seem so stupid now. She shook her head, gripped the knife tight in her hand. Memory stirred again: she hadn't always owned this knife; she'd gotten it somewhere, if she could only . . .

Look up, Little Cat. Look up and see the—

"Wait!" said Spock. He drew back against a boulder. The colony lay behind them now. Fallen rocks blanketed the last five hundred feet to a sheer rise of cliffs that formed the mountain's face. "Spock to *Enterprise.*" The channel's whistles cleared.

"Yes, Mr. Spock. We're still reading you, but just barely."

"Can transporter room lock on to these coordinates?"

"Mr. Scott says yes. That is a YES, but any closer and . . ."

"Mark our position. We will investigate and return here."

"We copy, Mr. Spock. Good luck!"

"Acknowledged. Spock out." He took a bearing, aligning the rock where they stood with two peaks of the mountain range. "Saavikam," he showed her, "remember this boulder. If we become separated, return here at all costs and call the ship." She looked terrified but said nothing as they went on. Those old collapsed mine shafts the expedition had found impassable lay further to their right, but Saavik wasn't taking him that way. She moved nimbly over the treacherous terrain, heading straight toward an outcropping in the wall of solid rock. A tremor shook the ground, and a rain of dust and pebbles scattered down the mountain. When it cleared, Saavik was nowhere to be seen.

"Saavik!" Spock shouted. "Saavik, where are you?"

He shone the light across the cliff. She was standing in a narrow gap, a rift behind the outcropping. Still it looked like nothing more than a natural crack in the mountain's face. He made his way cautiously, wording sharp reprimands in his mind, then forgetting them when he reached her and saw her face. This crack in the mountain was well-hidden, and much wider than it seemed.

"There," she whispered, pointing. "Down there."

"No, I must see *Spock!* Call him at once—or take me to him!"

"Can't do that, Mr. Achernar." Nelson's hand settled firmly on the butt of his phaser as the door to sickbay slid open. "Your appointment's with Dr. McCoy. Now let's go, sir."

"Young fool! This is—"

"Just a little check on how you're doing," McCoy said, coming forward to meet them. "Now you go in and make yourself comfortable. I'll be right there." He gestured to the examining room. Nelson's considerable presence blocked the corridor. Achernar paused, eyes traveling from one to the other, then he sighed and did as he was told. When the door shut behind him McCoy engaged the lock. "All right, Nelson. What's he on about?"

"I don't know, sir. He wanted to see the gardens, so I walked him down to Botanical. He looked out the viewport and got real agitated. Started talking wild, ordering me to take him to his ship. Tried to *bribe* me, sir—called me a fool for refusing. Now he wants Mr. Spock, if you please. And right away."

"He saw that little ship in our tractor beam?"

"No, sir, and not that planet either. Nothing's off to starboard but deep space. He won't tell me why, just says we're all in danger if we don't let him go. You think I should report this to the bridge, sir?"

"That he'd like his ship back, thankyouverymuch? This is the Romulan *Empire,* Nelson! Of *course* we're in danger! I'll let the bridge know what he said." McCoy started for the examining room, then turned back. "By the way, what went wrong with his ship?"

"The stabilizer, sir. Engineering replaced that whole unit. Stress fracture in the warp interface casing, but they don't know how it happened. Not enough stress to account for it, Mr. Scott says. Says Achernar might've done it on purpose. Only that wouldn't make *sense,* would it, sir?"

"Not one damn thing makes sense around here, Nelson."

"You think that could be important, about his ship?"

"Maybe. For God's sake, don't let him know it's fixed."

"But . . . he *does* know, Doctor. Found out last night. Sir, you want me in there to—"

"No, no. You sit tight. But if he comes out and I don't, you shoot him or something, hear?" McCoy went into the examining room, sizing up his patient.

"Doctor! Where is Spock? I must speak with him at once!" Achernar paced the floor with long, impatient strides.

"He's real busy, Achernar. You can tell me what's—"

"Call him here, or take me to him!" He lowered his voice and moved in on McCoy. "I know where we are, Doctor. I know these stars. And your ship is in grave danger."

"Uh-huh." McCoy ignored the implicit threat and consulted his scanner. "Blood pressure up, heart rate up . . . not good . . ." He tut-tutted and adjusted a hypospray. "Have you been having any dizziness? Nausea? Numbness in the hands or—"

"Listen to me, man! You—" Achernar's eyes turned cold and angry. A bone-crushing grip clamped over McCoy's wrist, setting the hypo quivering in his hand. "What is that drug?"

"This! Dammit!" McCoy fumed, "is your last X-9 Series *immunization!* Wit*hout* which, mister, you do not leave my *sickbay!* And the only danger *I* see here is a *patient!* Snapping off his doctor's *wrist!* Now you *sit up* and *behave* yourself, mister! *You hear me?"*

Achernar drew back and released the doctor's hand. He settled himself on the table. "Apologies, Doctor. I am concerned for the safety of your ship."

"Well, so am I." The spray hissed against Achernar's arm. "And it's high time *some*body did *some*thing—"

". . . Doctor . . . you . . . *fool* . . ." Achernar's eyes rolled up in his head as he toppled over. McCoy eased him down, lifted his feet to the table, and locked its restraints around his legs and arms.

McCoy stepped back to admire his handiwork and reached for the intercom.

* * *

". . . yes, Doctor, he'll be glad to hear that." Uhura turned with a smile. "Sulu, Dr. McCoy reports our Romulan guest says we're all in danger. But it seems he had a funny reaction to some medication."

"No kidding." Sulu tried to manage a grin. "Best news I've had all day. Too bad that other one—"

"Damn!" Chekov swore into the science station's viewer. "Tremor on the planet, Sulu! Seismic pressure building at the core. It is not so good they go underground."

"Get him back, Uhura."

She bent to her board, trying, and finally shook her head. "It's that field. There's too much interference now."

"Then inform Mr. Scott about the tremor. That's something he needs to know. Spock'll call in when he can." Sulu wished the captain were here. The command chair felt big and lonely.

On the screen, the scoutship trailed below them—a loose end. Sulu didn't like loose ends. He glanced over at Chekov, caught his eye.

"Pavel," he muttered, "it's not up to me. So we wait." The question was how long.

The tunnel wound down and down beneath the mountain. Spock shone his light on rocky walls where passages branched off on either side. More tunnels, some with mining carts and tools, some locked off by iron bars set in stone. He used his tricorder as a camera; at distances of more than a few inches its scans were as scrambled by the damping field as *Enterprise*'s sensors. A series of readings close against the tunnels' walls finally got results.

Deposits of that anomalous form of silicon were bound up in the iron ores at this depth. A substance native to this planet had been discovered, studied, engineered into a living virus—*that* was the reason for this colony where none should have been. And now he could prove it—if they ever got out of here alive.

Saavik walked beside him, clearly lost on her painful journey back in time and struggling for control. His quiet murmurs of discoveries did nothing to allay the waves of suffocating terror, hatred, emanations of a mind bent on vengeance. Another tremor rumbled through the mountain. He knew the danger, but it was far too late to send her back.

The floor sloped downward, turned sharply to the right, and ahead the tunnel turned again. Spock switched off the light, for now it was no longer dark. At the turning a painted sign banned the use of particle-beam weapons, and the jagged walls gave back a light of their own, flickering in colors. Suddenly he realized Saavik was no longer at his side. She stood farther on, bathed in that wavering light, knife glinting in her hand. "Saavik! *No!*"

She walked into it and disappeared.

"Saavik, come back! I *order* you . . ." but she was gone. Spock reached the bend at a run—and stopped short at what he saw: here the tunnel widened into a huge cavern supported overhead by a network of steel grids, a warehouse lit by what it stored.

Boxes. Rows upon rows of them, stacked in walls higher than his head, built with deadly bricks of weaving, iridescent light.

But Saavik was nowhere to be seen. He tried his scan, got useless jumble and looked down a score of glowing corridors, pausing to record disturbances in the dust—four empty spaces in one wall near the tunnel where the bricks were missing. He checked the chronometer built into his tricorder: fifty-one minutes since he'd called the ship. By now they should be heading to the surface, to finish the job *Enterprise* had come to do. Whatever tortured impulse sent her in that lighted maze might bring her out the other side. *"Saavik!"*

No answer. No choice. He chose an aisle and started walking.

Caught. Slung upside down over a shoulder. Hauled like a dead thing by hateful guards with hurting hands . . . pain ripping through her chest, blood bubbling from her mouth and nose, a dark trail dripping on the ground . . . that was how she came this way before.

Caught? No, she was *never* caught! Part of Saavik's mind was still asking questions while memories came bursting in her brain.

Pain. Eyes swimming, watching: a moving hip, clanking belt, a tiny shine of metal. Arm dangling, fingers reaching— shining knife! Dizzying pain. Then sliding off a shoulder, falling to the ground. Guards cursing—not seeing how she curled into a ball and pushed the knife inside the rags around her waist. Sharp boots kicking, laughing, lifting. Darkness taking everything away . . .

And she was here again—in this trap with the walls of eyes, lights that moved like dust in the suns, this place of nowhere to hide. But she had tried, huddled in their sickening brightness with blood welling in her throat. Saavik looked around and found herself alone. *Not move, not now, not ever make a sound* . . . no, that was *after*—after what she'd done. Shame opened in her like a wound. She couldn't remember why. Her heart thudded, pumping fear, and madness closed around the edges of her sight. In some other far reality, someone called—a voice that should not be calling here. She knew she should be answering, but the screaming in her mind grew with every step she took, swallowing her voice, drowning out her name. It was all happening again. Boots tramped, voices called, death hunted in these halls of light . . . *make It never see me* . . . *make It never hear me, make It* . . .

IT . . . had *lived!*

She *remembered* that, and blood ran freezing in her veins.

Because It . . . was *real. It was still here.* And she felt Its presence now, waiting for her in the dark, waiting at the end of all the light . . .

"Saavik!" Spock left the corridors behind, calling, adjusting his eyes to the gloom. Hulking contours of machinery loomed in the ambient light: canisters, gauges, conduits feeding down to a generator shaft drilled deep into the cavern's floor and spanned by a catwalk overhead. He considered an attempt to nullify the forcefield—and rejected it: a time-consuming task, even if the catwalk held his weight. And something else disturbed him.

This was a factory gathering dust, its automation hidden, encased in steel, its enclosed conveyor belt halted long ago. But there weren't adequate safeguards for dealing with these deadly products. One finished weapon still rested on a platform; others were piled on a wheeled cart nearby, and down inside the shaft power cells still glowed, charged by geothermal energy from the planet's core. Production here had ceased abruptly. The place had been abandoned in disorder, as had the colony above. Ahead the cave stretched on in shadows. More equipment, laboratory counters, lined one wall, and beyond that . . . shapes.

Many of them. Shadowy outlines with faint points of light, tall, oblong . . . he moved forward with a sinking heart, suddenly knowing what he would find. His light pierced the dark, tricorder whirred, and Spock came face to face with the horror that was Hellguard: test chambers. Test subjects. Rows upon rows . . .

The Vulcans had been here all along, those ill-fated crews of *Perceptor, Criterion, Constant,* and *Diversity.* The men and women of science and peace, who set out to map the stars so long ago, were missing no more.

Saavik felt her way along the cavern wall, seeing things that were no longer there: machinery clanked and hummed beside a shaft of fire. Dust rose around the generator's pit like smoke, red in the glowing air. She felt guards' bruising hands pinning both her arms, heard their spiteful laughter as they dragged her, kicking, biting, scratching, to this place inside her dreams.

Remembering made her cold. Shivering, she crouched behind a laboratory counter, dug knuckles into eyelids to make it go away, but she couldn't stop the seeing. She raised her head, looked through cloudy vials and beakers where a parting beam of light swung among the pillars of the dead, where memories took shape and walked, and burned their sad, despairing eyes into her soul.

Quiet Ones. Not so many standing all together, but more of them than guards—Bastard Guards! Stupid Quiet Ones not to fight, not to know how they were going to die . . .

". . . *resisting, Lord. They refuse to move.*"

"*They always do, at first,*" said a man in a long black cloak. Guards shouted, shoved, afraid of going near those dying places themselves. Quiet Ones didn't listen. They knew. Death was in their eyes, sorrow when they looked at her, all sunken faces, naked bones . . . why did Quiet Ones always die? Her own guards jerked her forward into a ring of light. She struggled, ached to reach her knife, stole a glance at it. And that glance froze her struggles and her heart. The knife's bright point poked out through the rags around her waist, rags that were coming untied.

"*Then they must learn,*" the voice sighed, annoyed. Black Cloak flowed, turned toward her. "*Centurion! What is this?*"

"*Nothing, Lord, your pardon. Little bitch made trouble up above.*" Iron hands twisted, held her fast. Cloak moved closer, looked down with cold, dismissing eyes. Then It smiled—an evil, horrid smile. She cursed, spit at It, screeching empty threats.

"*KILLS YOU FACE! KILLS YOU EYES! KILLS YOU BASTARD—*"

—and earned herself a reeling blow across her head. Its eyes looked over her, angry at her guards. "*Shut her up. We've trouble of our own—but none that can't be solved.*" Quiet Ones moved all close together, pretending not to hear. Black Cloak rustled. Its finger pointed in their midst. "*Take that one first . . .*"

He didn't look afraid. A soldier seized him, dragged him out, ripped away the tatters of his robe.

"*FIGHTS! YOU FIGHTS!*" Saavik screamed. A stinking hand clamped across her mouth. She fought for air, felt the *knife begin to slip, then catch again and hang heavy at her waist.*

That Quiet One never changed his face, not even when a sword sang through the air and sliced away his arm. Blood spurted, sprayed, pooled upon the ground. The blade went up, came down. Again. Again. Again. Screams rose, congealed in Saavik's throat. She couldn't look away. Her world turned spattered, green and dark. Finally he fell. The sword struck one more time. His head rolled free, eyes wide and staring in pieces of himself. Then everything was quiet, no sound but rasping whimpers as she sucked in air through fingers of a smothering hand. Black Cloak sighed.

"A pity," It said, "such a waste. The chambers—now!"
And still they did not move.

"I will not be disobeyed!" It screamed. "If I must . . . no! No need!" The Cloak rippled, whirled. Eyes lit on what they sought, and the face contorted in Its smile. Hand lifted, finger pointed straight at Saavik. "Take that one next, take her . . ."

Spock's hands shook. He steadied them. Grief blotted out his thoughts, and in its wake a towering rage. Hundreds of Vulcans and their children looked out from stasis-chamber tombs, a broken box in every one, and on every door a data plate showed how long each subject took to die. Blackened faces froze in agony, the last vestige of control torn from them at the end. He forced his mind to logic: their torture ended long ago; their knowledge of this place was forever lost. He walked the aisle running down the center of the rows and paid them homage in the only way he knew—by recording everything. He retraced his steps, noting that the chambers hung suspended on cables from the gridwork, safer than resting on this planet's shifting ground. They bore no names. But there were dates, beginning in the rows farthest back nearly twenty years ago. Later victims, many of them children, had died much quicker deaths. The row in front was not entirely filled; open chambers waited, empty but for a glowing, rainbow box.

That last entry—Spock converted it to Federation stardate. It could not be coincidence.

On that very date more than six years ago, *Enterprise* heard a signal coming from the Neutral Zone, and his fingers rested on a dying woman's face. Brave, doomed T'Pren. For her, for so many, that signal came too late. But not for a handful of misbegotten children, the last of a generation born to feed these chambers. One of them had seen this place and lived—and so might worlds if there was time. No, T'Pren did not die in vain. And Saavik . . .

"Saavik!" he shouted. "Saavik, answer me!"

A sound. It might have been a footstep.

"Saavik . . . ?" It came again. Definitely footsteps. He probed the shadows with his light, knowing she could dodge it if she chose—then knowing something else, a fact he always took for granted until now. Saavik made no noise when she walked.

The footsteps shuffled closer from the recesses of the cave, far beyond the rows of chambers. Spock shone his light between them, caught a movement in the dark: something tall, draped all in black.

It wasn't Saavik.

". . . that *one next, take* her . . ."

Yesyes! Takes me! Takes you bastard hands away and—

"NO!" someone said. She never knew which One it was. The word rang into silence. All their eyes were on her for a moment, then the Quiet Ones turned away, moving all together, going where It wanted them to go, all because of her.

NOT! she tried to scream, NOTNOT! FINDS KNIFE! KILLS FOR YOU! KILLS THEM ALL! . . . but the hand across her mouth kept the words inside. Clear doors slid shut, one by one. In each chamber came a blinding flash of light. Now their faces changed. Quiet Ones writhed in their dying places, beating hands against their walls, but their mouths made no sound—while It walked up and down and watched the little changing lights. Then Quiet Ones stopped. Little lights stopped. It stopped, turned again . . . and smiled.

"So. This served a purpose after all. Get rid of it."

BASTARD! LIAR BASTARD! Madness exploded in her head. They dragged her by the arms to an empty chamber, across a floor awash with blood. She thrashed and kicked and fought, forgetting how she hurt, forgetting how she couldn't win, forgetting everything.

The rags around her waist gave way. The knife dropped out, clanking on the stones, lay there shining in the light. "Well, well. What have we here?" It said, laughing at her little knife.

"Bitch!" the rightful owner swore, and made his last mistake. He loosed his grip an instant, bent to snatch it up. She twisted like an eel, and by the time his fingers reached the ground, the knife was buried in his belly, ripping, jerking free. He gasped and moaned, clutched his middle, stared in disbelief at entrails spilling through his hands. Her other guard lunged. She let him come and stuck the blade clean through his heart.

They all came at her then, and she fought with killing frenzy. Blood sprayed, soaked her hair and slicked her skin as she gouged and slashed at anything in reach. Something dark loomed behind her, came down like death in billowing black. Hot breath whispered on her neck, the throaty sound of laughter.

She drove the knife upward through blinding layers of cloth, raked it sideways with all her might. Black Cloak fell shrieking to Its knees. Blood poured down Its face, fingers clawed at where the eyes used to be, and It screamed . . . oh, how It screamed . . .

Saavik ran, from rushing guards and rows of chambers, past wide-eyed workers at their pit of fire. Shouts rang; footsteps pounded after her; hoarse, racking screams filled the air. Quiet Ones died, because of her . . . It still lived, because of her . . . and nowhere, nowhere left to hide. She plunged into the flickering maze, darted this way, that way, any way . . .

And woke. Drenched in blood, huddled in a labyrinth of

light trying to remember why. But someone was screaming, so loud she couldn't think; something was coming to find her, kill her, for whatever she had done. Make It never see me . . . *but someone did.*

RUNRUNRUNRUNRUNRUN . . .

It lived. She must remember that, and It would hunt her down no matter where she ran, how hard or fast or far. Those walls of eyes would watch forever, and It would always be here, waiting in the dark, while It screamed and screamed and screamed . . .

It was a specter, an empty shell, the shadow of what used to be a man who felt his way along the aisle between the chambers. His cloak was threadbare, torn, and Spock saw why he never flinched against the light. Beneath the hood and hair gone white a scar gouged that wraithlike face, sliced across the empty sockets of his eyes. He sensed a presence, stopped, drew himself up tall. Some remnant of authority still lingered in his bearing. When he spoke his voice quavered, and his language was Romulan.

"Who comes here?" he called.

"Sir," Spock answered him in kind, the courtesy souring in his mouth. "I come . . . to serve."

"Ah . . . you come back at last! I have waited! I have kept it all in order! See," he gestured blindly, "how well my work is done? First sends for me now? It is time for my report?"

Who? To whom did he report? "Yes," Spock said, "it is time."

". . . report . . . ah!" The man tottered a few steps closer, still far down the center aisle surrounded by rows of tombs. "My work, my discovery of the ages! No one—no *world* can stand against it! I told him long ago how it would be: many ships, many new worlds . . . report? Is it time? I keep this place for him . . . keep it all in order. See . . . how well my work is done?"

Spock swung the light about searching frantically for Saavik, wondering how best to get them both aboard. This man's mind had long ago descended into madness, but whatever knowledge might remain must be preserved. The voice droned on, and the ravings took a dark and angry turn.

". . . or my work of so many years! They *left* me here, you see? Aaaiii!" he moaned and touched his face, tortured by some memory. *"You* see, but I do *not!* You—are you still there?"

"Yes." Spock moved closer, anxious to keep him talking. "Tell me of your work. There was . . . some accident here?"

"Accident?" he shrilled and began to laugh, a hollow, dreadful sound. "Yes *accident!* A *child,* an insignificance— she tried to run away! But my guards caught her. Yes, many guards once . . . told me how they caught her! Oh, she died for what she—"

"LIAR!" A scream split the air.

Saavik's shadow fell between them halfway down the aisle as she stepped into the beam of light. Spock caught a glimpse of streaming hair, the face of an avenging fury, and the glint of metal in her upraised hand.

"Saavik! *No!"* he shouted. But she was beyond hearing, screaming out the hatred of a lifetime.

"GUARDS LIED! YOU LIED! YOU HATEFUL, MURDERING *BASTARD!"*

He backed away, helpless and afraid. "Who comes—"

"I DO!" Her voice rang. "THE ONE THAT GOT AWAY! BUT I'VE COME BACK! AND YOU ARE GOING TO DIE!" Her spirit soared. She tasted blood—and triumph— and she wasn't running anymore; she would never run from anything again. Her arm swept up—

"No, *Saavik! No!"*

—and something dark loomed behind her, came down reaching for her hand. She knew this; it had happened all before, it was all happening again. With a howl of rage, she whirled, blade slicing through the air . . . and the present crashed into the past.

Shining knife, Starfleet uniform, and . . . Spock. Somehow, she wrenched the blow aside. It glanced off his shoulder, tearing fabric, not skin. *Oh, Spock . . . and his face never changed, not even when* . . . Saavik flung her knife away, hurled it far into the dark, heard it clanging somewhere on the stones. The cloaked figure swayed, backed away pawing at the air, and his moans rose to hoarse, haunted screams. She lunged; Spock stood in her path.

"Saavikam. We must leave this place."

"They—" she stared around at the chambers, her hands clapped over her ears to stop the sound, "—wouldn't *fight!* They just—*walked in there!* Because of *me,* Spock! Because he—*he did this!* And he's getting *away!* Don't let him *live!* Let me—"

"Think, Saavik!" Spock shook her by the shoulders. "Think of what he *knows!* Think of the *lives* at stake! *Think!"*

But Saavik couldn't think. She did the only thing she could: she ran. Away from the dead and the enemy, away from Spock, and away from herself, while shrieking reverberated through the cave.

And with a frustrated glance in the direction of the receding screams, Spock went after her, stopping only once along the way.

"Correct, Mr. Sulu. Three graduated containment canisters. Beam them down at once. The return cargo will be triple-sealed, but isolate transporter room's life-support until it is safely aboard. Then secure it in lab one."

"Yes, Mr. Spock, I certainly will." Sulu swallowed hard and nodded at Uhura to relay the orders. That cargo could turn *Enterprise* into a ghostship. "Canisters on the way, sir. Now, about that survivor, you say he might know—"

"That remains to be seen. He is less than competent. I will bring him out with me when I complete our task. Mr. Scott—"

"Twenty minutes more, sir," Scott broke in from Engineering, *"an' I cannot do it faster. We're addin' extra shieldin'—an' hope to heaven it's enough! That planet's shakin' in its—"*

"I am aware of the seismic activity. Please proceed."

"Will Saavik go with you, sir?" Sulu asked.

"No. She will beam up shortly. Prepare to receive cargo."

"Standing by, Mr. Spock. We'll confirm."

"Sulu . . ." Chekov turned, pointing down at his scan's display. Sulu came to stand over his shoulder. At the edge of the screen three points of light were winking, moving slowly into the grid. Readouts flashed in one corner.

"Mr. Spock, we just picked up three ships on scan, no data yet on size. They're heading this way. At present course and speed, ETA is . . . four hours, twelve minutes. Is that enough—"

"It should be, Mr. Sulu. If not, you have your orders."

"Sulu," Uhura reported, "transporter room confirms."

". . . yes, sir. And that cargo, Mr. Spock. It's aboard."

"Set delay for two hours, Mr. Scott. And hurry. Spock out."

The bridge was very quiet. Sulu stared at the scan's blinking dots, then at the main screen where the scoutship hung suspended in the tractor beam. *Like a loose end,* he thought, *just waiting to come unraveled.* He thought about his orders if Spock didn't make it back in time. He thought about that cargo now on board the *Enterprise.* He wondered why he'd ever wanted a command of his own.

"Sulu?" Uhura whispered. "Hurry with *what?*"

"The bomb," he said. "Spock's going to blow that mountain."

Spock signed off, his eyes on Saavik, who gave no sign of awareness at his presence. She huddled on the ground, her face hidden against the rock where he'd told her to wait, it seemed an age ago. He knelt beside her, and when she didn't pull away, he touched his fingers lightly to her temple. Memories flowed raw and clear now across the surface of her mind, all the way back to the beginning. *Look up, Little Cat,* said a voice from the past . . .

. . . different from the others, that Quiet One with the angry eyes. She was not so quiet. She watched and hated too—and found ways to fight. "Take my food, Little Cat, so you stay fierce and quick . . . Guards are coming, Little Cat,

so run away and hide . . . Someday, Little Cat, I will get you out of here. I must tell my people. I must find a way . . ." *And She pointed at the sky and talked about a place called Home, where Quiet Ones and Little Ones belonged, where there were no guards or people dying in the night, where food was free and children slept and no one was afraid. Home was* that *one,* there, *with all the others shining in the night.* "Stars, Little Cat, you must always watch the stars. They are the only things of beauty on this forsaken world. Watch them, for they watch over you." *Time went by. Ships came, took workers with them when they went away, leaving angry guards behind, and they kept all the food.* ". . . you are starving, Little Cat, and all I have to give you is the stars. You are like them, brave and bright. Remember that, when you are hungry and afraid. No matter how dark and terrible the night—look up. They all belong to you. Remember to look up, Little Cat. Look up, and see the stars . . ." *But the last Quiet Ones disappeared, the night that ship came down blasting dust across the plain. Saavik searched in all Her places, sobbing in despair. Gone, gone like the others, never coming back. So Saavik watched the ship that night, guards drinking, walking carelessly away. And then a voice came calling on the wind.* "Here! Over here, Little Cat!" *She was* there! *A shadow in the shadows of the ship.* "Run! Run, Little Cat! We are going home!" *So far, so far . . . stones cut sharp in running feet. Guards heard, came shouting, pounding, hard and close behind. Beams of fire flared past her head, torched the ground, scarred the metal of the ship. They would burn Her, ship and all—and She would die and They would win . . . NOTNOTNOT! NOT* THIS *ONE!*

Saavik stopped running. She turned and threw herself at them as they came rushing past, knocking both off balance, scratching, biting, clawing for their throats. "Live! Live, Little Cat! I'll come back for you! Oh, forgive me, Little Cat . . ." *Fists slammed and fire guns whined. Bones crushed and engines roared. The ship lifted whipping dust, hovered for a moment, then soared off into the night. And they went on beating her, screaming curses as the blows rained down. And slung across a shoulder as they carried her away, she saw the little cowards lurking in the rocks: other children watching, doing nothing and afraid. But those trails of light kept climbing, higher and higher in the dark, and part of her climbed with them until the sky itself went out . . .*

Spock saw it all: the horror in the cave; the hours hiding in the tunnels until the guards were gone; the days of bleeding, hanging between life and death while fever ruled her mind and hunger ate away her bones. But somehow Saavik lived, to throw her knife and curse her world and always watch the stars, and tried to never fall asleep so she wouldn't hear the screaming.

He saw the new lights shine across the waste and Quiet Ones walk the world again, and maybe they had food . . . he listened with her at the tent: *Those children, Spock, should never have been born . . . Vulcan nature torn apart and shamed . . .* and felt a nameless dread as he shivered with her in the wind, trying to remember why. And finally, he heard himself: the Quiet One different from the others, the Quiet One who was not so quiet, that night he talked about a place called Home . . . *I know now, Saavikam . . .*

Spock drew back his hand. His mind sought itself again in cool, well-structured rooms of thought where logic reigned and chaotic things stayed locked away, but he found no solace there. His privileged life rose before him, and its own small struggles paled. His disciplines seemed empty now, denials mere conceits. Encyclopedic knowledge came to nothing here; the old equations failed. Because Saavik was in pain, alone in the dark, and he would give anything, anything he owned, to stop it. But short of wiping out her hard-won memories along with the suffering they caused, he knew no way to do that. And it seemed wrong that he didn't know. It seemed to him the greatest failure of his life.

Hellguard's wind blew gently now, gusting, chasing dust along the ground, and overhead the stars burned cold.

"She . . . gave me food," Saavik whispered, "and I never knew her name. Was she . . . my mother, Spock? Did she ever find her home?"

Yes, he longed to lie, *home and safe* ... "T'Pren. Her name was T'Pren. I knew her for a moment. She was brave, Saavikam, almost as brave as you." And as they watched the bright, indifferent stars, very quietly, he told her the truth. ". . . no, she was not your mother. But she would have been. She would have searched the Universe to find you." That caused Saavik to turn her face away.

"So you found me. You gave me everything—and I—I almost—"

"But you didn't. Don't cry, Saavikam. It is over now."

"It is *not* over!" she raged. "It will *never* be over! I want to *kill* him—I will want it *all my life!* And if I ever get the chance . . ." She looked at him with tears spilling down her face and no pride left to make them stop. "Forgive me, Spock, for failing you, but I can never be a Vulcan. *This . . . is what I am.*"

"There is nothing to forgive," he said, as he brushed the hair out of her eyes. "There never was. Except a teacher who kept his failure to himself. Come with me, Saavikam. See what I see, know what I know . . ." *Yes, I am what I am,* he thought as he reached out to her. For once in his life, absurdly, he was glad.

Saavik wept as though she would die. Spock's uniform was wet, soft against her cheek. His fingers smoothed her hair and reached deep to smooth her mind. So strange to feel another heart beating with her own, another breath inside another life. So bright, this warm, quiet curtain that fell between herself and pain. It gave her new eyes, new sight, a lens moving into focus . . .

Suddenly it came to Saavik that she had not made her world; like children everywhere, she just happened to be born . . . why had she never thought of that? She thought of other, stranger things. Questions washed like waves upon a shore. Did the Vulcans walk into those chambers *grateful* that the chance to save a life gave meaning to their deaths? Did T'Pren find the courage to cling to life so long in a child who turned and fought and chose to stay behind? And did that one brave moment change this world she never made and events of years to come? . . . the questions became her own. Spock's hand rested on her face. His arms wrapped around her, and time was standing still. She was not afraid. It was so warm here, so bright inside his mind. And there were rooms—wonderful rooms. Libraries of a lifetime, universes of knowledge in mathematical precisions, abstractions of refined clarity—and a door.

One perfect, beautiful door. Never opened. Never reached.

Your answer lies elsewhere, Spock . . . and a vast indifferent Mind—a Voyager incapable of brightness—kept reminding him why it was so. But that perfect door remained. His rooms understood all this. People came and went, adding equations in their passing—and one never left, that one who scrambled Spock's equations on purpose, laughing, illuminating. The walls assimilated even this, growing taller, stronger, finding equilibrium. And then . . .

An impossibly familiar child stood in the dust. Holloweyed, naked, starving. Proudly claiming ownership of nothing less than all the heavens. *Spock! Tells me somethings new now! Firsttime!* The rooms took on uncertainty, disarray. New matrices formed hastily, deleted themselves, formed again. Errors occurred. Dreadful screechings of computers. *Look, Spock! I DID it!* . . . and equilibrium became a state of flux. But brighter. Shining in secret on such tiny things: eyes wide with wonder; clenched fists that didn't strike; small fingers thriving, stroking helpless creatures, prying into everything—but one box high upon a shelf.

Oh, I meant to tell you—on the ship in a drawer . . . Victory. A battle won. A promise kept, that knife left lying there.

But all my mistakes—are turning inside out! You begin to understand.

And another drawer, secret as the light, that held another knife and an old bit of paper: SPOCK NOTGO . . . , a holo of her scowling face and a file tape from the Academy: EXAMINATION/EVALUATION OF FEDERATION CITIZEN SAAVIK. So much light inside that drawer, spilling over distances, pouring through the years. No failure, no shame, only Saavik—asking, learning, winning every day.

But that is only what I am—and it is not enough! Ah, yes. The door.

Brightness could cast shadows. Light could blind, betray. It gathered overhead into a sun. Sun of suns, day of days. Quietest Ones of all serene in robes, carven stones beneath their feet, voices chanting song: *Here on these sands our forebears cast out—*

—the light, Spock? Yes. And the dark. The rooms, the people, the one who laughs . . . and you. Everything. For that door.

Perhaps, for half-Vulcans, it just takes a little longer . . .

The rooms strained at their confining walls, yearning for new dimensions. Voices chanted on the air, sun on ancient stones—

—and something was happening to Spock, happening in his then and now. Saavik sensed it, grew afraid. Felt his hand go cold, his breathing cease, his mind turn toward the song. His heart no longer beat with hers; it scarcely beat at all. *I don't belong here,* she tried to say. But arms held her, arms and light.

Your answer lies . . .

Behind that door, Spock, that beautiful—

Elsewhere! said Spock, once and for all, to his sun and stones and voices of Vulcan. He breathed deep and free. *I seek no Truth that cannot be taught, no Peace that cannot be shared. I am what I am. And some things—I choose—not to leave behind.*

And then it was all gone, the sun and stones and singing. An empty space trembled where memory had been, with nothing left in it but silence, arms and light, and a perfect, beautiful door . . .

Opening. Opening wide.

And on its threshold all the walls came down, bemused, objective even in their dissolution. *Inside out. Fascinating . . .*

Light streamed and rippled as they walked—strange, for

they were standing still, and the stillness played a music of its own. The brilliance flowed around them beckoning, enfolding, sweeping them away. She knew this place she'd never seen: a continuum of light and dark, a woven spinning balance in crystal harmonies of thought. Enigmas came unraveled here, where Past and Future, Plan and Chance, Time and Distance lost their shapes—and found them. Equations refracted into prisms extending to infinities. It was ship and stars, journey and destination, going toward it and being there all at the same time. And they were not alone.

Everyone was here. Every soul Spock ever touched, every being he had ever known: mother, father, captain, friends . . . and T'Pren—whole and peaceful, safe and home. And there were multitudes Spock had never met who knew him just the same: wistful legions from a past before his time began, spirits waiting to be born in a future he would never see. Life touching life touching life, meeting here in this forever of the mind. Spock stood among them exactly as he was—in the dust of Hellguard after all, holding what he would not leave behind—and no one seemed surprised.

The meaning comes differently . . . the reasons for being born. And Saavik understood how their difference made their Truth the same. How it was enough to be standing where they were, who they were, doing what they must and living in their days, while they all walked together here inside the light. Enough and so much more. *We all are what we are, and we are all each other* . . . even in the dark and dust. She must remember that. How once she saw this place of no anger, no pain, no halves of anything anymore; how once, just once, she belonged. How Spock gave her even that. *I'll remember, Spock, I promise. But I know it will be over soon* . . .

As that errant thought strayed through her mind, Saavik also knew she was still crying, Spock still stroked her hair, and only minutes had passed. The brightness lingered even as the ground took shape beneath her feet again. Dust still blew. Stars still glittered in the sky. Identities divided slowly, each to its own form, but neither of them moved. She searched for thoughts to ask about that light, what it was, where it came from—

I do not know, Saavikam. Only that it shines. And something else, terribly important, that Spock was about to tell her—

But his communicator shrilled, a sharp, urgent sound. He let her go, steadied her on her feet. The ground trembled, and Saavik felt a sinking dread, an aching in her heart. *I know . . .* Spock was putting his own tricorder in her hands, sliding the strap around her neck . . . *I know what it was! He was telling me . . . good-bye . . .*

"You will beam up, Saavikam. Give this to Mr. Sulu. It must reach Starfleet Command. Do you understand?" She nodded, dazed, in no condition to argue. ". . . Spock here."

"It's ready, sir," said Uhura, *"but Mr. Scott wants—"*

"Don' do it, sir!" Scott broke in. *"That planet's in for a major quake. The cave's on a fault, and pressure at the core—"*

"Mr. Scott," Spock stepped a few paces away and lowered his voice, "please confine your speculations to the equipment for which you are responsible. Did you preset the timer?"

"Aye, for two hours. It's locked in, an' once the sequence starts, nothin' ye can do will stop it. But leave it above ground, sir! Beam up with Saavik! If ye go back in there—"

"It will be placed correctly, Mr. Scott, at the greatest possible depth. A surface detonation will not ensure success. And there is a survivor below who has information—"

"Ye'll be killed, man! The quake is comin'! If ye're caught down there, ye'll not make it out alive!"

"Must I remind you, Mr. Scott, of the gravity of our mission or the loss of life if we should *fail?* Beam down the device. *Now.* Prepare to beam Saavik aboard. And Mr. Scott, I would prefer you at the controls for both transfers."

"Aye, Mr. Spock! We'll bring the lassie back, safe an'

sound. But the rest—I don't like it! I'll do it—but I don't like it!"

"Understood, Mr. Scott. And noted. Spock out."

A giant silvery cylinder materialized in the air. Three meters tall, one in diameter, it floated just above the ground on its built-in antigravs. Spock moved it aside.

"Come, Saavik," he said easily, "I will follow soon." She nodded, gave no argument. She understood, which made him proud.

She walked to him, then paused. "Mr. Spock, I would like to ask a question. How will this work? Will it blow up the cave?"

"That is two questions, Saavikam, however . . ." she had earned them, and she had a right to know. ". . . stand by, Mr. Scott, one moment more." Spock shut his communicator and began examining the mechanism's controls as he explained. "Not *up,* Saavikam—down. To destroy the arsenal without contaminating surrounding space. Mr. Scott has constructed a gravitational bomb, in effect a planetary depth charge. The initial firing propels a shaped antimatter charge into the planet's mantle, which then detonates with the force of one hundred photon torpedoes. Massive thermonuclear meltdown will result, causing all matter within fifty kilometers to collapse inward upon itself. The iron ores in those mountains will liquify and form a molten crust. So, you see, it *will* be over, Saavikam," he said gently. "The place you knew will be gone. You may observe the event from the bridge, I promise. Now—"

"And that cave is deep enough?" Saavik peered over Spock's shoulder at the device as he tilted and maneuvered it, testing its antigravs' balance. Then he knelt to examine the tapered nose containing the magnetic bottle with its antimatter charge. The arming switch and timer's display were halfway up under a latched panel, clearly marked, and already coated with a film of dust.

"Yes," he said, testing the latch. It worked smoothly. "And time is short. You must go now, Saavikam. Please understand."

"I do," she said, as her hand dropped to his shoulder and her fingers dug into the nerve plexus at the base of his neck.

He crumpled; she caught him before he hit the ground.

"I do understand—" *Ye'll be* killed, *man . . . not make it out alive!* "—and no more Vulcans will die here!" She laid him gently in the dust, took his tricorder from her neck and slid the strap under his head. His communicator had fallen to the ground; she retrieved it, placed it carefully in his outstretched hand.

"I couldn't think of any other way," she said, as if he could hear. "You won't forgive me this, but you will live. Live long, Spock. Live forever!" She wiped fresh tears out of her eyes, then raised her fist to the starry sky. *"Not this one!"* she screamed into the wind. *"You won't get him, you bastard world! I've sold my soul to see you die! And I'm coming to kill you—myself!"*

She got to her feet, her own tricorder secure, her own communicator in her belt, and started off, guiding the lethal cylinder, ignoring the rumbling land. It shuddered, shifted. Wind blew in her face, and dust stung her eyes, but she kept on walking into the dark. She never saw the crack that opened in the earth behind her, widened, ran its zigzag course along the ground inches from Spock's head. And by the time his communicator began to beep, she was too far away to hear.

Spock heard. He could open his eyes now, see the communicator in his hand and his arm extending over a fissure that didn't exist a moment ago. He willed his arm to move, fingers to close. Nothing happened. Nothing would for some time; Saavik was always an apt pupil . . . the fissure deepened into a gulf. Stones and dust poured in with every liquid motion and jolting of the ground. The communicator went on beeping, even when it slipped through his useless fingers, winked once in the starlight, and was gone.

Far above the planet, imprisoned in *Enterprise*'s tractor beam, the pilot of the Romulan scout watched three moving specks on his scan, fuzzy motes in the beam's interference.

He waited out the minutes until they were close enough to read his warning. He'd taken great care not to alert the enemy, but he had not been idle. His small warp drive's generator cables were clipped, its emergency backup manually disabled. The magnetic insulation's only source of power now was the ship's main itself.

It was time. He looked out at the huge underbelly of the invaders' leviathan, and beyond it to the stars of home. He threw a switch, drew one sweet breath of air, and asked the gods to look well upon his death. Then he saw them smile.

". . . still no answer. Something's wrong, Mr. Scott," said Sulu. "Lock on and beam them up. We'll send Spock down again."

"Laddie, there's no lockin' onto anythin', not with the planet jumpin' around. Ye don' want 'em back in pieces."

"Then when you can, sir. Shields stay up till we find them." Sulu signed off, quietly desperate. "Uhura, keep sending. Stay on sensors, Pavel. Maybe the tremors will affect that damping field. Bobby, look sharp. If our friend out there even sneezes—"

Harper frowned at his screen. "Mr. Sulu, he just cut *power!*"

"What?"

"Yessir, support systems and everything. That ship's *dead.*"

Suddenly, Sulu got it. "No! He's— KILL THAT TRACTOR—"

The scout burst in a blinding, actinic flash as the magnetic field between matter and antimatter collapsed in its warp drive. *Enterprise*'s shields absorbed the impact, deflected bombarding gamma rays. But the electromagnetic pulse, already traveling into the void at the speed of light, had passed along the tractor beam through the ship, instead of bouncing off its insulated hull. Circuits fused in nanoseconds, faster than breakers could trip; suppressors overloaded, and megavolts of transient power surged through electrical systems, all the way to the computer's core.

Boards redlighted. Screens flared, winked down to sickening dots. Lights flickered, dimmed, went out. The main viewer glowed for an instant with incinerating debris tumbling in space, burning to black. Then it went blank.

". . . I *hate* loose ends!" said Sulu in the dark.

Chapter Eleven

IN THE RED WASH of emergency light, status reports filtered to the bridge over crackling inship channels. As backups and secondary systems cut in, monitors came back to life, attempting diagnostic routines. Comm frequencies squealed feedback. Warp drive and weapons systems failed to respond. Viewscreens stayed dark, and sensors were dead. *Enterprise* was deaf and blind.

"No visual up here, Mr. Scott." Sulu felt smothered by the claustrophobic blankness. "No short-range on the planet, no scan on those ships. And the computer's gone crazy. Subroutines are running that shouldn't be, and diagnostics read a system clear one minute, malfunctioning the next. We don't know what to believe."

"None of it, lad!" Scott shouted over the static. *"Core damage—memory banks in main an' backup, an' no knowin' how far it goes. The systems are still there—but we can't get at 'em. Take whatever ye can off line—"*

"We're trying that, but overrides are unreliable. Manual won't always engage. We need those sensors, Mr. Scott."

"Ye'll have full power an' visual soon enough. But sensors —no. The radiation, laddie. I'll need two days just to—"

"You mean . . . we can't get them back?"

222

"Not by scannin'. We can lock onto a signal. Transporter's shielded. That's not the problem."

"Then . . . explain, Mr. Scott. I must be missing something."

"Those ships comin', Sulu! They're scannin' us by now, an' they'll be comin' fast. That scout sent up a proper flare, just as he meant to do. We won't win a fight, lad. Spock's orders say we'll be headin' out of here." From the tone of his voice, Scott didn't like those orders either.

Protect mission status; do not engage enemy fire; leave orbit—take Enterprise *across the Zone if situation deteriorates* . . . the situation had done that. A bead of sweat ran down Sulu's face. He felt everyone listening at his back. Priorities. Choices . . .

"I—I am delaying those orders at present, Mr. Scott. I need this bridge working and whatever firepower you can give me. Send us some help up here. I won't leave without them—not while there's a chance. Sir, you have the right to relieve me."

"Now why would I be doin' that? We'll find 'em, lad, if we have to send down shuttles. Aye, an' then we'll have a wee bit of explainin' to do."

"Yes, sir. I sure hope so."

Saavik balanced on the catwalk that spanned the generator shaft, using all her strength to steady the metal cylinder as another tremor shook the cave. The catwalk shuddered. Dirt and pebbles spilled between steel girders overhead, and behind her the maze of light glowed beneath a hanging cloud of dust. When the tremor subsided she looked down: *the greatest possible depth,* that's what Spock had said, and this shaft was wide enough. Power cells burned faintly, beyond them blackness without end.

Her hand inched upward, opened the latch, turned the key, snapped the latch shut. 01:59:59, 01:59:58, 01:59:57 . . . seconds flowed by in the timer's display. The bomb moved at her touch. She guided it out over the catwalk's railing and held it steady, feeling its energy, feeling her own heartbeat. Then she let it go. It drifted slowly through her hands, shining in the light of the power cells past ropes of dust-coated cables and conduits, then beyond them and out of sight.

She climbed off the catwalk and sank to the ground. Her knees were jelly, but her mind was clear. The fear that Spock might follow her subsided; she conjured an image of him safe on the bridge, willed it to be so, and struggled to her feet. Ahead the chambers loomed like sentinels, but this time no ghosts walked. Past and present were separate now, distinct, as if a veil had lifted from her sight. She saw events as they had been, saw how they had twisted in her dreams: *It* had never hunted her; It would never hunt again. She relished Its torment, rejoiced that this place would blast to atoms and that her hand dealt its death. She felt elated, invincible. She wasn't going to die—that was only a dream. She was going to *win*—and only one more thing to do.

Along the jagged cavern wall, past the silent tombs, she squeezed behind laboratory counters and dead computer banks, as she made her way toward the recesses of the cave. Another tremor struck. Its vibration became a clatter, then a roar, showering dirt and stones. Test chambers swung, creaking on their cables; glass beakers rattled, rolled across the counters, and shattered on the ground. She ducked, clung to the back of a console until the shaking died away. The quakes were getting worse. And this unit she was touching—she recoiled, touched it again.

Warm. Alive with *power. And stored data? . . .* She keyed her tricorder to visual and moved around it. Then she saw. *Logical,* her mind said, but her soul cried out for blood.

The food synthesizer was still functioning. *Food.* Children had fought and killed for it, grew up starving for it—most never grew up at all—while their murderers ate from a machine that could have fed the world. Blood drummed in her ears. She backed away, her mind reeling, and her foot struck something metal.

The knife lay where she'd flung it, shining on the ground. She picked it up, took back the only thing this place had ever given her and moved on, a deadly hunter in the dark.

Far back beyond the rows of chambers the cave branched into catacombs. In one of them a black-robed figure sat in a high carved chair. His back was toward her. His hand held a wine cup and rested on the chair's arm. The only light came from a fire flickering in a ring of stones, and a peculiar scent filled the air. Saavik crept closer, fingers twitching on her knife, her free hand flexing at her side. She wanted to kill him more than she ever wanted anything in life—but slowly. Oh, so slowly.

"Get up!" Her voice bounced back from the walls. He didn't move, gave no sign he even heard. "I said *get up!* You *bastard,* you deserve to *die!*" Her knife rose, driven by some will of its own. *Think, Saavik, think . . .* and firelight danced along its blade. *Think of what he* knows*! Think of the* lives *at stake! . . .* and something stayed her hand. Shaking with the effort she forced it down, longing for the kill, telling herself that somehow she had won. An unsatisfying triumph, but a kind of winning all the same. "Live a while longer, *bastard,"* she hissed, "and come with me! There will be a *trial! Justice!* I will tell them *everything! And everyone will know what happened here!* GET UP, DAMN YOU—"

The cave began to shudder. The fire flared in bright tongues of flame shooting to the ceiling. She struck the chair in fury, and the wine cup fell, smashed against the floor with a rising odor of bitter almonds—and something else, pungent, familiar—

Saavik threw herself at the grate, plunged knife and hands into the fire, scattering coals, ashes, melted squares of plastic that were once computer tapes—knowledge that disintegrated into sparks before her eyes.

She whirled cursing, dragged him from the chair. Her fingers dug into his throat. The hood fell back from his scarred unseeing face, and the scent of bitter almonds clung about his cloak.

Cyanide. No pulse beat beneath her hand. He hung limp and lifeless, cheating her even in death. Cheating Spock. Cheating everyone . . .

Saavik's screams echoed through Hellguard's rumbling caverns, damning him to eternity and beyond. The bones in his neck snapped like twigs. The knife flashed, the madness took her mind . . . when it faded, she saw what she had done. And she was not ashamed. She drove the knife into his heart, left it there, where it belonged. Then she hurled the body on the fire. Flames caught quickly, turned the cloak into a blazing shroud, crackled as they ate his flesh and bone. And Saavik wept with rage because he couldn't feel it. She wept for justice lost and knowledge gone in easy deaths of poison and fire—and because she was to blame. Out there among the dead she had warned him, given him time to—

Time. She'd forgotten about the *time*. She ran for open air. How long had it been since she began the countdown? *Mistakes,* she cursed, her heart pounding, *I am making mistakes, and Hellguard is winning . . .*

It began again as she reached the cavern: at first silence, chambers swaying on their cables, dust shifting in the air, then a rumble like approaching thunder. Steel girders groaned as the mountain cracked and shivered. Sections of the roof collapsed in rains of rock and dust. She fought her way between the rows of chambers, colliding with them when they swung into her path, and saw the shadow of the catwalk loom against the weapons' glow. She ran for it, past it, onward to the light, and overhead the mountain roared. Girders screamed and twisted, snapped apart. One crashed down across the generator shaft, slicing the catwalk in two. A tidal wave of dust went rolling through the cave.

Saavik ran, ran for her life, thought and motion slowed to the tortured tempo of a dream. Her heart thudded, bursting in her chest. Lungs labored, breathing dust. Icy sweat poured down her face, burned when it seeped into her eyes, and made her cold, so very, very cold. Walls of boxes higher than her head shook and rattled, and all the world was dusty light, deadly corridors of light, colors that only came . . . *the dream!* she thought, panic stabbing at her mind. *Something about the dream, something I forgot! Mistakes, too many mistakes . . .*

She left the maze behind, reached the turning for the tunnel—and the ground opened up in front of her. She jumped, fell sprawling on the other side, then regained her feet, coughing, choking on the dust. She gasped for air—and looked back.

The walls of light were toppling. Boxes dislodged, shattered on the ground. And the cave was turning dark, because everywhere their lights were going out. Saavik ran. Up the twisting, narrow tunnel, until the light was swallowed up and she saw nothing more at all. She felt the blasting dust, the stinging spray of flying rock as tunnel walls caved in behind her—but it was only in her dreams that she could run so freely in the deep and roaring dark.

Now the twists and turns were unfamiliar, darkness absolute and all sense of direction gone. She pushed on, one hand fending off a wall of jagged stone, the other outstretched to feel her way. The ground rose steeply, the wall curved deep—this was it, the last turning. There would be fresh air blowing through the entrance to the cave. Any second now, air and sky and—

A wall that wasn't there before. A wall of solid earth and rock. She groped in all directions, pounded with her fists, clawed at stone and dirt with her bare hands. Skin tore from her fingers. Blood ran hot, sticky down her arms. The mountain heaved and thundered, and a pouring river of loosened rock knocked her off her feet. There was nowhere left to go. Terror swept over her, a wave of cold despair. And as Hellguard's dust burned her throat and lack of air dimmed her mind, Saavik remembered what she'd forgotten about that dream, the thing that drained her will away, turned her heart to ice: It always won. It always got her in the end. Because she couldn't run forever, and this place was a trap. With no way out.

She was going to die.

Spock didn't see the flare of light or shower of burning debris in orbit overhead. As the tremor subsided and dust began to clear, he saw only his immediate predicament. The patch of ground where he lay was now an island, one of many in a sea of new-formed chasms. Landslides crashed and thundered in their depths; dust rose and churned inside their walls. The mountain and its rocky outcropping that masked the entrance to the cave towered in the distance across a canyon five hundred feet wide. It was beyond reach, and so was Saavik.

She lived—he sensed that; perhaps she reached the cave. But unless the quake disturbed that damping field, her communicator was useless, and sensors couldn't find her there.

Sensors hadn't found *him*. They should have by now. During lulls between the tremors, Scott should have tracked his life reading, beamed him back to ascertain his status. Scott hadn't, which meant he couldn't, which meant something had gone wrong on board. And there was absolutely nothing Spock could do about it.

Sensation returned slowly to his arm and fingers. He pushed back from the precipice, even as its edge gave way. The ground around him crumbled, but his tricorder hung safely on his neck. If only Saavik had taken such care with his communicator! He doubted that she planned her ill-considered deed. But he should have seen it coming, should have sent her back at once, tears and grief and all. Their mindlink had held hidden costs—as did all emotional indulgence—and this was not a price he would have paid. Which was always the trouble with trading something for something.

Through the haze of dust a red dawn was rising in the sky, and its coming light revealed a land laid waste. Nothing at all remained to show that people ever lived on this obscenity the Romulans had called a world. Whatever the Empire believed, the colony here had not failed; it was never meant to succeed.

Spock wasn't sure why he watched the mountain, but that was where he sent his thoughts: *Saavik, when I get you home—*

The ground heaved again, a long, sustained temblor that sent more boulders toppling down the mountain, crashing in the canyon below. The rocky prominence cracked and fell away, exposing the cave's entrance—but only for a moment. Slides of loose stone flowed down the mountainside, and when the dust settled, the cave was no longer there. Saavik would not be coming home.

Live, Saavik, he thought, against all reason. *Live . . .*

. . . Live! The word rang in her mind, but the air was gone, and the voices she heard . . . *Live, Saavik . . .* couldn't help her now. *Look up, Little Cat . . .* but there were no stars in here. *No matter how dark and terrible the night, remember . . .* she did, she remembered everything from the very moment she was born. But the darkness was dragging her down, and the dust was choking her, cheating her, killing— *Look up, Little Cat!* She tried—*Remember to look up*—she tried again, pushing death away. *Look up! And see the—*

Light.

A tiny point of light shining far above her head. She reached for it, grasped and clawed. Dusty sunlight shafted in, and *air.* The mountain shuddered. Debris poured inward, widening the hole. Saavik climbed the mound of sliding rock, sucked air into her throat, then looked out into the blinding light where howling winds were blowing the dust away. No ground remained beneath the entrance to the cave. Her escape route was a landslide spilling into an abyss. And across its yawning gulf—

Spock. Stranded on a rocky pinnacle, a dreadful silhouette against the rising suns—but that was *wrong!* Why?

Why? . . . He saw her then, held out his hands—empty hands—and Saavik understood. She dug her communicator from her belt, wiped her bloody fingers.

"Enterprise!" she shouted. *"Enterprise!"* The communicator might as well have been a stone. *"ENTERPRISE!"* No one answered. No one would—something about this mountain . . .

"Spock!" she screamed, struggling for a foothold as pieces of the mountain fell around her. Boulders crashed into the canyon from above; the ground was sliding out from under her. She fought for balance, judged the distance and the wind, felt the communicator's shape and weight in fingers slippery with blood. She wanted to wipe her hand again. No time. Her vision narrowed to the point in space between Spock's empty hands. In all the Universe nothing else mattered, nothing else existed but a piece of metal, 150 meters, and Spock.

Saavik threw.

It sailed, tumbling through the air, flashing in the suns.

She never saw what happened. The mountainside came down on top of her, sealing up the cave again. Light disappeared. Rocks pressed down, cut deep into her flesh. Dirt forced its way inside her mouth and nose, ground into her eyes. The weight grew, smothering, crushing . . . then stopped . . .

. . . and began to fall away. There was someone shouting—

"Got her! An' half a mountain, too! Stand back—back! . . ."

—and a deafening noise as the wide column of earth and rock was released by the transporter and collapsed to the platform in a roiling cloud of dust. Saavik stood in the middle of it, coughing, somehow standing on her feet. The doctor was saying something, trying to help her down, and a tall, familiar figure stood frozen in her path. His anger hit her like a wave.

"Where, Saavik? How long ago?"

"Deep . . . shaft. Don't . . . know . . ." she gasped between breaths.

"And you are alone." He radiated disapproval.

She wanted to explain, but it wouldn't matter. She wanted to hold on to something, but there was only her tricorder, still about her neck—incredibly, still running. *The food machine,* she remembered vaguely, *forgot to turn it off* . . . it would tell him—and he would never speak to her again. She held it out.

He took it, shut it off. "Cadet, report to the bridge."

"Over my dead body!" McCoy shouted, waving at the dust with the scanner in his hand. "You're both a mess! I want her in—"

"Out of the way, Doctor!" Spock brushed him aside to reach the comm. "Shields up, Mr. Sulu! Take us out of orbit, warp—"

"Impulse, sir," Scott intervened, "the drive's down."

"Best speed, Mr. Sulu. I am on my way. Scott, come with me!"

And then she was in the lift, with Mr. Scott talking about sensors and explosions and ships, and the doctor arguing that someone was in shock. Saavik leaned against the wall and wondered who, wondered why she was here at all—unless for some public proclamation of her guilt. *Yes,* she thought, *that must be it* . . .

On the bridge the lights were bright. Instrument boards and circuitry lay exposed at every station. Faces lit with relief changing to alarm. Spock was coated with dust, his clothing stained and torn. Saavik saw there was no skin on her hands, and blood welled green through layers of dirt, dripped on the tatters of her Starfleet uniform. It was of no importance. She looked to the screen, where Hellguard's image dwindled.

"View aft, Mr. Chekov. Magnify and enhance." Spock took the command seat, and the screen leapt into close-up. Dust clouds from the quake were visible, drifting over shadows of the mountains cast by rising suns. Nothing happened for a moment.

Then the mountains trembled. A dull-red spot began to glow and brighten, expanding underground in waves of concentric rings.

"Bull's-eye!" Scott crowed. "I'll be seein' to the engines—"

"Alacrity would be advisable, Mr. Scott."

McCoy snorted irritably at the screen. "Well, that's dandy! Now if you two are finished, can I just—"

"No, Doctor. The cadet made a bargain. She may keep it."

Then Saavik understood: *I've sold my soul to see you die.* So he heard her after all. And he was permitting her this . . .

At the instant of detonation, the cave and colony and all she knew of Hellguard vaporized. Land mass began collapsing inward, forming a giant crater on the surface. Mountains toppled, melting into a vast neutronium sea. As the wave front spread, the second charge penetrated the planet's mantle all the way to its unstable molten core. The added depth of the explosion multiplied its force exponentially, exceeding Spock's predictions. Continental plates tore and shifted. Magma came spewing to the surface as the crust fractured into veined networks and bled in rivers of fire. Deposits of gases trapped far below the ground ignited in chain reactions, opening volcanic rifts and sending firestorms sweeping across the land. Hellguard was burning. Its rocks, its dust, its secrets and its dead—even its air would be consumed before the holocaust was done. No life could exist there for millennia to come, only a blackened cinder, welded shut, orbiting 872 Trianguli in a cold and empty night. And what Saavik felt as she watched the dying of her world was the closest thing to joy she had ever known.

Enterprise drew away, impulse engines straining. At last the screen switched to the view ahead, but a fiery afterimage hung before her sight. A sudden stillness came into her mind, a huge descending silence she'd never heard before. Someone's hand was on her shoulder, a quiet voice speaking in her ear.

"Come on, honey, you're losing blood. It's all over now . . ."

The bridge's lights seemed very close, and colors burnt her eyes. Shapes, textures, faces stood out in sharp relief—edges of existence that were beautiful and clear. Everything was clear.

". . . sickbay, Spock! And don't try to—"

"Yes, Doctor. Dismissed."

All over. She had been a visitor here, and it was time to go. But Spock lived, and she lived, and Hellguard lived no more.

And the screaming had finally stopped.

"Mr. Spock—" Sulu was pointing at the starfield, areas that distorted, wavered. Even without sensors, the aberration was familiar. "We've got a problem!" The distortions took on color, then form. Two garish, painted battlecruisers materialized out of rippling space, maneuvering into positions around *Enterprise* . . . then a third, larger ship dead ahead and coming at them. Sulu didn't need sensors to know their torpedoes would be loaded, their phasers targeted and locked.

"Go to Red Alert—and full stop, Mr. Sulu. Weapons' status?"

"Red Alert!" Uhura was saying over the comm. The klaxon began to blare. "Red Alert! Battle stations! This is not a drill . . ."

"Not good, sir. Shields, but no phasers, no photon torpedoes . . ."

"Come on, Saavik," McCoy said, hustling her into the lift.

". . . controls frozen and overrides won't work. The tractor—"

"Yes, core damage. It renders all systems unreliable. Repairs will take some time. Mr. Scott," said Spock into the comm, which still sputtered, "we have company. Estimate on warp drive?"

"At least an hour, sir. Give us time to— Bloody hell!" he swore as Spock keyed the screen's image to his comm.

"As you see, it is not mine to give."

"But they're not firin' on us!"

"I suspect they want this ship. Do your best, Mr. Scott."

"Sir," Uhura turned, "they're hailing us."

Spock sat down in the captain's chair.

"On-screen, Commander."

Praetor Tahn stood on the bridge of his flagship, staring aghast at the Federation behemoth on the screen, trying not to let his officers see that he was quaking in his boots. This was not part of his plan, which had gone so well up to now. Exactly as his old friend said to do, he'd arrived on station—ostensibly to inspect his ships—surrounded by his loyal guards and feeling the eyes of the First's assassins everywhere on the docks. They would wait until the time was right, when ships were gone and guards relaxed and no witnesses remained. And then some regrettable "accident" would befall him as he was returning home.

So he didn't. That was the genius of it. He simply stayed on board—to lead his troops on this mission of utmost importance. Ah, such devotion to duty. Such bravery. Such a *beautiful* plan.

But he'd heard the whisperings on subspace channels: secret meetings in the Empire, rumors from the outposts, coded data dumps from probes seeded in the Zone. Federation ships were massing beyond the Line, causing consternation in high places and carefully worded queries about what such activity might mean.

Tahn knew. Gods, he knew. And then that ominous sensor flare sent them rushing headlong to their destination, only to find the enemy already here and planet *Thieurrull* burning in the night beyond, blazing like a torch. One, just *one* of their ships could do this to a world? *O Gods . . .*

"They do not fire!" he said to his commander. "Why?"

"Scanners show power in their weapons, Lord. It could be some kind of trick. But we are three, and they are one. We can destroy them—if that is what you wish, Lord."

And bring a thousand ships across the Zone and down around their ears? Gods, no . . . "I will hear your strategy," Tahn said, thinking himself adroit. "What else might I wish?"

"To capture them, my Lord. To take the ship for yourself, and prisoners for the Empire, and to come home victorious. Bring these criminals to justice, and the Empire will be forever in your debt. With such a deed and such a ship, you would rule the fleet. There is much glory here. And honor, Lord."

And such a ship would need such a commander, would it not? thought Tahn, who was not a total fool. But things had changed since he set out; one plan failed, so he must have another. And this might work, it just might . . . "Speak to these invaders," he said, and saw his ambitious commander swell with pride. "We will take their ship and spare their lives. Tell them so."

Long moments passed. Then a face came on the screen that set Tahn's stomach churning.

"Federation Invaders," barked his young commander, "you trespass in sovereign space! You destroy an Imperial vessel! You lay waste to a world! You mock your treaty with the Empire—but you will never escape! My Lord is prepared to be merciful. Lower your shields, surrender your ship, and we will spare your lives."

"I shall consider it," said the Vulcan.

The screen went blank. Tahn's mouth was dry.

"He is arrogant, Lord. And indecisive. We must persuade him."

"What do you propose?"

"We fire—not to destroy, but to break their shields. Then we send our troops aboard to conquer the invaders. We must not show weakness. Shall I give the order, Lord?"

Tahn's stomach heaved; his hands were trembling, so he hid them beneath his robe. This glory business was not easy on one's nerves. "Commence fire," he said.

* * *

"—playing with us, sir," said Sulu, as the bridge rocked under bombardment from three sides. "Those phasers are only half power, but our shields won't take it for long."

"That is the object of the exercise, Mr. Sulu. How long?"

"Maybe twenty minutes, sir. Without instruments it's hard—"

"Understood." Spock touched the comm. "Mr. Scott, report."

"On the drive, sir?" Scott shook his head at another failed attempt by his crew. "We'll not align new crystals with all this knockin' about! Forty, fifty minutes of peace—and maybe we could—"

"Our shields will not hold that long. Delegate the tasks, Mr. Scott. Your presence will be needed on the bridge."

There was a moment's silence, then a heavy sigh. "Aye, that it will. On my way. Keep at it, lads. McInnis, ye're in charge."

"Sir?" Fear showed in his eyes. "Do we have a chance?"

"What kind of talk is that? Get on with it, man!" Scott stepped through the revolving door and its decontam field. He went to the monitoring board where Obo sat with all its fingers and toes buried in the circuitry. Readouts were finally beginning to appear on the screens. "Leave it, laddie," he said, "an' come with me."

"Didn't *fffinish!*" Obo protested.

"Aye. But ye'll want to be with Mr. Harper now. And I'm thinkin' he'll want to be with you." He took a last look at his engines, and headed for the lift. Obo trailed close behind.

"Dammit!" McCoy swore and steadied the patch of syntheskin he was applying to Saavik's hand. Cleaning open wounds, sealing ragged tears, grafting skin cloned from her own cells (a routine culture begun days ago)—all this was tricky enough without the pounding they'd been taking. It was incessant and getting on his nerves. With single-minded annoyance, he shut danger out of his thoughts by blaming the whole thing on Spock.

"Keep talking to me, Saavik. What happened then?"

Her emotionless, factual account of being trapped underground in an earthquake was hair-raising, but talking was better for her than that glazed, isolated silence . . . *and what the hell was* wrong *with that damn Vulcan anyway?* McCoy was in the transporter room when the signal came, Spock's voice shouting coordinates not his own. Then he came back alone, naked grief and fear on his face as that column of rock six beams wide began materializing on the pads. But no "glad to see you, kid"—not one kind word. And hauling her up to the bridge like that—an injured *cadet,* for God's sake! Never would've happened if Jim—

"—hold it!" he said suddenly, his attention caught by her words. *"What* was that?" But she'd stopped talking, retreating again into some reality of her own. "The cave," he prompted, "you were trying to get out—and *what?* Say again!"

But the comm interrupted, and Spock's voice filled the room.

"Bridge to all decks. This is Spock. As you are no doubt aware, we are under fire from three Romulan ships—without warp drive or weapons' capability to resist them. Enterprise *would be destroyed by now, if that were their intent. It is not. Listen:"*

". . . grow tired of these games!" The foreign speech echoed in English through the translator. *"Your shields are buckling! You cannot escape! Prepare to be boarded, and surrender your ship to the person of Tahn, noble Praetor of the Romulan Empire—"*

"Less than fifteen minutes of power remain in our shields," Spock went on. *"It will then be my duty to commit this vessel to Starfleet General Order Six, paragraph fifteen. I shall do so . . . with the utmost regret. Remain at your posts. Spock out."*

"Dammit!" McCoy swore at the comm. "Now Saavik, this is real important! *What* did you see down there? Tell me again!"

Slowly, mechanically, she did.

"You're *sure?*" he nearly shouted. She nodded, puzzled. "You stay right there!" He was already out the door. "I'll be back!" echoed from the corridor, but Saavik knew otherwise.

As his footsteps died away, she gazed around the sickbay and saw that she was not alone.

On the far side of the examining room, a black-cloaked figure opened his eyes and stirred, testing the table's restraining bands. They held him fast. He met Saavik's eyes and smiled.

"Hello, Little Cat," he said softly. "Tell *me* something now. What is the meaning of this General Order Six?"

Saavik regarded him coldly, no longer caring what he called her. It never crossed her mind to summon the guard standing watch outside the door. "It means," she said, "among other things, that enemies do not capture Federation starships. Ever."

"Then Spock will destroy us first?"

"Of course." She watched him tug at his restraints.

"And what if I told you that no one needs to die? Listen to me, Little Cat—I can *solve* this! Let me go, and I will."

She turned away. His words were treacherous, false.

"Ah, friend Saavik, I sense that you do not believe me."

"You are no friend of mine, Mr. Achernar." She slid off the table and came closer to confront him. "I dislike you. You smile, you lie, you watch us—and you are hiding something. Perhaps you planned against us all along. Oh, I believe you want your ship—so you can save your neck. No life concerns you but your own."

"So," he nodded, resigned, "you do not like me, and I want to save my neck. Is that such a crime? This is not my fight, Little Cat. Would it matter so much if I got away? No, but I remind you of what you are. *That* is what you do not like. And for that I am to die. My life is in your hands—but what if you are wrong?"

He kept twisting at his bonds, and Saavik felt a foolish rush of pity. *To die helpless, trapped . . . his smile is just a smile. His cloak is just a— What am I thinking! I have made enough mistakes today to last a lifetime!* But there would be no lifetime.

"I know what I am," she said, "and I am not wrong. No, I do not like you. But—" . . . *so much blood is on my hands, so much hatred in my heart. And how could he harm us now?* . . . "—but I do not cause your death." She reached the lever, unlocked his restraints. "Save your neck, then, Mr. Achernar—if you can."

"Come with me!" He sprang to the floor, grasped her by the shoulders. She froze at his touch, wondering why she didn't kill him. "The Universe is wide," he whispered, "and you were meant for better things. Come with me, Little Cat—you do not have to like me. I can show worlds you never dreamed of. I can give you anything—a ship, a home, a fortune—whatever you desire." His face was close, his hands were gentle, and his smile was real.

"A home . . . you lie. No one can give me that."

"I can buy you mansions—worlds! Home is only where you're standing. Didn't your precious Vulcans ever tell you that?"

"Yes. Today. And I stand here, Mr. Achernar. With these people, on this ship. Now go. You are wasting time."

"And you, Little Cat, are a *fool!*" He dropped his hands and sighed. Then, with a swirl and billow of his black cloak, he was gone.

After a moment Saavik left the sickbay, stepped over Nelson's unconscious form, and walked down the empty hall. Where it ended at Deck 7's outer corridor, she found what she was looking for, a small viewport set into the bulkhead. As her hand touched the window, another blast of phaserfire shuddered through the deck. She sensed a soul in this ship that should have flown forever, felt the fears and griefs of all aboard about to lose their lives. No sight of the enemy from here, not even when she pressed her forehead to the port and looked out at the night.

A warm, familiar presence brushed against her mind. She knew it could only be a memory, but she held it close and sent it one last thought: *I wanted to be a real Vulcan, Spock. I wanted to be . . . like you.* Then she let it go. And when she stood alone to meet the end, there were only stars.

"Computer may not execute, Mr. Scott, but we must try."

"Aye, sir. An' take the villains with us, I'll warrant!"

That was small consolation to Spock as he stared his ultimate failure in the face. After searching for a way out since those ships first shimmered into sight, all his calculations had dead-ended, and two constants remained: *Enterprise* must not fall into enemy hands; and despite the tempting offer to spare their lives, he knew too well what could happen to prisoners. If the computer refused the destruct codes, his failure would be compounded by disgrace: *Enterprise* turned against the Federation she was built to serve, and her people condemned to a life of servitude at best. Scott and Sulu stood behind him at the science station. The others watched, forgiveness in their eyes. But Spock did not forgive himself. Jim Kirk would not forgive him either.

"Computer. This is Spock, first officer in command of *Enterprise*. Request security access, and confirm function."

There was a long pause. "WORKING," the computer finally said.

"Computer. Destruct sequence one. Code one, one A."

The words read out on screen; the computer waited.

Will it hurt for long? Uhura wondered, and wondered if anyone else was wondering too. *Captain, I'm not frightened anymore . . .*

". . . Commander Montgomery Scott, chief engineerin' officer. Destruct sequence two. Code one, one A, two B."

And again the code confirmed without a hitch. *It's going to happen,* Chekov thought, *this time it's going to happen . . .*

"Computer. This is Lieutenant-Commander Sulu, weapons and helm officer. Destruct sequence three. Code one B, two B, three." Sulu looked across the bridge, saw Chekov watching him.

"DESTRUCT SEQUENCE COMPLETED AND ENGAGED—"

"Spock!" The lift doors were opening, their security alert

dead. Red-faced and shouting, McCoy burst onto the bridge. "Don't do it! *Stop* that thing, dammit! I found the *answer!"*

". . . FOR ONE-MINUTE COUNTDOWN."

"She *saw* them, Spock!" He shouldered his way past Sulu and Scott. "But she *didn't die!* Spock! Are you *listening* to me?"

The bridge rocked as phasers hit the shields again.

"Yes, Doctor, but as usual you make no sense. What answer?"

". . . SEQUENCE COMPLETED AND ENGAGED. AWAITING FINAL CODE—"

"Stop that thing and *listen,* dammit! She was underground, the roof was falling in. She saw those things *breaking*—but *she didn't die!* She was *choking,* Spock! Her lungs were full of *dust!* Don't you *see? There must be something in the DUST!"*

Spock did see. "Even if you are right, Doctor—"

"Hell, yes, I'm right! Those things were going *off,* smashing on the ground! Their lights were going out, just like they did back home! But she's *still alive*—and half that mountain's all over our damn transporter room! We can *find* it, Spock! Whatever saved her, we can *find* it—*in that dust!"*

"DESTRUCT SEQUENCE COMPLETED AND—"

McCoy never let up. "We don't need to go to war, Spock! We can stop it! And save Earth—and *Jim!* We'll just analyze the—"

"Doctor, we are about to be—"

The ship pitched again. Damage indicators flickered to life this time, and a siren began to wail. Chekov turned to report.

"A hit, sir. Shields two and three are down."

"Doctor, enemy troops will board this ship. We have neither numbers nor weapons to resist them. Any suggestions?"

"DESTRUCT SEQUENCE COMPLETED AND ENGAG—"

"Yeah, Spock! Get us *out* of this!" McCoy glared at him and delivered a final shot. "That's what *Jim* would do!"

"Sir," said Uhura, "they're hailing us again."

"Dammit, tell them—" McCoy turned, then looked past her to the lift. *"Wait* a minute! What the hell is *he* doing here?"

Achernar leapt from the opening doors, black cloak flying.

"Stay where you are, friends!" He towered over Uhura at the comm station. "Answer them!" he told her.

"Sorry," she lifted her chin, "I don't take your orders."

"Answer the hail, Uhura," Spock said quietly. She did.

". . . and abandon this foolishness!" A new, older face frowned at them on the screen. *"Or prepare to die! I offer mercy, and—"*

"Greetings, Tahn!" Achernar called out. "I see you keep your appointments." The frown on the screen changed to astonishment.

"Old friend! You've come! But how . . . ?"

"At great risk, friend Tahn. These idiots intend to—"

Sulu and Scott went for him, then stopped short. Achernar had jerked Uhura from her seat. A phaser gleamed in his hand, rested at her temple, and the last shred of hope died on the bridge. *Enterprise* was out of time—and the enemy was already on board.

". . . SEQUENCE COMPLETED AND ENGAGED. AWAITING FINAL CODE *. . ."*

This is ridiculous! Uhura thought. At the corner of her eye the phaser blurred in her peripheral vision. She blinked—

"They intend to destroy this ship! And that would be a pity, friend Tahn, because I have accomplished our mission!"

—blinked again at what she saw: that phaser wasn't set to kill. *It wasn't set at all.* "Mr. Spock! He's not—"

"Silence!" Achernar thundered. *"I give the orders now!"*

And in the hush that followed:

"Code zero, zero, zero . . ." said Spock.

Chapter Twelve

"DON'T BE A *FOOL!*" Achernar hissed. "I can get us *out* of this! He does not want your ship—I *know* what he wants!"

Spock paused, suspending time. No one moved.

"What is that you say, old friend? How came you with these—"

"I found what you seek, Tahn. And how I came to be here is a long, expensive story. But you will never get their ship. They will blow it up if you attempt to board. In fact, they may do so on general principles, even as I try to persuade them otherwise. So stop your target practice, and let us talk some business."

One more blast burst against *Enterprise*'s hull, causing the screen to snow and orders to be shouted on the Romulan bridge.

"That's it, Mr. Spock," Chekov said; shields were down.

The screen cleared, the channel crackled. *"Talk, old friend,"* the words came through. *"I am listening."*

"And so are they, Tahn. My ship was disabled in what they claim is 'their' space. They kindly took me aboard. So I am here—but what you want is on my ship. A pretty problem, is it not? Perhaps we can arrive at a mutual solution."

"Computer," said Spock, very quietly. "This is Commander Spock of the U.S.S. *Enterprise.* Code one, two, three, continuity. Abort destruct order. Code one, two, three . . ."

A sigh went around the bridge, an exhalation of relief that suddenly stuck in every throat.

"59 . . ." said the computer. "58 . . . 57 . . ."

Eyes went wide. Faces froze. This couldn't be happening. "56 . . . 55 . . ." But it was.

Achernar disregarded the situation he could not control —and seized upon the one he could. He plunked Uhura back in her seat and strolled to the command chair, where he lounged with apparent unconcern. "But first, Tahn, the matter of my commission . . ."

Uhura thought fast: if the Romulans knew their danger, they would blow *Enterprise* to bits. She narrowed the viewer's angle, tried to damp the electronic voice counting them all down to destruction. No indicators registered to tell her if it worked.

"Computer. Override." Spock's fingers were beating a tattoo over pads and toggles; his voice was calm, as if he were speaking to a wayward child. "Code one. Two. Three . . ."

". . . 50 . . . 49 . . ."

"No overrides, sir!" Scott began hitting key combinations without results, muttering about core damage and random glitches.

". . . 47 . . . 46 . . . 45 . . ."

Spock felt something bump against his knee. He ignored it, repeatedly keying commands. The computer refused to disengage.

All of them knew ten seconds was the countdown's point of no return. Nothing in the world could stop it then—

And nothing was stopping it now. The computer refused to disengage.

". . . 41 . . . 40 . . . 39 . . ."

The bump at Spock's knee came again, became a tug. He looked down into glowing, neon-yellow eyes that peered through the forest of legs around the science station.

"Eeeasy fix?" a small voice asked.

"By all means!" He sprang from his seat as Scott boosted Obo up. Hands and feet flew to work prying up panel covers, playing over the components and circuitry above and beneath the counter. Obo's toes and fingers seemed not to be touching anything as their filament extrusions traced pathways, probed energy patterns. With instruments, that would take hours. Spock's hand rested on Obo's head, sending images, information . . . but there was no time, no chance.

". . . 29 . . . 28 . . . 27 . . ."

"—but that is robbery!" Tahn shrieked. *"We agreed—"*

"—that I could name my price, friend, and forty percent it is. If you knew what I have been through . . ."

"Quick, Obo!" Harper whispered urgently. "Just make it stop—any way you can!"

"Thirty-five percent, Tahn—not a gram less!"

"Outrageous! Fifteen! And even that—wait! What is that marking time? I want that ship—what are they doing?"

". . . 17 . . . 16 . . . 15 . . ."

"Twelve seconds, Obo," Spock said.

"Now it seems they are trying *not* to blow us up. So all our discussion may be in vain, friend." Achernar glanced over his shoulder. On the screen curses echoed behind Tahn's horrified face. The Romulan ships began falling back. "But in case it is not, I make a great concession: thirty-three percent."

". . . 11 . . . 10 . . ."

"That's it then," Scott said, defeated.

Spock withdrew his hand. "A brave attempt," he murmured. Harper's eyes met his, glistened.

". . . 8 . . . 7 . . ."

"C'mon, Obo!" Harper kept urging, "You can do it!"

". . . 5 . . . 4 . . ."

"Lad," Scott touched Obo's shoulder. "It's over."

"Nnnooo!" cried Obo. "Didn't fffin—"

". . . 2 . . ."

Voltage arced through Obo's body as a shower of sparks sprayed from the console. Its eyes flew open, glowing bright.

Its body jerked, stiffened as current danced blue around it, but one hand stuck fast inside the panel's workings. Acrid scents of ozone and burning flesh filled the air. Scott forcibly restrained Harper. Spock reached to pull Obo free, but the charge knocked him to the deck.

". . . 2 . . ." the computer said again. ". . . 2 . . . 2 . . . 2 . . ."

Then power tripped. The science station's screen went blank.

And neon eyes went dark. Hot smoke curled from the hand still adhering to the panel. As Obo slid from the chair, singed flesh and cartilage disintegrated, and fingers tore from their webs. Clear, iridescent liquid oozed onto the deck, and helping hands reached to break Obo's fall. Its limp form was icy cold.

"Obo . . ." Harper knelt beside it.

"Medics!" Uhura shouted over inship. "To the bridge! Medics!"

"Hold on, son. Let me . . ." McCoy pushed forward, reaching for his medscan, swearing under his breath when he remembered where it was—on the table beside Saavik in sickbay. *Of all the damn times . . .* but his hands and experience told him what he already knew: internal injuries would be far worse than severed fingers. A sustained electrical charge inflicted massive tissue and brain damage, and Obo had absorbed too much current for too long. Even in stasis, there wouldn't be anything to save. No vital signs . . . he stopped probing and swore again; the hardest part of being a doctor was knowing when to let go.

The computer began beeping and grinding. Its screen came back to life with code patterns racing in multicolored squares across the display, then resolving into the readout of sixty seconds ago. "WORKING," it announced. "DESTRUCT SEQUENCE COMPLETED AND ENGAGED. AWAITING FINAL CODE FOR ONE-MINUTE COUNTDOWN."

"Computer. This is Commander Spock of the U.S.S. *Enterprise.*" He hauled himself up from the floor, clung to the counter, and took a deep breath. "Code one—two—

three. *Continuity*. Abort destruct order." The whistles and grindings continued. "Repeat. Code one, two, three. Continuity. Abort destruct order."

The noise stopped. The code sequence wiped off the screen.

"DESTRUCT ORDER ABORTED."

"Computer. Disengage. Screen off."

Again, it obeyed. Obo had done the impossible, but McCoy looked up, shook his head, and his face said that the Belandrid's brave act had been its last. Spock sighed.

". . . out of the question, Tahn!" Achernar was protesting. "Damn you, man! I've had *expenses!* Thirty percent . . ."

"Obo," whispered Harper, gathering it gently into his lap. He held it like a child and began rocking back and forth. "I know it hurts, but you're gonna be all right . . ."

"Son—"

". . . 'cause we're gonna make you all well—aren't we, Doc!" Harper insisted, refusing to acknowledge McCoy's grief.

"Mr. Harper, you do not under—"

"No, Spock. Let him be."

"Sir?" Harper smiled up at Spock as he cradled Obo on his shoulder. His eyes shone with tears and pride. "I just knew you wouldn't be sorry. See, Obo can fix anything, sir—honest."

". . . twenty-five percent, Tahn. And that is my final—"

"—but the *ship!*" Praetor Tahn felt the mutinous stares of his commander, centurions, the soldiers on the bridge, who had no idea why they were ordered here, no idea that his fortune and his future were held hostage by these deadly foes. "What about the—"

"They wait. To see what you will do. They can annihilate it at a moment's notice. They will never let you board—and need I remind you, Tahn, that this vessel's fate is also mine? *Let us not play games here, friend! Twenty-five percent. Your silence until we cross the Zone, and I will return with what you seek."*

And what will I do then? Tahn wondered, sweating beneath his robe and staring out at planet *Thieurrull* in flames. The invader ships would come, reducing all his little plans to ashes. There would be no good life for him now—there would be no life at all. Even if his officers did not turn against him, even if he survived in this vile, airless night, the First would learn the truth and hunt him down— unless . . . *unless* . . .

A desperate thought occurred to him, the beginnings of a plan so daring that his blood surged with the boldness of it. No ship, no prisoners, no glorious arrival home—but Tahn *did* have something to give the Empire: the *reason* for those massing ships, the treachery and purpose of the Grand Design. He could go and tell them—everything! He knew no names—but he knew something better: the time and place of that next meeting. All of them, together in one room, where soundshields could be tampered, doors could be broken down. There would be a chance then, for the Empire, for himself. A new life, on a new world, where sun was warm and wine was sweet—and perhaps no one would notice if he lived especially well. Yes, bargain first for mercy, and then there was a chance that he could have it all . . .

"Twenty-five percent. Done!" he said. "Explain these terms to the Vulcan. Then I will speak. Advise him to listen well."

"One moment, Tahn. I must ask if he will speak to you . . ."

"Lord!" His commander's eyes were dangerous. "This is treason to the Empire! These are our enemies! They have no weapons, no shields! We can destroy them—or let them destroy themselves! Whatever paltry thing you bargain for—"

"Silence." Tahn drew himself up tall. "You know nothing of what I bargain for! You know nothing of our mission here! Do you—do *any* of you—wish to answer to the Empire if my orders are disobeyed?" Eyes dropped, shifted; clearly no one did. Tahn vowed then and there to make the Empire a gift of his dank, disgusting house and lands, his costly ships and surly troops—and most of all this viper of a commander.

That Vulcan face came back onscreen. Its hooded, ruthless eyes made the skin crawl at the nape of Tahn's neck.

"Agreed," the Vulcan said. *"You wish to speak further?"*

Tahn thought of gold and sun, the gleam of precious rubies and all that they would buy. He was not given to gambling, but he must gamble now, with everything to gain and everything to lose.

"Yes," he said, "a warning to your Starfleet. We see the result of your presence in our Empire. We know your ships mass beyond your borders. We know you plan to attack. You may burn our worlds, but you will never conquer us. What say you to that?"

Not a flicker in that face. *"That I will stop it, if I can. And return your friend to his ship. But I shall do neither of those things here."*

"Old friend? Does this Vulcan keep his word?"

"I believe so, Tahn. You know that I keep mine. He has promised to repair my ship. We shall rendezvous here as planned."

"Then go. There is nothing to stop you between here and the Line. Beyond that, I cannot say. Old friend, I will be waiting."

Tahn broke the link and gave terse orders to his commander, who relayed them with a new respect. The alien ship moved away, leaving its damage behind. *Thieurrull.* Tahn had never been there, only heard its name whispered down the years through voice-changers from beneath black cloaks. To the government it was another failed colony; to The Ten it was the Grand Design; to soldiers it was the worst duty in all the Empire.

"Lord," his commander whispered, "what *was* our mission here?"

"That." He nodded to the distant fires. "The invader did it for us. Learn to use your enemies, Commander, lest they learn to use you." The lie came so easily that Tahn knew it for the truth. An evil place, a danger best undone—and there must have been some reason why the soldiers called it "Hellguard."

"I don't believe this, sir," said Sulu from his station at the helm. "They're doing it! They're letting us go!"

"Aye," Scott looked away from the limp body in Harper's arms. "I'll go see to the engines."

The medical team arrived in one lift as Scott was departing in the other. McCoy waved them aside, put an arm around Harper's shoulders. Spock came to stand beside him.

"Mr. Harper. You must go with the doctor now."

"Yes, sir . . . c'mon Obo, you're gonna be just . . ." He saw everyone watching and tried to smile. "One tough kid, huh?"

"Indeed, Lieutenant," Spock said quietly. In a gesture of respect and grief, he laid his hand on Obo's head. And raised an eyebrow. "Doctor," he said, "you are neglecting your patient!"

"What?" McCoy snatched a scanner from the nearest medic, who was transferring the severed arm into a cryo-unit. ". . . Well, I'll be—don't just *stand* there, Harper! *Move* it! Medics! Get that unit—"

"That's okay, guys. I can manage."

"Guess he can at that." McCoy fussed over his patient. "Easy does it, Harper. Sickbay!" he ordered the lift as they all piled in.

Spock switched on the comm, and started issuing instructions to the transporter room and science lab. Work crews began arriving on the bridge. With them came Nelson, rubbing his neck and expecting reprimands. Achernar walked forward to meet him, and to Nelson's acute embarrassment, returned the phaser with a smile.

"Forgive me, friend. You did not seem amenable to persuasion. And you, Commander . . ." He turned to Uhura with an apologetic bow. "I sincerely regret the inconvenience. Friend Tahn would not have believed me without some show of force."

"Crude," said Uhura, "but effective."

"And Spock," Achernar gazed at the floor where Obo had fallen, "I also regret . . . I had hoped to prevent damage."

Spock nodded. "Mr. Nelson, escort Mr. Achernar to his ship. He may ready it for departure, and his transmitter may be removed. Do try to remain conscious."

"Aye, sir," Nelson mumbled.

"Achernar, if and when we reach safety, you are free to go. Your cargo will be returned. Since the logs of our encounter were erased, its presence without yours would be difficult to explain. It seems that today at least our interests have coincided."

"They do," said Achernar, "more often than you might think. These hostilities are tiresome—and so bad for business."

When Nelson left the bridge with his charge, Spock moved down to the helm, studied the main screen, and spoke in a low voice.

"Mr. Sulu. If I understand the sequence of events, some time elapsed between the scout's explosion and my beam-up. Correct?"

"Yes, sir." Sulu knew what was coming. "Power was out for a while, but I think it was about two hours. Sir."

"And although warp drive was inoperable, you were aware of approaching enemy ships and you did have impulse power. Correct?" Sulu nodded. "Then in fact you could have left orbit. You could have carried out my orders, yet you chose not to do so. Correct?" Another nod. "And you undertook this action on your own?"

"I did, sir," said Sulu, calm as any Vulcan.

"This will be reported, Mr. Sulu. Relinquish the conn to Mr. Scott when he returns. I shall be unavailable."

"Yes, sir." Sulu kept his eyes studiously on the helm, but Uhura and Chekov glared openly at Spock. Several techs working on the bridge wisely kept their mouths shut, even after the lift doors closed and Spock was out of hearing.

"Maybe he'll get over it, Sulu," Uhura muttered, from under a snarl of cables at her station. "After all, you saved their lives—and those ships would have caught us anyway. He *knows* that."

"Not the point," Sulu said without rancor. "I had my orders. Fact is I just couldn't do it. He knows that too."

"You are in good company," Chekov spoke up loyally. "Neither could the keptin. But 'Ensign Sulu' does not sound so bad."

"It's a little early for jokes, Pavel. The bridge is a wreck, we're on impulse power on the wrong side of the Zone, and our scanners are fried. So look sharp, and keep us out of trouble."

"I am trying, Sulu. But vhat is Spock doing? Vhy isn't he—"

"I don't *know!*" Sulu glared.

That silenced everyone. For the next hour, repairs proceeded. Someone brought up trays of sandwiches and coffee. Senior crew had been on duty almost around the clock, but no one talked about relief, and the stars outside barely changed position as *Enterprise* crawled through space. The snail's pace frayed their nerves. As Uhura cleared interference on ship's channels, her board began beeping steadily with incoming calls: departments checking in, duty officers reporting systems back on line, and Dr. McCoy from sickbay. His news sent a cheer around the bridge.

"*. . . Obo'll make it! That little fellow's got two brains—when one shuts down, the other keeps going. Couldn't reattach the fingers, though, too much tissue damage—but Obo doesn't seem to mind. It woke up and talked to Harper for a minute, then went back to sleep. Now what I want to know is—*"

"We'll pass the word, sir." Sulu's attention was on Scott, who had just stomped onto the bridge looking like a thundercloud. "Got to go now, Doctor. Tell Harper to take his time."

"*Harper's not here,*" McCoy growled. "*Spock came and got him! And Saavik's not here either! Now I want to know—*"

"She's not up here, sir. We'll send her back if we see her,"

Sulu promised, switching off. "The conn's yours, Mr. Scott, and—"

"Aye, laddie, I know. The beastie's livin', and our drive's back on line." But Scott wasn't celebrating. He poked about at the engineering station and finally seemed satisfied with what he found. "Warp one, Sulu. Let's see how she goes."

She went, and the crew cheered once more. Warp one became warp two, then warp three, and the bridge was breathing easier as they entered the Neutral Zone. When Chekov spotted two patrols bearing down on them, *Enterprise* accelerated again and left the Romulans blasting at her emission particles in frustration. She sped on across that no-man's-land of space a single light-year wide, but Scott's mood lightened not at all, not even when Sulu and Chekov gave mighty sighs and sagged in their chairs with relief.

"Entering Federation space, Mr. Scott," Sulu said quietly. "We made it, sir. We're home. And sir, I ought to tell you . . ."

"Bridge to all decks," Uhura broke the news over ship's channels. "We made it, folks. Just thought you'd like to know."

". . . so I think I'm on report, sir." Sulu finished the account of his exchange with Spock, and Scotty snorted in disgust.

"Ye'll sit helm, lad, where ye belong!" He muttered some choice oaths in Gaelic, inspected the progress of repairs, then he shooed the techs off the bridge.

"There's something ye don't know," Scott announced. "We may be close to home, but we've not made it yet. An' I can't say we will. Our Mr. Spock's taken leave of his senses! He and Harper—"

Scott stopped. The lift was arriving, and its passenger was yelling. As usual.

"For *once!*" McCoy shouted, as he charged through the opening doors. "For *once,* will *some*body tell me what the *hell*—"

"Scotty was just about to," Uhura said. *"Weren't* you, sir."

"Aye," Scott glowered, "'tis against orders, but I can't keep it to myself. Spock and the Harper lad sealed off lab one. They're in there with one of those bloody Romulan boxes! They're workin' in suits, testin' bits of rock an' dust. Containment barriers, feeder lines, oxygen—I set 'em up, but I don't like it. If he's right, all's well, he says. An' if he's wrong . . ." Scott shook his head.

"If he's wrong—*what?*" McCoy demanded. "Go *on*, dammit!"

"Ye'll not breathe a word of this, Doctor!" Scott snapped. "Nor any of ye, understand? If it goes wrong, we lay in a course on the computer, then send out the logs and abandon ship—aye, leavin' Spock an' Harper behind, alive or no, for if containment breaks, there'll be no way to bring 'em out. We'll drift in the pods till someone picks us up. An' if Earth's no better'n we left it, this plague aboard cannot be stopped. Now, nary a word, mind you! Or Spock'll have my—"

"Indeed!" Spock's voice tolled behind them; this time no one had noticed the lift. He and Harper walked onto the bridge, minus their helmets, but still clad in white environment suits that were covered with a powdery, glittering dust. Harper wore a look of quiet triumph and rushed over to McCoy, asking about Obo. Spock held a computer tape in his hand and went straight to Uhura's station, ignoring the grins and exclamations of relief.

"Break radio silence, Commander. Admiral Nogura, Eyes Only. I trust your Rosecrypt can confirm our ID without question?"

"Mr. Spock," Uhura took the tape and began encoding, "you just leave it to me."

Spock watched her work, and Scott hovered at his shoulder.

"Sir," he prompted, "might we be knowin' what ye found?"

"The antidote was in the dust," said Spock. "Dr. McCoy was correct. Fortunately, as his theory was the only clue we had."

"Well, I'll be damned!" swore McCoy, grinning broadly.

"I have no doubt of it," Spock agreed. "Nevertheless, in this case your deduction was actually logical, a watershed of sorts in your career. May I assume that your patient is stable, Doctor? Since you are here engaging in idle gossip?"

"Spock, Obo is being watched by the best staff and every working monitor in my sickbay! And I wouldn't *need* to be here, if someone'd just told me what the hell—"

"Message sent, sir," Uhura interrupted. "What do we do now?"

"We have done all we can. But you may hope, Commander, if you wish. Hope that we were in time. Call relief personnel to the bridge. Mr. Sulu, move us off from station. Mr. Scott, we hold here for repairs. I shall return shortly. Perhaps," he looked from Scott to Sulu as he started off the bridge, "you can carry out *those* orders without creative embellishment."

"Oh, aye," Scott muttered, trailing after him. "But sir, about Sulu bein' on report. The lad misremembers, sir. I pulled rank on him, I did. I said—belay that, laddie!" he warned, as Sulu opened his mouth to protest. "Ye'll not be contradictin' your betters! Here's how it happened, sir: 'We'll find 'em!' I said, 'if we have to send down the shuttles!' Now," he looked around for confirmation, "is that not what I said?" All heads but Sulu's nodded on cue. Spock turned; his eyebrow hung like an icicle.

"And what *I* said, Mr. Scott, is that Sulu's actions will be reported. As will the performance of each member of this crew . . . to the captain, of course. Given his own creative tendencies," Spock sighed in resignation, "I have little faith that discipline will improve. I shall be on the hangar deck."

"Not so fast, Spock!" McCoy stood in his path. "Your Saavik's walked out of my sickbay, and I want her back. If you see her—"

Spock's expression hardened. "That is most unlikely, Doctor," he said and strode past McCoy into the lift.

The bridge erupted with questions and congratulations. Harper began a blow-by-blow account of their lab experiments, and Scott and McCoy converged on Uhura to see the contents of that message.

"I don't understand it," she said. "Just a formula and some directions. Sounds simple, if they've got this stuff back home."

"But this——" Scotty frowned at her screen, shaking his head. "Oh, lass, they've got a-plenty. Starfleet's been sittin' on the answer all along. But I can't believe it! The stuff's worthless!"

"No, sir," Harper assured him. "Not anymore."

"Welcome aboard, friend Spock." Achernar sat in the padded splendor of his ship, checking readouts on his instrument panel. "My compliments to your crew. My ship is repaired and undamaged."

"It was powered down at the time of the explosion. And no doubt your hull is shielded . . ."

Spock climbed through the hatch, inspecting the interior with interest. Scott was right: the ship was a delight, obviously custom-built, and no expense had been spared. A single-unit transporter occupied the aft main deck, extravagant in so light a craft. Pearl gray and chrome, plush furnishings, hand-tooled wood trim, a sensor array Spock wished he could study. All of it was far more lavish than a Vulcan would consider tasteful, but the elegance and workmanship surpassed any he had seen. A music tape played softly. The only feature out of place was a gaping hole in the center of the deck, which revealed an empty cargo hold.

". . . as it will need to be," Spock added. "The Zone is a dangerous place at present."

Achernar shrugged. "It always is. So you keep your bargain?"

"Yes. What intrigues me, Achernar, is how you plan to keep yours. What is this thing of value that Tahn thinks you have?"

"A fortune," Achernar smiled, "which he made by embezzling funds from a certain 'organization.'" An organization, Achernar thought to himself, that is about to be dissolved forever. "I assisted him over the years to render his assets more . . . liquid, shall we say. But then this organization demanded his ships and troops, and that very night twenty chests vanished from his locked cellar. Tahn saw his days being numbered. He wanted to escape, but without wealth he could go nowhere. So he commissioned me to get it back. It is worth more to him than any ship—even yours." Achernar leaned back in his custom-crafted chair and gazed at Spock. His smile broadened.

"So . . . something for something," Spock murmured.

"Always. The secret, you see, is in knowing what."

"What I see, Achernar, is that you bargained in bad faith. You have no twenty chests. No fortune."

"You do not believe me."

"No," said Spock, and found himself oddly disappointed. "We rescued you in Federation space. We searched your ship. You carried only contraband. Your word is your affair, of course."

"And I am not accustomed to having it impugned!" Achernar's eyes flashed. "I find that troubles me. So, friend Spock, I too shall make a trade. Look again." A hand brushed under the flight panel, but Spock never saw it. His eyes followed Achernar's pointing finger to the cargo hold, where a second bay had opened up beneath the first. This one wasn't empty.

The belly of the little ship was lined with gold. And silver. And the fiery shine of Romulan rubies scattered over gleaming mounds of coins, goblets, bars of pure bullion . . .

"Do not blame your crew, friend. When searchers discover a full cargo hold, they seldom think to look further. And what use would my expensive scan-proofing be if it failed to work?"

"Fascinating," said Spock.

"Damnably complicated!" Achernar frowned in annoyance. "A pernicious nuisance! I stole Tahn's treasure myself, you see—oh, come now, Spock. A fool and his gold are soon parted anyway, are they not? Better I should steal it than someone else. He would come to me for help. I would return it, charge a modest sum for my efforts, and meanwhile satisfy a certain client on your side of the Zone who has an inordinate craving for rubies."

"And the locked cellar?" Spock's glance shifted aft.

"A transporter needs no keys. Sensors locate precious metal. But I only converted Tahn's ill-gotten gains. I never asked him where they came from. Such curiosity would be unseemly. No, I knew nothing of his absurd politics until he summoned me, certain his great leader had found him out, removed his gold, and appropriated the soldiers who could defend him. I could hardly contradict him, could I? So I sent him off with his troops. We planned to meet at *Thieurrull*, and I went about my business—but that cursed gold was too damned heavy. Ruined my stabilizer, and left me to the likes of Starfleet. I even tried to warn you, once I learned where you had taken us, but your doctor drugged and trussed me like a chicken rather than listen to good sense. This whole transaction," he complained peevishly, "has been nothing but *politics* from beginning to end. Avoid politics, friend Spock. They are dangerous, and very bad for business."

"I abhor your business," Spock said, "but I take you at your word—against my better judgment. A question, if I may—"

There was the whine of electric carts outside and the sound of footsteps, then a knock on the hatch's rim. "Your cargo, Mr. Achernar, and I did like you said with the . . . oh. Mr. Spock."

"Mr. Nelson, gentlemen. Proceed." The security team loaded the contents of their carts into the hold, which now appeared as empty as before. It did not escape Spock's notice that two items were missing: the Romulan ale and the Glenlivet. He sighed and refrained from comment; for once, he simply didn't want to know.

"Now," said Achernar when they were gone, "something still puzzles you, friend. What is your question?"

"Why did you do it? Mr. Harper said you knew your ship was repaired. I am not clear on how you escaped from sickbay, but you could have come here instead of to the bridge. You took a risk."

"Yes." Achernar's face softened. "And so did the little cat who set me free—against her better judgment. She dislikes me. She vowed," he recalled fondly, "that if harm came to your ship she would hunt me down and rip my heart out. Let us say that I believed her." He delved into a pocket and took out a coin. "Romulan gold," he murmured, holding it to the light. "None finer in all the galaxy. Give her this for me someday, to remind her of her worth." He laughed at Spock's hesitation and pressed it into the Vulcan's hand. "I shall deduct it from my commission, of course."

"Of course. And someday perhaps she will appreciate it. Safe journey, Achernar. You did us a service."

"I did. One that I expect to be returned should our paths cross again and should the need arise. As the humans say, friend Spock, you owe me. And unlike Vulcans," he grinned, "I call in my debts." He was still grinning when Spock reached the bottom of the ramp and turned back to lift his hand.

"Live long, Achernar, and . . . prosper."

"I endeavor to do both. Prosper, friend Spock. Live long!"

Spock felt a sudden chill as the hatch swung closed. The hangar deck was cold; no doubt he was tired. From behind the observation window he watched the ship lift off, a black needle darting into a black night.

". . . yes, sir, that's what it says." Lieutenant-Adjutant Michaels stood nervously at Nogura's desk. "But your order went *out* already, sir! By now those ships—"

"Where's the verification on this?" Nogura snapped, furiously calculating subspace time-lags and his fleet's distance from the Neutral Zone. "Are we sure it came from *Enterprise?*"

"Confirmed, sir." Michaels keyed in the transmission data and analysis. "And she's not in enemy hands. This overrode every priority sequence in the network. Even if the

Romulans had our new code, they couldn't do that. This was sent by an expert, Admiral. It repeats three times, each cross-ciphered by a different date—the date the Treaty was ratified, then the date *Enterprise* was commissioned, then . . . well, that's your birthday, isn't it, sir?"

"Science got all this?"

"Yes, sir. But it'll take a while to find enough of that stuff to pulverize and beam into the air supply—"

The intercom shrilled: Komack. Again.

Nogura stared at the data on his screen. A war was beginning, a hundred years of peace ending because a message came too late. If the message was right, that didn't need to happen. But if it was wrong—

". . . one moment, sir." Michaels covered the tiny sensor of the comm's remote with his finger. "Sir, Admiral Komack's shuttle is docking, and he wants to see you, sir—about why you delayed the attack. He wants to come up here. He wants to know what the, uh, hell you're doing. Sorry, sir. That's a quote."

Nogura nodded. Across the room, his willow's branches stirred in a breeze from the air vent. Surviving. Bending. Constantly reminding him that life would be easier if its owner did the same. But trees weren't admirals. Life wasn't easy. And right now he'd rather be looking at an oak.

"Turning some ships around," he said, reaching for his encoder, "is what the hell I'm doing. Tell him that, Michaels." He began tapping on the keys.

"Aye, sir." The young adjutant gulped, muttered miserably into the comm and winced during its lengthy reply. Then he covered the sensor again. "Admiral, he—he says you can't *do* that, sir!"

Nogura's fingers kept tapping; he didn't look up.

"Sir, he says the Council *voted!* He says he'll write a *report!* He says—"

"Michaels."

"—sir?"

"Put him on hold."

Chapter Thirteen

SAAVIK SAT IN a dark corner of the observation deck, where she'd spent the return voyage watching the stars, speaking to no one, and considering how her life had changed. Spock had not sent for her, and she felt no desire to hasten the moment; it would come soon enough. After days of soul-searching and casting some fiercely held assumptions aside, she found much to wonder about in this new life that lay before her. But of one thing she was certain: There was no place in Starfleet for her now, not for any cadet who disobeyed orders and assaulted her commanding officer. Regulations were quite specific on that point—and Spock was also bound by them, as she knew very well at the time. It changed nothing. She had done what she must, and he would do the same.

Dr. McCoy appeared every day, ran his scanner over her, and examined the healing layer of synthetic skin that covered her hands and arms. He made approving noises, sprayed something cold on her wounds, and showed a delicacy she never suspected he possessed by leaving her alone. Uhura came once, sat with her awhile, then touched her on the shoulder and went away again.

And Bobby Harper brought her the news. He found her

here that first night and every night since, and in his quiet, gentle way began to tell her of each day's events, never asking questions or expecting a response. She heard how Achernar was a legend now and Obo was a hero; and how halfway across the Neutral Zone, the whole Federation fleet turned back when the answer came in time.

". . . and it worked," Harper was telling her now. "Word came from some admiral today. HQ and Life City are open. Memorial services are tomorrow, and we're almost home. We made it, Saavik, we stopped a war. And Earth's safe again. So whatever you did back there, well, it made a difference. I just wanted you to know."

Saavik was still silent, but Harper thought she seemed a little less distant than before. And she'd listened hard when he told her how Obo was getting well. So maybe it did some good to keep talking to her like this. She didn't seem to mind, but it was always hard to tell with Vulcans.

"Funny, though, about that dust," he mused, settling back with her to watch the view. "Mr. Spock said it immunized the whole planet and he should have known. The machines that made the weapons weren't designed to keep the virus *in,* but to keep the dust *out.* All those iron and sulfur compounds—the air was full of 'em. But one, FeS_2, actually breaks down the virus's molecular structure. Starfleet really was sitting on the answer, and so was Life City. See, in the old days people came out to California prospecting for gold, and lots of folks lost everything on good old FeS_2. Iron pyrite. It sure looked pretty, but it wasn't the real thing. That's why they called it 'fool's gold.' I wonder what they'd think now if they knew it saved the world."

"Mr. Harper," said Saavik softly, the first time she'd spoken in days, "I would like to ask a question. What do humans do when they . . . lose everything?"

Harper wished he knew. He hadn't lost everything, of course; Obo was doing fine. But this morning Mr. Spock offered him a permanent assignment to the *Enterprise,* said to think it over and to let him know. *There's nothing to go back to,* he'd been telling himself all day. *Mom's gone, and home won't ever be the same* . . . and he had to quit seeing Jessie Korbet's face in his dreams and wishing for things that might have been. *But there's Obo. What about Obo?* . . .

"Everything?" he put his mind to Saavik's question. "You mean like fortunes, or homes, or . . . people we love? Things like that?"

"Yes." Saavik nodded, eyes on the stars. "Things like that."

Harper thought about those prospectors and pioneers long ago. He thought about shining domes and childhood haunts and growing up in a city that made a thousand worlds his home. He thought about his mother, all those awards hanging in her office, all the work she never got to finish—and he thought about Obo. And suddenly he knew what he'd be telling Mr. Spock.

"Well, when we lose everything," he said quietly, "we rebuild it, that's what we do. We begin again, and we start over as often as it takes. I almost forgot that. I had to decide something important today, and now I know what to do. Thanks, Saavik."

"For what, Mr. Harper? You knew the answer."

"But I didn't *know* I knew it," he smiled, "till you asked the right question. Humans aren't logical like Vulcans. We always look for happy endings. And when things don't turn out that way, we just try again. So we keep our old stories, like the one about Pandora, because we need to believe something *was* left inside that box. A chance to win, I guess, against all the evil in the world."

"Hope."

"Yeah. And sometimes we win. But other times . . . we sort of get rained out. Vulcans don't believe in hope, do they?"

"I do not know. I have not experienced it, but there are many things I have not experienced. For myself," she said slowly, "I believe that people make their own evils—and the result is not a matter of chance. I believe a box *opens*, Mr. Harper, because that is its *nature*—and curiosity is ours. Trusting in gods does not keep it shut, and hope does not keep its evil from getting into the world. The only way to do that . . . is not to make the box."

"But someone always does. You think people can change?"

"I think those who look for happy endings must insist upon it. And I *know* people can change."

"Now that," he smiled, "sounds a little like hope, Saavik."

"No," she sighed, "it is very hard work. But every time I fail, I'll remember what you said, Mr. Harper. And I *will* begin again . . ." she turned back to the stars, retreating into her own thoughts as she whispered to herself, ". . . as often as it takes."

And after a while, Harper slipped away to find Mr. Spock. He still didn't know what happened to make her so sad. Come to think of it, he didn't know much about Saavik at all. Except that she was "the Photon Torpedo." He'd seen her pitch three perfect games without even wrinkling her uniform. And he didn't think someone with an arm like *that* would ever fail—at anything.

"Spock, come take a look at this." McCoy bent over his scan. "I swear, that little critter's tougher than anybody thought. It's growing new fingers, see? Cellular regeneration's already advanced. Now how the hell does it *do* that?"

Spock studied the screen a moment. "Easy fix, no doubt."

"And very quick! But what happens to Obo now? And what will you do about Harper?"

"Mr. Harper has asked for a transfer to Life City, and I shall expedite his request. His knowledge will prove invaluable during the restoration. I am recommending the Belandrid to the museum's authorities for a position there as well. So Mr. Obo's stated preference—to remain with Mr. Harper—stands every chance of being honored. I can see no logic in separating personnel who perform more efficiently together."

"Well," McCoy said, relieved, "it's about time your logic made some sense!"

Spock went to the door, then hesitated. For a Vulcan, McCoy thought, he was almost dithering. "Doctor," he finally said, "I came to inquire about Saavik. What is her condition?"

"She won't have scars, if that's what you mean. Not on the outside anyway. As for what goes on in her head, you know better than . . . Spock? Won't she talk to you either? I just assumed—"

"I have not seen her, Doctor. I have waited, but she has chosen to miss her tutorial every day since—"

"Miss her . . . she got buried *alive!* Came within an inch of *dying* down there! And *you* worry about her goddamn *schoolwork?*"

Spock stiffened. "I requested a medical opinion, Doctor."

"And I'm giving you one! Not that you ever tell *me* what's going on! But my guess is that besides everything else, maybe she remembered whatever it was she forgot. And maybe it was just too much information, too fast. Give her a rest, Spock, for God's sake. She won't feel like learning anything for a while."

"That is unacceptable," said Spock flatly.

It was the last straw for McCoy. "Now you listen here, you green-blooded son of a Vulcan! You took her down there! You nearly got her killed! And now you don't have the decency to ask *her* how she's doing? Well, since you're so damn *concerned,* she's up on the observation deck, looking like her *life* is over! I don't know why, but you're the only person she gives a damn about. So get up there, and do whatever it takes to *cheer her up!* YOU HEAR ME?"

"Surely a rhetorical question, Doctor. And as you correctly point out, I am ill-suited to the task. Which of course I knew in the first place." The bleakness in Spock's face took McCoy by surprise. His anger evaporated, leaving him gruffly apologetic.

"Aw, you'll think of something. God knows you've had enough practice over the years. Just do what you always do, Spock." A note of affection crept into his voice. "Just . . . be yourself."

Spock raised an eyebrow and considered this a moment. Then he turned and left McCoy talking to himself.

"What am I *saying?* I just told the Big Bad *Wolf* to go cheer up Little Red *Riding Hood!*"

A fine gold dust still swirled in the air at Starfleet Headquarters as workers in suits and masks went about the long process of cleaning up. Federation Plaza swarmed with shuttles landing empty, lifting off with sealed black coffins draped in Federation flags. The dead were going home for burial to cities on Earth and to worlds far away, with medals for their service and escorts to do them honor. But from all the tragedy had come one hopeful piece of news: For the first time in history, the Romulan government used a subspace channel to speak directly to the Federation Council. This unprecedented contact signaled new hope for a dialogue. They had not known of the plot, they said, until certain information came to light; the traitors had been dealt with; no one wanted war. So the peace of the galaxy, which teetered on the brink for a while, had righted itself again.

In his Spacedock office Nogura frowned at his comm, where two security guards were checking in from Administration's Room 2103.

"She wants to take *what* with her?"

"A book, Admiral," Renn broke in, *"just a book. Sir, we got a call from Starfleet Medical—I knew Admiral Kirk wasn't taking care of himself! Is he going to be all right, sir?"*

"Yes, Doctor. It's just exhaustion. What about that book?"

"Well, they said he keeps talking in his sleep about a book and a little brother. And they asked if we knew what he meant. We don't, but this was the only book around. It belonged to that ensign who died at the front desk. So I asked Security to bring it over. We'd like to take it to him, sir."

"All right. But you'll have to hurry. You two are going out

to Life City. They need help restoring the exhibits—and a computer jockey. The hours will be better, I dare say. And you're both getting well-deserved commendations. Doctor, Mr. Kinski, your shuttle is waiting. You're dismissed, with thanks." Nogura switched off and took his next call. "Yes, Michaels?"

"That ship's been decontaminated, Admiral. All the weapons are destroyed. They tested its fancy cloaking device. Didn't work, sir. Power drain blew all the warp enabler circuits. And Enterprise *is in system, Admiral. She'll dock within the hour."*

"I'll be there."

Nogura shut down the comm and went to water his bonsai, blooming now against the blue oceans of Earth. It was one task he never delegated, and he was leaving tonight. Tomorrow he would speak at the memorial service and dedicate a monument to Starfleet's fallen; he'd insisted on that. A new tree would grow in Federation Plaza. Nogura would plant it himself.

And he'd made damn sure it would be an oak.

". . . but you can't quit *now,* Kinski," Renn argued. "Not when Life City needs us. That's just *bad timing!"*

They sat in the shuttle's back seat as it climbed through the gathering clouds over San Francisco.

"Admiral Kirk told me to think about it, and I have," Kinski declared. He was sounding much more sure of himself lately.

"Then think about it some more!"

"Okay, and I don't mean I'm quitting *now.* But how do I know what's bad timing, anyway?"

"I guess you don't," Renn sighed. "It's just luck."

"Say, Mr. Kinski," said their pilot from the front seat, "when we get to Life City, why don't you take a walk outside, look up at the stars? That helps you think. It's what I did the last time I was there."

The pilot turned and looked at them with solemn blue eyes.

"By the way," she said, "my name's Jessie. And let me tell you a story about *good* timing . . ."

Admiral James T. Kirk watched the approaching storm from his window in Starfleet's Medical Tower. Thunder rolled. Lightning jagged across the sky, and fat drops of rain began spattering his view of the brightly lit Plaza below. He remembered very little of his rescue from the Vault. It was all a blur of kind hands, hushed voices, and drifting in and out of unconscious sleep. In the past few days he'd slept a lot, celebrated all the news. *Enterprise* was safe. Earth was safe. The Federation was safe—

And Heihachiro Nogura still had him guessing.

Why? Kirk wondered. *Why did he do it? When I'd promised? When he had me, fair and square? I'll never figure him out . . .*

Nogura had delayed his ground assignment. Kirk's orders still listed him as Admiral and Acting Captain of the *Enterprise.* Nogura was letting him off the hook—but *why?* Time to find a replacement? A simple act of kindness? Maybe both, but it was something else as well: a short string.

And Kirk already felt its tug. Because this time it wouldn't be for long. Soon the day would come when Nogura would call him home—and he would go. No tricks, no games, no way out. Word of honor. *Damn that Nogura . . .*

I'll take what I can get, he told himself, but a cold, gray weariness had seeped into his bones. "Exhaustion," the doctors said. Or maybe he was just . . . getting old. Maybe the day would come when he knew Nogura was right. Because strings pulled, and clocks didn't stand still, and everyone had to grow up sometime.

Kirk turned the book in his hands. He'd been sleeping when they left it. Arguing loud enough to wake the dead, the night nurse told him, as she brought in his uniform for the memorial tomorrow.

A new dress jacket. With medals and ribbons and gold braid that hung like chains.

Kirk didn't want to think about that tonight. He settled

into the chair by the window and opened the book. Tomorrow he'd find that little brother, but tonight he wanted to read the story one more time—all about another Jim, forever young, who ran away to sea. Tonight he wanted to forget about gold braid and promises. He wanted to be ten years old again, and to have it all in front of him . . .

> *If sailor tales to sailor tunes,*
> *Storm and adventure, heat and cold,*
> *If schooners, islands, and maroons,*
> *And Buccaneers and buried Gold . . .*

Kirk read on into the night, while the storm beat against the window and tossed the trees outside. He hardly noticed. And it must have been the print that caused his eyes to water and sent an occasional trickle down his cheek, but he hardly noticed that either. It just seemed like part of the rain.

Spock had been standing there for some time, but Saavik's back was turned. She leaned on the viewport's railing watching their approach to Earth, and if she sensed his presence, she was waiting for him to speak.

"It was poorly planned," he said finally. "No doubt you have had time for second thoughts. If you wish to express regret for your actions, that would be most appropriate. You may proceed."

She faced him then, cool and detached. If this moment caused her anxiety, she didn't show it. She appeared resigned, at peace, entirely Vulcan. For some reason, Spock found that disturbing.

"I regret my error, Mr. Spock," she said calmly.

"Indeed."

"Yes. I should have called the ship, told them you were unconscious, and had you beamed aboard. I . . . didn't think of it."

"You violated orders, attacked your commanding officer —and that is the extent of your apology? It lacks a certain remorse."

269

"Yes. The task required no great strength or expertise. There was no point in asking your permission, since you would not have given it. My duty was clear, Mr. Spock. I saw no other way to accomplish it. I believe I acted logically."

"Starfleet regulations do not allow for such logic, Saavik."

"I never thought they did. But some things are more important than Starfleet. Sir, you would not have survived."

"In your opinion."

"I was there."

"I see. Have you anything else to say?"

"Yes. I do not regret my actions. And whatever happens now is no more than I deserve, because I would do it all again."

"You are not helping your case, Saavik."

"I have no case. I gained more than I lost, and I can never lose what you have taught me. I know now . . . what it means to be a Vulcan. I saw it. And what I saw may always be beyond my reach. But I think that is beside the point. I am going to try—and keep on trying, Mr. Spock, every minute of my life. Because there is no better thing to be." She took a deep breath. "That is what I wished to say. I am finished now."

"But I am not," Spock said. "I take no pleasure in what I am about to tell you. As an officer of Starfleet I deplore what you chose to do. As your teacher, however, I must discuss a matter I have obviously postponed too long. Which reminds me, Saavik," he fixed her with a disapproving gaze, "you have been neglecting your studies. Dr. McCoy believes you are somehow incapacitated. That hardly seems the case. I have taken a month's leave to conduct a seminar at Starfleet Academy and will personally instruct you. Be advised that I do not appreciate absences, in regular classes or private ones. Now, to the matter at hand . . ."

Spock seated himself and showed all the signs of embarking on a long lecture. Saavik was too overcome to speak. She turned away to hide her confusion, wondering wildly whether she had just imagined it all. But no . . .

". . . when personal duty does take precedence," he was saying. "But proper planning is *imperative* when one must disobey orders. Decisions hastily reached are invariably flawed. Every result must be envisioned, every contingency provided for—including, I feel compelled to mention, planetquakes and lost communicators. 'I didn't think of it' is precisely the sort of thing one does *not* wish to say to Starfleet Command. Regrettably, I speak from . . . ah, this subject is quite distasteful to me, Saavik, and I shall address it only once. Do I have your attention?"

"You *do,* Mr. Spock!"

"Very well. Then listen carefully and try not to interrupt. In my case the charge was mutiny, and I was guilty of that crime. I forged orders to an illegal destination, abducted Fleet personnel and forcibly appropriated this starship and crew as means of transport. My *planning,* however, with one exception—"

"Hijacked?" Saavik gasped, forgetting herself completely. Her eyes were wide as saucers. Her newfound calm was gone. And when the word went unchallenged, a delighted smile lifted the corners of her mouth. *"You,* Spock? You *hijacked* the *Enterprise?"*

Spock took his time about answering. With monumental patience he folded his hands in his lap. "I believe," he murmured, "that is what I just *said.* Do I take it you find this interesting?"

Saavik's smile vanished as quickly as it came. She caught her breath and managed to recover her composure, but not the eyebrow that climbed her forehead. *"Fas*cinating!" she said.

This isn't right, Uhura decided. She wasn't expecting cheers or fanfares or a fleet of ships to greet them as there had been sometimes in the past. But the bridge was deserted. Spock, Scotty, and McCoy were off somewhere ignoring the view or savoring it in private. Sulu and Chekov sat at their posts pretending it didn't matter and this was no big deal, just another homecoming. It was more than that, this chatter of normal traffic, this swarm of satellites winking in their orbits, this sight of their gemstone planet turning under its rings of cloud. And Uhura felt some ceremony was called for, some sense of occasion, whether anyone else thought so or not. Besides, she had the conn.

"That's right, Approach Control, once around before we dock." She nodded to the helm. "Gentlemen . . ."

"Permission to maneuver, ma'am?" Sulu grinned at Chekov and flexed his fingers over the controls.

"Do it, Sulu, with *feeling* . . ." She touched a key, and as the strains of a symphony swelled through every level of the ship, Uhura began to sing.

> *"Goin' home, goin' home,*
> *I'm a-goin' home*
> *Quiet-like, some still day,*
> *I'm just goin' . . . home . . ."*

"What is that music, Mr. Spock?"

"Terran. An ancient symphony called *From the New World.* Those words were set to its theme by one of the composer's students. I find the symphony sufficient, but the folk song has also endured."

"It is very . . . emotional."

"Indeed. The music honored a young country, its natives, and the immigrants who came to make new homes in a freer land."

"They . . . *made* homes? How did they do that?"

"The same way they do now on worlds across the galaxy. Study the humans, Saavikam. They believe it is possible to belong anywhere. It is also their custom, and perhaps it is their best, to welcome strangers to Earth's shores."

"Yes. They are generous. And adaptive. And they have some good ideas, as well as some very foolish ones—"

"Mmmm . . ."

272

"—but they take so much for *granted*. Just look at their world. It is so beautiful, and they are so fortunate. Do you think they *know*?"

"They learn, Saavikam. Slowly, but they learn."

"Oh. Well, in that case, Mr. Spock, I would like to ask a question . . ."

THE STAR TREK
PHENOMENON

more on next page...

THE
STAR TREK
PHENOMENON

_____ **VULCAN ACADEMY MURDERS**
64744/$3.95

_____ **VULCAN'S GLORY**
65667/$3.95

_____ **WEB OF THE ROMULANS**
70093/$4.50

_____ **WOUNDED SKY**
66735/$3.95

_____ **YESTERDAY'S SON**
66110/$3.95

• •

_____ **STAR TREK– THE MOTION PICTURE**
72300/$4.50

_____ **STAR TREK II– THE WRATH OF KHAN**
67426/$3.95

_____ **STAR TREK III–THE SEARCH FOR SPOCK**
67198/$3.95

_____ **STAR TREK IV– THE VOYAGE HOME**
70283/$4.50

_____ **STAR TREK V– THE FINAL FRONTIER**
68008/$4.50

_____ **STAR TREK: THE KLINGON DICTIONARY**
66648/$4.95

_____ **STAR TREK COMPENDIUM REVISED**
62726/$9.95

_____ **MR. SCOTT'S GUIDE TO THE ENTERPRISE**
70498/$12.95

_____ **THE STAR TREK INTERVIEW BOOK**
61794/$7.95

**POCKET
BOOKS**

**Simon & Schuster Mail Order Dept. STP
200 Old Tappan Rd., Old Tappan, N.J. 07675**

Please send me the books I have checked above. I am enclosing $_____ (please add 75¢ to cover
postage and handling for each order. N.Y.S. and N.Y.C residents please add appropriate sales tax). Send
check or money order—no cash or C.O.D.'s please. Allow up to six weeks for delivery. For purchases over
$10.00 you may use VISA: card number, expiration date and customer signature must be included.

Name_____

Address_____

City_____ State/Zip_____

VISA Card No._____ Exp. Date_____

Signature_____ 118-26

STAR TREK
THE NEXT GENERATION

- ☐ STAR TREK: THE NEXT GENERATION: ENCOUNTER FARPOINT 65241/$3.95
- ☐ STAR TREK: THE NEXT GENERATION: #1 GHOST SHIP 66579/$3.95
- ☐ STAR TREK: THE NEXT GENERATION: #2 THE PEACEKEEPERS 66929/$3.95
- ☐ STAR TREK: THE NEXT GENERATION: #3 THE CHILDREN OF HAMLIN 67319/$3.95
- ☐ STAR TREK: THE NEXT GENERATION: #4 SURVIVORS 67438/$3.95
- ☐ STAR TREK: THE NEXT GENERATION: #5 STRIKE ZONE 67940/$3.95
- ☐ STAR TREK: THE NEXT GENERATION: #6 POWER HUNGRY 67714/$3.95
- ☐ STAR TREK: THE NEXT GENERATION: #7 MASKS 70878/$4.50
- ☐ STAR TREK: THE NEXT GENERATION: #8 THE CAPTAIN'S HONOR 68487/$3.95
- ☐ STAR TREK: THE NEXT GENERATION: #9 A CALL TO DARKNESS 68708/$3.95
- ☐ STAR TREK: THE NEXT GENERATION: #10 A ROCK AND A HARD PLACE 69364/$3.95
- ☐ STAR TREK: THE NEXT GENERATION: METAMORPHOSIS 68402/$4.95

POCKET BOOKS

Simon & Schuster Mail Order Dept. NGS
200 Old Tappan Rd., Old Tappan, N.J. 07675

Please send me the books I have checked above. I am enclosing $_____ (please add 75¢ to cover postage and handling for each order. N.Y.S. and N.Y.C. residents please add appropriate sales tax). Send check or money order—no cash or C.O.D.'s please. Allow up to six weeks for delivery. For purchases over $10.00 you may use VISA: card number, expiration date and customer signature must be included.

Name_____

Address _____

City _____ State/Zip _____

VISA Card No._____ Exp. Date_____

Signature _____ 100-06